ADDY'S

REDEMPTION

A Novel

by

JULIANA ORMSBY

CCB Publishing
British Columbia, Canada

Addy's Redemption: A Novel

Copyright ©2012 by Juliana Ormsby
ISBN-13 978-1-77143-038-8
First Edition

Library and Archives Canada Cataloguing in Publication
Ormsby, Juliana, 1948-, author
Addy's redemption : a novel / by Juliana Ormsby. -- First edition.
Issued in print and electronic formats.
ISBN 978-1-77143-038-8 (pbk).--ISBN 978-1-77143-039-5 (pdf)
I. Title.
PS3615.R57A44 2012   813'.6   C2012-908603-7

Cover artwork by: Ray Kalani Kelly (kalanikelly@gmail.com)

Disclaimer: This is a book of pure fiction, a product of the author's imagination, and does not represent any persons, living or dead.

Publisher: CCB Publishing
              British Columbia, Canada
              www.ccbpublishing.com

Blessings and thanks to my devoted family and friends for inspiration, encouragement, and editing, particularly when my eyesight failed. A special thank you to Paul Rabinovitch of CCB Publishing for his advice, infinite patience, and kindness.

"Men never do evil so completely and cheerfully
as when they do it from religious conviction."
— Blaise Pascal (1623-1642)

Some describe Post World War II United States as the best time
in our country's history, when more families could fulfill
their "American Dream." My story is set during this optimistic
world of sugar-coated civility. Yet, these tales are not unique;
we find them in every life. The struggles between good and evil;
sin and forgiveness; shame and pride have existed throughout
history and are integral parts of the human condition.

Chapter I

Lifting the Veil

Addy glanced around the living room, noticing she had left her needlework on the wing chair by the fireplace. As she had done so many thousands of times during her marriage to Lionel, Addy whispered to herself, "I'd better put that away before Lionel gets home."

Lionel loved order. Part of his obsession had come from his having served briefly in the military. He could not bear to have anything out of place. Although they could have well afforded to hire a housekeeper, Lionel always emphasized that because Addy did not work, she was responsible for keeping the place spotless. On one level, Addy believed this was a fair bargain, but Lionel was extreme in his demands. He expected, without exception, a picture-perfect house, shirts pressed and starched as if they had come from the laundry, beautiful meals on the dining room table at six o'clock sharp, children's faces scrubbed and shining, and newspaper and slippers waiting for the Master when he arrived home from work. After all, had he not provided Addy a fine home with an all-electric kitchen, three bedrooms, and a rumpus room?

Once Addy left her job to get married she became, essentially, a scullery maid. Most neighbors seemed not to suspect what her life was really like. On the rare occasions when company came to her impeccable house for unforgettable dinners, they raved about the "perfect" Addy. Lionel would puff up with pride, give his wife a perfunctory peck on the cheek and boast, "That's my Addy-girl."

Addy's mother and father had been in a gruesome car crash when she was only three years old. Her maiden aunts, Sophia and Hazel, obligated to be her caretakers, always clucked about

1

how fortunate it was that Addy had not been in the car. Sometimes, when she was in her deepest depression, Addy wished she hadn't been spared. On the night of the accident, Sophia and Hazel were babysitting for little Addy. Her parents were on their way home from a Christmas party they had attended at the home of Dad's new boss. Although her parents rarely left Addy with a sitter, Daddy had probably felt an obligation to attend the gathering despite the inclement weather. All Addy ever knew about the accident was "black ice; dead on arrival."

Sometimes she repeated these words over and over again in her head. Because she was a precocious child with a wide vocabulary and lucid mind, she continued to have foggy memories and sensations of her lovely parents. Daddy was a tall, slender, dark-haired man with twinkling brown eyes and warm smile; Mommy a pretty, brown-haired woman with bright green eyes and an equally beautiful smile. Of course, Addy had seen photographs of her parents, but she was convinced she actually remembered them. Some nights as she drifted off to sleep, a wave of comfort and security washed over her. She was sure it was Mommy and Daddy's love. They doted on the child they had tried so hard to conceive. Life was complete when their sweet Addison was born. After their cruel and senseless death, Addy quietly seethed with rage—why were her joyful, healthy parents ripped so violently from her life? Why did she end up living in a sterile, guilt-ridden environment with her old-maid aunts, Sophia and Hazel? They were Daddy's sisters and Addy's only living relatives. Dutifully, they took over raising the frisky, chubby, happy little Addison. Oh, her life before the accident had been so good. After that, a small leech was persistently sucking the vitality from her soul. Sometimes, Addy dared to wish she had been put up for adoption; maybe she might have had a fair shake at having some normal parents. She would immediately ask God to forgive her because, after all, her aunts did the best they could.

Living with two cheerless Catholic spinsters, who probably should have entered a cloistered nunnery, Addy was clueless about the opposite sex; and the aunts made certain she stayed that way. They always lectured her that it took only thirty seconds to ruin your life. Addy never really understood what that meant, but she knew it had something to do with not being alone with a boy. When she finally realized the aunts were talking about the amount of time it takes to conceive a baby, she was already engaged to Lionel. He gave her a Catholic marriage manual that discussed "conception." As Addy now looked back on that book, she laughed aloud. Copulation was for procreation. A boy should not slide down a banister because he may inadvertently commit a sin of sexual arousal. At the time, Addy accepted this crock of bullshit as the way things are with everyone. Yet, she often wondered if her parents had conducted their lives in that manner. She remembered them as being so happy, and rather than naming her after a saint, they chose the name "Addison." One thing Addy did like about herself was her name. It suggested that Mom and Dad were a loving, bright couple looking forward to raising an optimistic, confident girl. Oh, if they could see what she had allowed herself to become.

Addy had graduated from college with high honors, but the aunts were growing older and frailer so it was now her responsibility to take care of them. Often Addy wished she was a strong, independent person like her secret friend, Helena Kurowski, Addy's favorite classmate throughout their education at St. Mary's Catholic School for Girls. Helena took shit from no one and always lectured Addy that she should not feel obligated to the aunts; she owed them nothing. After all, it wasn't Addy's fault that her parents died in a car wreck. Helena begged Addy to move to New York so they could find jobs and get an apartment together.

The aunts never approved of Helena and literally forbade Addy to see her friend outside of school. Helena's parents were divorced, and Helena lived with her mom, Mary. God only knows where the father had gone. In the eyes of Addy's aunts, both Mary and Helena were "damaged goods," but this view of Helena and her mom just did not make sense to Addy. Mary worked very hard as a nurse, went faithfully to Mass every

Sunday, and did not have men in her life. It wasn't Helena's or her mom's choice for the dad to have left them. True to her word, Helena moved to New York City, and Addy eventually lost touch with her. As Addy grew older, she often wondered what her life might have been like if she had dumped "the two old bags" and moved to New York with Helena.

In spite of her resentment toward her aunts, dutiful, well-bred Addy dared not abandon them. She despised Hazel and Sophia for sheltering her so much. If they had not, maybe she could have found the happiness she suspected her parents had known. Now she was well into her twenties and could not pursue work in her field because she had to stay at home and look after the aunts. Theirs was a small, backward Connecticut town with few opportunities for employment so Addy had to settle for a job as a clerk in an office supply company. Yes, here was the perfect, respectable, sterile environment for the nice Catholic girl Sophia and Hazel had raised. Inside, Addy raged with hatred for the two old bitches.

When Addy was a young girl, Sophia and Hazel frequently entertained porky, self-indulgent, egotistical priests after Mass. It sickened Addy to watch them disgustingly gobbling the pastries and coffee cakes she had baked. In fact, baking was the one thing Addy knew she could do well. She often dreamed of opening her own bakery one day, but she knew that would never happen. She just wasn't spunky enough to strike out on her own. Besides, she was not a lucky girl. Things never work out for people who are born unlucky.

Celibate Catholics often stir up a hungry sexual undertone when in each other's company. Something about these Sunday morning gatherings was repugnant, but naïve, young Addy could not put her finger on it. All she knew was she had to don her finest frocks, and her aunts dolled up as well. The priests would hold court and be treated like royalty. Sophia and Hazel rarely laughed when they were alone with Addy, but when the priests came a-calling, the aunts behaved like silly schoolgirls. They hung on to the fathers' every word, giggling at the oddest moments. It was so confusing. Some of the priests ravished young Addy with lecherous glances. Of course, many of them did not care about her at all because, as she later figured out, they favored men or even young boys. How did she not know about homosexuality? She was in shock when she found out that there are men who prefer men, and, even more curious, women who love women. Of course, Addy had heard the expressions "fairy" and "sissy," but she thought that meant men who acted effeminate. Girls who hated to do things girls do, as wearing pretty dresses and playing with dolls were "tomboys," but Addy, in her wildest dreams, never imagined some of these girls would grow up fancying other girls. She remained in the dark about this unusual way of life well into her thirties. By then she had read about famous creative bohemians who followed their hearts at all costs. In real life, however, she had never met anyone of this persuasion.

One Sunday after Mass, Father Jean-Paul Roberge brought his younger brother, Lionel, to the aunts' house after Mass. In retrospect, Addy suspected this was a pre-arranged meeting, although Sophia and Hazel would never admit to it. Addy was getting older, and the aunts realized she needed a good Catholic man to take care of her. Sophia and Hazel had lived on money inherited from their parents and their brother's life insurance, but aside from the house, very little remained for Addy. Although Addy had a job, it paid not nearly enough for her to support herself. The aunts were enamored with Lionel. After all, he was a successful Catholic businessman who could definitely be trusted with their pure niece.

Lionel began courting Addy, frequently delighting the aunts with candy or flowers. Addy was rarely alone with him, but a few times when he came for dinner, and the aunts had gone upstairs to bed, he held her hand, put his arm around her shoulders, and kissed her. Although Lionel was not bad looking and had a muscular build, Addy wasn't particularly attracted to him. Admittedly, when she received these first kisses, Addy felt unfamiliar tingling in the area of her body where she received monthly visits from Mr. Red.

She had been only ten when she panicked to see blood in her

panties. Embarrassed by having to speak about the subject, her aunts hastily reported that from then on, Mr. Red would visit her every 28 days. While Hazel rushed to the drugstore to buy a sanitary belt and napkins, Sophia forewarned Addy that with Mr. Red arriving every month, she would be able to have children. Could this be the reason why girls, especially those who had begun menstruation, could not be alone with boys? While Addy made this connection, she was still unaware of what a man and woman had to do to make a baby.

After seven months of courting her, Lionel presented Addy with a small diamond engagement ring. Although in her heart of hearts Addy knew Lionel was not the kind of man she had always dreamed of marrying, what else could she do? When Lionel first kissed Addy, it felt to her that she had wet her pants. Burning up inside, face flushed, mouth salivating profusely, Addy just closed her eyes and accepted the kisses. Lionel himself didn't awaken these new sensations; the response arose automatically. It could have been any man kissing her. In fact, Lionel often repulsed her, particularly when he started ranting about his distaste for non-Catholics. He was a boorish, unsophisticated know-it-all who never questioned the teachings of the Catholic Church. Addy wondered if he had read any books by the literary masters or listened to classical music. She, on the other hand, kept a secret diary of poetry and nourished her heart with stories of true love, like that of Elizabeth and Robert Barrett-Browning. She knew that romance like theirs came along only rarely, and Addy was, after all, an unlucky girl. Feeling her options in life were altogether limited, she floated along blindly as the aunts prepared a small bridal shower in anticipation of Addy's new life as a homemaker. Lionel had enough money to plan a rather lavish wedding at the elegant Westport Inn. In spite of the shallowness of his character, he did know how to put on the dog to impress people.

When the day of her wedding arrived, Addy was literally sleepwalking. Surely, this couldn't be happening. At any moment, Mommy and Daddy would swoop down from Heaven, whisking her away with them. From the books and papers they had left behind, Addy knew her parents were erudite, polished people. If they had lived, they would certainly chide her for abandoning her dreams and allowing the aunts to force her into settling for Lionel as a spouse. After all, he was not of her caliber.

Remarkably, Lionel's eyes shone with pride as his brother, Father Roberge, escorted Addy the virgin bride, down the long aisle of St. Michael's Cathedral. This was, in fact, the first time Lionel ever noticed how truly beautiful Addy was. She had always dressed modestly, wore no make-up, and was awkward and shy. With her long chestnut hair swept sophisticatedly into a French braid, Addy wore a crown of flowers fashioned from dainty seed pearls and crystal beads with a short veil covering her face. The same glistening crystals and pearls adorned the entire top of Addy's wedding dress. Cascading from the pointed bodice were layers and layers of chiffon dotted with the same crystals and pearls. The billowing skirt enveloped Addy's petite frame. Had Lionel ever noticed that Addy's figure was perfectly proportioned 34-24-34? In one of her long, graceful glove-covered arms, Addy cradled a Bernhardt bouquet of calla lilies. For the first and only time in her life, Addy felt like a princess; a prima-ballerina; a prom queen. She blushed to think that she might be, after all, a pretty girl.

As Addy approached the altar, a whisper of awe brushed over the crowd. Lionel could hardly wait until the priest finished the Mass so he could lift the veil and own all that this culminating act symbolized to a man like him. As Lionel lifted the veil, Addy's large green eyes widened with fear and sudden revelation. She now belonged to Lionel for better or worse, and after the wedding, she would officially be his wife and have to share a bed with him. She received a beautiful long lace nightgown and peignoir set for her shower. It finally dawned on her what these fancy bedroom clothes meant.

Lionel had chosen filet mignon for the wedding reception menu. This may be the last time Lionel would splurge on such an expensive meal. As Addy tried to swallow a small bite of steak, she felt as if her throat was closing. The idea of a honeymoon with Lionel frightened Addy to death. Perhaps Lionel provided this swanky wedding as payment for the right to ravish her barbarically that night and forever more. Sophia and Hazel, eyes dewy with tears of joy, had absolutely no clue.

* * * * *

"That's my Addy-girl." Lionel always said that in front of company and gave her a pretentious peck on the cheek. Addison cringed inside from his touch. Of course, that did not mean she had stopped being available for sex. She dared not refuse him. When he was ready for her, he would pinch her bottom hard, sadistically twisting the skin, and she'd awaken, legs spread, ready to receive his nasty member. Lord knows he probably had other women when he was on his business trips, and maybe even closer to home. Addy hoped he would never give her syphilis. She had read that the disease could make a person blind, crippled, and always led to an early demise.

Once she risked bringing up the topic of using rubbers, even though it is a sin for Catholics to practice birth control. Lionel, of course, turned things around to make her look as if she was the offending party.

"How do you know about safes? Don't you trust me? You think I've been unfaithful? You call yourself a CATHOLIC? You know I live by the seventh commandment, in case you forgot it, 'Thou shalt not commit adultery'. How dare you question my faithfulness? Maybe YOU are the one who's running around. I see how you look at the lawn boy. You lust after him; I know it. I'll bet my last nickel that you've already fucked him. How do I know what you do all day when I'm at the office working hard to support your cheating ass? You whore! Now I know why you know about rubbers."

His anger escalated out of control. Eyes narrowed; lips clenched; body grew taut.

Oh please no, thought Addy desperately as she witnessed Lionel's all too familiar demonic transformation. Lionel's voice became louder and louder; the insults more offensive and lewd.

8

Then he smacked her hard across the face. The blow left an angry red welt on her right cheek, and Addy whimpered like an injured puppy. As Lionel began to calm down, he cradled her in his arms, tenderly kissing her bruised cheek. Addy loathed him and the ugly scenario that had taken place countless times over the years. She knew well what would come next. He would take her by the hand, lead her to their bedroom, lift her skirt, unzip his fly, and fuck her. Sometimes he would force his penis up her anus, then immediately after, push it into her vagina, then her anus again, rhythmically alternating between her two openings.

Addy suffered repeated urinary tract and bladder infections. Although the urologist may have suspected why she ended up in his office so frequently, he was always tactful about it. He advised her to use a squeeze bottle filled with a sterile washing solution every time she urinated. In spite of her fastidiousness, the infections continued. The urologist finally prescribed long-term, low-dose antibiotics. She hated taking the medicine because she developed yeast infections and a raw stomach as side effects, but those problems were better than being in pain every time she peed.

It had been almost twenty-five years since Lionel first lifted the veil. Addy knew she was too intelligent and sane to put up with the rapes and beatings, yet she had no way to escape. It was like her hopeless dream of having her own bakery. The dreams of unlucky girls never come true. Such unfortunate souls do not have the confidence or spunk necessary to change their lives.

A few magazines were brave enough to publish articles about wife beating. Addy could identify with the women criticized for staying in abusive relationships. Her spirit had died long ago, so what did it matter if her shell was battered? Lionel had also indirectly threatened her life. After he beat her then cuddled her, he would whisper, "Now Addy-girl would never think of leaving her daddy, would she? She knows what happens to naughty little wives who try to run away, doesn't she? There's nowhere for them to hide. You know it's a man's world. Men stick together. Have you ever heard of any guy arrested for belting his wife? Hey, I know plenty of cops who keep their women in place with a good smack."

Addy was convinced that no matter where she fled, Lionel would track her down. Because he was such a glad-handed phony, he had associates all over the country. He even had their neighbors and friends fooled. After all, he was a deacon at church, coached Little League baseball, and golfed with his neighborhood buddies and co-workers. Addy learned early on that he didn't want her to get too close to the women in the small circle of couples they knew. If he found out she had been for coffee or lunch at a neighbor's, he would fly into a rage, pointing out the housework she had failed to do. Eventually, Addy understood this was his way of keeping her from spilling her guts about the abuse. Addy learned to stay home, working around the house all day and reading women's magazines when her chores were completed.

As Lionel constantly reminded her, she was so lucky to have a nice house and a beautiful yard maintained by Tim, the neighborhood youth Lionel had accused her of fucking. Yes, Addy did use those words in her head, keeping herself entertained by her rebellious thoughts. Wouldn't Aunt Sophia and Aunt Hazel have died a much earlier death if she had dared let the "F" word slip from her lips? Actually, she had never heard the "F" word until Lionel used it with her. Addy was puzzled how a man who portrayed himself as an upstanding Catholic could use such filthy language in the bedroom.

Addy eventually settled upon the opinion that Lionel was crazy. He fashioned himself after the imaginary "Father Knows Best" radio program where the wise, infinitely patient, and loving dad would come home to his happy, zany family. In Lionel's house, they had to be seated around the dining room table at precisely six o'clock, no exceptions. Addy and the children internalized all of Lionel's rules in order to keep the peace.

Things might have been okay, really, if only Lionel were nicer. Addy would love to pamper a good man. She imagined her mom had probably spoiled her dad because he looked like a man who treated his wife lovingly and respectfully. At least that is what Addy gathered from her aunts' descriptions of her father. In fact, Sophia and Hazel had often shed tears over how much they missed their little brother and how sweet he had been to them.

One afternoon, Addy was reading a true story about a woman whose husband beat her regularly, even while she was pregnant. At least Lionel's attacks lightened up while Addy was expecting. She often wished she could have been one of those Catholic baby-machines constantly knocked-up so Lionel would be less violent. Addy had three children: Peter, James, and little Mary. Although Lionel was excessively strict and militaristic with the kids, he did refrain from hitting them.

Lionel seemed to time Addy's thrashings when the children were not around. He frequently revealed his demonic temper to the children by shouting and slamming things, but he never laid a hand on them. Maybe he sensed that if he hurt the kids, his submissive little Addy would rise up, a wounded mother bear, and somehow find the courage to rip him to pieces. The children did learn early on though, to "walk on eggs" so as not to set Daddy off. What if they weren't asleep on the nights he attacked Addy? Whenever that thought rose in her mind, Addy immediately dismissed it. Her children were her reason to live; her angels; saviors; her precious charges, and she tried to shield them from pain and ugliness.

The magazine article Addy was reading that afternoon went on to describe the many horrible things this man did. If he did not like what his wife prepared for dinner, he would smash the plate of food on the floor. At least that had never happened to Addy. She learned to cook exactly what Lionel favored so he usually approved of the meals presented before him.

Some compassionate nuns helped the abused woman to escape to a safe place, but the woman soon went back to her husband who eventually beat her to death. This story made Addy's stomach turn, yet she could understand. When you feel you have lost all hope, it is sometimes easier to lie down and give up.

Chapter II

Confession

Some people who go to Catholic school hate nuns, but Addy did not. Her teachers at St. Mary's were very intelligent and treated her gently, perhaps because she was an orphan. In addition, many of these women had been missionaries and shared vivid stories about the difficult circumstances they encountered when sent to poor countries to establish hospitals and schools.

Nuns take vows of poverty and chastity, and for the most part, seem to lead humble, simple existences. Helena had always reminded Addy that the nuns had the lowest position in the Catholic Church acting as maids to the priests.

When Addy recalled the over-stuffed, pompous priests who visited with Aunts Sophia and Hazel after Mass, vows of poverty and chastity never came to mind. On the contrary, those priests lived lives of luxury, with collections of fine china and crystal, summer homes, trips to the opera in New York City, and frequent vacations abroad. When Addy got older, she was shocked to learn that the Church never defrocked errant priests but simply transferred them to other parishes or positions. This information made her secretly hate those priests, but of course, she never shared her feelings with Lionel. Parish-funded hedonism ... that is how Addy viewed the life of a priest.

Naturally, Lionel loved the priests. In many ways, he was like the worst of the wicked among them: hypocritical, self-indulgent, and vile. Addy, always fair-minded, however, knew that not all priests were bad. She had read that in the olden days, Catholic families felt especially blessed if their sons became men of the cloth. Many poor parents saw the priesthood as the only hope for their sons to receive an education as well as free room and board. Addy wasn't sure, but she suspected these priests were probably decent fellows. Still, she hoped her sons Peter and James would never consider a religious vocation. Lionel, on the other hand, would have loved if the boys chose the priesthood. Then he could puff up even more while he played the role of the devout, humble deacon. What Lionel didn't know was that Addison viewed God as a vengeful puppeteer watching his pathetic creation limp along in suffering and pain. After all, hadn't she prayed for an end to this living nightmare of life with Lionel? She knew she had to stay for the children's sake. She stopped praying about the abuse and just wished Lionel would die.

Lionel's beliefs about God were straight out of the Baltimore Catechism. Addy still remembered that thin, blue-covered book: the doctrine for Catholic children. When she was a child, the drawings of two bottles of milk had intrigued her. One bottle held plain white milk, but the other contained black flecks. The dirty milk represented the soul of a sinner. After all these years, Addy still recalled the rote responses she had memorized:

Question: "Who made us?"
Answer: "God made us."
Question: "Why did God make us?
Answer: "God made us to show forth his goodness and to share with us his everlasting happiness in Heaven."

All Catholic children learn about two kinds of sins: mortal and venial. Mortal sins are transgressions against the Ten Commandments, whereas venial sins are less serious. Addy's eyes filled with tears when she remembered herself as an innocent little girl confessing she had "stolen a grape" from the grocer's display. She did not want to take the grape, but Helena put her up to it. Addy admired Helena so much; she would do almost anything to maintain their friendship.

Although to the outside world, Addy's may have appeared the ideal Catholic life, how comically far from the truth. Lionel had made her "damaged goods," just like the aunts' view of

Helena and her mother, Mary Kurowski. Addy was certain that Helena and her mom had never participated in the smutty things Lionel forced her to do. The few times she protested, Lionel made it clear that, as a Catholic wife, she must submit to her husband. Aunts Sophia and Hazel had often praised Lionel for coming along and saving Addy from the life of sin and degradation she might have faced if she had moved to New York with Helena...what irony.

When Catholics go to Confession, they name their sins, and the priest gives a penance of prayers to recite according to the severity of their transgressions. Addy wondered what Lionel's confessions were like. When he was not out of town "on business," he went to Confession every Saturday afternoon. Addy went along just to appease him, but she gave the same list of sins each week: "I ate meat on Friday. I missed Mass on Sunday." Most often, her penance was three Our Fathers and three Hail Marys. Of course, Lionel and Addy never went to Confession at St. Michael's because Lionel was so involved in that parish; the priest may have recognized his voice. Lionel took Addy around to various Catholic churches in the area, using the excuse that he wanted to get a peek at them.

Lionel must have rationalized that God forgave his sins, at least until his next Confession. One Saturday Lionel drove her to a church in Middletown. Drowning in depression and self-loathing, the last thing Addy wanted to do was to stir up even darker thoughts as she searched her mind for sins. Her gloominess came about last night when she and Lionel attended the wedding of their neighbor's son. Addy observed just how tenderly some men danced with their wives. Why was she stuck with a beast?

Addy knelt in the dark confessional and waited to hear that familiar yet frightening sound of the priest slowly opening the panel on his side of the confessional. At that moment, Addy's heart beat so rapidly she was sure she would faint. The screen that blocked her view of the priest consisted of a strange material Addy had never seen anywhere else. It was a corrugated, perforated partition covered with a thick, yellowish waxy substance. Only a Catholic who has knelt in a confessional would recognize the distinctive odor of this veil-like window through which you could see the shadowy outline of the priest.

"Bless me Father, for I have sinned," Addy began mechanically. "It has been two weeks since my last Confession. These are my sins." Then, almost as if someone else were speaking, Addy blurted, "I want to divorce my husband."

The priest was silent for a moment then replied, "The Catholic Church does not approve of divorce under any circumstances."

Choking back her tears, Addy whispered, "But he beats me."

Cold and matter-of-fact, the priest answered, "Make an appointment to see a Catholic marriage counselor. It is sinful to even think thoughts of divorce."

Addy left the confessional in disbelief and walked zombie-like to the altar. Her deep hatred for the Catholic Church rose inside like a raging fire. She wanted to run through the sanctuary screaming, "DEMONS. YOU ARE ALL DEMONS."

Instead, she glanced over at Lionel with his fat head bowed in holiness.

"You fucking son-of-a-bitch," ranted Addy in her head. "If this is your religion, you can stick it up your ass, just like your fucking filthy dick you love to stick up my ass."

Addy no longer felt guilty about the foul rebellion that played out in her head. It was what kept her sane. She knew that her marriage was very wrong and unhealthy, but she had no way to escape. If she killed herself, the children would have to stay with Lionel, and God knows what he would do. As difficult as it was to go on, Addy had to be an anchor for her beloved Peter, James, and Mary.

Chapter III

Memories of
Sound View Beach, Connecticut

During the ride home from Middletown, Lionel suddenly announced that he was planning to rent his co-worker's summer cottage in Maine.

Oh, hell, thought Addy. How will I be able to tolerate him all day every day for a week?

"Charlie says he has two weeks available," he continued.

TWO WEEKS, Addy thought with alarm. What a perfect penance.

"Of course, I can't take two weeks off from work, but you and the kids can go."

Addy straightened up and replied, "Of course. What weeks will we be going?"

"August 14th through the 27th. I'll be in Denver, but I think you can manage the kids all right without me. After all, it's about time you started to show some responsibility."

She was dumbfounded. Had she heard him correctly? Did he say he would be in Denver? Does that mean he will be letting us go without him? Maybe there is a God after all. As soon as they got home, Addy would start crossing off the days until vacation on the calendar.

The last time Addy had stayed in a cottage by the shore was when she was a child. It was at the ocean that she felt truly alive. Although Addy did not realize it at the time, as a child, she believed there was something wrong with her because she had lost her parents. That was a very unlucky thing. Aunts Sophia and Hazel used to take her to Sound View Beach to stay with some Italian friends who rented cottages in a little Italian enclave every summer. During those two weeks, Addy became

16

someone else. She spent her days floating in the ocean, collecting shells, digging in the sand, and fashioning elaborate castles with canals and moats. All the kids would hunt for snails, and the women would boil the hapless creatures for supper. They would use an open safety pin to dig out the snail's body. Addy just could not stomach the snails. Fortunately, there were always other delicious choices like homemade raviolis or veal cutlets.

The women, joking and laughing, standing over huge pots of boiling pasta, and brushing the hair away from their sweaty brows with bent wrists, could have been a Van Gogh painting. Addy didn't know Italian, and the women knew very little English, but no one cared. At times, a look of sadness clouded the women's happy faces as they observed Addy, commenting, "Poveretta." Addy later learned that translates something like, "Poor little thing." They felt sorry for Addy because she was an orphan, but they treated her as if she was one of their own children. Even Addy's aunts loosened up at the shore, smiled more, and treated Addy with greater warmth. In Addy's mind, Italians were magic. They loved life, no matter what the circumstances. Food, wine, music, children, nature.... these were the treasures of those beloved people.

In addition to the snails, the kids collected buckets of indigo blue mussels, and the Italian men would pry open the shells, then slurp and swallow the slimy orange bodies of the mussels live. Addy nearly threw up at even the idea of this practice, but she had to admit, the mussel-slurping men stirred admiration for what was to Addy a solely masculine pastime. There was so little masculine influence in Addy's life.

The Italian ladies were fat, but they didn't seem to care. They all wore long, dark swim dresses, rubber bathing caps, and water shoes. Later in the day, when the cooking was done and the sun less intense, the women would wade into the shallow water, link hands, and sing in their broken English, "Ring arouna da rosy." They coaxed the children to join the circle, and when they came to the verse, "Ashes, ashes, all fall down," everyone would dunk into the water, squealing with laughter.

Addy was sure this was how life was supposed to be.

The old Italian ladies would jokingly call Addy, "Cigar Mail." Well, at least that was how it sounded. Addy later learned they were saying "Zia Carmela," which means "Aunt Carmela." The practice she shared with this "aunt" was to change her bathing suit every time it got wet. Addy hated when the sand collected in the rear of her suit, making it droop, as if she had a load in her pants. Thankfully, her aunts did acquiesce to this one simple pleasure and brought along an ample supply of swimwear for Addy. Some suits had coordinating bathing caps decorated with floppy rubber flowers.

The grown-ups warned the kids not to track sand into the cottages, so when Addy needed to change her suit, she rapped dutifully on the wood frame of the screen door, hoping to get the attention of one of the adults inside. Sure enough, "Cigar Mail," amused by their mutual habit, brought out a fresh suit from Addy's dresser drawer. It happened to be one of Addy's favorites: it had a gray background printed with small yellow flowers and a flounce around the bottom.

Addy thanked "Cigar Mail" politely and then ran down to the changing rooms. This little group of shorefront cottages owned by a short-tempered Italian widow who rented to the same group of Italian families every year boasted outdoor cold-water showers and rustic wood privacy stalls with long doors that latched from the inside.

When Addy grabbed the handle on one of the changing stalls, the door flew open. Apparently, a woman had forgotten to slide the latch to secure the entrance. Addy stood there frozen, gaping at a sight she would never forget. She had never seen anyone naked, but in her wildest dreams, she couldn't have imagined anyone's backside being so enormous, saggy, and pink. The poor woman said kindly, "Closa da door, honey, closa da door."

After she changed her suit, Addy spent the entire afternoon floating on her back in a plump tire inner tube. She bobbed along on the waves, humming her favorite tunes, heart bursting with joy and thanksgiving for the gift of her ocean. She had usually remembered to head for shore before high tide, but this one particular day, she was lost in dreams of mermaids and mermen in their underwater kingdoms. Voices calling to her from the shore shook her abruptly from her fantasy. Glancing toward the beach, Addy saw her aunts, the Italian women, and the kids motioning for her to come back.

Addy never learned to swim and was scared of deep water. She tried to turn over on her stomach with the tube ringing her waist so she would be in the best position to paddle back to shore. As she shifted her body, the tube began flipping. Panicking, Addy lost hold of it. She was sinking, realizing too late that the tide had come in, and she was very far from land. The tiny figures on the shore waved frantically but helplessly because none of them knew how to swim either.

Addy's mind raced with what she knew to be true: "If you go under three times, you will drown." Addy was drowning. As she disappeared into the bottomless sea, she knew this was the end. How surprising to die so young. Yet, she was not afraid. She often thought that maybe Mommy had become a mermaid and Daddy a merman now living under the magnificent sea. Perhaps she was going to join them.

Suddenly, she felt a strong arm grab and pull her. Someone was rescuing her. The trip from way out in the ocean and back to shore was a blur. All she knew was that a strong, hairy Italian man had jumped in, lit cigar and all, to get her. The strangest part of this near-death experience was neither Addy nor her vacationing Italian friends had ever seen this man before and never saw him again. She was convinced a cigar-smoking angel saved her life.

In the evenings after dinner, the kids would walk to a nearby concession stand for Italian ice. There was a merry-go-round, too, with a long metal arm that dispensed brass rings. As your horse whizzed past the outstretched mechanical contraption, you had to lean far out to try and grab a ring. Most rings were silver, but if you caught the rare golden one, you got your next ride free. Addy strove to catch a ring but was frightened she might fall if she leaned too far off her horse. This was after all, a very fast-spinning carousel. One time, the merry-go-round attendant cheated and placed the golden ring in Addy's fingers. She never forgot how proud and special she had felt that night because of that man's simple act of kindness.

There was a penny arcade where the kids could play all kinds of games such as pinball and skee ball and stuff themselves with popcorn, candy apples, and cotton candy. Aunt Sophia and Aunt Hazel did not want Addy to spend too much time at the arcade because the older boys always hung around there. The Italian kids could go out alone, but as expected, the aunts chaperoned Addy on these evening excursions, which put a damper on things. In spite of her "shadows," Addy had great fun. As the sky darkened, and they all walked back to the cottages, the kids felt exhausted but exhilarated. All day in the salty water and hot sun erased every thought from their minds. With the cottages' windows open, the drowsy, sunburned children drifted off to sleep to the reassuring music of the waves rolling gently to shore.

Addy kept these precious recollections of the Sound View Beach vacations locked up in her heart and took them out when things got tough. The two weeks at the shore were her redemption, her escape from a flat, gray existence into a short chapter of her life that was once brimming with vitality, hopes, and dreams.

As Lionel drove toward town, she thought again about the poor woman she had burst in on at the changing stalls at Sound View. To a small child, an enormous derriere is a shock, but Addy suspected her own ass was probably that large by now. As some men often say about women, she had "let herself go."

* * * * *

Addy's reminiscence suddenly shattered with a sharp remark from Lionel.

"Earth to Addy. Earth to Addy. Are you listening?"

Startled, Addy replied, "Of course. You said we would be going to Maine from August 14th through the 27th, and you'll be in Denver." Hallelujah! She thought mischievously.

Summer finally arrived, and the kids were ecstatic, counting the days until their first real vacation. School usually got out in mid-June, but by the end of July, the children were usually bored already. This year they had something marvelous brewing; Mary took charge of crossing out the days on the calendar.

Weeks before the vacation, Addy started to iron and pack. Her petite figure ballooned in recent years, and one thing she dreaded was shopping for a new swimsuit. God knows she would never fit into the relics she had saved in case she lost weight. Food was Addy's drug. She turned to it when she was nervous, stressed, or depressed, which was most of the time. Lionel and the children loved dessert after dinner (and she did, too) so she continued to bake. Lionel golfed and lifted barbells in the basement, and he hadn't blown up with age like Addy. He criticized her weight, but that did not keep him from wanting sex nearly every night.

One morning, Addy reached up to the closet shelf to take down a suitcase Lionel no longer used for his business trips. He had recently purchased a new set of expensive leather luggage for his travels. Addy had no need for suitcases because she and the kids never went anywhere. Inside the suitcase was a piece of paper that looked like a receipt of some kind. Before discarding it, Addy noticed it was a voucher for Mr. and Mrs. Roberge for two nights at the Broadmoor Hotel in Colorado Springs.

As much as Addy despised Lionel, her heart sank. So he had a woman in Colorado. That must be where he was going. What infuriated Addy was imagining how he probably treated this woman. Broadmoor was a luxury hotel featured in one of Addy's magazines. Lionel, in his warped sense of morality, might think one woman outside "the holy sacrament of marriage" was not as bad as having several, particularly if he were "in love" with this person. Addy doubted if this lady was his only lover. Over the years, he traveled to several cities for business meetings, and his drinking escalated. He must have picked up his share of bar flies.

I wonder if this woman knows Lionel is married with children? Addy mused. She was undoubtedly married and did not give a hoot. On the other hand, maybe she was attracted to his charm and lavish spending habits, thought Addy sarcastically.

"What a joke," Addy laughed, crumbling up the receipt, and then rushing to the bathroom to flush it down the toilet. If Lionel suspected Addy knew something about his conniving to go to Colorado, he might explode and cancel her vacation with the kids. Their first real vacation...she just could not believe that James, Peter, Mary, and she were about to share two whole weeks together without Lionel. Could it really be possible?

Chapter IV

Wells, Maine

Early on the morning of August 14, they loaded the car for the long ride to Maine. Lionel's blood boiled as he watched the kids putting their bags helter-skelter into the back of the station wagon. True to his militaristic form, Lionel made the kids remove their belongings, and he rearranged everything like a perfect puzzle.

Addy had never learned to drive. She longed to get her license, and Lionel had once encouraged her to do so. Although she passed the written portion of the driving test, she was just too nervous to use the car, fearing Lionel's wrath if she ever had an accident. It was maddening to have to rely upon Lionel to transport the kids and her everywhere. He was a rude and impatient driver.

Before getting on the road towards Maine, they stopped at First National Market to pick up provisions for the vacation. Addy had made a shopping list so that she and the kids could zip through the aisles and not keep Lionel waiting. It was pathetic how automatically Addy responded to every situation that might spark Lionel's temper. What a way to live.

Because the cottage was actually a summer home, where the owners planned to retire one day, it had a fully equipped modern kitchen and other amenities. Lionel said the beach was only a few minutes' walk, and there was a small grocery store nearby. The children, well trained by Addy not to get on their father's nerves, were quiet during the endless trip to Maine. They amused themselves looking out the windows as they whizzed past parts of New England they had never seen. When they finally pulled into Beach Plum Lane, then the driveway of a lovely home, Addy was suddenly overwhelmed with feelings of nervous anticipation and joy. Fighting back the tears, she excitedly asked Lionel, "Is this it?"

"Yep," he grunted. "Charlie has a gorgeous place here, and he never rents it out to strangers. He did it as a favor to me so you're darned lucky."

The house was actually two cottages joined together in a U-shape. It looked as if there had once been a freestanding garage between the bungalows, but a large part of the garage had been redesigned to increase the size of the O'Malley's place and add the master suite. There was still an attached garage for the O'Malleys with a door leading directly into the other residence. Lionel said that portion of the U-shaped configuration was still very much a beach cottage. Charlie had the "luck of the Irish;" an old woman sold him the two houses for a song, with the stipulation that she could use the cottage side for two weeks a year for the rest of her life. Apart from those two weeks, Charlie rented out the cottage side as an income property.

Once again, Lionel emphasized how fortunate Addy and the kids were to be able to stay in Charlie's side of the property and warned the kids not to mess anything up. Addy wondered if Charlie knew that Lionel wanted to spend these two weeks with his woman in Colorado. After all, Charlie was often on the road with Lionel.

When Lionel turned the key to open the door to this beautiful home, Addy was speechless. The house was something Addy may have seen in one of her magazines. Light streamed into the many windows, illuminating the space with a happy glow. Darker hues were popular when Addy and Lionel's house was constructed several years ago, but now their home seemed gloomy and dated. Lionel never wanted to spend any money on improvements. As Addy walked through Charlie's house, one space after another entranced her. The floor plan was very open with living room, dining room, and kitchen flowing into one another. The kitchen contained white cabinets with glass doors, a white tiled floor, and a counter that looked out into the living room. There were stools on one side of the counter, and a large dining area extended from the kitchen. Off the dining room was the huge master suite with its own bath. On the nightstand, Addy spied a photograph of Charlie O'Malley and his wife. Charlie was a tall, handsome, athletic-looking Irishman whose eyes seemed to twinkle with warmth. He looked like a mischief-maker, holding back a good laugh. Charlie's wife on the other hand, was plain and serious-looking, almost homely. Not that Addy was any beauty, mind you, but she often wondered how some unattractive women won the hearts of gorgeous men. Just how Charlie's wife, Kathy—Addy thought that was her name—held her head, Addy knew that if Charlie ever dared stray from her, she would raise holy hell. With her sixth sense about people, Addy knew immediately that Charlie loved his wife, and he was not a cheater. She had to turn away from the photo quickly. Pictures of happily married couples stirred up a mixture of envy and sadness in Addy's heart. She knew that envy was one of the seven deadly sins. Although she held such disdain for the Catholic Church, Addy still tried to be a good person and avoid the worst offenses: Pride, Envy, Anger, Sloth, Greed, Gluttony, and Lust.

The children shouted with delight as they discovered that the sliding glass doors on one side of the dining room led to a sun porch, the brightest space of all. The white wicker furniture sported new blue, yellow, and white printed cushions. Adorning the sofa and chairs were hand-hooked throw pillows with images of shells, starfish, and seahorses. There were huge jalousie windows on three sides and a ceiling fan overhead.

The fireplace mantel in the living room held numerous photos of Charlie's family and friends. Addy glanced at them briefly and decided they represented a slice of a very happy existence: beachside barbeques and lobster roasts; Charlie, his wife, and another couple smiling as a waiter carried out a glowing birthday cake; pictures of the kids at various stages of their lives. Addy just had to stop looking. She vowed to avoid studying these photographs too closely during the vacation.

Lionel hated when Addy would drift off into her dream world. He said sharply, "There's a restaurant near the beach parking lot. I thought I'd take you and the kids there for lunch."

Addy figured Lionel might be feeling a slight pang of guilt for leaving them while he went off to Denver, but no. He wasn't that selfless. She suspected the real reason for his sudden generosity was that he wanted a lobster roll.

Although the restaurant was within walking distance, Lionel drove them there. Addy saw him check his watch several times; he must be on a tight schedule. They drove to the parking lot of Wells Beach, and then walked over to McKenna's Sea Side Grill. The intoxicating smell of fried fresh seafood mixed with salt air immediately brought back memories of Addy's summers at Sound View Beach. In fact, the whole place resembled a scene from a 1920s picture postcard.

The kids ran quickly to save a picnic table by the sea wall. You could walk down some stone stairs to the beach about thirty feet below. Hot dogs and fries for the kids, a lobster roll for Lionel, and a fried scallop roll for Addy; what a delicious break from their normal routine of always eating at home. The children's faces were already pink from the sun, but they didn't mind the heat. A soft breeze played gently with the wisps of auburn hair that framed Mary's sweet face. Anyone watching Lionel, Addy, Peter, James, and Mary eating lunch by the sea would assume they were a normal, happy American family. When Addy noticed the impatient look in Lionel's eyes, she knew she had better eat faster.

While they rode back to the house, Lionel spouted inane directions, which he always assumed she needed. "Don't lose the keys to the cottage; make sure the kids shower outside so they don't track sand into the house; leave the place as spotless as you found it; be sure to wash all the towels and sheets after stripping the beds ... and blah, blah, blah."

Lionel immediately jumped out of the car as soon as they returned to the house and didn't even bother to walk inside with them. Tousling the boys' hair, and giving Mary a quick peck on the cheek, Lionel reminded them he would be back to pick them up on the 21st around 6:00 p.m., and he wanted them all packed and ready to go. He glanced toward Addy, then reached into his pocket, took out his wallet, and handed her a fifty-dollar bill.

"This is in case you guys want to eat at McKenna's sometimes. Now don't think you have to spend it all."

"Thanks," Addy said cheerfully, trying to disguise her eagerness for him to leave. Once Lionel's dark spirit had gone, the true sweetness and light of this enchanted cottage could shine through at its brightest. There were two other bedrooms so the boys quickly called "dibs" on the one with matching twin beds. That made more sense since the other bedroom had one double bed. By the time they unpacked their clothes and made up the beds, it was nearly four o'clock. "Can we go to the beach now, Mom?" James asked excitedly.

Addy hesitated ... she thought, after all, dinner would be at six, and that wouldn't give them much time. Just before responding, Addy had a revelation: Who said we have to eat dinner at six? Lionel isn't here, and we four are on VACATION.

"Sure. Go change into your suits." The boys raced to their room, digging through their dresser drawers to find their swim trunks. Addy had to stop herself from saying, "Hey, we just finished putting everything so neatly into the bureau, and now your clothes are all scrambled up."

Before the words tumbled automatically from her lips, she made a silent vow to herself that the kids were going to have the time of their lives, and it didn't matter if the drawers were neat. She really wasn't a stickler for tidiness but had to conform to Lionel's expectations. He controlled every aspect of the kids' and her life. Rejoice! Rejoice! He's not here to see!

Mary tended to be neater than her brothers were. She knew exactly where she had placed her beautiful new bathing suit. She had picked it out herself. It was a pink and yellow floral and butterfly print trimmed at the top with a small pink ruffle. The pink straps crossed in the back and were held together by a lovely appliquéd butterfly.

Addy struggled to pull her new old lady's dowdy swim dress up over her thunderous thighs. Suddenly the picture of the Italian lady's huge rump flashed again across her mind. Laughing aloud, Addy said to herself, "Now I know how she felt."

Addy gathered up a beach blanket, towels, fruit, and some bug spray. She asked the kids if they would like sandwiches for dinner after they got home from the beach. The spontaneity of the situation was too rare a treat for the kids to comprehend at first.

"Sandwiches for dinner?" Peter questioned. Then, three birds trilling with joy, chirped, "Sure, Wow, Great."

Addy, too, already felt lighter inside. She had spent so many hours of her life making dinners for the family that putting sandwiches together for supper was going to be a new experience. Maybe she would place all the fixings in assembly-line fashion on the counter so the kids could create their own sandwiches.

Addy didn't want to walk down the stone stairs to the beach just below McKenna's Sea Side Grill. It was not a very pretty beach; the sand looked rough, and it was still crowded with noisy people. When she had flipped through the O'Malley's loose-leaf notebook that contained restaurant menus and other tidbits of information about the area, she found a flyer for Wells Town Beach. If you had a sticker on your car, you could park free in the beach lot all summer. Of course, walkers entered the beach free any time of the day. The kids divided the towels and other beach gear and trudged over to the Town Beach. There were just a few cars still left in the lot. A long wooden board pathway wound its way through sand dunes to the ocean. It was quite a hike up the inclined trail to the water. Addy was out of breath, but her slender kids bobbed along cheerfully. Why had she "let herself go?"

On the horizon, Addy saw the peacock blue water sparking in the late afternoon sun. She stepped out of her beach slippers and let the sugar white sand sift through her toes. Addy felt as if her heart would erupt. Yes, the Connecticut shore was nice, but something about this Maine beach was so different. It felt timeless, eternal ... Antique maps; spyglasses; young men shipping out on fishing vessels; women waiting breathlessly at the wharf's edge to greet their sweethearts returning home from sea voyages ... Connecticut had the same maritime history, but the Maine coast was more rugged, wild, confirming the passion and ceaseless transformation of nature. As she watched her three beautiful children race to the water, Addy suddenly felt ashamed of herself. Why did she continually wallow in self-pity? Look at her perfectly formed, smart, sweet babies. She spent so much time locked up in her own head or trying to dodge Lionel's barbs; she rarely stopped to realize how lucky she was to have the children. Lionel had given her that one good, spotless gift. In fact, if you did not know beforehand they were Lionel's children, you would never have guessed he was their father. Addy wondered why Lionel hadn't accused her of having had sex with at least three different men because the children each looked so different.

The eldest, Peter, or Pete, his preferred moniker, was tall and lanky with blonde hair, large brown eyes, and skin that tanned easily. He was smart, easy-going, and very athletic. Lionel favored him, but Pete never took advantage of his father's preference. On the contrary, he was loyal to Addy, James, and Mary, and would always rush to their aid. James, who preferred "Jimmy," was very different from his brother. He also had skin that tanned easily but had curly dark brown hair and vibrant blue eyes. Addy remembered how surprised she was to give birth to a child with dark hair and light eyes. Elizabeth Taylor, supposedly the most beautiful woman in the world, was famous for her raven-black hair and violet-blue eyes. These traits made a rare combination. Jimmy preferred books to sports, but to satisfy his father, Jimmy played on the town's soccer and baseball teams. He was also an excellent writer and artist. Unfortunately, Lionel did not view Jimmy's gifts as "masculine." Addy worried that as Jimmy matured, Lionel might bully him. For now, Jimmy's role as altar server kept him safe.

Mary ... sweet little Mary ... had Addy's dark brown hair, hazel eyes, and fair complexion. There was something ethereal about Mary. Delicate and sensitive, she loved nature and had an amazingly compassionate heart for such a young girl. Addy hoped wolves would not mistake Mary's sweetness for weakness.

All the children were tall for their ages, and that was another thing that surprised Addy. Lionel was on the shorter side, and Addy herself was only 5 feet 3 inches. Everything about her children was wonderful: each was attractive, smart, considerate, and seemingly well adjusted. Who knows what the future held for them. How could they grow up with a father like Lionel and not end up on the psychiatrist's couch? Was having a dad like Lionel better than having no dad at all?

After her near drowning experience at Sound View, Addy promised herself that if she were ever a mother, she would make sure her children learned to swim. She watched her three fish frolicking in the waves and felt more at peace than she had in years. When was the last time she enjoyed her children with such abandon without worrying about what Lionel would do next? Her chest tightened when he came to mind, but she wanted to embrace new experiences and promised herself to squelch all thoughts of him during the vacation. It would be difficult, but she resolved to keep her vow to herself. After all, an opportunity like this may never come along again.

The sun was setting, but the kids were still in the water. Addy called to them, asking if they were ready to go home. "NOT YET," they shouted. She could hear the unfamiliar ring of freedom, joy, and harmless defiance in their voices. Soon enough, the children got cold and ran shivering to the blanket, quickly wrapping themselves in their beach towels. Addy gave them each a spritz of mosquito repellant, they gathered their things, and started down the wooden walkway. Addy could tell the kids had had a good workout in the water because they strolled at a pace she could match.

"How stupid of me not to bring a flashlight," Addy chided herself as they stumbled along to the parking lot in the dark. The warm glow of the cottages dotting their route home lit a flicker of security and hope in her heart. These sweet dwellings seemed oblivious to any pain or sadness. They glimmered with unquestioning confidence that life has infinite goodness to offer.

When they reached the house, Addy and the kids all huddled together under the spray of the outdoor shower. Warm water in a beach shower ... what a treat. Addy shuddered while recalling the torture of the freezing cold water of the outdoor showers at Sound View Beach slapping against her little sunburned body. Because the mean landlady strictly forbade sandy and dripping wet kids inside the cottages, Addy had no choice but to endure this suffering. That was the only unpleasant memory she had of that place.

When the children and she went inside, Addy had the kids take warm showers and change into their pajamas straightaway. She rinsed out their suits, hanging them on the clothesline in the lovely backyard. Addy wished she could have a clothesline at her own home, but they lived in the suburbs, where outdoor clotheslines were unpopular. She remembered how fresh the sheets used to smell when she was a little girl growing up at her aunts' house. Addy had never even seen a clothes dryer. Maybe some rich people owned them, but all the families in her neighborhood hung their wash outside. She remembered her aunts even going out into the winter snow to hang the clothing and linens. Sometimes everything would be stiff as boards when Addy helped pick the wash off the line. They would bring the clothes inside and thaw them near the radiators. At the time, Addy was irritated that her aunts hung the sheets outside even in the winter, but now she finally understood: fresh air at all costs.

It was nearly nine o'clock, and they had not had dinner yet. The kids were starving. Just as Addy planned, she lined up paper plates and plastic cutlery, bread, cold cuts, cheese, tomatoes, lettuce, mustard, and mayonnaise on the kitchen counter. She had small bags of State Line potato chips, a Massachusetts-made treat loved throughout New England. She had brought a tin of her homemade chocolate chip cookies for dessert.

The kids rushed through the cafeteria-style line, assembling their sandwiches, then climbed up on the counter stools to feast. They laughed and joked, even talking with their mouths full. Addy sat alone at the dining room table with her chair turned to face the children. When had she ever seen them this happy at dinnertime? It was nearly eleven o'clock when they finished eating, and the kids could barely stay awake to brush their teeth. Addy tucked in Mary first, who whispered a spontaneous little prayer, "Thank you, God, for this vacation." Addy felt the same. When she got to the boys' room, they were already fast asleep.

Addy retired to her "suite" to get ready for bed. At first, it felt so unnatural to be using another woman's bathroom. She could not help peeking in some of the vanity drawers; in one, she found packages of rubbers and some petroleum jelly. Hmm ... the O'Malleys practiced birth control. Then, her heart sank as she imagined what it must be like to make sweet love with your husband instead of tolerating barbaric violation. From all the women's magazines Addy had read, she understood that some couples enjoyed lovemaking well into the later years of their marriage. In fact, the magazines had begun to provide "tips" on how to remain attractive for your husband and please him in the bedroom. For a split second, Addy thought, maybe Lionel cheats because I am no longer appealing. She immediately scolded herself, not only for thinking of Lionel while on her vacation, but also for conjuring up such stupid thoughts. He had treated her in the same way ever since their honeymoon when she was still young and maybe pretty. After her bath, Addy was too tired to read or even think much. She pulled back the covers of the huge bed, hugged her pillow, and fell into a deep, dreamless sleep.

The weather remained perfect for the first three days of their vacation, and they spent each carefree day at the beach, even bringing a picnic lunch with them one day. As she watched the children dig in the sand, collect shells, and make sandcastles, she recalled her own happy days at the seashore. Had she and the children died and gone to Heaven? Every day was peaceful and filled with joy. She dared not count their remaining days of freedom.

That evening as the children played *Sorry!* and Addy read her well-worn copy of a collection of the works of Jane Austen, strains of Bach's "Brandenburg Concerto No. 5," one of Addy's favorite pieces of music, drifted through the sun porch windows.

She looked up from her book, curious to see from where the

music was coming. Addy caught a glimpse of the man in the cottage next door. He was sitting alone on his porch, reading a newspaper. She had never noticed him before and quickly brushed aside the image of his beautiful profile with the thought that his wife must be inside.

Something about the aura of this man stayed with Addy as she bathed and prepared for bed that night. He was, from what Addy could see, breathlessly handsome ... the kind of man that could marry any woman he chose, and he had probably done just that. Addy imagined a striking, slender blonde waiting for him inside the cottage. How are some women so lucky?

After this first glimpse of the man, Addy kept looking over at his house or on the beach to see if she could spy him once more. She never noticed him on the beach, but one evening, she saw him sitting alone on his porch as he had done that first night. On Thursday of their first week, it started to rain. The kids grumbled, but Addy suspected they were actually relieved to get a break from the hot sun. New Englanders, fully aware of the long, cold winter ahead, dare not squander a sunny day at the beach. Yet, sunburned bodies secretly crave clouds and rain. Because they did not have to rush out to the beach that morning, Addy fussed with eggs and bacon for breakfast. They had barely finished eating when someone knocked on their door. The children looked wide-eyed at one another, trying to imagine who it could be. After all, they knew no one in Maine.

Chapter V

New Friends

Somewhat hesitantly, Addy called out, "Who is it?"

A man's low voice answered, "It's Greg from next door. May I talk to you for a minute?"

Although his voice was deeply masculine and assured, there was a sense of urgency about it.

Without thinking about how messy she must look, Addy rushed quickly to the door. When she opened it, there he was ... the beautiful creature she had seen sitting on his porch at night, yellow rain jacket draped over his wide shoulders. He's a triangle, Addy thought spontaneously. She didn't know why, but tall men with broad shoulders and narrow waists secretly thrilled her. Maybe it was because as a child she had a set of brightly colored wooden men you could balance and stack. They seemed to be wearing business suits so Addy called them her "Gentlemen."

The rain dripped from the hood of the raincoat of this Narcissus, who most probably had not spent his life gazing at his own stunning reflection. In fact, he appeared to be oblivious to his good looks.

Blushing with embarrassment, Addy said, "Please come in."

Thrusting his large hand toward her, the man said, "Hi, I'm Greg Finn from the house next door." His handshake was firm and confident. Addy was touching a dream.

"Hello. I'm Addison Roberge, and these are my children, Peter, James, and Mary."

The kids nodded, looking the stranger over with pleasant curiosity.

"I'm sorry to trouble you, but I need to ask a favor. I have an interview this afternoon, and my sister was supposed to come up to watch my daughter. She just called to say her kids woke up sick so she doesn't dare bring them up here. She's afraid Allison, my daughter, might catch what they have. Allison can't be around sick children."

Addy was speechless? Where was his wife? What was wrong with his daughter? How could this perfect specimen of a man have any troubles in his life?

Addy said quickly, "Would she be comfortable staying with us? The kids would love the company."

At first the man looked hesitant and then said, "That's a great idea. I shouldn't be gone that long. Well, unless they decide to hire me on the spot." He broke into a broad Irish smile, his straight white teeth glistening.

Greg asked if he could bring Allison over around one o'clock. His interview was in Portland. Addy forgot how frumpy she looked and said cheerfully, "We'll be waiting." The kids looked at one another excitedly. What new adventures awaited them on this rainy day? The tension vanished from their neighbor's face. "I can't thank you enough." He said as he turned and sprinted back to his cottage.

Addy showered and changed into the only decent summer outfit she had, white slacks and a navy blue top. Ugh. Why was she so fat? Shut up, stupid, she chided herself. You could never attract this man, even if you were young and single. He was simply out of her league.

At precisely one o'clock, Greg arrived at their door. He was extraordinarily handsome in his raincoat, but in a pinstriped oxford shirt and khaki pants, he was indescribable. A tiny redheaded girl, who looked to be about six years old, stood nervously next to her father. Addy was so relieved to see the child showed no obvious signs of illness. Aside from being rather thin and a bit pale, Allison looked perfectly normal. Mary came straight to the door to greet Allison.

"Come on in. Want to play *Mr. Potato Head*?"

Allison immediately forgot she was with strangers and replied excitedly, "I love *Mr. Potato Head*."

Greg said, "She has had her lunch." Addy asked what foods,

if any, Allison could not have.

"None," Greg smiled, "... if you can get her to eat anything."

As he turned to leave, he reiterated, "You don't know how much this means to Allison and me."

Addy blushed and managed to fumble her way through, "I hope you get the job."

"Thanks. Wish me luck!"

Allison proved to be a delightful child. As Addy watched her playing with the kids, she wondered about Greg's wife. Would Addy ever find out why he was alone with his daughter? The afternoon wiled away slowly. Mary even got Allison to eat a sliced apple and some cookies. The boys seemed to enjoy Allison as much as Mary did. They teased the girls harmlessly while Mary and Allison laughed over-dramatically as girls sometimes do around boys.

About five o'clock Greg knocked on the door, and Allison yelled excitedly, "It's Daddy."

There was Greg standing in her doorway, arms full of grocery bags. Addy asked immediately, "How did it go?"

"Well, they didn't give me the final word, but I think I got the job. This was my third interview." He suddenly turned shy. "By the way, I hope you don't mind. I brought steaks and chicken to put on the grill for dinner."

Embarrassed, Addy protested, "Oh, you shouldn't have done that."

In spite of her response, Greg sensed she approved.

"Do you like red wine?"

Although Addy did not drink, she did not want to seem a fool. What if the kids told Lionel a man had wine with their mother? For a moment, she was lost in confusion and fear.

"Sure. I love it," she quickly lied. Addy did not care if Lionel beat her to death. She had to spend time in the presence of this Greek god.

Greg put the groceries down on the counter and then scooped up Allison in his arms.

"Daddy, Daddy, I had fun," she exclaimed.

"Does that mean you want to go home now, sweet potato?"

Greg teased.

"No, Daddy. Let's stay here please."

Addy was relieved that Allison wanted to stay for supper. Greg seemed the kind of dad who would put his little girl's wishes before his own. He asked Addy if there was any charcoal in the garage. She was too embarrassed to let him know she had not even tried the grill, and Greg must have noticed her discomfort.

"Never mind. I'll get some charcoal from my place."

The rain had disappeared by six o'clock. Now a cool breeze blew away the clouds, revealing a deep blue canopy of sky.

"Look outside, kids. There's a rainbow," Addy declared excitedly.

The kids pushed their way to the door to see. Tears welled in Addy's eyes, as she thought, maybe this is a good omen, but immediately dismissed the thought as ridiculous. Even if this was the only night she ever spent with Greg and Allison, Addy would be grateful.

Greg insisted that he do the grilling and told Addy to relax. First, he wrapped baking potatoes and ears of corn with tin foil and let them roast directly on the coals for quite a while before placing the meat on the grill top. As she slowly sipped her wine, Addy began to unwind and thought dreamily, all that, and he cooks, too.

Why doesn't this man have a wife? Wait. Maybe he does. That's it. She could not come because she is traveling for work, Addy thought pessimistically. She accepted the fact that she was a masochist. Any woman who continues to live with a sadistic man like Lionel has to love suffering. Why was she allowing Lionel to burst this magic rainbow bubble?

After dinner, the kids played kick ball in the yard while Addy and Greg watched them from her sun porch. Addy noticed that Allison was having a hard time keeping up with her kids so she shouted, "Let Allison have the ball!"

Greg turned to Addy and said, "Thanks for being so considerate. Allison doesn't look sick, does she?"

"Not at all," Addy quickly remarked but did not want to pry

about what was wrong with Greg's daughter. He in turn offered the information on his own. She has leukemia."

"Are there any cures for it?" inquired Addy gently. Greg suddenly looking sad said, "Not yet. There is a lot of research going on, and there are some treatments ... but no cure. Allison has been lucky so far. She is in remission," and looking panicked, he added, "or I would never have left her with you." For a moment, it seemed Greg felt guilty for not telling Addy about Allison's condition beforehand.

Addy tried to change the subject and said with half-hearted optimism, "Maybe by the time she is older, they will have found a cure."

For the first time, Greg looked depressed. "As long as she is in remission, she's OK. I have resigned myself to the fact that I am slowly losing my daughter. That's why I want to change jobs and move up here permanently. Things always seem so much better by the ocean, and Allison loves Maine."

Trying to lighten the mood, Addy became animated. "You are so right. My best memories are of summers by the sea."

Greg looked over at Addy as if he was seeing her for the first time. He saw a deeply private sadness in her hazel eyes and wondered what had caused her sorrow. She was, after all, a lovely woman. Addy felt self-conscious as she felt Greg studying her face. She looked away. The questions she burned to ask were about Allison's mother. Was she dead? Certainly, a perfect man like Greg could not have this much bad luck.

As if reading her mind, Greg continued, "When my wife found out about Allison's disease, she just couldn't deal with it so she moved away. We eventually divorced, and Allison never again saw or spoke to her mother."

Addy's heart was breaking. "Does Allison ask about her mother?"

"All the time," Greg added. "I tell her that her mom is working on a secret project and cannot write letters or visit. It's a dumb lie, but Allison seems to accept it."

Addy instantly hated this woman. What kind of mother would abandon her child?

"Oh Greg," Addy said sincerely, "I am so sorry."

He smiled at her and said, "Well, at least I have my little girl for a few years. That's a lot more than some people have."

He's an optimist, Addy thought. I had better not be too negative or morose around him. He has enough on his mind. Greg checked his wristwatch and said, "Wow. It's late. I had better get Allison to bed."

Addy was dreading hearing these words. He was going to leave.

Greg called to Allison, and all the kids came running.

"Can Allison come over and play with us another day?" implored Mary.

"Why sure," said Greg, his beautiful smile brightening his face. "She is lucky to have found some kids to play with. She's sick of just her old dad."

Allison went over to Greg and hugged his legs. "That's not true, Daddy."

What a sweet child; just like her father.

They said their "good nights" without making any plans. Greg's optimism was contagious, and Addy knew they would all be together again. The wine had gone to her head, and she fell asleep that night, imagining herself cradled in the safety of Greg's arms.

The sun was already bright by eight in the morning. After breakfast, the kids asked excitedly, "What are we going to do today?"

They had no sooner spoken than a knock came at the door. There was Greg, standing sheepishly, but illuminated like a pure-hearted knight. Addy had been too shy to study him closely, but this morning she could not take her eyes off him. He wore a navy blue T-shirt with a small yachting logo on it, khaki Bermuda shorts and boat shoes with no socks. Such fine legs. Allison was standing next to her dad. Dressed in blue shorts and a red and white striped shirt, she looked rested and happy.

"You two look like sailors," Addy laughed.

"I hope it's not too early," Greg said, "but we wanted to invite you to come out on our boat with us today."

Addy's kids, still in their pajamas, looked amazed. A boat! Addy was, of course, afraid of deep water, but at that moment, she didn't care. The kids ran to their rooms to get dressed. Greg's beach wagon was waiting out front. All four kids piled into the back seat, leaving Addy to sit next to Greg. She watched how carefully and confidently he drove.

"The boat is docked at the Webhannet River boatyard."

Addy dared not display her ignorance about the geography of Maine, or boating, for that matter. She had never been in a boat. When they arrived at the marina, other boaters waved and shouted at Greg and Allison.

Greg's boat was a beauty. It was wooden, about 26 feet long, and the well-waxed mahogany gleamed in the sunlight. Although the boat was an older one, someone had lovingly babied it. There were padded benches along the sides of the top deck, and a kitchen, bathroom, and bedroom below.

"This was my dad's boat," Greg said proudly. "I had to eat my words when I told him I would never have a motorized boat. I used to sail, but this boat is better now that Allison and I are co-captains."

Greg helped the kids fasten their life jackets. Addy was relieved when he gave her one, too. The sea was calm, the sky blue, the breeze gentle; a dream of a day for boating. Is this what people who believe in God see as proof of his benevolence? Yet why does Allison have to suffer? Why does Greg have to stand by helplessly watching his little girl's health decline? Addy raged. She looked over at Greg as he handled the boat so firmly and capably, and wanted so much to ask him what his take on God happened to be. She did not.

Only Greg knew that this boat ride held a surprise for the children ... he was heading to Old Orchard Beach, the first and longstanding New England ocean side amusement park. The kids suddenly caught sight of the ferris wheel and looked at Greg with amazement.

"Are we going THERE?" Jimmy asked.

Greg replied, "We sure are, buddy. Do you think you'll like it?"

Addy panicked. She didn't have enough money with her to fund a day for her three children at an amusement park.

She turned to Greg to protest, but he said, "By the way, this day is on me. Allison and I are so happy to have made some new friends in Maine."

Why is he so nice? Why is he such an angel? How could he be so benevolent when he was, after all, unlucky?

Their time at Old Orchard Beach whizzed by in a blissful blur. The seductive smells, sounds, and sights enraptured Addy, as they had done all those years ago at Sound View. Allison and Mary rode the carousel, trying to catch the golden ring. All of them went on the ferris wheel, high in the air with the ocean right below. Greg knocked down stacks of wooden milk bottles so that Allison and Mary could win Teddy bears, and the boys, American flags. They stuffed themselves on foot-long hot dogs, sticky red candy apples, and puffy pink cotton candy.

Addy pleaded with the God she did not trust to never let this day end. Please let us stay forever with Greg and Allison.

As the sun began to set, Greg said, "We have to start getting back."

The kids groaned, but they were nice children who had already learned that all good things must eventually end. On the trip back to Webhannet River Marina, everyone was quiet. The sleepy children went down below and all plopped on the big bed. Addy sat next to Greg as he steered his boat. Had he stole a glance at her a time or two? Of course not... that was impossible. No matter how bad his luck, he was, after all, a triangle. He was just too handsome and perfect for her, and besides, he was probably an unquestioning Catholic like Lionel.

LIONEL. It would be just a matter of days until he came to pick them up. What would she do? How could she go with him? What if the kids told him about Greg?

Frightened, Addy thought of the cruelty she would suffer if Lionel knew she had spent time with a man. Then, she remembered her promise not to think of Lionel during the vacation. He could beat her as hard as he wanted. She had never kissed another man, and she wanted to kiss Greg. If she was going to be smacked around for doing nothing, why not enjoy herself?

Addy turned to Greg and smiled the coy smile that women use instinctively when flirting with a man, and he warmly drank it in.

Yes, Addy thought, I am going to kiss him.

The next morning Addy awakened with a feeling of dread. It's Saturday. Lionel would be coming for them in a week. She wanted to spend every precious moment until then with Greg.

What an ass I am, she chided herself. How can I think a man like him would want to kiss me?

Self-loathing was one of her favorite pastimes. After all, she had lost both her parents, and then married the mental case, Lionel. She was plainly and simply an unlucky person trapped in hell.

As she rolled over on her side, Addy stopped thinking along that negative line for a moment.

Wait. Greg is unlucky. I know nothing about his parents, but fate handed him a set of losing cards ... dying daughter, runaway wife ... Why wasn't he morose and depressed like she was? He didn't seem to feel sorry for himself at all.

The kids were awake, and Mary skipped into Addy's room. Always quiet and polite, she said softly, "Mommy, can we have breakfast now?"

"Of course, sweetheart. How would you like blueberry muffins?"

Addy had brought along a container of baking mix so she could whip up muffins in a cinch. As she bustled around in the cheery kitchen, she felt grounded in the present ... coffee perking, aroma of blueberry muffins drifting through the lovely home, and her precious children.

After breakfast, Addy waited longingly for a knock on the door, but it didn't come. It was about ten o'clock, and the children wanted to go to the beach. Was Greg still here? Is something wrong? Is he even real?

Addy and the kids trudged along to Wells Beach. Maybe Greg would be at the beach, but he had not been there thus far.

The sun was probably too hot for Allison's fair skin. Addy spent a greater part of the afternoon reading on the blanket while the kids played in the water. What if she never saw Greg again?

By two o'clock, the sun was hotter than it had been all week. It was Saturday and even Wells Town Beach was crowded. Many of the sunbathers were speaking French. Greg had told her that Maine is a favored vacation spot for the French Canadians. Compared to the Atlantic coast of Canada, Maine's water was tropical. In spite of her efforts to slather the kids with suntan lotion, all three looked red.

"Do you want to go back?" she called to them. Surprisingly, they said, "Yes." She was relieved. Maybe Greg had stayed home today.

When she arrived back at the house, she noticed Greg's beach wagon in the driveway and another car parked in front of his house. You idiot, Addy. He must have a girlfriend. How could he not? At that moment, she vowed to stop behaving like a lovesick schoolgirl. Addy and the children had lunch, and then the three kids actually went to their rooms to take naps. They were exhausted from the blistering sun.

Addy sat on the porch reading her latest "Good Housekeeping." No Jane Austen today. Austen's works were too romantic, and the last thing Addy needed right now was to read love stories. She thumbed through her magazine restlessly, distracted by the thought of the wagon in front of Greg's house. She looked out and saw a lovely, tall, graceful woman taking things out of the car. How could I have ever been so stupid? Addy thought. How dare I think a man like Greg would find me attractive?

Astonishingly, the woman was heading toward Addy's door. Addy vowed not to answer it, but the woman was persistent. Don't be a baby. If Greg has a girlfriend, good for him. He deserved happiness. Addy slowly opened the door, and the woman smiled. "Hi. I'm Caroline, Greg's sister."

Greg's SISTER! When would this miracle end?

Relieved, Addy said, "Please come in."

Caroline sat on the sofa in the living room and said, "Greg

tells me you have three children, but it's so quiet in here. Addy laughed, "The kids are actually taking naps. The sun was unbearable today."

Caroline agreed. "Today is a scorcher, but tomorrow is supposed to be much cooler." Addy could see Caroline's resemblance to Greg and instantly liked her. She was unassuming and appeared to be oblivious to her own beauty.

"I am so sorry that I couldn't make it up here to watch Allison the day Greg had his interview. He told me you let Allison come over to your house, and I just wanted to thank you. What would he have done without you? We have had our cottage for years, but the people who used to summer in the area have moved on. Greg has no one around to help him."

A worried look came over Caroline's face. "That's why I'm concerned about him living up here alone with Allison."

Much like Greg, Caroline quickly shrugged off the worry. "It is the best thing for both of them, so I'm sure they will meet some people. Are you going to be staying long in Maine?"

"No, we have to leave this coming Saturday," Addy responded sadly.

"Oh, what a shame. Allison seems like she loves your family, and Greg does, too."

Did Addy notice a twinkle in Caroline's eye?

"Listen ..., since it is supposed to be cooler tomorrow, I want to make a deal with you."

Addy suspected Caroline needed a babysitter, too.

"To repay you for being so nice to my brother, I want to do something for you. There is a small, old zoo with a few rides in York. That zoo has been there since I was a child. How about if I take your kids to York for the day?"

Addy was confused. Did she mean she wanted Addy, Greg, and their children to go along?

"Did Greg tell you I have a ten-year-old son, Alex, and an eight-year-old daughter, Sarah? My brother is completely devoted to Allison but hasn't had a break in years. I do try to take Allison as much as I can, but she and Greg live in Boston, and I live in New Hampshire."

Addy was still lost ... so she wants ME and both our sets of kids to go with HER to York for the day? That would be fun; Caroline seemed very pleasant.

"I thought Greg and you might enjoy spending some time alone together away from the kids."

Caroline burst out laughing when she saw the look of terror on Addy's face.

"Have no fear. My brother isn't an ax murderer; he asked me to arrange it this way, but don't tell him I told you."

Addy was speechless. Greg wanted to be alone with HER? Didn't he or his sister care that she was married? What did all this mean?

"Maybe you two could have a nice dinner at the Gray Gull. It's just a stone's throw from here ... or maybe not. You might just want to stay in and put steaks on the grill. I'll take the kids around one o'clock and probably won't bring them back until after dark. Don't worry ... I can handle a brood ... I was a teacher before I got married." Caroline laughed and rolled her eyes.

Addy was suddenly terrified. What if Greg wanted to have a sexual encounter with her? She was so fat, while Greg had a perfectly toned body. Well, she was a grown woman and could refuse.

She briefly drifted off into one of her self-absorbed comas. Caroline sat patiently then said, "Look, my brother has been divorced for three years now, and in that time, he has yet to spend an evening out with a lady. You may well be married, but your husband is obviously not around. It would be a harmless dinner. You both seem like you could use a little diversion."

Addy said, "I will have to ask the kids."

Caroline wrinkled her nose and scowled, mimicking how a mad face looks.

"They don't have any say. They are going to York whether they like it or not. I won't breathe a word to the kids that you will be with Greg."

Caroline must be very liberal-minded. How could she set up her brother with a woman about whom she knew nothing? On the other hand, perhaps Caroline wasn't liberal at all. Maybe she just wanted her brother to be happy at all costs.

Addy went through the motions of preparing dinner and watching TV with the children that night. She finally worked up the nerve to bring up Caroline's proposal to take them to the zoo in York.

"Hey kids," Addy blurted, "Allison's aunt wants to take you to York to the zoo."

The kids were engrossed in a cartoon show and nodded distractedly. She didn't think they heard what she had said.

"Do you want to go to the zoo tomorrow?"

Pete turned to her for a second and replied, "Sure," while Mary and Jimmy nodded their heads in agreement. She would wait until tomorrow morning to let them know she was not going. If they decided they didn't want to go, she could not force them. Otherwise, their memories would be vivid and unpleasant, and they might slip and tell Lionel. Addy tossed and turned all night. What if the kids changed their minds about going? Bless Caroline; at least she had tried.

The next morning, Jimmy asked, "Hey, Mom, are we still going to the zoo today?"

Addy rarely fibbed, but she said, "You know, I had coffee after dinner and didn't sleep a wink last night. Would you feel comfortable going with Greg's sister Caroline, her kids, and Allison?"

"What about Greg?" Jimmy queried.

Again, another lie. "Well, I think he's going too."

"Sure Mom, stay home and rest. You always work so hard," Pete decided aloud.

Bless you, my dear Peter.

At one o'clock, Caroline arrived at the door with her two children, Alex and Sarah. They appeared to be nice kids, just like Allison and Addy's children. As the kids looked each other over, she sensed excitement from her three. This was not only their first vacation, but every day provided a new adventure. As the kids walked over to Caroline's car, Mary asked with concern, "Where's Greg?"

"My daddy has an appointment today," said Allison proudly, "but he said I can go with you guys."

Mary readily accepted Allison's reply, while Caroline said, "Pile in troops. We're off to York."

Caroline looked back at Addy, and out of earshot of the children said, "Stop worrying. I'll take good care of them and will feed them dinner. Greg and you relax and have fun."

The decisive moment had arrived. Caroline, Greg, and she had all lied just to arrange some kind of clandestine rendezvous for Addy and Greg. Shame consumed Addy for a moment.

What the hell are you thinking? All you wanted to do was kiss him.

Maybe that was all Greg wanted, too. Or maybe he wanted no part of kissing her. Maybe he was a devout Catholic. Lost in her reverie, Addy was startled when Greg suddenly appeared at the door.

"Hi, Addy," he said rather shyly. "Don't mind my sister. She's always worried that I spend too much time alone so she's up to her old matchmaking tricks. I told her you probably have a husband, but she didn't care, so here I am. How about having lunch with me?"

Addy breathed a sigh of relief. Lunch. She would not have to get undressed after all. Her heart beat joyously.

"Sure, just let me change."

"Oh you can wear what you have on, if you like. The Gray Gull is casual at this time of day."

Greg never mentioned another word about her having a husband. They were simply two parents who needed a respite from their kids. The waiter at the Gray Gull led them to a table with a view of the ocean. Greg suggested she order the pecan-crusted haddock, one of the specialties of the house, if she liked fish. They both ordered that dish, and Greg asked, "Do you like white wine with fish?" Lying again, Addy said she did.

Addy cut up her salad nervously, hoping not to have a long leaf of lettuce hanging from her mouth if Greg looked over at her. As they ate, they talked about where they had gone to college and what majors they had chosen. Addy was ashamed to tell him she had never used her English and Journalism major, nor had she ever fulfilled her dream of opening a bakery. She let him do most of the talking.

"I had a double major at Boston College—architecture and THEOLOGY. Strange combination, right?"

Addy suddenly felt girlish and witty. "Not really. Architects build structures and theologians build beliefs." Oh God. What a stupid thing to say. He must think I am a complete ass.

Greg chuckled. "My parents wanted me to be a priest, and I even considered it for a while. I never wanted to be a parish priest, though ... more like a Benedictine monk. But, the draw of the flesh was too strong for me ... I ended up getting married," he laughed aloud.

Convinced the next question out of his mouth would be, "Are you married?" Addy quickly thought of something to keep him from uttering those dreaded words.

"Do you believe in God, Greg?"

Greg looked surprised at first, pondered for a moment, and then responded, "You know, Addy, I do. I was brought up Catholic and have made it my business to deconstruct the dogmas of the Catholic Church. There are so many tenets I disagree with."

Addy instantly replied, "Me too."

"Yet," Greg continued, "when I look at the beauty of the ocean or the stars at the beach at night, I can't help but think there is an inscrutable force at work in the universe. I once read that for humans to question God is like pairing up a baby with Einstein to discuss the theory of relativity."

What an insightful image, Addy thought, smiling at Greg shyly.

By this time, the waiter brought them the dessert menu, and Greg suggested they order coffee and the apple crisp.

Addy felt obligated to belittle herself about her weight and say, "Like I need dessert."

She wanted Greg to know that she was fully aware of her fatness and that she should not be, and was not always, fat.

Greg brushed aside her comment saying, "Women worry too

much about weight. As for me, I prefer a more Rubenesque woman. String beans just don't appeal to me."

Addy felt a load lifted from her shoulders. Maybe he actually found her body attractive.

After enjoying homemade apple crisp with ice cream and coffee with Addy, Greg asked the waitress for the check. Smiling, he turned to Addy and said, "Ready to go?"

Both were quiet and nervous during the ride back home. Greg finally said, "Addy, it was warm in that restaurant, wasn't it?"

Addy agreed. Although the windows at the Gray Gull had been wide open, it was a humid day.

"I'm going to stop at my house and jump in the shower. Would you like to stop over at my place in a bit?" Greg inquired innocently. Addy felt her throat closing. Was she allergic to haddock?

She managed to utter softly, "Sure. I think I will take a shower, too."

They both returned to their respective homes. As soon as she unlocked the door, Addy raced for the bathroom. Was she going to throw up from anxiety? STOP IT. She would never want Greg to smell vomit on her. Shaking with apprehension and excitement, she stood under the warm shower, making sure she scrubbed her sweaty body over and over again. She feared she may not be fresh "down there," so she grabbed the bottle of "My Sin by Lanvin" from Mrs. O'Malley's vanity and guiltily sprayed it between her legs. Now she had even stooped to stealing perfume, but the spritz of perfume aroused her. Whatever she might be about to do may cost her life, but for one selfish moment, she didn't care. She had dreamed only of kissing Greg. Now she wished he would passionately consume her. She knew he was not capable of ravaging her in a cruel way. He would surely be tender like the men about whom she had read.

She put on her yellow sundress, which actually felt loose on her, and walked over to Greg's. He was sitting on his sofa wearing only white Bermuda shorts. Addy gazed at his naked, tanned triangular upper body and sat down next to him.

Neither of them spoke. He looked at her longingly, taking her face in his hands and sweetly began kissing her mouth and eyelids. Passion swelled and overwhelmed them both ... two lonely, unlucky people. How could this one blissful moment be wrong? Addy responded boldly to his kisses, by thrusting her tongue in his mouth. He returned the kiss passionately, touching her full breasts and then reaching up under her sundress. Greg stopped and took Addy by the hand, leading her to the bedroom. Addy was afraid. What if she didn't know how to perform the act of love? She had always kept her mind tightly shut, detachedly leaving her body, when Lionel had sex with her. LIONEL? Get the fuck out of here, monster ... pig. I wish you were dead.

Addy focused her body, mind, and soul on Greg. He removed her sundress, bra, and underpants; removed his shorts; pulled back the bedclothes; and guided Addy to lie down on her back. What he did next was something Addy had never known. First, he tenderly kissed her erect nipples, calling her name, "Oh Addy, Addy."

His lips moved slowly down her body, kissing her all over, until he reached her vagina. Oh God, I hope I smell and taste good, Addy worried.

He kissed her there with such gusto, as if he was really enjoying it, using his tongue and mouth to savor her juices. She became wetter and wetter. He kissed her again on the mouth, and she could taste her intimacy on his lips. Having never experienced this before, Addy lost herself in white heat. Greg's penis was hard, and he entered her cautiously. He moved slowly, and Addy's body moved in rhythm with his. How did she know how to do this so naturally? Greg then pulled his penis out and returned to savoring her vagina with his tongue. Time stood still, as he became more and more aroused, gently thrusting his penis back into her vagina. Both of them began moving as one, entering a dimension of ecstasy she had never before visited. Simultaneously, the two lovers cried out in joyous rapture, while Greg's copious sperm filled Addy. Fluid exploded from her as well.

Wrapped in a coverlet of ecstasy, Addy thought, this must be an orgasm. Greg pushed her hair back from her face and looked deeply into her eyes, drinking her in ... Addy, with all her pain and flaws ... Addy, the unlucky girl ... Addy, the wounded spirit. Addy tried to suppress her sobs. Looking alarmed, Greg asked, "What's wrong? Oh, Addy, what's wrong? Did I hurt you?"

Looking sincerely into Greg's eyes, Addy said, "Oh no. You made such beautiful love to me. I have never known such love."

Greg got a warm washcloth from the bathroom and tenderly sponged off Addy. An urge came over Addy, and she found herself at Greg's penis, licking it, sucking it, and pushing it gently down her throat. Yes, she did know how to do this, but with Lionel, she hated it. He would push her face hard against his penis, choking her. Greg lay back and closed his eyes. Almost immediately, his penis swelled again, and he reveled in the sensations of Addy's lips and tongue on his penis. Greg tasted sweet, and Addy wanted to pleasure him forever. He suddenly drew his penis out of her mouth and placed it in her vagina. Once again, they moved in unison, and once again, they exploded in orgasmic pleasure.

Greg placed Addy's head on his chest. Neither of them spoke. There was no regret, no shame, and no thought. They silently embraced one another for what seemed like an eternity.

Addy suddenly realized that the room had grown dimmer.

"Oh, Greg. Caroline will be bringing the kids back any time now. We better check the time."

Tragically, it was already after six o'clock ... time for Cinderella to run away from the prince.

Greg asked Addy if she would like to take a shower with him. This was another first for her. She loved how Greg soaped her body up as if she was his baby.

After they got dressed, they went into the living room and sat on the sofa, gazing at one another.

"Whew," Greg said, "we just made it. Addy, I know this is probably the wrong time to ask you, but do you have a husband?"

Addy felt as if she would heave. She lowered her eyes, and

said, "Yes."

A shadow fell over Greg's face, but he continued, "Is he good to you?"

As her eyes filled with tears, Addy answered in a small voice, "No. Not at all."

Looking angry, Greg asked, "Does he hurt you?"

Addy shook her head "yes."

"Does he hurt the kids, too?"

Addy shook her head "no."

"You know, Addy, ever since I first met you, I've noticed a sad look in your eyes, and I suspected something was wrong. What are you going to do?"

Addy shrugged her shoulders forlornly. "I don't know. I just don't know. I'm afraid if I leave him, he will find me and kill me. He threatens me all the time."

"Addy, you have to get away from him somehow. You are too wonderful a woman to live like that ..."

Addy couldn't listen anymore and said, "I have to go now, Greg. Thank you for being so kind."

Greg took her in his arms and protested, "No, Addy. It's you who have been kind to me. I have to help you. I want to figure out a way to help you."

Greg walked Addy back to her house. Embracing her, he gave her one last kiss. She couldn't speak. She did not want to cry; she wanted to be brave and happy so that Greg would see her as a strong woman. Lost in thought, Greg walked slowly back to his house. How could he rescue this sweet woman from the clutches of a beast?

Just as Addy sat down on the sofa, Caroline arrived at the door. The kids looked happy and spoiled. "How was your day?" Addy feigned innocence.

"Great! Fantastic!" they all chimed in.

"After the zoo, Caroline took us to watch the lobster boats bringing in their pots," said Pete excitedly. Apparently, her kids had gotten along well with Caroline's.

"How was your day, Mom?" Pete asked innocently.

Calmly, Addy replied, "Restful."

Caroline caught her eye and grinned with the secret neither she nor her brother would ever reveal.

If Addy had died that night in her sleep, she would have been content. Of course, that wouldn't be fair to the kids. She didn't really mean it, but she was so fulfilled. Never in her life on this earth had she felt so complete.

The days of the second week of their vacation flew by. Caroline and her kids, who stayed on to spend the whole week at Greg's, planned such fun activities every day ... barbeques in the yard, badminton, hunting for fireflies at night. Addy had never seen her children so happy. Allison seemed to thrive as well.

Shadows gathered as the days and hours approached six o'clock on Saturday, August 21. That was when this fairytale would end, and Addy's real life would begin once again. Until then, she and the children soaked up every drop of joy and normalcy. It was foolish, but she felt, yes, someday Greg would rescue her.

Like the grim reaper, Friday inevitably arrived. Lionel would be here tomorrow. After this heavenly vacation, how could Addy return to Connecticut with Lionel? Wouldn't it be better to be dead? Yes, her sense of hopelessness and despair frequently spawned urges of suicide, but her responsibility to the children saved her. She lived for them alone.

Addy got out of bed, pulled on her robe, stepped into her slippers, and shuffled to the kitchen to make coffee. The kids were still sleeping because they had gone to an outdoor movie in the town square last night. The house was as silent as a chapel. She looked around the O'Malley's residence, thinking, "Why can't this be my real life?"

Immediately, her Catholic conscience jumped in, scolding, you should be grateful you even had this vacation. Stop wishing for what you don't have. That's coveting. The smell of coffee percolating on the stove drew her back into the moment. Someone was knocking on the door.

Oh, God, thought Addy, panicking. Don't tell me Lionel has decided to pick us up early.

She went to the door, and there was Greg, holding Nolan's

Doughnut Shop waxed bags in both hands. Everyone who vacationed in Southern Maine knew about Nolan's. What had started as a small insignificant bakeshop had risen, literally, as an empire of "dough."

Addy immediately felt self-conscious about being in her bathrobe but laughed to herself, *he's already seen you naked, you fool.*

Looking around, Greg saw the kids were nowhere in sight and kissed her on the lips. Addy immediately felt aroused and wished she could lead him into her bedroom this time. He said, "Caroline and the kids are still sleeping so I hoped I could sneak a cup of coffee with you. Mmm ... I smell it already. Did you read my mind?"

Although Addy and he had made such passionate love, Addy still blushed when he looked at her. "We're leaving tomorrow, Greg. I'm so glad you stopped by this morning. Tomorrow I'll have to start cleaning early, and we wouldn't have time for coffee together in the morning."

Greg's beautiful smile faded as he, too, suddenly realized the halcyon days were ending. He would return to his lonely existence, maybe never to see Addy and her children again. Addy took out two sets of placemats, napkins, cups and saucers, plates, and a large platter for the doughnuts. Simply setting the table for Greg lifted her spirits. Oh, if he were her husband, how she would spoil him. As Greg spread the doughnuts on the platter, he said, "I hope the kids like my selection."

The doughnuts were still warm, and their sweet smell transported Addy to Sunday mornings after Mass at Sound View Beach. The Italian men woke up very early on those special days, hurrying down to the doughnut shop. It wasn't a bakery with glass cases but simply a building with a Dutch door. Once all the doughnuts were gone, the door was shut until the next Sunday morning. The Sound View doughnut spot was as successful as Nolan's, paying for all the Panetti children to go to college.

"They're perfect," Addy replied. "I love glazed, Pete loves plain, Jimmy loves jelly, and Mary loves any kind. Thank you so much, Greg. How thoughtful of you."

Greg got up to pour his own coffee, but Addy insisted, "You sit right there. I'll get it for you. That's the least I can do."

When she picked up his cup to take over to the counter, her hip brushed against his arm. She could finally understand what it means to want to just grab someone and make love to him right on the kitchen floor. Simply brushing by Greg set Addy on fire. How would she ever lie next to Lionel again, awakening to his cruelly pinching her bottom to signal that he wanted sex? She knew Lionel was a brute, but she had never had any other sexual experience for comparison ... not until Greg.

She brought Greg's coffee to him, this time trying not to brush against his arm. Why torture herself? The kids would be awake any minute. Greg had no sooner placed a glazed doughnut on his plate, than Jimmy came out of his room, rubbing his eyes.

"Doughnuts!" he shouted.

Greg and Addy glanced at each other across the table. They knew they had enjoyed their last quiet moment together. Shortly, Pete and Mary were awake, pouring orange juice and picking over the doughnuts. For the first time in the lives of her children, Addy resented them. Why had they stirred and spoiled her last precious seconds with Greg?

Greg said, "Well, I had better be getting back to my place."

"Take the rest of the doughnuts with you," Addy insisted.

"Are you kidding? I have two more bags for our brood in the car. You guys enjoy them."

Addy reminded the kids to thank Greg. She knew all three of her children had become very fond of this special man and his daughter. Greg was easygoing, patient, funny, kind, nurturing ... all the things their father was not.

In a melancholy tone, Mary asked, "Will I see you again before we leave tomorrow?"

"Of course," Greg answered cheerily. "Why don't you come over today and play with Allison?"

Mary beamed. The weather was cloudy, and it looked like rain. Allison loved Mary; they got along so well.

"May I, Mom?"

"Certainly," Addy replied. "Your things are so organized; you can just get them together tonight. "Will you help me scrub the cottage before your father comes tomorrow?"

"I love to clean," Mary answered.

Not to be outdone, the boys said, "We'll help, too."

Addy smiled at Greg, proud that he knew what good kids she had. Greg smiled back. He pounced toward Jimmy, tickling him, snarling in a pretend sinister voice, "You kids better help or I'll put you in a lobster trap for bait."

Jimmy squealed and Mary ran screaming, pretending to be scared.

Pete said wryly, "Hey ... at least you would get to stay in Maine."

Addy and the children had fallen in love, not only with Maine, but also with the simple, cheerful glimpse of life Greg and Caroline had given them. Greg said once again, "I had better get going; the doughnuts are probably melting all over the seat as we speak."

Hesitating, Greg thought for a moment ... "Hey, I have an idea. Since it's not a nice beach day, why don't you all clean up part of the house today? The weather is supposed to clear up by this evening, and there may be a starry sky. How about if I make a bonfire on the beach? We can roast hotdogs and marshmallows."

The boys looked at each other in amazement. A bonfire on the beach? They had had a brief stint with the Boy Scouts, but the only time they went camping, it rained, and the Scout leader could not make a fire. They had to eat the peanut butter and jelly sandwiches they had brought just in case.

Mary looked worried, "Will I still be able to play with Allison today?"

"Why not?" Addy answered, feigning cheerfulness.

She wondered if Greg was planning the bonfire to spend his last evening with her. At least that is what she hoped. Her self-confidence had left her long ago. In fact, she never really had any self-confidence. She still could not fathom that Greg had chosen to make love to her. Maybe he was just a lonely seducer;

an opportunistic rogue. Oh my God, Addy. What a fool you've made of yourself.   How could you have ever thought this gorgeous man actually found *you* attractive?

Greg's deep voice roused Addy from her masochistic reverie when he said, "Will that be OK with you, Addy?"

Narrowly escaping from her coma of self-hatred, Addy looked up, her eyes meeting his sincere gaze. Why couldn't she trust that Greg was for real? He had proven his honesty and goodness so many times during this vacation. There was a sense of urgency in Greg's words; almost as if he were pleading with her to say, "Yes." Perhaps he really did want to spend their last evening together. Addy returned his look and an overwhelming feeling of love rose unexpectedly from her heart. She couldn't hide her yearning.

"Oh, Greg," she said, almost in tears, "you think of the nicest things to do. We would love a bonfire on the beach."

Greg smiled with relief. "Great! Caroline and I will get all the food, so don't worry about anything except getting the house ready to pack up. Bring a blanket and some bug spray, and we'll be good to go. See you around 7:30."

Picturing herself seated next to Greg on a star-lit beach inspired Addy to get busy. The boys hurried to their room, looking around in confusion, not knowing where to begin. They didn't even complain that Mary wasn't cleaning. Addy had always had to guide the boys about housework. Admittedly, she had let the boys mess up their room all they wanted because Lionel was not there to bark orders.

"Don't worry, boys. I'll help. First, gather up the toys, games, and books and put them in the laundry basket we brought them in," Addy assured Jimmy and Pete.

There was a washing machine in the house so Addy had kept up pretty well with the laundry, thank God. She told the boys to collect their dirty clothes and put them in the basket near the washer.

The day flew by. Mary had lunch at Allison's, while Addy and the boys stopped cleaning for only fifteen minutes, just enough time to gobble down sandwiches for lunch. The refrigerator was filled with groceries, but Addy would give them to Caroline and Greg. They had been so generous; how could she ever repay them?

When Addy dusted the fireplace mantel, she could finally look at Charlie's family photos. Yes, maybe they had a happy life; yet, the thought of their happiness did not stab her in her heart as it did when she had first seen the pictures. Although too brief, Addy had a taste of what it might be like to have a loving husband, and even if she never saw Greg again, she would carry him in her heart forever. Her whole being was suddenly flooded with the light of gratitude. When she had first arrived in Maine, she was a zombie, going through the motions of living but possessing no soul. She had never found solace in religion, at least not the religion force-fed to her. The glow of thankfulness emanated from her spirit, stretching out in all directions, kissing the universe. Her soul ... had it returned? Was there a compassionate side to the Catholic God she had rejected so long ago?

When she was in college and began to question her faith, Addy read extensively in philosophy and religion. One of her free-thinking college classmates, Gracie Steer, suggested the controversial course, "The Bible in Literature," offered by the brilliant professor, Richard Berridge. Dr. Berridge encouraged his students to dig beneath the surface. Amazingly, Addy learned that Herman Melville had drawn deeply upon the King James Version of the Bible when he wrote *Moby Dick*. In fact, the work was an allegory representing the author's tormented search for God.

When Addy mentioned some of the things she was learning in college, the aunts were appalled. Every good Catholic knew the Bible was solely for priests, and the King James Version was for Protestants. Addy could not understand why the readings and gospels at Mass were from the Bible, yet the laity was discouraged from even touching a Bible. Sometimes the aunts regretted having sent Addy to college, but they knew that was what Addy's parents wanted.

For college graduation, Gracie presented Addy with a

beautifully framed illuminated script printed in calligraphy with these words from Philippians 4:8 (KJV):

Whatsoever things are true,
Whatsoever things are honest,
Whatsoever things are just,
Whatsoever things are pure,
Whatsoever things are lovely,
Whatsoever things are of good report,
If there be any virtue,
And if there be any praise,
Think on these things.

The idealistic college-aged Addy treasured that framed quotation and tried to live her life by its words. Her aunts viewed Lionel as the good Catholic knight who had come along to rescue Addy from blasphemous philosophy. After Addy married Lionel, she eventually stored the framed Bible verse in the basement along with all the other things that were once so precious to her: classical records; volumes of poetry by Blake, Emerson, Whitman, even Rilke. The words of these masters illumed her heart and soul ... they were messages spanning time ... celebrating the beauty and mystery of life. There were her art books ... paintings by Botticelli, Cassatt, Cezanne, Degas, Rembrandt, and Van Gogh. Lionel thought interest in "old" things was senseless, so gradually Addy's prized books and other possessions relating to the masters wound up in the mold of the basement.

As she stood in the kitchen of Charlie O'Malley's home in Wells, Maine, far from Lionel and Chester, Connecticut, Addy closed her eyes and saw Lionel before her. She imagined she had a whip in her hands and was striking Lionel repeatedly, shouting, "You bastard. You ruined me. I was once smart, pure, good ... you raped my body and mind ... my filthy life with you stole my beauty." As she whipped Lionel violently in her fantasy, Pete asked her a question. Addy came to and answered him. She still wished Lionel's plane from Denver would crash or maybe he would get into a car wreck while he was driving to Maine to pick them up.

Everything suddenly became clear: Greg embodied those qualities described in the illuminated script. Although the Church and the world would accuse her of the sin of adultery, Addy felt just the opposite. Greg's lovemaking made her feel clean and worthy for the first time since she had married Lionel. In spite of the hardships he was facing, Greg maintained noble qualities. He was not bitter or broken. Maybe he prayed to a God who gave him strength, courage, and peace. If only she could hold on to the optimism Greg stimulated in her.

Around seven o'clock, Caroline came over to sew up some details about the evening's "Good-bye" bonfire. "Wow," she exclaimed, "this place is sparkling! I'll bet it's cleaner now than when you came."

Addy laughed, winking at her sons. "I couldn't have done it without these guys."

Caroline was a perceptive woman; she had observed the sadness in Addy's eyes. Nothing in the world would make her happier than to see her brother Greg get together with Addy. Caroline knew Addy had a husband, but she also sensed this guy was not worthy of Addy. Greg and Addy deserved each other. Caroline's heart ached momentarily thinking about her brother up here in Maine alone with Allison and Addy returning to God-knows-what in Connecticut.

"The picnic basket is all packed, and Greg's down at the beach collecting driftwood for the fire. Mary, Allison, and my two are walking down to help him. Can your boys come now?" Caroline asked.

Panicking, Addy said, "I'm not quite ready. I still have to take a shower after all this cleaning." Addy suspected Caroline, as always, planned this move so Addy could dress in peace. Dear, kind, Caroline ... she was so much like Greg. Caroline must have known Addy wanted to take her time getting ready to look her best for Greg on this last night of her vacation.

The boys were eager to go with Caroline. Addy looked around—the place was shining—just as it had when they arrived.

All she would have to do tomorrow is wash the bed linens and towels, and maybe a few breakfast dishes. She suddenly had an idea. Lionel had given her a few extra dollars for food, but Greg had paid for almost everything so Addy still had money left over. If she and the kids ate lunch at the Sea Side Grill, they wouldn't mess up the kitchen before leaving.

Whoops ... lost in thoughts again, and it was almost 7:15. She went to her bathroom in the master suite to shower and dared to look at her naked body in the full-length mirror she had avoided. Greg saw this, she thought, so maybe I should look. Her body was not as bad as all that. Granted her breasts sagged from nursing the kids; her stomach protruded, and her thighs were just plain fat. Yet, overall, she still had somewhat of an hourglass shape. For the first time in longer than she could remember, she did not hate her body completely. After all, hadn't this same form participated in sublime pleasure?

Addy lathered herself all over with a bar of pink Camay soap ... then fretted .... What if the mosquitoes eat me alive? Stop worrying, Addy. You have to smell enticing. She washed her hair with Breck shampoo then dabbed herself again with "My Sin" after the bath. The shampoo and perfume actually belonged to Mrs. O'Malley, but Addy used just a little. In addition, Charlie had told Lionel everything in the house was for their enjoyment.

Addy dressed in a long-sleeve white oxford shirt and pair of blue dungarees. When she glanced at herself in the mirror, the woman staring back at her was not Addy at all. Instead, here was an attractive woman, face tinged pink with sunburn, auburn wisps of curls framing her slim face. Yes, slim. When Addy first arrived in Maine, she felt so fat and ugly; delighted her new dungarees fit, she believed she had lost weight without even trying.

When she arrived at the beach, to which she could now walk without gasping, everyone was there. The kids had gathered plenty of firewood; the blankets and beach chairs were set up around the fire pit. In addition to the picnic basket, Greg and Caroline had brought big thermos bottles, one filled with coffee, the other, with wine. Now the adults could "tie one on" without the kids noticing. Addy, Caroline, and Greg knew this was their "good-bye" party, and they intended to celebrate. By the time the fire got going really well, it was around 8:30. The kids helped Greg find long green sticks, and he whittled the ends of the sticks to a point with his jackknife.

When it came time to roast the hotdogs, Greg instructed the children about sitting far away from the fire, not putting the hotdog directly into the flame, and turning the sticks so the hotdogs would brown on all sides. The kids followed Greg's instructions exactly. Soon there were six golden hotdogs on a paper plate. The grownups thought the kids would each want to eat the ones they had made themselves; instead, the kids begged to roast the dogs for everyone. Greg covered the plate containing the first batch with tin foil. They needed four more for the adults, but each child wanted to roast one so now they had two extra. That was an understatement. The kids kept roasting until everyone had a least two or more each. They were all stuffed, but Greg threw more wood on the fire. After all, they still had the marshmallows to roast.

The coffee thermos remained untouched while Caroline, Greg, and Addy imbibed the thermos of wine. Caroline said, "Hey, what's a campfire without songs? I know plenty of tunes from when I was teaching."

Greg added, "And I know more from all my years at Boy Scout camp." He dared them, "Who is brave enough to start?"

Everyone giggled with embarrassment, but no one volunteered. In spite of the fact that Addy felt tipsy, her self-consciousness rose, and she knew she would die of shame if forced to sing. She used to belt out songs as a kid, but once Aunt Sophia said, "Addy you are so off key. I hope that's not the way you sing in music class." So much for Addy's singing career.

Greg said, "OK, you chickens, I'll start—this song is called, 'I'm A Nut,' and you sing it to the tune of 'I'm a Little Teapot.'"

The boys looked at each other and groaned; they all knew that dumb teapot song.

Greg ignored them and said, "This is how it goes ... I'll sing the lyrics, and you join in on the chorus."

The little ditty was hilarious. Addy suddenly remembered singing a different version in Girl Scouts, so it was Addy's turn for the next round. She never sang in front of anyone but tonight was her night. Besides, it would be impossible to make a fool of herself with this kind, loving group.

Caroline was next with "A Thousand-Legged Worm, The Ants Go Marching, and Ten Little Men in the Bed." By this time, the kids loosened up and giggled like crazy. The boys even added their rendition of "Ten Beer Bottles on the Wall." Addy wondered where they had learned that song, but tonight she didn't give a hoot. She felt carefree and relaxed after drinking so much wine.

By this time, it was pitch dark. Just as Greg predicted, thousands of sparkling stars filled the ebony sky.

"Time for the marshmallows," Greg said enthusiastically.

He whittled fresh points on the kids' sticks and slid two marshmallows on each stick. The inevitable luckless marshmallows dropped into the fire and burned black, but the children just laughed. The aroma of burnt marshmallows was pleasant. Few things in life come close to roasted marshmallows, crispy, hot, and golden brown on the outside, with gooey sweet whiteness dripping from the center. Everyone had more than their share ... sticky faces, hands, even hair ... tonight none of it mattered.

A collective silence fell slowly over the small, carefree group. They were all aware that the marshmallow roast marked the last event of the beach campfire night. Each stared solemnly at the fading glow of the embers. What were the children thinking? Addy wondered. Did they dread going back home as much as she did? The silence was deep and poignant; the sky, winking with diamond stars, was helpless in soothing their pain. At last, Mary's sweet voice broke the heavy silence.

"I have a song," Mary said timidly.

Mary? Addy thought. Shy little Mary? Addy didn't recall ever having heard Mary sing. She was in the children's choir at church but repeatedly turned down the choir director's request that she do a solo. Everyone around the campfire turned to look at Mary, and this made her even more nervous. Nevertheless, she opened her mouth to sing. At first, nothing came out, and then her voice cracked. Almost simultaneously, Greg, Caroline, and the kids quickly looked away. They were sensitive enough to know that if they looked directly at Mary, she would be unable to sing. What happened next was something Addy knew none of them would ever forget. As if some angel had suddenly inhabited the body of little Mary, she sang strong and clear the words from the song the mice in the movie *Cinderella* sing about dreaming.

Addy, and most likely the rest of the group, had tears in her eyes. "Mary," Addy asked quietly, "where did you learn that song?"

"It's from *Cinderella*, Mom, don't you remember? That's the part where she is singing to the animals when they wake her up early in the morning."

"I have the record and kept listening to it over and over until I knew all the words by heart," Mary continued proudly.

Oh, how Addy hoped her kids still believed in their dreams. She had abandoned her castles in the sky long ago; yet in Wells, Maine, she briefly experienced an unimaginable dream. Caroline, always so clever, told Addy and Greg she would get the kids back up to the houses, if Addy and Greg didn't mind packing up the rest of the stuff. The kids were tired, and Addy started to protest.

"Don't worry. I'll wait while your kids shower at your house, then they can come over to our house in their PJs while my two get ready for bed. After all, it's their last night together so they won't mind staying up late."

Addy's kids never objected to Caroline's ideas. They seemed to be enthralled with her.

Addy knew Greg and she could not linger too long on the beach because her kids, especially Pete, may grow suspicious. Her children were very naïve and innocent, and she doubted they would ever "get the wrong idea." Still, she had to protect them as well as herself from Lionel's Spanish Inquisition. She never wanted to make them feel they somehow had to cover for anything she did. Immediately after the group trekked back to the houses, Greg took Addy in his arms and kissed her passionately. It was so easy to lose herself in his kisses. A picture flashed across her mind ... imagine if, like in the movies, they could make love on the beach under the stars. Soon Greg was unbuttoning her blouse, pulling down her bra straps, and sucking tenderly on her nipples. She could see how aroused he had become, and knowing she had this intensely erotic effect upon him, Addy felt attractive, desirable, and incredibly aroused, too.

Unzipping her dungarees and pulling them down over her hips, Greg first used his fingers to play with her vagina, then his tongue to moisten her even more. When he felt she was ready, he unzipped his shorts, pulled them down over his tight, muscular behind, and thrust his penis into her hungry opening. How could this be? How could she become aroused so quickly? Before she knew it, her body was moving in perfect synchronization with Greg's, and soon, they both flared into orgasm. Greg and Addy began laughing.

"I just don't believe this, Greg, we are like college kids."

He laughed in agreement. "I am sorry, Addy. This was so quick and clumsy, but I couldn't bear not to have you one more time before you leave."

They both knew what that meant. In less than twenty-four hours, Cinderella would lose her slipper on the stairs of the castle. This time, the prince would not find her; she had already found him.

Addy and Greg gathered up the remnants of the night and started slowly back to their homes. They did not speak. What more was there to say? When they got back, Caroline had the kids bathed and in their PJs. Allison was already asleep, and the rest of the kids were dozing.

"Oh Caroline," Addy exclaimed, "I can't thank you enough."

Caroline gave Addy her famous omniscient smile. "It has been my pleasure, and I hope *yours*."

Greg and Addy looked nervously at one another, and then

burst out laughing. Greg helped Addy guide her sleepy kids to their beds. After the children were all tucked in, Greg, sounding more serious than usual, said, "Look, Addy. I would prefer not to be around when your husband comes to pick you up tomorrow. Caroline and I have made plans to take the kids into Ogunquit in the late afternoon. We'll wander around ... they have a phenomenal candy shop there. Then we will stay for dinner in town. The traffic between Ogunquit and here is brutal in the evening, so I'm sure we won't be back before six o'clock." Addy was touched that Greg remembered what time Lionel would be coming to get them.

Just to stall him a little longer, Addy said, "Oh, Greg, I forgot. My refrigerator is full of food. Would Caroline and you like it? Everything is still good, and I hate to throw it out."

Greg smiled, "Of course. When should I come by to get it?"

Addy said she planned to eat only breakfast in the house, and then clean up everything and have lunch at the Sea Side Grill. Part of her wished he would say he'd join them, but she knew she was just trying to stretch their last moments beyond what would be judicious. Anyways, he had just said they were going to Ogunquit.

"How about if you come by about eleven o'clock? Hopefully the kids will be awake and have eaten by then."

Greg looked deep into her eyes and whispered, "Good night, Addy dear. Thank you for making me so happy."

Addy could say nothing. She looked at him as a lost soul, tried to smile, but large tears rolled down her cheeks. "Oh no, Greg. Thank YOU."

Greg took her into his arms and held her tightly. Addy was sure she felt Greg's tear drop on her face. Saying nothing, he turned to go.

When Greg came in the next morning to get the groceries, he was his usual seemingly cheerful self. Allison and Caroline were with him. They all hugged and kissed. Allison asked Mary sadly, "Are you coming to see me again?"

Mary turned her innocent face up to Addy and questioned earnestly, "Mom, will we ever come here again?" catching Addy off guard. She truly doubted Lionel would ever do this for them. Trying to sound cheerful, Addy said, "You never know. Remember your special song '... a dream is a wish your heart makes'. Let's keep on dreaming and wishing, OK?"

Allison was silent. She was used to disappointment, even rejection. After all, her own mother had abandoned her. Caroline tried to change the subject quickly, saying, "I know we will keep in touch and meet again. Wow. Thanks for all these groceries. We won't have to shop all week." Greg gave Addy one last, long, loving look. The three turned, walked back to their house, and that was it.

Once Greg, Caroline, and Allison left, everything seemed to change. The kids became very quiet. Addy suggested they go in the yard to play so she could put the finishing touches on the beach house. She washed and dried all the sheets and linens; scrubbed both bathrooms; made up all the beds; placed all the dishes and cooking utensils in the exact spots where she had found them; and polished the counter and stovetop. She worked constantly until nearly two o'clock. The kids were getting hungry and asked when they would be eating lunch.

"Very soon," she said. "Guess what? We are eating at McKenna's so we won't mess up the kitchen."

"Yippee," the kids shouted in unison. They loved the idea, particularly because there was a penny arcade near the restaurant. Addy had jealously guarded the $50 Lionel had given her, and now was the time to spend the rest of it. First, they would have lunch, and then she would give the kids a load of change to spend at the arcade. She figured that if they went there soon, they could pass enough time so that when Lionel arrived at 6:00, they would be ready and waiting, just as he had ordered.

Addy and the children took their time walking over to the restaurant. They still had a few hours in Maine, and Addy tried hard not to sacrifice these precious moments to the fear and dread of returning home. When they reached the Sea Side Grill, the children ran to save a picnic table while Addy ordered fried clam platters for the kids and a scallop basket for herself. As they ate, they watched the waves rolling in, splashing on the shore below. Whenever Addy was at the beach, even as a child, she realized that waves had rolled in for thousands of years before her and would continue to roll for thousands of years after she was gone. It wasn't that the ocean was indifferent to human life. The sea was simply doing what it was made to do. Wouldn't life be easier if we had a definitive answer about why we were made?

Addy laughed to herself at these deep thoughts. Greg, the lovemaking, Maine...they had worked a spell on her, opening a door in her mind that slammed shut as soon as she married Lionel. Oh, in the beginning she had tried to share some of her thoughts and interests with Lionel, but he dismissed her as sentimental, bookish, and, inevitably, foolish. As the years went by, Addy internalized Lionel's view of her as "less than."

While Addy and the kids took their time eating lunch, Addy asked, "Did you kids have a good vacation?"

"Good?" answered Pete. "You mean GREAT."

"What did you like best, Mary?" Addy questioned.

Mary took no time in answering, "Allison. She's the best new friend I have ever made."

"How about you, Jimmy?" Mary asked.

"The campfire on the beach last night. Definitely the campfire."

"Pete?" Addy asked.

"I liked watching the lobster boats unload their catch. And I loved Greg's boat."

While the kids reminisced about their day at Old Orchard Beach, Addy was suddenly consumed with terror. What if the kids told Lionel they had spent a good part of their vacation with a man? She would just have to try to brush it off, saying a neighbor's family had invited them to some activities. Maybe if Lionel had had a piggishly good time in Denver, he wouldn't bother to ask the kids about their vacation.

Lunch was finished, and Addy gave each of the children a handful of change. "It would be better if you didn't tell your dad about the arcade," Addy warned. "You know how he feels about wasting money on things like this."

Addy watched the kids at the arcade for a while, and then she wandered over to a beach shop. In the window was a lovely purple swimsuit with metallic gold threads woven into the fabric, and a matching purple cover-up, bathing cap, and beach slippers. One of her idols, the amazing swimmer, Esther Williams, would likely wear an outfit like that. She wandered over to the candy shop and bought some Tootsie Rolls. By the time Lionel got there, the kids would be hungry, and these candies would not make a sticky mess.

As her watch approached 5:00 p.m., Addy's heart began to pound. One more hour. She walked over to the arcade to fetch the kids. They were in the midst of one of their favorite games, but she told them they had only fifteen minutes left. She still had to check the house to be certain she had not forgotten anything. The children joined Addy soon enough, and they all trudged back to the house. Was there lead in the kids' shoes? They seemed to have lost that carefree jaunt so typical of youth. Addy suspected that Pete, Jimmy, and Mary were as reluctant to see Lionel as she was.

Chapter VI

Back to Reality

When they reached the house, they carried their suitcases into the living room and sat waiting for Lionel. Those last few minutes before six o'clock were very tense. Finally, the clock struck six; Lionel pulled up in front of the house, hurriedly got out, walked around to open the back of the station wagon, and then rapped on the door. The moment of reckoning had arrived.

"Did you have a nice vacation?" he asked absentmindedly, directing his question to no one in particular and not waiting for a response. "Let's get going."

The kids carried their bags out, placing them on the ground next to the wagon for their father to create the perfect packing configuration. Lionel didn't even bother to inspect the house before they locked up the place. As always, he was eager to get going. They all piled into the car and started for home, riding in tense silence for several miles. Addy hoped it was because the kids were tired, not depressed. Lionel was completely preoccupied with something. Maybe he was wishing he could have stayed in Denver, just as much as Addy wished she could stay in Maine.

As they finally approached Connecticut, Lionel asked if they had eaten dinner. "We had a late lunch," Addy responded quickly so that Lionel would not say she was irresponsible for not feeding the kids.

"I'm going to stop at the next Howard Johnson's," Lionel said.

He must have been hungry himself, or he wouldn't have mentioned dinner. The kids perked up when they heard "Howard Johnson's." That place had the best macaroni and cheese.

Addy thought if she sat across the table from Lionel, her face might reflect fear or guilt. Strangely enough, she looked him square in the eye without a hint of emotion. In fact, she felt stronger simply knowing she had a delicious secret hidden deeply in her heart. Lionel glanced at her briefly and mumbled, "You look suntanned. Did you have nice weather?"

"Great," Addy feigned cheerfulness.

The kids sat in another booth, and Lionel could not question them.

Addy quickly changed the topic by asking Lionel how his trip to Denver was. He rolled his eyes and said, "Busy, busy, as usual. No vacation for me."

By this time, the waitress delivered the food. Thank God, Addy thought with relief. She truly doubted there would be any further conversation about Maine.

When they arrived home, the children were exhausted, but Lionel insisted all suitcases be unpacked and clothes put away, in either the dresser drawers or hamper. The beach toys had to be stored in the garage. By the time all the unpacking was done, it was after midnight. Lionel never gave the kids a break. A reasonable man would have known that Addy and the kids were tired, and the unpacking could wait another day. After all, school hadn't started yet.

The kids were so tired, they did not want to take baths so Addy quietly told them to "wash up," quickly brush their teeth, and then hop into bed. They zipped through their bedtime preparations and were asleep within minutes. Addy, exhausted too, took her time taking a shower, washing and drying her hair, and getting into her nightgown. Her hope was that Lionel would be asleep by the time she crawled in next to him. How could she ever tolerate the degradation of having sex with Lionel after the elation of making love with Greg?

The angels were with her that night. By the time she went to bed, Lionel was snoring loudly in a deep sleep. All night she kept hoping the bruising twist of her skin from Lionel's pinch signal for sex would never come. Eventually she fell asleep, and by the time she awoke, Lionel had already left for work. This was probably the first time in their married life he had not awakened her to make the coffee. Oh, if only his ignoring her would continue.

Addy went downstairs to make coffee. Lionel must have stopped for breakfast at the diner on his way to his job. Lord knows, he had never put the coffee on for her. As she looked around the dark, outdated room, the sunny kitchen in the Maine house flashed across her mind. Had it all been a dream? Everything about the vacation was bright and happy. Aside from the summers at Sound View Beach, Addy had never experienced such joy. Of course, the births of Pete, Jimmy, and Mary were indescribable gifts. Each time her three-week hospital confinement for childbirth ended, and it was time to take the baby home, Addy wished she could either stay in the hospital or run away. Lionel was not warm or patient with the children. He probably viewed them simply as acquisitions along his road to material success.

As Addy sat drinking her coffee, lost in thought, the kids came running downstairs. They were all very cheerful, particularly because Lionel had left early for work, and they didn't have to sit and have a formal breakfast with him.

"What would you like for breakfast this morning?" Addy asked.

Pete said, "We haven't had Belgian waffles in so long. Do you feel like making them?"

"Of course I do. Pretty soon, you will have to go back to school, and we won't have time for homemade waffles in the morning. Jimmy and Mary, would you like waffles, too?"

"Sure," Jimmy said, "but don't remind us of school."

Mary chimed in, "I love waffles AND I love school."

The boys rolled their eyes in disgust then went back upstairs to wait for breakfast.

Addy loved cooking breakfast. She had the waffle recipe down pat and assembled the ingredients in no time. Lionel didn't like waffles so they hadn't had them in ages. The sweet smell of Belgian waffles slowly baking on the waffle iron filled the gloomy kitchen. Addy went over to the window and pulled the curtain as far back as she could to let in the sun. At the beach, Addy had thought about how the waves lapped the shores of countries around the world, had done so for centuries, and would continue to do so for as long as the earth existed. The sun was the same. It was shining in the kitchen in Maine, just as it was shining through her window in Connecticut—impartial, systematically, methodically. How could it be the same sun illuminating such different places?

The smell of the waffles getting brown shook Addy out of her philosophical frame of mind. She called to the kids, "Waffles are ready."

She had a round waffle iron that made one-fourth of the circle for each person. As soon as Addy placed the quarter of the circle on their plates, she poured the batter for the next batch. The kids quickly passed the butter and maple syrup around the table.

"Mmm, mmm ... Mom—these are DEE-WISH-US," Jimmy said with his mouth full, while Mary and Pete laughed.

It was almost as if they were all back in Maine ... free, happy ... looking forward to the next adventure.

Addy knew she would have to spend the day cleaning but didn't want the kids trapped inside, too. The phone rang, and Pete jumped up to answer it. Of course, if Lionel were home, Pete knew never to leave the table without permission. The kids acted one way when they were alone with Addy and another when Lionel was present. It was truly amazing how the kids learned to live with this dichotomy. The phone call was for Pete. It was his friend Ron Avery asking if all the kids would like to come over to swim.

Addy said, "As long as Ron's mother will be home." Pete asked Ron about this, and then shouted, "Yes. Can we go, Mom?" The other two pleaded to go as well. Pete said, "Ron's mom will pick us up." Addy just couldn't refuse. It was supposed to be a scorcher today, and Ron always invited Addy's children over on hot days. The Avery family often remarked how much they love Pete, Jim, and Mary.

Pete finished making plans with Ron; Addy kept dishing out

the waffles, and, for the moment, all was right with the world. Joan Avery, as well as the other neighborhood moms, knew Addy would not accompany the children. Addy suspected that by now, the women knew there was a problem in the Roberge household, but no one spoke about it.

The kids wouldn't be going until after lunch. Addy suddenly realized they had not stopped at the grocery store on the way back from Maine so she would have to improvise for lunch and dinner. She had the ingredients to make tuna sandwiches for lunch, but what would she make Lionel for dinner? She would think of something. Since she didn't drive, she often had to use her imagination to create dishes from what she had on hand. Somehow, everything came out delicious. She had a gift for that.

The kids were thrilled to think that on their first day back from vacation, they were going to go swimming. Addy knew just how they felt. On rare occasions, she had experienced feelings of joyful anticipation, as if life was truly happy, reliable, and safe. As she mixed the tuna salad for lunch, she reached back into the recesses of her mind and stumbled upon a time when she was a Girl Scout. Thank God, Aunts Sophia and Hazel approved of that organization and allowed her to participate. Addy would have joined ANY club as a child just to get out of the house. The aunts had failed to check out her troop carefully and never realized that, not only was her friend Helena Kurowski in her group, but Helena's mother Mary was one of the leaders. Addy often thought that if the aunts had given Mary Kurowski a chance, they would have seen what a wonderful woman she was. In fact, it wasn't until her aunts were long dead that Addy could say in her mind, "Mary Kurowski was better than my aunts." No one ever knew Addy named her own daughter after this courageous, kind, and intelligent woman. How she hoped her sweet little Mary would develop some of those characteristics as she grew into a woman. Addy shuddered, what kind of an example am I, meek, trapped, unlucky Addy?

Chapter VII

Memories of Girl Scouts

Addy quickly went back to thinking about Girl Scouts. They had so much fun earning badges for cooking, sewing, and all sorts of other positive, life-enhancing skills. While they were working on their nature badges, their troop took a fall hiking and camping trip to Lake Goshen. Although this was a Girl Scout summer sleepover camp, the director allowed troops to use part of the facilities in the fall. What a stroke of good luck that Mrs. Sarno, a robust, cheerful Italian woman, came to the house to talk to the aunts about the trip. If Helena's mom had come, the aunts would refuse to let Addy go camping and may have even pulled her from the troop.

Mrs. Sarno explained that there would be one chaperone for every four girls, and for safety, the husbands of the troop leaders were also coming along. Because Columbus Day was on a Monday that year, the girls would be leaving early Saturday and returning late Monday afternoon. Nine-year-old Addy listening to Mrs. Sarno from the other room, held her breath until she heard Aunt Sophia reply, "I don't see why Addy shouldn't be able to go, do you Hazel?"

Hesitating, Hazel answered, "Addy is shy. Maybe she will be afraid."

Addy, forgetting she was hiding and secretly listening, burst into the living room shouting excitedly, "I am not scared. All the other girls will earn their nature badges, but I won't if I don't go. I love the outdoors. Please let me go."

Mrs. Sarno laughed, gave Addy a hug, and then said to the aunts, "What do you say?" Hazel and Sophia looked at one another in agreement. "She can go, as long as you promise there will be no boys there, and Addy will be safe."

Addy retorted, "This is a GIRL Scout camp, right Mrs. Sarno? No boys are ever allowed in a GIRL Scout camp."

Mrs. Sarno replied quickly, "She's right. Boy Scouts have their own separate camps FAR from any Girl Scout camps. That settles it then. I'll be over to pick Addy up at 8:00 on Saturday morning."

The girls were given a list of items to bring with them so Addy and the aunts went shopping at the local outdoor equipment store to purchase an inexpensive sleeping bag; knapsack; flashlight; jackknife; bug repellant; and a tin dinnerware set. The gear added up to quite a bit, and Addy worried the aunts would complain about the price. They didn't.

When Saturday morning finally arrived, Addy awakened early and dressed in her red plaid flannel shirt and gray dungarees. The cuffs of the dungarees rolled up to reveal the same plaid flannel lining. Of all her clothes, this outfit was her favorite, but she rarely wore it. With everything packed in her new knapsack, Addy fidgeted, waiting for the Sarnos to come for her. The aunts had gotten up very early to prepare a hearty breakfast of bacon, eggs, and toast so, as they said, she would be strong enough to hike. A feeling of guilt swept over the young Addy. The aunts were kind and did their best. She must try harder to love them.

Just as Addy finished her breakfast, Mrs. Sarno knocked at the front door. As always, Mrs. Sarno was cheerful, greeting the aunts warmly and patiently waiting for Addy to gather up her things and kiss the aunts "good-bye."

Of course, Aunts Sophia and Hazel's last words were, "BE CAREFUL." Mrs. Sarno reassured them that Addy would be home safe and sound on Monday afternoon. She handed them a slip of paper that had the director of the camp's phone number, "just in case." Mrs. Sarno always did the right thing at the right time.

Mr. Sarno drove, and Mrs. Sarno sat next to him in the front. Four girls were crowded into the back seat, but Mr. Sarno's hilarious jokes all along the way to Camp Goshen made the girls forget how squished they were. When they arrived at the camp,

Addy immediately spotted Helena and her mother getting out of their car. Helena ran over to Addy, calling, "We're in the same tent!"

Addy just could not believe how lucky she felt that day. The weather was perfect. It was warm for October, and the vivid reds, yellows, oranges, and even magentas and pinks of the autumn trees were almost blinding. The contrast of the sapphire sky against these indescribable hues was overwhelming. Tears welled up in Addy's eyes. How can anything be so beautiful? she thought.

Feisty Helena looked over at her and said, "Are you crying, Addy?"

Addy knew that she could explain her love of autumn to Helena, and Helena would understand, but right now Addy had to be a brave camper. "No," Addy said, embarrassed by her own corniness, "I think I have something in my eye." She reached up, wiped her left eye, confirming, "Yes. There it is. I'm fine now."

The girls claimed beds in their assigned tents and unrolled their sleeping bags on top of the cots. Luckily, the other two girls in Helena and Addy's tent were nice. After the scouts stowed away their gear, the troop leaders and their husbands led the girls on a short hike around the camp to get the lay of the land and collect pretty leaves. Then they all returned to the tent area. For lunch, they had sandwiches, which the leaders had prepared in advance but for dinner that night, they were going to cook over the fire. The girls were excited about that.

After lunch, everyone went to the large log cabin that served as the dining hall during the summer. The leaders had told the girls to bring all the leaves they had gathered during the hike because they were going to work on a surprise activity. On the stove in the cabin kitchen, containers of wax were melting over a low flame. Once the wax melted, the adults distributed the containers to several tables and told the girls to take turns dipping a leaf into the warm wax, preserving the leaves forever. Addy's little heart overflowed with joy. Forever. How rarely she felt secure enough to imagine "forever."

The afternoon meandered along until the sun began to set.

The girls had previously signed up for various tasks for each day. Some of the girls helped the leaders start the campfire with wood the fathers had picked up on their hike. The leaders had also brought their own wood, just in case the branches in the forest were damp. The supper menu was, "Campfire Stew and Banana Boats." Addy had signed up to help with dinner that night and just couldn't believe the huge black pot bubbling over the fire contained their supper. Soon the smell of the stew simmering drew the girls out of their tents. The fresh air and exercise had made them as ravenous as bear cubs.

Finally, the stew was ready to serve. The girls waited in line with their bowls as Helena's mom ladled out the hearty stew. The sky was growing dark, but the glow from the fire and large lanterns embraced the innocent girls with peace and safety. The banana boats were something Addy would remember for the rest of her life. She memorized the recipe by heart:

Cut a slit in your banana and the peel, the long way, keeping the peel attached on the other end. Do not remove the banana skin. Scoop out some of the flesh of the banana under the slit peel. Fill the scooped out part of the banana with marshmallows and squares of a Hershey's chocolate bar. Replace the peeled back skin then tightly wrap the banana with tin foil. Place the foil-wrapped banana on the grill over your campfire for approximately 8-10 minutes or until the chocolate and marshmallow melts. Once cooked, remove the bananas from the grill. (Be careful as they will be hot. Wear oven mitts.)

What an amazing dinner ... all cooked over a campfire. The girls cleaned up their dishes after they ate, then sat around the campfire singing songs. When it was time to go to bed, they sang "Taps."

Addy looked up and saw millions of stars. Having never been in the woods at night, Addy never realized how many stars existed in our galaxy. This meant that even when Addy couldn't

78

see the stars at home, they were still shining brilliantly in the dark woods. Somehow, that thought made Addy feel invulnerable.

The girls went back to their tents to get their toiletries. Flashlights guided the giggling crew to the shower house. It was too cold by now to take a shower so Addy used the toilet, and then washed up and brushed her teeth. When she returned to her tent, she slipped into her sleeping bag to undress and put on her pajamas. It was awkward, but all the girls did the same, violating no one's modesty.

The leaders made the rounds to the tents to be sure the girls were in bed. One of Addy's tent mates wanted to tell ghost stories, but much to her relief, the other girls said, "no." The chirping of the crickets lulled the campers off to sleep.

On Sunday morning, the girls made "Campfire Breakfast Muffins," which were simply a mixture of ham, cheese, eggs, and shredded potatoes cooked in a muffin tin over the fire. They were delicious. Food cooked over a fire always tastes so much better.

After breakfast, the leaders took the girls on a hike down to a waterfall. They walked a long way and were tired and thirsty. However once they reached the falls, they forgot about their fatigue. The water tumbled over the rocks into the swiftly moving river below. Everyone stopped talking and stood there listening to the music of the waterfall. Once again, tears welled up in Addy's eyes. Helena looked over at her, but this time she said nothing. They sat by the waterfall, resting and eating their picnic lunch. As the cheerful bunch sat chatting and laughing, the leaders noticed the sky suddenly darkening. Not wanting to alarm the girls, they said nothing about a possible thunderstorm. Although the weatherman had predicted sunny skies for the entire weekend, the weather in New England inevitably does what it pleases.

By the time they hiked back to camp, the sky was even darker, and it began to rain. The girls ran to their tents while the leaders gathered to discuss what to do. Streaks of lightening ripped through the sky, the rain poured down in sheets, and the wind picked up to at least fifteen miles an hour. Some of the girls screamed. The storm was getting worse.

Soon the leaders ran around to all the tents to give the girls an update on the rest of the weekend. Because of the weather, the leaders felt it was a bad idea to stay at the campground. Instead, they would return home, but the good news was that the girls would be camping out in the leaders' living rooms.

The girls gathered in the dining hall while the leaders phoned all the parents to inform them about the change in plans. Some of the parents had already panicked and called the camp director to check on their daughters.

More than anything, Addy wanted to sleep at Helena's house. Yet, how could she do it without the aunts finding out? Fortuitously, Mrs. Sarno assigned Addy to Helena's house. She just had to talk to Mrs. Sarno. From out of nowhere, Addy found the voice to speak up.

"Mrs. Sarno, may I speak to you in private?"

"Sure, Addy. Let's step out into the hallway."

"Mrs. Sarno, I want to stay at Helena's house, but my aunts do not like me hanging around with Helena. I don't want to lie, but is there any way I could stay at Helena's without my aunts finding out about it?"

At first, Mrs. Sarno looked confused. Then, as if she instantaneously understood what Addy was asking, she said, "Don't worry, honey. I'll figure something out."

"Oh, thank you Mrs. Sarno, thank you!"

Addy drove back with the three other girls who were her companions in the car on the way to the campground. The storm raged violently, but Mr. Sarno assuaged the girls' fear by cracking jokes all the way home. As the Sarnos pulled into Helena's driveway, Addy could barely contain her delight. She had never slept over at anyone's house, and now she was going to be pretend camping on her secret friend's living room floor. When Mrs. Sarno was leaving, she said to Helena's mom, Mary, "We'll come over and pick up Addy tomorrow afternoon." Mary started to say, "I will drive her," but by some miracle she said instead, "Sure. That will be great."

Addy burned with shame, hoping Mary Kurowski didn't know why Mrs. Sarno had to be the one to drive Addy home.

Helena lived with her mom in an old farmhouse that had been in the family for quite some time. There were acres of land surrounding the large home, with apple trees, a beautiful pond, and several farm animals. The atmosphere was serene and welcoming. Helena met Addy at the front door, escorting her into the living room to join the others. The storm raged on so Mary was quietly grateful they had decided to leave the campground. She got some clothesline rope from the garage and strung two lines across the living room. Then she got blankets and threw them over the ropes. She figured each clothesline tent could accommodate two girls. Mary searched through the Girl Scout Campfire Cookbook to find recipes adaptable for use on the stovetop.

As evening came round, the girls took turns taking baths because they were still grubby from their time in the woods. The best part of this Sunday in October so many years ago was Addy's chance to share a tent with Helena. How Addy admired Helena's spunk and intelligence. It seemed Helena could do anything and feared nothing. The friends whispered for most of the night, sharing their hopes and dreams for the future. Helena wanted to move to New York just as soon as she was able, while Addy wanted to open her own bakery. These two days—one in the woods—the other at Helena's house, were memories of happiness following happiness.

Chapter VIII

The Burning of the Roast

The chiming of the clock on the mantle shook the grown-up Addy out of her reverie. Damn. It was already four o'clock. What would she make for dinner? The phone rang, and it was Mrs. Avery asking if the children could stay for supper. Mr. Avery was going to cook hamburgers and hot dogs on the grill. "Would you like to join us, Addy?" Mrs. Avery asked hesitantly.

"Thank you so much for asking me, Joan. I have to cook for my husband, but the kids would love to stay—if it's no bother."

Mrs. Avery was quiet for a moment. She sounded disappointed and said, "I understand, Addy. It is last minute."

By 4:30, Addy began to get flustered as she tried to figure out what to make Lionel for dinner. She already knew he would be in a foul mood because she had given the kids permission to eat at the Avery's. The phone rang again. It was Lionel calling to tell her not to hold dinner for him because he had a meeting and was going out with the guys in the office. Sweet Mother of God, Hallelujah and Amen!

Addy couldn't remember when she last had the house all to herself. She fixed herself a peanut butter and Marshmallow Fluff sandwich and then sat down in her armchair next to the fireplace. Now she would deliberately conjure up memories of Greg. After returning from Maine, she had been afraid to allow herself to think of Allison and him. Addy closed her eyes and recalled the afternoon of lovemaking and the spontaneously sweet connection by the campfire on the beach. If a compassionate God existed, maybe he wanted her to find happiness. Just in case, she sent up a prayer that Lionel would get home very late.

The children returned flushed and excited because they had

lit sparklers before they left Ron's house. Happiness upon happiness, Addy thought as she shooed them upstairs to get ready for bed.

Addy's little prayer must have been delivered. By 11:30 p.m., Lionel still wasn't home. Addy showered and went to bed, never hearing what time he came in. He didn't even bother her for sex.

The cherished last days of summer flew by, and the children soon had to return to school. Addy missed them terribly at first but eventually settled into her routine of cleaning, cooking, and reading. Lionel had resumed his hard pinching of her behind when he wanted sex; Addy was able to shut down her mind completely as he convulsed on top of her like a rabid dog. For all he cared, Lionel could be fucking a hole in a log. When Lionel groaned repulsively, Addy knew it was over.

One Monday evening in late September while the family was eating dinner, Lionel announced that he was having his new boss over for dinner on Wednesday night. He told Addy he would drive her to the grocery store in the morning before he went to work. She was to pick out the best filet mignon roast in the butcher's case. What? Addy thought. He hasn't sprung for an expensive cut of meat like that since our wedding reception. He also warned the kids to be on their best behavior when the boss came.

After the children were off to school, Lionel told Addy to get ready to go to the market. He wanted her to make mashed potatoes, fresh green beans, butternut squash, a salad, and chocolate cream pie for dessert.

Addy rushed around the store, collecting all the items to make the dinner Lionel had ordered. She would be cooking all day. Lionel drove her home, helped unload the groceries, and gave a last warning, "Remember, everything has to be perfect."

Addy was a nervous wreck and hardly slept Tuesday night. In the morning, she made the crust and chocolate pudding, and when cooled, put the assembled pie into the refrigerator. She would wait and whip the cream just before serving the pie. The day passed so quickly, but by three o'clock, she had completed all the prep work. When the children arrived home from school, she asked them to be sure their rooms were in order. They were to take baths and then dress in the outfits she had ironed for them.

Things were going along smoothly, thank goodness. Addy went upstairs to bathe and change into a green dress Lionel had once said he liked. She went downstairs to start the roast, using a recipe she had found in a cookbook. Because they did not ordinarily have such fine cuts of meat, Addy was insecure about cooking tenderloin. She tried to follow this recipe exactly:

**One 4 to 5 pound tenderloin,
tied and trimmed at room temperature
One large clove garlic sliced in half
Lots of fresh ground black pepper**

Instructions: Preheat oven to 500 degrees. Rub the tenderloin all over with the garlic. Then rub it liberally with the pepper. (Save salt for after meat is cooked. Salt draws out meat juices during cooking.) While you are doing this, take note of how thick the meat is. Place the meat in a roasting pan, stab a meat thermometer into the center of the roast and place the pan in the oven. Immediately turn the heat down to 225 degrees. If you have decided you have a thin tenderloin, start checking the temperature on the meat thermometer after 30 minutes. If you have a thicker tenderloin, start checking the thermometer after 50 minutes. The thermometer should read 140 degrees for rare meat. When the meat is done, remove it from the oven and let it stand for 10 minutes. Don't forget to put salt on the table. Yield: Serves 8-10

Addy had read the recipe quickly and put the meat into the 500-degree oven. She called to Mary to help her set the table. Addy took out her best china and silverware, and she and Mary laughed and joked as they got the table ready for company.

Mary was reminiscing about the fun they had in Maine with Allison and Greg. As soon as Addy heard Greg's name, she instantly drifted to another realm. She stood there daydreaming, but then Mary said, "Mom, I smell something like burnt meat."

Addy dashed to the kitchen. Smoke billowed out from the oven. Oh God. She had neglected to turn the heat down to 225 after putting the roast in the oven. What could she do? She could not drive to the market to get another roast. Terrorized, she tried to calm herself with the thought that the center of the roast may still be pink. The outside of the meat was charred black, and the meat thermometer read 170 degrees. Addy turned off the oven, hoping to keep the roast warm until Lionel and his boss arrived.

Before long, she heard Lionel's key in the door and then the sound of laughter. She could swear she heard a woman chuckling as well. Addy quickly removed her apron and walked into the living room. Lionel introduced her to his new boss and the boss' WIFE. Addy had no idea the wife was coming, too. From that moment on, the night was a blur. Addy knew that Lionel was furious at her for serving burnt meat. The rest of the meal met with his expectations, but as she watched Mr. and Mrs. Styles politely gnawing on the shoe leather meat, she knew she was in for trouble after the guests left.

Lionel kept it together until after the kids were asleep. Addy tried to stall going to bed, but tonight Lionel was waiting up for her. She climbed in beside him, and he immediately started his tirade. Addy trembled with fear because she knew what was coming.

"I had you buy the most expensive cut of meat for my boss," he began calmly. "So what do you do? You burnt the fucking meat. You burnt the fucking meat (his voice was getting louder) on the night my boss and his wife came to dinner. What is wrong with you? You are a worthless fucking piece of shit."

He put his hands around her neck, shaking her head and choking her. Addy gasped for air, struggling to stay alive. She was almost unconscious when he stopped. He belted her in her right arm, punched her in the stomach, and smashed her across the face. Addy whimpered like a puppy.

"Go ahead and cry you good-for-nothing baby. If divorce were allowed by the Church, I would have been long gone."

Lionel turned over, and Addy went into the bathroom to weep soundlessly. She had bruises around her neck, a burning black and blue on her arm, and she felt like vomiting. She sat on the toilet for a long time, crying as quietly as she could. Greg would never be capable of such violence against a woman. If Greg were there right now, he would tear Lionel to pieces.

One day faded into another, and Addy did her best to hide the bruises. The weather had grown cold so a turtleneck jersey covered the marks on her neck.

* * * * *

During that fall, Helena's mother, Mary Kurowski, passed away. Mary had a weak heart, and Helena tried to no avail to get her to come live with her in New York City. Mary, however, wanted no part of New York. She was perfectly content remaining on the farm that had been her home ever since she was a child.

One brilliant autumn day, Mary was picking apples from the trees planted by her long-dead parents. Feeling a bit tired, she walked over to rest a while on her glider next to the pond. Her devoted Irish setter, Woodrow, ran over to sit at her feet. The maple trees reflecting in the pond looked like a million golden coins. Suddenly Mary felt an unbearable heaviness and pain in her chest. She was too weak to get up and call anyone so she just sat there, realizing that this was probably the end. She blinked back the tears, wishing she could say "good-bye" to her daughter Helena. Then one of Mary's favorite prayers rose in her mind. It was from St. Teresa of Avila, one of Helena's favorite saints when she was child:

Let nothing disturb you,
Let nothing frighten you,
All things are passing away:
God never changes.
Patience obtains all things.
Whoever has God lacks nothing;
God alone suffices.

Even as the pain overwhelmed her, Mary was not frightened. She would go quietly to the Heavenly realm into the loving arms of Jesus.

Mary's neighbor, Mr. Paget, while driving home from work, happened to glance over at the farm. He was disturbed to see Mary slumped on her glider, while Woodrow jumped on her, barking frantically and licking her face. He pulled into Mary's driveway and ran over to the glider crying, "Mrs. Kurowski, Mrs. Kurowski!" The front door of Mary's house was open so Mr. Paget ran in to call the ambulance.

While the ambulance siren screeched into the driveway, Mr. Paget hurriedly tried to locate Helena's phone number. He found it in Mary's address book next to the telephone. Helena had not been back to stay in her childhood town since leaving home for college.

Chapter IX

Helena

Mary Kurowski used to take the train to meet Helena in New York, where mom and daughter would have glorious times shopping and dining. Helena took Mary on a few cruises and once to Fatima in Portugal, where the Virgin Mary had appeared to three shepherd children and revealed secrets to them. Her prophecies were recorded in documents locked away to be opened in the future. Rumor had it that when one of the Popes opened the letters, he cried because the predictions were terrifying. As Mary Kurowski grew older, Helena could not convince her to travel much more. Helena wanted her mother to move into a retirement home closer to New York. Mary, however, was strong-willed and determined to live out the rest of her life on her own.

When Helena first moved to New York, she worked long hours at night as a waitress while searching for a job in journalism during the day. In the same navy blue suit and pumps, Helena went to one interview after the other, never hearing back from any of the companies that said, "We'll call you."

Weeks turned into months and soon Helena had been in New York for a year. How could she ever admit to her mother that she was still slinging hash? Her pumps had holes in the soles, and her feet were freezing as she walked to yet another interview, this time for a proofreader's position at a small publishing firm. Here goes nothing, she thought gloomily.

Much to her surprise, the owner of the company was sincerely interested in her, and they talked for over an hour. When he finally offered her the job, she was speechless. Of course, the pay was not much, but at least she got her "foot in the door." She thanked him profusely and went immediately to the restaurant to give her notice— no more greasy-smelling uniforms and hair. Helena did not have a wardrobe of clothes to wear to an office, but she would manage. It certainly was not a luxurious place.

Helena enjoyed her new job, and the people who worked with her were decent. She had not been out on a date since moving to New York, and her office mates were always trying to fix her up with someone. She had no time for such frivolity; her goal was to get ahead in the world of publishing.

One afternoon, a truck driver came into the office to get a signature for a delivery. Everyone else was out to lunch, so Helena looked up absentmindedly from her work to see what the man wanted. Wow. What a looker. He was tall, well built with sandy blonde hair, chiseled features, and piercing blue eyes. When he smiled a broad, impish Irish smile, the gutsy Helena suddenly became feeble. She composed herself and walked over to the counter to sign the delivery receipt, trying not to look this fellow in the eyes.

She returned to her desk after signing the form, but the man did not leave. He just stood there staring at her and smiling. "Is there anything else I can help you with?" Helena said in her most professional tone.

"Sure," he answered in a thick Irish brogue. "Give me your telephone number." After several minutes of playful bantering, Helena gave him her number. She could not believe what she did and immediately regretted it. Well, she would just not pick up her home phone at all for many days. He would soon get the message that she was definitely not interested in him.

When she got home from work that night, the phone rang, and going back on her word, Helena answered it immediately. It was him ... Edward Callahan, the man she saw at her office that afternoon.

He called her frequently until she finally agreed to meet him for lunch on a Saturday. Helena realized she was lonely, and gorgeous Edward was there to fill the void. She had been to college, but Edward had not. Still, he was decidedly masculine, handsome, and seemed to possess a natural intelligence (or so Helena convinced herself).

Edward told her Irish folk tales and recited funny limericks. Gifted with an enchanting tenor voice, Edward could make any woman swoon. The Irish lullabies were Helena's favorite. While they were dating, their relationship was idyllic. They picnicked in the park; held hands and took long walks together; and went to the picture shows on Saturday nights. Laughing, joking, constantly together; they were unable to live without one another.

After a seven-month courtship, Helena and Edward wed. Mary had doubts about her daughter's choice. Edward reminded Mary of Helena's father, who also seemed wonderful in the beginning. Alcohol, a violent temper, and another woman had broken Mary's heart. It was lucky that Mary's husband abandoned them while Helena was too young to get to know him. Still, if her daughter Helena loved Edward, Mary would be happy for her.

Helena's pals at work were delighted with her good fortune to marry such a handsome, charming Irishman. As can often be said of the Irish, they either write or drink—Edward chose the latter. Sadly, he was no James Joyce who mastered both the bottle and the pen.

At first, Edward drank only when in the company of his huge Irish family or with his friends at the Casey Belgard Club. All the Irishmen socialized at Casey Belgard's, and the club even sponsored a baseball team called, "The Casey Bs." Of course, their uniforms were emblazoned with shamrocks, not bees. The men played endless games of darts at the club, tossing back their whiskey as evening lapsed into morning. Helena loathed dart matches and found baseball tedious.

After the first few games of the season, the wives and children were sent home at the close of the ninth inning so "the boys" could either celebrate their victories or drown their sorrows. The score of the games made no difference in the evenings' outcome. Helena began to leave earlier and attend less frequently. Edward didn't seem to mind. After all, he had "the boys," with their big plans, unrealistic ideas, their whiskey, and buxom barmaids.

Helena had no children to show off, no recipes to exchange with the women, and hated the redundant conversations about concoctions to clean windows or whiten the wash. Helena was certain her lessening appearances didn't make much difference to the wives and their broods.

Oh, Edward and Helena were still in love, held hands, and took walks. He still spun fanciful tales, but now as he held her in his arms and sang Irish lullabies, their faces were both tear-streaked—his with unfulfilled dreams, hers with regret. He had promised, and she had believed.

Just around the time of their second St. Patrick's Day together as husband and wife, Helena discovered she was pregnant. Edward was delighted, as was his entire extended family. Maybe the much-dreaded Sunday dinners at Momma's would be less strained, now that the relatives would not be inquiring why Helena was still not with child. Perhaps Edward and she could move out of their cramped cold-water, third floor, walk-up flat in Hell's Kitchen, only two blocks from Momma's and the rest of the tribe. At first, Edward treated her like fragile Irish crystal, but life resumed, as it always does.

The dart games grew longer, and soon it was baseball season. There were wins and losses. The games had turned into something more than just a fun pastime for "the boys." When the team lost, Edward came home in a terrible mood and took out his frustrations on Helena. There were the reprimands Edward was receiving from his new boss at work; the bills they could not pay; the worries over where the money would come from to buy the things the baby would need.

As the stress in his life escalated, so did Edward's temper. Once after coming home from a game his team had lost, he had words with Helena and slapped her across the face. Edward immediately took her into his arms, sobbing, vowing never to touch her again. Still, when Edward played baseball, Helena hoped for wins.

Edward's vow never to touch her again was another empty promise. That first slap set a precedent, and it was now easier for Edward to continue slapping her. The slaps turned into punches; the handholding into shoulder grabbing and wall slamming.

Helena had just received a small salary increase at work. She didn't tell Edward about it but opened a bank account to save some money for the baby. The girls at work were whispering about a baby shower. Maybe between her savings and the shower, Helena would be able to get all the sweet things a baby needs.

The baby was growing inside her, and Helena was exhausted. It was getting more and more difficult for her to make that trek up and down the three flights of stairs. The heat in the apartment was stifling, and the open windows made no difference.

Helena did not bother to wait up for Edward after the baseball games anymore. In this way, she was safer from the ugly repercussions of the losses. One Saturday evening, Helena was fast asleep but awakened to a sudden, loud crash. Edward was home, sprawled on the floor muttering something about "dirty cheats." Oh no. They had lost. He attempted to get up but fell head long into the faded cast-off over-stuffed chair, tripping over his bat or glove; Helena wasn't sure which. She dared not turn on the light. Then the unthinkable happened. She giggled and tried desperately to choke back the laugh she felt bubbling up in her throat.

In spite of his drunken stupor, Edward heard her. He stumbled to his feet, a seething demon. The bat was leaning against the chair so it had to have been the glove that tangled in Edward's feet. By this time, Helena had gotten out of bed, hoping if worse came to worse, she could run out of the apartment. Edward grabbed for her nightgown, but Helena quickly stepped away. He caught her wrist and then yanked her toward him, shook her violently, then smashed her into the wall. He was weaving crazily, unsteady on his feet. Helena was terrified. The shamrocks on his baseball shirt seemed to be spinning and dancing as he shook with rage.

The baby within her suddenly turned or rolled over. Her hands flew automatically to her belly and she wondered if "Little Eddy," as Edward always referred to their baby, was reacting to the quivering shamrock dance as well.

Helena was hysterical, but as often happened when she was either overjoyed or frightened, Helena snickered, and before she knew it, she was laughing aloud. Helena immediately moved one hand to cover her mouth, Edward stepped forward, grabbed the hair that had fallen across her face and slammed her head against the wall. She saw stars. Her vision began to dim, and then cleared but dimmed again. Edward was standing in front of her. His body steadier and more rigid now, he had somehow managed to hold the bat in his hand. His face contorted with blind rage, Edward stabbed the bat into her bulging stomach. The pain exploded, and Helena's knees buckled. Edward kicked her in the back. As he lurched past her, the blackness receded.

Helena had a throbbing pain in her stomach, and her head felt like it was going to explode. Before her eyes fully focused, she heard a sound all too familiar to her. Edward was puking on the floor. In the dim light of the streetlights below, Helena saw Edward lean out the window, vomiting uncontrollably. The room reeked with the smell of cheap whiskey.

Her head was spinning, but her fury at what he had done to her left no room for pity or forgiveness. Slowly and quietly, Helena got to her feet. The bat was propped there next to the window. She grasped the bat with both of her shaking hands, remembering how "the boys" had swung in all those nauseating baseball games. Edward was still choking and vomiting pro-fusely into the alley below. She crept forward, shouldering the bat. Sensing her behind him, Edward quickly straightened up, turning to face her. Rage strengthening her swing, Helena swung as hard and as fast as she could. With a large cracking sound, the bat connected flawlessly with Edward's temple. The impact lifted him off his feet, and he fell partially through the open window. Helena dropped the bat, kicked it under the sofa, then grabbed Edward's feet and stuffed him the rest of the way out the window. She did not look. She knew what awaited him—a pool of his own vomit and blood on the filthy heat-baked asphalt, three stories down.

Helena went back to bed and slept peacefully. Hours later, the police rapping at her door awakened her. Word of the terrible accident spread throughout the neighborhood.

"Oh my. And pregnant she was. Poor little thing."

"No, she'd best not view the body. He landed on his head, after all. His brothers will see to the arrangements."

People came and went that first day. After the "accident," things were fuzzy, and Helena was not sure just who had stopped by. "In shock," they whispered. "Put her to bed," they suggested. Three days later, her baby was dead. "Spontaneous abortion," tongues wagged. "The shock of the accident," they told each other.

Helena buried Edward along with her baby girl, Catherine, at St. Bernard's Cemetery a week later. Her boss was so kind and understanding. In fact, the entire company displayed an outpouring of sympathy and compassion. In a few weeks, Helena returned to work. During her first week back on the job, something amazing happened. Helena received a visit from a stranger, an insurance adjustor. He brought papers for Helena to sign, then handed her a check for $4,000, a veritable fortune.

Edward's company had a union, and part of the workers' dues went toward life insurance. This was the payout benefit for Edward's accidental death, the bespeckled gentleman quietly explained.

Helena's mind was reeling. Now she could escape from that horrid little flat. Though she never thought about Edward while she was there, it was stifling, cramped, AND three flights up. She soon made plans and found a small one-story duplex apartment in Brooklyn with a tiny yard and garden. When she moved, she threw out nearly everything, including the freshly scrubbed bat she had found under the sofa. The lumpy over-stuffed chair, the gaudy dishes "Momma" had presented to her as a wedding gift, the cheap hand-me-downs from Edward's relatives—gone, all were gone. The Salvation Army accepted Edward's clothes, shoes, and, of course, baseball glove. She was free of it all—all of it. No lullabies tonight or ever again.

Helena continued working at the small publishing firm and remained happily alone for the next four years. One day at work, she met John Sylvan, a struggling young author. He was a gentle soul, a well-educated thinker, so unlike Edward. John and Helena began having lively discussions over coffee and lunch. Their friendship blossomed into romance, and they were eventually married in a quiet ceremony in the pastor's study. She was, after all, a widow, so her remarriage was acceptable in the eyes of the Catholic Church. Her mom had misgivings about Helena's choice of a second husband, but Mary kept her doubts to herself.

John had begun writing a tortured novel prior to their marriage. While Helena worked, John wrote. Alternatively, he tore up lots of papers at least. Finally, Helena got tired of supporting John, and they divorced amicably. Some nine plus years later, Helena ran into John in Greenwich Village with his latest queer young lover at his side. The novel was still unfinished, and Helena chuckled to herself, "I doubt if this guy knows how long John has been working on his masterpiece." Then she laughed aloud, thinking, "No wonder we never had any kids. I thought John was too tired from writing all day."

Although she never told Mary why, Helena was able to get her marriage to John annulled. Truthfully, Helena did not give a damn about the Catholic Church; she just wanted to make her mother happy. After all, Mary had been an excellent mother. Embittered by the rejection both Mary and she suffered because Mary was divorced, Helena harbored resentment toward all religion. Although Mary had been able to annul her marriage, in those days people viewed divorced women as "sexually promiscuous, loose ... the gay divorcee" because they had already been through the hands of one man. Why, then, were widows held in such high esteem?

Helena had first married for puppy love, then for intellectual compatibility. Two strikes out were enough for her. That is why when she met R. James Smithfield at a party for a retiring editor, Helena thought nothing of having a drink with him later that evening after the party. She never went on dates, but this man was twenty years her senior so he would be safe. She was, after all, terminally single and called this gentleman, "Mr. Smithfield."

Mr. Smithfield proved to be extremely intelligent, well-travelled, and witty. He was a widower who, like Helena, regretfully, had no children. Although he made his fortune in the cotton industry, his first love was literature, and he had helped develop several reputable publishing houses. Apparently, Mr. Smithfield found something he liked about Helena and invited her to dine with him the next evening at a lavish New York restaurant. Helena was admittedly lonely. She could use a fine dinner and some good conversation. One dinner led to many, and soon Helena was calling Mr. Smithfield, "James."

James took Helena to see "The Nutcracker" ballet at the New York City Center. Helena felt particularly light-hearted that evening. She glanced over at James' face as he stared intently at Clara performing her sweet dance with the small wooden nutcracker. Although James was older, he was very distinguished, levelheaded, and handsome. Helena somehow couldn't take her eyes off him that night. He must have felt her gazing at him because he turned to her, almost embarrassed, and flashed a warm, white smile.

They both agreed that, no matter how many times they saw *The Nutcracker*, the Christmas tree growing dramatically before their eyes never ceased to amaze them. After the ballet, James took Helena to "Dominic's," their favorite coffee shop where the espresso and homemade Italian pastries were divine. James ordered a small tray of sweets for them to share. The rotund Chef Dominic, as always, beaming with pride in his culinary expertise, personally delivered the tray to their table. Piled high on the paper-doily covered silver tray were Florentines, Sfagliatella, Pignoli, Cucidati, and other delights, whose names Helena had yet to learn. As Chef Dominic placed the tray in front of Helena, she noticed a small dark blue velvet ring box on the edge of the tray.

Chef Dominic quickly left the table, laughing all the way to the kitchen. James removed the blue box from the tray and gazed lovingly at Helena.

"My darling, here is a gift for you because you are my greatest gift," James said, handing the box to Helena. Independent, resilient, strict Helena actually blushed. She opened the ring box to find a dazzling diamond solitaire engagement ring.

"Helena, I love you and want to marry you."

Helena knew that if you feel like crying but did not want to allow yourself to cry, gaze upward. She looked up at the ceiling, dabbed her eyes, and said, "Oh James, I can't; I just can't."

James looked heartbroken.

Helena could not bear to hurt him. He was the nicest man she had ever known, and she suspected she loved him as well. Helena said, "It's not you James, really it's not. It's me. I have a terrible track record with men."

James looked relieved. Laughing, he said, "Well, I have a solution for that. We will just have to take you out of the race."

Helena tried on the ring and never took it off. Already flabbergasted by her daughter's choice in men, Mary Kurowski received the news of Helena's engagement to a man almost Mary's age. Yet, Mary had a different feeling about James, Helena's third husband. He was kind, stable, generous, and he absolutely adored Helena. Mary sensed that the marriage would last, and it did.

When Helena looked back, she always remembered her years with James as the happiest, most fulfilling in her life. Of course, some jealous people said James was Helena's father figure, and so what if he was? With him, Helena could relax, exhale, and be vulnerable. He made her feel beautiful, special, and sexy.

One brilliant blue and gold morning while they were vacationing in Miami Beach, James suffered a massive stroke. Helena was devastated. The only other time she had felt such grief was when she lost her baby daughter, Catherine. Day after day, Helena sat by James' hospital bed, hoping that the therapy he received might restore his faculties. Helena consulted the best specialists she could find, but the verdict was always the same: too large an area of his brain had been damaged. Eventually, Helena placed James in an exclusive private rest home in Boca Raton and visited him as much as she possibly could. Although James' face seemed to brighten when she was there, Helena doubted if he knew who she was—what an undignified way for James' life to end. Sometimes Helena wished his heart would stop. He would be so embarrassed if he could see what he had become. Eventually, Helena's wish came true. James passed away quietly in his sleep one night, his beautiful spirit freed at last from the prison of his useless body.

Unlucky in love, Helena was luckier in her career. Mary, however, reminded Helena her success was the result of hard work not simply good fortune. After Edward died, Helena continued doggedly at the small publishing house where she had begun as proofreader. She had received incremental promotions over the years until, as their junior editor, she made a priceless discovery: Joshua Mannings Harrison, an idiosyncratic, reclusive author with a first novel so powerful, it literally leapt off the pages, grabbed the reader, and never loosened its grip until the entire book had been devoured.

Helena's skin rippled with goose bumps as she stayed up nights reading and rereading Harrison's manuscript. The deranged murderer performed his grisly crimes with stealth and cunning. As she read, Helena had flashbacks of her own crime but pushed them out of her mind. After all, Edward had killed her daughter.

Harrison's plot twisted and turned, doubling back upon itself. The clues were nonexistent. Rage seethed from the novel—the rage of the stalker-murderer and the anger of NYPD's Senior Detective, Dennis McGonagle felt toward himself because of his inability to solve these gruesome homicides. A devout Catholic, Detective McGonagle believed he was morally obligated to protect the innocent and seek justice for victims.

Helena's bosses were astounded at their good fortune. Harrison's first novel rocketed to the top of the New York Times Bestseller List where it remained for months. Of course, a second novel truly validates an author. The second manuscript swiftly arrived on Helena's desk in her tiny office. At least it WAS an office—no more sitting behind the counter like a receptionist. Helena could have easily moved to a more prestigious publishing house, but she felt an allegiance to the men who had first given her a break.

Harrison's second work spun horrifying tales of murders and dismemberments, with the plot flawlessly weaving a pattern of deception and betrayal. The ending was a stunner, another mega-bestseller. Harrison kept writing graphic tales of murder and mayhem, and Helena, now a full partner in her firm, continued to represent exclusively the now-famous J.M. Harrison.

Helena made other literary discoveries along the way but none with the cult-like following of J.M. Harrison. As for Harrison himself, Helena loathed the man. As much as she had made a lot of money thanks to his masterpieces of suspense, she often wondered how any sane person could create such ghastly tales. Perhaps, as in the case of Alfred Hitchcock, Harrison's strict Catholic schooling had something to do with his odd personality and predilections. Hitchcock was equally eccentric, but his films were not as gruesome as Harrison's novels. Critics sometimes suggested the sublimated sexuality in Hitchcock's movies entranced audiences. As a director, Alfred Hitchcock had to adhere to the regulations of the Production Code Administration, but as a novelist, Harrison could openly titillate his readers with sexual sadism scenes.

As Harrison's wealth and fame burgeoned, his lavish lifestyle became more depraved. Helena attended gatherings at the Harrison mansion, and what she witnessed there was not only X-Rated but also scarier than one of Harrison's novels. Harrison was a homosexual and among the top most drunken authors in America. At least he was a high-functioning drunk. Halloween at his home was particularly wanton. Harrison had amassed a collection of bizarre friends, most of whom were parasites feeding off his fortune. To receive an invitation to one of Harrison's Halloween bashes was like winning the Irish sweepstakes. The sprawling mansion, one of the first castles built in America, boasted heavy, imposing, gothic furniture upholstered in forest green, maroon, and dark blue velvets ... a perfect backdrop for Halloween.

The prospective party guests started planning their costumes months in advance, keeping the designs a secret until the unveiling on All Hallows Eve. In the end, all that work was for naught, as most guests ended up naked, drifting off to the many "play rooms" with either man, woman, or a few of each. Furnished in a more contemporary style than the rest of the mansion, these rooms contained huge white leather sofas that accommodated several people at once. Crystal chandeliers hung from the ceiling, shedding the exact amount of light to keep things flattering, but sensual, to all the naked bodies that writhed on the sofas throughout the night. Pity the poor maids who had to clean up those rooms the next day.

As soon as the clothing came off, Helena made a rapid exit. Harrison could never quite "get" Helena, and she was glad she could not "get" him either. He was, simply put, a lunatic.

As James' wife, she held the purse strings to the Smithfield fortune, but Helena had also accumulated massive amounts of cash during her career. Sadly, the only thing she could not buy was health for her beloved husband, James. She would have given all that she owned for just a few more days of the happiness she had shared with James before his stroke. At least Helena had gotten it right with James, and his love would sustain her until the end of her life.

Chapter X

The Funeral

Immediately after Mr. Paget phoned her, Helena went into automatic pilot, a defense mechanism that never failed in times of crisis. Early the next morning, she robotically packed her suitcases, arranged with the post office to hold her mail, called her secretary to cancel all appointments until further notice, and contacted Blanchard's Funeral Home in Chester. Helena was on the road to Connecticut by 10 a.m.

Countless cups of coffee fueled the rest of Helena's day. It was dark by the time she finally arrived at the farm, and, disregarding the fact that she had not eaten anything since the previous day, Helena dropped into bed, exhausted. She hadn't even taken the time to cry.

What she did not know is that some overzealous, mediocre rookie reporter, with fantasies of hitting it big, wrote an article about Helena's return to Chester for her mother's funeral. It was good for the sake of the ignoramus of a newshound that Helena never picked up *The Chester Gazette*. If she read the article so blatantly violating her sacred privacy, the outraged Helena would waste no time speeding down to the newspaper office and demanding the reporter's dismissal.

The article hit the newspaper the day after Helena arrived in town with headlines, "Celebrity Hometown Girl Returns to Bid Final Farewell to Her Mother." The story described Helena Kurowski, now Mrs. Helena Smithfield, a spunky local girl who had headed for New York City at an early age and never looked back until now. The article provided details of Helena's climb to the top of the ladder of success in the exciting world of publishing to her position as literary agent for the outrageously popular master of suspense, J.M. Harrison.

* * * * *

At Addy's house, the children had gone off to school, while Lionel uncharacteristically lingered over his coffee. He noticed the article about Helena Smithfield (nee Kurowski) in the Gazette and slowly made the association with Helena, the daughter of the "gay divorcee," Mary Kurowski. Lionel vaguely recalled Addy wanting to be Helena's friend, but Aunts Hazel and Sophia forbidding it. Lionel remembered how Addy's aunts had praised him for saving their niece from the influence of that bad apple, Helena Kurowski. Well, well, well—Lionel thought as he read the newspaper—that slut Helena has really made a place for herself in the world.

The wheels in Lionel's devious mind began spinning. Wasn't St. Michael's parish eyeing Mary Kurowski's farm as a possible acquisition? Hadn't his brother, Jean-Paul, now a monsignor, dreamed of establishing a retreat house or retirement home for priests? Lionel could see it now, "Sanctuary of the Monsignor Jean-Paul Roberge," or even "The Lionel Roberge Retirement Home for Priests."

Maybe Helena would be interested in selling or even donating the farm to the church. After all, what would a rich, highfalutin New Yorker like her want with a farm in Chester? If Addy could cozy up to Helena again, maybe Lionel could step in and make a business deal. Orchestrating the purchase of this land would be a feather in Lionel's greedy, hypocritical cap.

Addy was standing at the sink with her back to Lionel, washing the kids' breakfast dishes. As usual, she was out of her body somewhere off in fantasyland. Whenever Lionel was present, Addy would find it necessary to escape from the moment.

"Addy," Lionel called to her—again, in a louder voice, "ADDY!" God how he loathed his imbecile of a wife whose mind was always somewhere else.

As if awakened abruptly from a deep sleep, Addy jumped. "Oh, yes, Lionel?"

"Do you remember that girl, Helena Kurowski, who went to St. Mary's with you?"

Did Addy REMEMBER her? Helena was the only true friend

Addy ever had. In fact, many were the times Addy mourned the loss of Helena and the dream of the life they may have shared if Addy had only been brave enough to go off to New York City.

"Of course, Lionel," Addy replied. "Why?"

"There's an article here in the paper about her—looks as if she's a big shot now."

Addy could have told him that. She always knew Helena was destined for great things.

Lionel continued, "The article says she's in town for her mother's funeral."

Addy's heart skipped a beat: Helena, in CHESTER? Unfortunately, Addy had lost touch with Mary Kurowski. How sad it was to hear that she had died. Addy always loved Helena's mom but had given up her efforts to see her long ago. In the same narrow mindset as her aunts, Lionel discouraged visits with "the gay divorcee." Addy smiled maliciously. Wouldn't the pig Lionel die if he knew his own daughter was named after the kind, honorable, devout Mary Kurowski?

Lionel was losing patience with Addy's inattentiveness. "What the hell is wrong with you, anyways? Why don't you ever listen?"

Oh God, thought Addy fearfully. Was he planning to go off on her? After all, they were alone, and he never stayed drinking his coffee this long.

"But Lionel," Addy answered nervously, "I heard everything you said."

"Well, I think we should attend the funeral. I'm sure it would be nice for you to see Helena again," Lionel said with an air of propriety.

What was he up to? Addy thought. She dared not think too long, though, or he would start getting mad again. She would have to save her thinking until after he left for work.

"Sure, Lionel," Addy said, feigning enthusiasm. "I don't know if Helena will remember me, but we can go to pay our respects."

Lionel got up from the table, smug with his own cleverness. "The paper says there isn't any wake, but there will be a prayer service on Saturday at 9:00 a.m. at Blanchard's Funeral Home with a Mass at St. Michael's at 10:00 a.m. and burial at the Heavenly Gate Cemetery."

"I'm leaving for work. Make plans to go."

As soon as Lionel was out the door, Addy sat down at the kitchen table to do her thinking. She was going to see Helena after all these years. Although excited, Addy also dreaded the reunion. She had gotten so fat since she knew Helena as a schoolgirl all those years ago. Helena was probably a gorgeous, sophisticated woman who would find Addy frumpy and dull. Still, Addy had to go to the funeral whether or not she chose to do so. Apparently, there had to be something in this for Lionel, or he would have never encouraged her to go to, of all people's, Mary Kurowski's funeral.

Addy was certain Helena would loathe her. Why hadn't Addy visited the ailing Mary in all these years? Hadn't Addy loved Mary more dearly than even her own aunts? Helena would definitely think Addy was a shallow, heartless, hypocrite.

Her neighbor, Joan Avery, was always someone Addy could count on if she needed a favor. Still, Addy felt anxious about calling anyone on the telephone. What a stupid coward I am, Addy thought to herself. She dialed Joan's number and nervously asked Joan about watching the kids on Saturday morning.

In her usual generous manner Joan said, "Why not drop the kids off here? You know how much my kids love your kids."

Addy hesitated before saying, "But Joan, we have to be at the funeral home for 9:00 a.m. Isn't that awfully early for your kids to get up on a Saturday morning?"

"Don't be silly Addy," Joan laughed. "You know my kids will be delighted. In fact, you could have your kids sleep over on Friday night, if you like. Then all the kids could sleep late."

Although Addy wanted to give an immediate, unconditional "Yes," she hesitated. Could she stand to be alone with Lionel on Friday evening? Would Lionel even let the kids go?

Addy hesitated and said, "Could I let you know after I see what my husband's plans are for Friday night?"

Joan Avery wanted to scream. Her suspicions that something was terribly wrong in the Roberge household had increased steadily over the years. Poor Addy. How could such a sweet woman be married to a creep like Lionel? Joan did not trust Lionel one bit and hounded her own husband, Frank, to quiz Lionel during their golf outings.

Frank, like most men, did not want to pry. Joan was frustrated that she knew so little about what Addy's life was really like.

On the other end of the phone line, Joan replied kindly, "Of course, Addy. You can let me know right up to the last minute. We don't have any plans on Friday, and I won't tell my kids about a possible sleepover until I know for sure."

Addy loved Mrs. Avery for always making things so easy. What a gem of a woman.

"Thanks so much, Joan. You are the best neighbor anyone could have."

Addy really meant that. Because of Lionel, most of the neighborhood women had dumped Addy, but not Joan Avery. Joan knew Lionel was a heel, but that made her try all the harder to be Addy's friend. Someone had to come to Addy's rescue, and Joan was not one bit intimidated by Lionel. She found him to be a boorish know-it-all who deliberately bullied timid Addy. God only knows what went on at the Roberge house behind closed doors—Joan's blood boiled to think that some men got away with treating their wives cruelly. Why, there were more laws to protect animals than women and children, as Joan frequently reminded her husband. Frank teasingly called her a "suffragette," but agreed with her wholeheartedly. Frank was a good man and was not all too crazy about Lionel himself. Unlike Joan, however, Frank accepted the simple reality that a person cannot change the world.

Much to Addy's dismay, Lionel never mentioned anything about having plans for Friday night. When Addy asked him if the kids could sleep over at Joan's, he snapped rudely, "No. They have their own beds." So much for a fun night for the kids. What a beast.

Addy cringed as she dialed Joan's number to tell her the kids would not be able to sleep over Friday night. What excuse could she use? Most normal people didn't agonize over such trivial matters, but Addy was not normal. Finally, she gathered her courage, picked up the phone, and slowly dialed Joan's number. Addy stammered as she gave Joan some lame excuse, and, of course, Joan understood.

"What if I pick up your kids before Lionel and you leave so they can spend the day at our house? That way you won't have to rush home after the funeral. You know they always have a luncheon afterwards; AND I can get my housework done."

Addy breathed a sigh of relief. Joan was truly an angel. She always knew just how to let Addy off the hook without shaming her.

Early Saturday morning, Addy dressed carefully in her high-neck pale yellow wool dress and jacket. It was the only outfit she could think of that would conceal the bruises on her neck and arms. Lionel, dressed to the nines, seemed excited rather than somber about attending the funeral—sick bastard, thought Addy with revulsion.

As Addy walked through the doors of Blanchard's Funeral Home, she almost fainted from the sweet, heavy scent of perfume hanging in the air. She loved flowers, but the smell of so many funeral bouquets clustered tightly in a small place was overwhelming. Addy had never seen such gigantic, elaborate funeral arrangements. Mr. Blanchard's eyes must have popped out of his head as the flowers arrived. Some came from Hartford, New York and even Florida. The names scrawled on the cards were familiar to anyone who read the *New York Times* or *Wall Street Journal*. This was definitely big doings for the Blanchard family business.

The rumor mill in Chester was working overtime, and the funeral home bulged with nosey townsfolk wanting to catch a glimpse of their new local celebrity, Helena Smithfield. Addy looked around in disgust. She knew most of these people did not know Mary Kurowski but came simply to gawk.

Lionel pushed his way through the swarm of people,

dragging the dutiful Addy behind him. As they reached the front of the line at last, Lionel mouthed words of sympathy while Helena looked at him blandly. Like so many others in the throng of "mourners," Lionel was just one more face in the crowd. Helena had no clue who he was but disliked him right away.

Immediately, Lionel launched into the "old school friends" and pushed Addy forward. Before Addy even opened her mouth to speak, Helena's steely blue eyes brightened as she instantly recognized her childhood friend. Neither woman spoke, but Helena's mind flooded with memories of two lovely schoolgirls sharing secrets, giggles, and dreams, while enduring the rigors of education at St. Mary's Catholic School For Girls—two outcasts, victims of circumstances beyond their control—Addy by the death of her parents; Helena by her mother's divorce. They were truly sisters of the heart, and the circumstances in which they found themselves made the bond between them even stronger than if they were biological sisters.

The intensity of Helena's gaze, the elegance of Helena's persona, the sudden, overpowering flashback of Addy's love and admiration for her loyal friend Helena; the sight of the body of beloved Mary now lying white and cold in a casket—all this emotion was too much for Addy to contain, and she suddenly burst into tears. Giving her a sharp look, Lionel guided her quickly to one of the last few chairs.

Monsignor Jean-Paul Roberge then led the prayer service, gushing on about Mary's devotion to the Catholic Church and blah, blah, blah. Lionel had probably given him the heads up about making a good impression on Helena. After all, the Kurowski farm was now in Helena's hands. Helena, of course, was unmoved. Why was it that even as her mom toiled as a nurse so that Helena could get a Catholic education, Mary and Helena never fit in? Now that she had attained wealth, all the townsfolk were there to brown nose, but Helena was too shrewd and sophisticated to put up with their nonsense.

The obligatory luncheon took place at a high-priced 1800s inn on the river. The building was once a gristmill operative for nearly 100 years converted to a lovely award-winning restaurant. Unfortunately, the weather was unusually warm on this Indian-summer day, and all the body heat in the old inn created a stifling atmosphere. Helena could not wait for the vultures to eat and get the hell out of the place.

Lionel worked the room with his brother the monsignor in tow, while Addy sat stiffly, planted where Lionel had left her. Although she was sweating profusely in her hot, itchy, wool ensemble, Addy could not remove her jacket. Her upper arms and neck were ringed with faded blackish-purple-blue and sickly yellow-green handprints that remained from Lionel's last beating. The bruises no longer hurt, but Addy was conscious of their presence.

From across the room, Helena studied Addy intently, and suddenly **SHE KNEW**. Rage consumed Helena as the long-buried memory of her first husband, Edward, puking out the window, raced across her mind. It was at that moment Helena decided there was some business that needed attending before she left town, and she would change her plans to stay in Chester indefinitely.

All the way home from the funeral luncheon, Lionel talked at a frenzied pace about the events of the day, while Addy sat in a stupor, not allowing herself to think about anything. She knew how upset Lionel got when she floated away, and she was not in the mood to endure his haranguing.

Lionel soon pulled up in front of Frank and Joan Avery's house, and Addy went to the door to pick up the kids. As always, Joan greeted Addy cheerfully and called for the children. Flushed with excitement and joy, Pete, Jimmy, and Mary ran to the door, but as soon as they got into the car with Lionel, they knew to keep quiet. Lionel announced they would be having sandwiches for dinner because Addy and he had eaten a big lunch. As always, Lionel determined what Addy was supposed to cook for supper. The kids were tired and went to bed early.

Lionel was preoccupied all that evening, and Addy was glad.

"Lionel, do you mind if I go to bed early too? Funerals exhaust me."

"What else is new?" he grumbled. "Go to bed. I have some paperwork to do."

Addy kept the shower running a long time so she could hide from Lionel in the streaming water and cry as much as she wanted. She just couldn't believe she had seen Helena once again. Accomplished, beautiful, sophisticated Helena had the world at her feet. What must she had thought of her mousy friend, Addy?

When Addy awakened Sunday morning, she was relieved to find a note from Lionel saying that he had left early to attend a charity golf outing and would not be home until evening. The kids would be happy to sleep late and not go to Mass. Addy and the children enjoyed a long, peaceful Sunday without Lionel.

On Monday after breakfast when the kids had gone to school, Lionel once again lingered over his coffee. The specter of gray dread consumed Addy. Why was he sticking around again? What was his evil little mind plotting this time?

"My brother and I have been talking about asking Helena Kurowski if she would like to see her mother's farm go to the church. Maybe St. Michael's could build a retreat house or retirement home for priests—what a dream that would be, "The Roberge Rest Home for Retired Priests" or "The Retreat House of Monsignor Jean-Paul Roberge."

Lionel stopped for a moment, and then continued, "I'll bet Helena would even DONATE the farm to the church. After all, she's loaded, and she probably still has a Catholic conscience about her sinful life. Once a Catholic, always a Catholic, I say. She could absolve herself by giving the land to the church," Lionel chuckled.

Flames of anger, stronger than her fear of Lionel, shot through Addy's heart. The rage she never dared speak aloud flew out of her mouth, ravens of hatred. "HOW DARE YOU JUDGE HELENA, YOU BASTARD. WHAT DO YOU KNOW ABOUT HER SINS?"

Surprised for an instant by the mouse wife's first-ever attempt to talk back to him, Lionel lunged for Addy, knocking over the kitchen chair. Addy ran toward the hallway telephone table, hoping she would get there in time to call the police. She just did not care anymore. Let the world know the truth about Lionel.

As she reached for the receiver, Lionel grabbed her wrist, twisting her arm behind her back. He threw her to the floor, and she landed on her back. Before she could roll over, Lionel kicked madly at her breasts, stomach, groin, and head. Addy screamed in agony, but no one heard. A dying insect, fighting for that last moment of life, Addy tried to roll over to protect her front side. In excruciating pain, Addy managed to make it to her side but lost all her strength. Lionel kept kicking—her back, her thighs. Addy, a bag of trash; Addy, a football; Addy beyond pain. Lionel pulled the lifeless ragdoll to her feet, punching her in the face. Blood spurted from Addy's nose, but Lionel was careful to avoid knocking out any of her teeth. Missing teeth could raise suspicions of a beating, but nosebleeds and bruises could result from a fall. Besides, knocking the little lady around wasn't really a crime. A lot of men did it when their wives got too big for their britches. Kevin Murphy, the Chief of Police in Chester, had been Lionel's buddy since grade school and attended Mass regularly at St. Michael's. In fact, both Kevin and Lionel were pillars of the church and community. Chief Murphy would never believe Addy's word over Lionel's. If Addy decided to run away, she would have no money for a place to live, and Lionel always threatened he would find her no matter where she went. Besides, she would never leave the kids.

Addy did not move. She could not move. Her body throbbed with pain she had never before experienced, not even in childbirth. This was the most brutal of all the beatings that had come before. The blood rapidly streaming from Addy's nose formed a large black pool on the ugly green carpet. Lionel went into the kitchen to get the morning newspaper and then calmly spread all the pages over the bloody mess. Addy closed her eyes, praying this was the end; surely the next strike would be the deathblow.

The newspaper pages were quickly soaked through with blood. Ignoring the pathetic figure of his suffering wife, Lionel went down into the basement to find the ragbag. There were still some old timers around who bought rags; Lionel had Addy save threadbare linen and the children's outgrown clothing to sell. As he dragged the ragbag up the cellar stairs, Lionel's mind raced. He had to clean up this mess before the kids came home, but luckily, it was still early.

He took all the rags out of the bag, picked up the bloody newspaper, and placed it in the now empty sack. Then he piled several layers of rags over the stain, pleased that the cloth soaked up the blood like a sponge. Shooting a glance over at Addy, he saw her nose still bleeding. He placed a rag loosely over her mouth and nose. Addy did not stir. She seemed to have lost consciousness, but Lionel saw that she was still breathing. Look at her, he thought with disgust. A whimpering little fool. Oh how Lionel wished he could get rid of her for good so that he could be with the woman he worshipped, a goddess whose boots he was not worthy to lick. Yes, she was his mistress, but she was also his "Mistress."

Wouldn't Addy be shocked if she knew that Lionel himself endured beatings at the hands of Mistress Irena? Lionel puffed up with pride the first time Mistress Irena commented upon his high tolerance for pain. She had assured Lionel that their next session would push him beyond the limits of unimaginable suffering. Lionel passionately anticipated his next meeting with Irena. In Lionel's mind, the whippings were saintly, secret "Mortification," a part of Catholic history the church no longer liked to discuss. In bygone times, some monks, ascetics, and nuns would inflict painful suffering upon their bodies as atonement for their sins. These saints would also endure flagellation by their superiors in mutual effort to ascend that much closer to Heaven. After all, Lionel rationalized, only Christ was sinless, yet he died for our sins. How fitting it is for a Catholic to suffer as Jesus had done.

As Lionel watched Addy's blood soaking into the rags, he slowly became aroused. Picturing himself lying on his stomach naked with wrists and ankles tightly bound to the bedposts, Lionel could almost feel the sharp blows of Mistress Irena's whip across his ass. Later she would grind the heels of her stiletto boots into Lionel's back. Irena lashed relentlessly at his tender, fleshy bottom while Lionel whispered under his breath, "Lord, I humbly offer my wounds to thee for the forgiveness of my sins." The more welts and bruises Lionel had, the holier he felt.

By now, his penis was getting hard. He looked over at the half-dead Addy and commanded, "GET UP," but Addy just moaned. "GET UP, I SAID."

Addy did not stir. Lionel glanced over at the rags to be sure they were still doing their job of absorbing the blood. Then he kneeled behind Addy's head, grabbed her under the arms, and began dragging her upstairs. Addy was too sick to think. Her head was spinning, and nausea rose in her throat as her body bumped over each stair. Suddenly, vomit spewed from her mouth, with some pieces hitting Lionel.

"Damned you," Lionel shouted. He dragged her into the upstairs bathroom, leaving her lying on the cold pink and black tiled floor. Lionel quickly removed his blood-and-vomit-stained clothes, and then jumped into the shower.

This just had to be a bad dream. Lionel couldn't be whistling "Unchained Melody" in the shower while Addy lay dying on the bathroom floor. Addy blanked out once again. Sharp pains awakened her as she realized someone was rolling her on to her side. Opening her eyes, Addy didn't see Lionel. Perhaps it was over, but how would she get up? Then she felt her bra being unfastened, her panties pulled down over her throbbing thighs. Lionel was stripping her.

He rolled her on to her back, grabbed her under the arms, and then dragged her into the bathtub. Would he be cruel enough to shower her off like a dog? What did it even matter? Addy was no better than a whimpering stray.

Lionel left her lying there in the icy tub for a moment while he went into the hallway to get a washcloth from the linen closet. Shivering with cold and fear, Addy screamed angrily at God in her mind. Why don't you just let me die now? What have I done to deserve this?

Startled by a spray of warm water, Addy looked up to see

Lionel standing over her, legs spread, and erect penis dangling over her head…a flashback of an image that haunted Addy since studying art history, the panel depicting hell in Hieronymus Bosch's nightmarish, "The Gardens of Delight." If Lionel placed her head under the shower, Addy would drown.

No, Lionel was too sneaky for that. If he drowns her, he would be unable to explain away all the bruises. He squatted down, his fat penis thumping her face as he moved. Overwhelmed with nausea, Addy fought the urge to vomit. If she puked on his penis, Lionel would resume his rage.

He seemed to be in a trance as he softly sponged Addy all over. "You were a very bad girl today. You shouted and swore at Daddy. You should know by now I will not accept such behavior from you. Now tell Daddy you are sorry."

Addy clamped her mouth shut tightly.

"I TOLD YOU TO APOLOGIZE!"

Addy still refused to speak. Lionel once again squatted over her face, took his penis in his hand, and tried to force it into her mouth. Addy was so weak, but she managed to keep her lips clenched tightly.

Surprisingly, Lionel stopped. He pulled Addy to her feet, grabbed the large, faded green bath towel, and wrapped it around her. He was eerily calm as he guided Addy into their bedroom.

Lionel gently helped Addy lower herself into the easy chair while he turned back the bedclothes. He rummaged through the neatly folded lingerie in Addy's bureau, pulling out a blue flowered flannel granny gown. As Lionel helped Addy to her feet, the towel that had been covering her ugly bruises fell to the floor. Lionel caught a glimpse of the swelling and welts. He left her standing there, helplessly naked, then remarked in a patronizing tone, "I hope you have learned your lesson and will never talk back to me again."

Addy began to sway, as if she was going to pass out, so Lionel quickly lowered the nightgown over her head. He put his arm around her back, leading her to their bed.

"You have had quite a day," Lionel said nonchalantly, as if

she had just returned from a shopping trip to New York City. "You had better get some rest."

Addy slowly lowered her head onto the pillow, and Lionel tucked the covers around her neck. Every inch of Addy ached. Her eyelids drooped as she drifted into the darkness of unconsciousness.

Like a dutiful nursemaid, Lionel whispered, "I'll get you some aspirin. That should make you feel better."

He went quietly into the bathroom, opened the medicine cabinet, removed two small containers, and then filled a glass with water. Lionel shook two aspirin from the bottle, lifted Addy's head from the pillow, and placed the pills in her mouth. He continued holding her head up as she slowly sipped the water. As Lionel lowered her head to the pillow, Addy dimly noticed the other medicine container on the nightstand. It appeared to be a bottle of petroleum jelly. What was he planning to do ... dress her wounds like Florence Nightingale?

Addy closed her eyes to rest. As she was lying there quietly, she felt a chill as Lionel pulled back the covers and then climbed into bed next to her. He whispered sultrily, "Turn over on your side, baby."

"I can't. I hurt too much to move," Addy rasped in a tiny voice.

Lionel ignored her and pushed her so that she was lying painfully on her right side. What could be happening? Was the torture continuing? What was he going to do?

"You know I like to take you in the rear end. Usually, I just go for it, but you have learned a good lesson today so I am going to give you a treat. Daddy is greasing up your asshole so his dick can slide in easier. It won't hurt as much."

The serpent no sooner finished hissing when Addy felt the full measure of Lionel's penis in her rectum. She cried out in pain, elevating Lionel's excitement even higher. Thrusting faster and faster, harder and harder, Lionel's whole, heavy, body slapped ruthlessly against Addy's back.

"Now, tell Daddy you are sorry."

"I'm sorry," Addy screamed in agony. "Please stop, Lionel,

please."

By this time, Lionel spiraled out of control, lost in the bliss of inflicting pain.

A loud groaning signaled his climax, and rivers of sperm spilled from Addy's bottom. Lionel lay still, breathing heavily. Addy was beyond numb: First the beating, now this humiliation. If she had the strength, she would run down to the kitchen, grab a carving knife, and slit the dirty bastard to pieces. Lionel could outrun her so such thoughts were fruitless. There was no way to escape from the beast.

Lionel jumped out of bed, sprinting to the bathroom to wash himself up. He brought another damp washcloth to sponge off the sperm dripping from Addy's behind.

"Wow," he laughed. "I sure had a great climax this time. Now that's the way a wife is supposed to satisfy her husband."

Addy had rolled over onto her back and shut her eyes. Lionel dressed hurriedly and then went downstairs to check on the carpet. The rags had done a great job of soaking up the blood. Although a dark spot remained, Lionel knew he could clean it up with pine soap. He gathered up the rags and shoved them in the same bag with the bloodstained newspaper. He would have to think about where to dispose of this mess permanently, but for now, he would put it in the old coal bin. The kids were afraid to go in there because they thought it was full of spiders.

He would tell the kids Addy had a terrible dizzy spell, fell and had a serious nosebleed. The doctor had ordered complete bed rest for a few days. In fact, Lionel would forbid the children to disturb Addy, even though he knew they would want to see her. He would emphasize how important it was for Addy's recovery that she stay in bed until the doctor said she could get up.

Lionel remembered that Addy's blood-and-vomit-stained clothes were still on the bathroom floor. He got the wet mop out of the broom closet, and then ran upstairs. After wadding up Addy's clothes into a ball, Lionel proceeded to mop the bathroom floor with bleach. Holding Addy's stinky garments at arm's length, he carried them down to the cellar and tossed them into the ragbag so cunningly hidden in the dark coal bin.

Clever Lionel even thought to pour liquid pine soap all over the newspaper, rags, and clothes to mask the repulsive odor rising from the coal bin.

By the time school was dismissed, Lionel had cleaned the house and started dinner. Mary was the first to arrive. Surprised to see her father home so early, she asked instinctively, "Where's Mom?"

In an uncharacteristic act of concern, Lionel kneeled down so that he was eye-level with Mary. "Daddy stayed home from work today because Mommy is sick."

Mary's little heart beat rapidly; her breathing shallowed.

"Is she in the hospital?"

"No. She's upstairs in bed sleeping. The doctor said no one is to bother her until she is stronger."

Mary began to cry, but Lionel barked impatiently, "There's no need to cry. Mommy's fine."

He lowered his voice, "How about if you help Daddy fix supper? We can start right now before the boys get home."

This was so foreign to Mary. Her father was never there when she got home from school. Mommy was always waiting for her at the front door. Then mother and daughter usually went into the kitchen to eat cookies and drink milk while Mary told Addy every detail of the school day. In addition, her father never cooked. "That's woman's work," he always said.

"What will we make?" Mary inquired innocently.

Lionel laughed, "Don't you think Daddy can cook? I learned to do lots of things in the Army. Let's make macaroni and cheese."

Mary's spirits lifted. She loved macaroni and cheese and had even learned to make it herself. Lionel insisted the family eat fish every Friday, but Mary just could not stomach fish. Since she didn't like fish, Lionel told her she would have to go to bed without supper. He eventually conceded to Mary's fixing macaroni and cheese for herself.

As Lionel and Mary walked to the kitchen, they heard the boys come tumbling through the front door. "MOM," they shouted through peals of laughter.

"MOM," Jimmy screeched, "PETE PEED HIS PANTS."

"I did not," Peter said with annoyance. "We had art class last period, and I spilled water on myself when we were cleaning up."

The boys ran to the kitchen and stopped cold at the sight of Lionel and Mary. Pete and Jimmy were speechless.

Lionel glared at them and murmured, "You two better shut your big mouths. Your mother is upstairs sleeping."

Old enough to realize that Lionel did not give a damn about Addy's welfare, the boys immediately grew suspicious.

"What's wrong with her?" Pete asked, no longer as afraid of Lionel as he had once been.

"She took a nasty fall," Lionel lied. "The doctor says she has to stay in bed for a few days, and you guys are not to bother her under any circumstances. Now get upstairs and change your pants, Pete, and don't either of you dare open your mother's door."

Pete did as Lionel said, but as he climbed the stairs, he noticed a large stain on the living room carpet. A feeling of nausea swept over him. What had really happened to his mom?

Why was there such a big spot on the rug? The furniture in there was pretty soft. Maybe it was the end table. Maybe the spot was so large because his fanatically clean father had scrubbed the carpet.

Pete had to stop thinking about this. He knew his father would never answer questions about the situation. He also knew his mom could never divorce the creep, but Pete wished his father would die. Pete had once said that aloud to his mom, and she was horrified.

"Pete, we can't wish for people to die. That is a terrible sin you must confess."

Pete knew his mother didn't really mean that. She said it because she hoped the kids still swallowed that Catholic garbage. His heartless father was an esteemed member of the church, yet he treated Addy so cruelly. How could that be good Catholicism?

Mary and Lionel made baked macaroni, steamed carrots,

salad, and crescent rolls. There was still some gelatin fruit salad and cookies left over from the previous night. While Lionel bowed his head to say grace, the children shot glances at one another. Each of them sensed that something was terribly wrong. They ate dinner in silence, then Pete, Jimmy, and Mary cleared the table and did the dishes.

After the dishes were dried and put away, Lionel went into the kitchen to inspect their work. Nodding with approval, he whispered, "When you go upstairs to wash up and do your homework don't disturb your mother." The kids did as they were told, each walking somberly to their rooms, like cloistered monks to their cells.

Lionel stayed home from work for several days, and during that time, the children never saw their mother. Meanwhile, Addy was healing nicely, as she had always done, and grew stronger each day. She was pale and drawn, but her face showed no marks of abuse. Her clothing could hide the parts of her body that were still swollen and bruised. She was eager to see the children because she imagined how worried they must be.

After the children left for school, Lionel brought breakfast up to Addy. He pulled the hassock up next to their bed and watched Addy hurriedly shoveling down her food. Lionel grew more impatient each day that Addy was incapacitated.

"How does it feel to get the royal treatment?" Lionel asked, ironically.

Addy thought, you bastard. If it weren't for you, I wouldn't have ended up like this.

Lionel repeated louder, "I SAID, how does it feel to get the royal treatment?"

"Great," Addy responded flatly.

"Now, if you had just heard me out that day, none of this would have happened. I was trying to tell you that I think you should start up your friendship with Helena Kurowski again. Maybe you can convince her to let the church have her mother's farm."

Addy knew enough now not to object to Lionel's suggestion. It was a command she must follow or risk having the stuffing knocked out of her again.

She thought for a moment then said carefully, "Do you think she will talk to me after all these years?"

"Of course she will," Lionel answered. "She doesn't have any other friends in this town, and she must be sad after losing her mother. Why don't you call her today and make plans to go out and see her at the farm? I'll drive you there."

Lionel got the telephone book, looked up Mary Kurowski's number, dialed, and then shoved the receiver at Addy. He was no fool. If left to her own devices, Addy might lie and say she had called Helena and got no answer.

Addy's heart was beating so fast. She hated to speak on the telephone to strangers and prayed Helena would not pick up.

"Yes?" a groggy Helena answered sharply.

Addy froze. Had she awakened Helena? How she hated to disturb people.

"YES?" Helena said a second time impatiently.

"Oh, hello Helena, this is Addison Roberge—I mean Addison Blake. I hope I didn't wake you up. Do you remember me?"

Helena recognized Addy's timid voice immediately. "ADDY," she said with a smile. "Of course I remember you. How ARE you?"

Addy forgot that Lionel was sitting right there listening to her every word.

"Oh, Helena, I am so sorry about your mom's passing. I didn't get a chance to talk to you at the funeral."

"Thanks, Addy. She was a great lady, wasn't she?"

Tears welled in Addy's eyes. "Yes, she was ... more than great."

Lionel glared at Addy. She knew what she had to say next. "Helena, could I come by and see you before you leave?"

Helena immediately recalled Addy's pale yellow ensemble, the same sickly shade of bruises in the last stage of healing. She was determined to not only see Addy, but to uncover Addy's secret.

"I'd love to see you, Addy, any time. What day would be good for you?"

Addy had to think quickly. She was not quite strong enough to visit Helena too soon.

"Will you still be here next week? I'm not feeling very well right now."

Lionel gave her a stern look. Thank God Helena responded immediately, "I've extended my stay here indefinitely so you just name the day."

"How about next Wednesday? Will that be OK for you?"

"Sure. Come for coffee around ten thirty."

Addy forgot her pain and glowed with anticipation. Helena had not made her feel uncomfortable. In fact, it seemed as if she really WANTED to see Addy.

"Great, I'll bring my famous sour cream coffee cake."

Helena laughed, "Thanks. You know what a lousy cook I am."

"You made good 'S'Mores' when we were Girl Scouts. It will be so nice to see you again, Helena."

Lionel smiled with smug self-satisfaction. After that bothersome setback of Addy's incapacitation, his plan to convince Helena to give the farm to the church was finally set in motion.

Lionel was too thick to understand just what a formidable force he was facing. The extremely intelligent and strong Helena had long ago thrown off the shackles of her Catholic upbringing. She viewed Lionel with utter disdain, and he was a silly fool if he thought he could wrangle with the likes of her. Still, for the sole purpose of somehow helping Addy, she would play along with whatever nonsense lie ahead. The news of seeing Helena again made Addy heal that much faster. Lionel continually blabbed about what she should say and do when she met with Helena.

On the Tuesday night before the day of her visit, Addy took down her recipe box and looked under "S" for the sour cream coffee cake. The ritual of baking was the only thing that made Addy feel competent. Most of the recipes in her treasured blue and white metal Dutch print file box had been tweaked to perfection. Addy always cut down on the salt and sometimes the sugar. When she made her unforgettable chocolate chip cookies, she substituted shortening for half the butter so the cookies would remain plump instead of spreading all over the cookie sheet.

Confidently, Addy gathered the ingredients. This was one cake Addy knew how to bake by heart. Since this was for such a special occasion, however, she read the stained recipe card carefully. Rarely was the house this quiet. The kids were in bed, and Lionel was out at an office party. For the first time since their vacation in Maine, Addy felt a warm sense of peace and safety. Synonymous with this emotion was the sweet memory of Greg.

Addy tried not to think about him very often. Although Lionel had no way of knowing what had gone on in Maine, Addy was always paranoid that Lionel could read her thoughts. As the aroma of cinnamon, brown sugar, and walnuts engulfed her, Addy drifted into a fantasy of Greg sitting right next to her at the kitchen table, drinking a cup of coffee. She saw him getting up, gently lifting her hair, and kissing her on the back of the neck.

"Mmm—you smell as good as that cake. You bake so well and make love even better," he'd whisper. "How I adore you, my sweet, darling, delicious Addy."

Addy would then become aroused and laugh. "Don't get me excited now. The cake will burn."

Greg would jokingly respond, "I'll wait, but you can expect to be on fire upstairs once you take the cake out of the oven."

"Don't you want to wait until it cools so you can have some?" Addy would answer coyly.

"I can wait till morning for that cake. I want to eat YOU now." Addy giggled at the double entendre and blushed. Feeling aroused, Addy blushed simultaneously in real life, too.

At that moment, Lionel burst through the unlocked kitchen door, shattering her fantasies. Lionel, plastered once again, slobbered, "What's wrong with you? You look like the cat that ate the canary."

"Nothing's wrong. I'm just waiting for my cake to bake. Remember I'm supposed to go and see Helena tomorrow morning?"

Lionel grinned, "Right. I will drive you. I'm going up to bed."

As he staggered toward the hallway, Addy wished he would fall down the stairs and die or at least be asleep when she went up. Usually when he was drunk, he didn't pinch her bottom to signal his demand for sex.

"Ding," the timer sounded. As Addy removed the cake from the oven, she was overjoyed to see how high her masterpiece had risen. She turned the tube pan upside down on a baking rack so the coffee cake would easily slide out of the pan in the morning.

With Lionel snoring beside her, Addy left her body and resumed the dream world of Greg. In her fantasy, Greg barely waited for Addy to remove the cake from the oven, and then took her hand, leading her upstairs to their bedroom. Her passion soared as he undressed her slowly. Leaving her standing there naked for a moment, he said, "God, I love you, my beautiful wife." Then he undressed himself. His penis was already erect, but he rarely thought about his pleasure before hers. Instead, he kneeled down and began to lick her vaginal lips tenderly. Addy closed her eyes, trembling with ecstasy.

Greg gently pushed her down on the bed and spread her legs wide apart so that her vagina was fully open. Addy felt no embarrassment as Greg gazed at the parts of her body that even in her wildest dreams, she never imagined showing a man. Greg was her husband in the most sacred sense of the word. She trusted him implicitly, and they shared nothing shameful. Addy never doubted for an instant that Greg was completely devoted to her. Lost in the taste of the woman he loved, Greg used his tongue to make rapid circular motions on Addy's clitoris. Because of Greg, Addy had discovered how sublime oral sex could be. She burned with pleasure, and then closed her eyes, smiling with gratitude for the gift of her beloved Greg.

As Lionel rolled over suddenly, he bumped Addy out of her illusion. Greg vaporized, and Addy remember where she was in reality.

The next morning, Addy got up extra early to remove her

coffee cake from the tube pan. She cut lightly around the edge of the cake with a butter knife, careful not to dig too deeply. To her relief, none of the cake had stuck to the sides of the pan. Next she cut gently along the bottom of the cake where it was attached to the tube part of the pan. Voila! Perfection.

Addy transferred the cake to the paper-doily covered crystal cake dish she had prepared earlier. Covering the beautiful coffee cake with tin foil, Addy placed her scrumptious-looking indulgence into her cake carrier.

Once the kids were off to school, Addy went upstairs to get ready to meet Helena. How she wished she were not so frumpy. Nothing in her closet cried, "Sophisticated, Elegant, Self-Assured." Addy finally decided on a long-sleeved white blouse with a stand-up collar, and a navy-plaid skirt. She had lost a couple of pounds while confined to bed but was still too fat to tuck in her blouse. She found a girdle in her lingerie drawer, wiggled her way into it, and struggled to push the tails of her blouse into the skirt. Barely able to breathe, Addy found a navy blue cardigan to cover the lump of fat hanging over the waistband.

Lionel, already in the car, tooted the horn impatiently. He was just so crude. Her aunts always told her how low class it was to beep a car horn while waiting for someone to come out of the house. Why were the aunts so eager for her to marry Lionel in the first place?

Addy did not rush. Lionel surely would not smack her before she went to Helena's. She walked slowly to the kitchen and carefully retrieved her cake carrier.

"Took you long enough," Lionel grumbled impatiently when she got into the car, but Addy just ignored him.

When they drove up to the farmhouse, Woodrow, barking loudly, and wagging his tail excitedly, ran to meet them. Addy opened the car door immediately, hoping Lionel would not try to walk up to the house with her.

"Call me at the office when you want me to pick you up." His last words to Addy were, "Now don't screw this up."

Chapter XI

The Farm

Balancing her cake carrier, Addy slammed the car door shut. Free at last, she walked up the creaky wooden front porch steps. Although Addy had been to Helena's house that one time when the Girl Scouts camped indoors there, she had forgotten just how lovely the farmhouse was. There were double front doors with glass windows and an ornately carved mechanical twist brass doorbell. Helena once told Addy the reason old Victorian houses had wide front doors was so the caskets of dead family members could be carried out. The front parlor had sliding wood pocket doors for the same reason. Before there were funeral homes, people used to hold wakes for the deceased right there in the formal front parlor.

While Addy was admiring the beautiful porch swing and swirled patterns etched into the frosted glass of the front door windows, Helena opened the door. She wore a long aquamarine silk dressing gown. Addy didn't have a moment to beat herself up for being so dowdy compared to her friend because Helena immediately hugged her warmly, saying, "Addy, I am so happy to see you. Sorry I'm still in my robe. Come in, come in."

Woodrow followed Addy inside, and then went straight to the kitchen and lay down next to the stove. His duty of greeting guests was complete for the day.

Addy set the cake carrier down on the kitchen table. Helena stood back, and said, "Addy, you look wonderful."

Addy hung her head in shame, but Helena, refusing to acknowledge Addy's inferiority complex, continued sincerely, "You haven't changed a bit!"

Relaxing a bit, Addy replied quickly, "... and you look so BEAUTIFUL."

Helena laughed, "That's what facelifts are for. Sit down, make yourself at home. I'll put the coffee on. That's the only domestic activity at which I am skilled," she joked, trying to sound like a stuffy English butler.

Helena took out Mary's old coffee percolator, the kind used on top of the stove. She had always wanted to buy her mom an electric percolator, but Mary would not hear of it. She insisted the stovetop percolator made much better coffee. "Just because they make things easier doesn't necessarily mean they make things better," Mary would quip. Helena had to agree with her on that one. At the farm, it always seemed time stood still; it was a good, secure, innocent feeling.

Addy sat quietly, looking around at the tidy, old-fashioned kitchen, with its converted coal stove, iron sink, and large pantry. Helena, so out of place in this bucolic setting, resembled an expensive, fragile porcelain figurine a farmer might have purchased for his wife's birthday.

As the coffee perked merrily, Helena lowered the flame, and then went to the china cupboard to get the cups and plates to set the table. Addy removed the coffee cake from its carrier.

"Wow!" Helena exclaimed. "I haven't had home-baked cake in ages. I plan to eat it all; with the exception of the one or two pieces I let you have."

"How do you stay so thin, Helena?" Addy inquired.

"It's called cigarettes, booze, and no food," Helena laughed. "Do you smoke, Addy?"

Looking down, Addy answered, "No."

"How about drink?"

Addy remained with her head down, and then responded, "Sometimes."

"No wonder you look so young. I'm trying to quit smoking, but I will never quit drinking—it's the only thing that keeps me sane in New York."

Not wanting Helena to think she was judging her, Addy quickly remarked, "New York is such a crazy place. I did try smoking once, but it just made me feel sick. I do have wine now and again."

By this time, the coffee was ready, and Helena carved out two huge hunks of coffee cake. Addy found it surprisingly easy to be around Helena, and she knew Helena was not judging her in any way.

The two friends dove into their slices of cake like two skinny schoolgirls who had not a care in the world. "This is to DIE for," Helena exclaimed. "Why haven't you opened up that bakery you used to talk about?"

Addy once again looked down. By now, Helena could feel Addy's insecurity and did not want to do anything to make it worse. Helena said quickly, "How inconsiderate of me for saying that. I don't have kids or a home to look after, and I obviously do not cook. I don't know how you do it all. I'm sorry."

"Some women are able to handle a family and a job, but I'm not one of those women."

"Don't be silly, Addy. You're so smart and competent. You could do anything you set your mind to do."

"... if my husband would let me ..." blurted Addy suddenly.

Helena knew she had struck a nerve. She wanted to hear about Addy's husband but did not want to pressure this poor soul. Her life was probably already a living hell.

Trying to divert Addy's attention to another subject, Helena said cheerfully, "Tell me about your children, Addy. You are so lucky to have kids. I wish I had some of my own."

Now Addy worried. If she talked about her children, would she make Helena feel sad? Addy would not talk about the kids. She would continue on the subject of Lionel.

"Helena, I've never told anyone before, but my husband beats me." The words tumbled effortlessly from Addy's mouth, but she instantly regretted what she said. Why had she revealed this to a person she had not seen in years? She was a stupid little fool, just as Lionel said.

Helena put her coffee cup down. Wanting to choose her words carefully, she sat there thinking for a long while. Addy looked away.

"Addy, I understand. I really do." Helena continued, "My

first husband beat me."

Addy's eyes widened in shock. Slowly placing her cup down, Addy said, "What did you do? What happened to him?"

"He's dead now, thank God. Men like him deserve to be six feet under."

The way Helena made these pronouncements had always been highly amusing to Addy. When Helena spoke, the kingdom obeyed.

This struck Addy so funny she began laughing aloud. At first, Helena was slightly taken aback, but she soon began laughing, too. The women laughed so hard, tears streamed down their cheeks.

"Don't, Helena," Addy protested, "please don't. I'm going to pee my pants. Where's the bathroom?"

Bent over with laughter, Helena pointed to a door off the hallway. Addy raced toward the bathroom while attempting to pull down her girdle on the way. As soon as her bottom hit the toilet, the pee gushed out all over. While Addy quickly cleaned off the seat with soap, water, and toilet tissue, Helena continued laughing loudly in the kitchen. Addy chuckled as she washed her hands. Catching a glimpse of herself in the bathroom mirror, Addy was almost certain she saw the pretty, pre-Lionel Addison Blake, Girl Scout par excellence.

When Addy returned to the kitchen, Helena was sitting at the kitchen table with her hands covering her face. Her body heaved with sobs. Was she laughing or crying? Addy worried.

Helena uncovered her face, and to Addy's relief, she could see Helena had been laughing. "Now, why was that so funny?" Helena asked breathlessly.

Addy began laughing again. "It's just the way you say things. You always made me laugh so much. Sometimes you did it on purpose just to get me to pee my pants, remember? It worked again this time after all these years."

Helena suddenly became serious. "Addy, we have to do something about your husband."

"It's not that easy. I know I shouldn't put up with the way he treats me, but I don't have anywhere else to go. I don't have money of my own, and I would never leave my children."

Helena understood. So many women were in the same boat. They may have given up jobs to be full-time homemakers and were completely dependent upon their husbands financially. If the marriage became abusive, what could these women do? Some were probably just too ashamed to tell anyone. Even if they wanted to run away from their husbands, where would they go?

Addy suddenly remembered why she had come to see Helena in the first place. She would not try to convince her long-lost friend to sell or give the farm to the church, not ever. Instead, she would reveal to Helena every detail of Lionel's devious plan.

Helena listened intently as Addy explained the whole story.

"Why that son-of-a-bitch," Helena said, shaking her head.

"He is a son-of-a-bitch, Helena. I hate the sight of him. I've hated him since the night of our honeymoon."

Helena thought for a moment, shook her head, and smiled slyly. "Addy, we are going to beat him at his own game. Don't you see? This is your ticket to freedom. You can just keep coming here, pretending you are slowly trying to get me to agree to give up the farm. If the fiend complains that it is taking you too long to convince me, you can just say that you first have to establish my trust. After all, I am a tough cookie, right?"

"Brilliant!" Addy exclaimed. "Just brilliant. You can't imagine how much it would mean to me if I could come here to see you often. It would make my life bear..." Addy stopped mid-sentence. "Oh, I didn't mean to say that. The kids are what I live for. They make things bearable, but coming here would be wonderful."

"It's settled then. We will plan to get together at least once a week. I would love for you to bring the kids to see the animals some time."

"They would like that so much. They've always wanted pets, but Lionel thinks animals are too dirty to keep inside, and our yard is not fenced in."

Addy looked at the old wooden pendulum clock that sat ticking on the kitchen shelf. It was already one o'clock. Where had the time gone?

"I'll have to call Lionel to pick me up soon," Addy said sadly.

"I can drive you home. That will give us more time together. How about if I take you out for a glass of wine?"

Addy's first instinct was to say "no." What if Lionel smelled wine on her breath?

Then she had the sudden realization that Lionel might approve of anything she did with Helena, so long as he believed Addy was working on breaking Helena's resolve. Why did he believe that Addy was up to the task? It was probably because she was the only person in Chester who had any concrete connection to Helena. It was either Addy or no one.

"Yes. I would love to go for a wine. I just have to be back by three o'clock when the kids get home from school. May I use your phone to call Lionel?"

"I'll run upstairs and change. It'll only be a minute." Helena felt as if she was getting a new lease on life. She loved intrigue and hated violent men. This was exactly what she needed to get her mind off her mother's passing. At least Edward was sweet and loving in the beginning of their marriage, but it appeared that Lionel had never been kind to Addy.

Poor kid. Suffering all these years at the hands of that tyrant. Helena was not ready to tell Addy about how Edward had died or about the baby girl she'd lost. She wondered if she would ever reveal her deepest of secrets to Addy. Time would tell.

Dressed in a stunning tangerine tweed pantsuit, Helena descended the staircase confidently and gracefully. The colors she chose for her wardrobe always complemented her sleek blonde hair. Addy still could not comprehend that this amazing looking, wealthy woman actually wanted to be her friend.

Helena suggested they take a ride to a café in Madison. It was once again a warm, Indian summer day, so they rode in Helena's custom-designed silver Rolls Royce convertible with the top down. With her eyes closed, Addy sat back and relaxed as the wind tussled her hair. Had she ever felt so wild and free?

The café was deserted, and the waiter recognized Helena immediately. "I was sorry to read about your mother," he said sincerely.

"Thanks. Could you bring us the wine list?"

The waiter quickly delivered a long brass-covered menu. "Would you ladies like to order something to eat?"

"We don't have a lot of time, but why don't you bring us shrimp cocktail. Do you like shrimp, Addy?"

"Yes, thanks."

Helena perused the wine list and decided upon a bottle of German Riesling. The waiter brought the shrimp cocktail out shortly, opened the wine, and poured some into a glass for Helena to taste. "That's fine, thanks," she said politely.

Their table was next to the window overlooking a beautiful marina. The deep blue water of early fall sparkled in the late day sun. Addy sipped her wine slowly, and Helena kept refilling both their glasses. Not long ago, Addy was lying in bed recovering from the most severe beating she had ever endured. Today she was sitting in an exclusive café by the ocean with a lovely woman she had thought she would never see again. Although Addy was not used to drinking wine often, she liked the sensation it gave her. She felt warm, alive, and almost hopeful. Maybe she was drunk.

The friends continued to chat and make plans for their next meeting. Fortunately, Helena was keeping track of the time on her stunning diamond and gold watch. About two thirty, she said, "We had better get going."

The place was still empty. Helena looked around for the waiter. He was leaning against the bar looking bored. Helena waved to get his attention, and rushing over to their table he asked, "May I get you ladies anything else?"

"Just the check please."

Addy saw Helena take two $50 bills from her wallet and stared in disbelief. Just wine and shrimp cocktail had cost one hundred dollars, almost a month's worth of groceries.

"Let's go," Helena said.

"I can't let you pay all that," Addy protested.

"That's not so much. If you want good wine, you have to pay for it." Helena laughed.

As they pulled up in front of Addy's house, Mary and her friend were approaching.

"That's my daughter, Mary," Addy said proudly. "Do you know I named her after your mother?"

This gesture touched Helena's heart. "She's beautiful. She looks like you."

"Thank God," Addy joked. "None of my children look like my husband. Imagine if I had to stare at his face times three?"

The two conspirators laughed happily at Addy's comment. Mary saw her mom sitting in front of the house in Helena's beautiful silver Rolls Royce. She ran up to the car and said, "Hi Mommy. What a pretty car."

Addy introduced Mary to Helena, explaining that Helena was a friend of hers from way back when she was a Girl Scout.

"I'm a Girl Scout," Mary said shyly.

"That's wonderful. Good for you," Helena said, suddenly thinking about the little girl she had lost. "I live on a farm and have some animals there. Would you like to come see them with your mom someday?"

"I love animals," Mary replied. "Could I go to her farm, Mommy?"

"Of course, sweetheart," Addy replied. She knew Lionel would now approve of anything related to Helena. Mary excused herself and ran into the house to use the bathroom.

As the boys came rambling home, they spied Addy sitting in the Rolls. Only in magazines and movies had they ever seen such an amazing car. They ran over to Addy in disbelief.

"Hi Mom. What a car!" Peter exclaimed, and Jimmy was equally impressed.

After Addy introduced her sons, Helena said, "Your mom and I were friends when we were in school. I have a farm and animals nearby. Would you like to come visit the animals someday?"

Both boys shook their heads "yes" but were fully engrossed in checking out every detail of the car. Laughing, Helena continued, "When you fellows learn to drive, you can take this buggy out for a spin."

Peter and Jimmy stared at each other in disbelief. Imagine them tooling around town in a Rolls. They'd get tons of girls for sure. Addy broke the trance, saying, "Boys, you should go inside now and start your homework."

Peter and Jimmy reluctantly bid "good-bye" to Helena, and she said, "I hope I'll see you at the farm soon."

After the boys went inside, Addy said, "I had better go now so I can fix dinner. Thank you so much for everything, Helena. I had such a lovely day."

"No, thank YOU for the coffee cake. I know what I'm having for supper tonight. Will I see you next Wednesday, same time, same place? I can come pick you up so you don't have to trouble your dear husband to drive you," Helena said raising her eyebrows.

Addy laughed. "I'll call you Tuesday afternoon to let you know if he insists on driving me, OK? We don't want to upset the apple cart, do we?" Addy smiled.

"Heavens no," Helena said sarcastically. "We will follow 'his majesty's' orders to a T."

As Addy got out of the car, she thanked Helena once again, saying she could not remember when she had laughed so much.

"Me too," Helena agreed. "See you next Wednesday. Bye." As Helena stepped on the gas and flew away, Addy hoped the police did not stop her for speeding. After all, the two women had drunk a whole bottle of wine.

When Lionel came home from work, the first words out of his mouth were, "Well, how did it go today?" Addy was facing the stove with her back to Lionel. She didn't want to get too close to him for fear he might smell the wine on her breath.

"Things went fine," she answered.

"What do you mean? Did you bring up the topic of the farm?"

"Of course," Addy lied. "I planted the seed today, but Helena is a long way off from even considering the option of letting the church have the property. She said she doesn't know what she is going to do with the farm, but she's staying on in Chester indefinitely. I don't think she wants to live in the farmhouse. I suspect she wants to go back to New York. Anyways, she asked me to come over again next Wednesday. I knew you wouldn't mind if I agreed because I'm getting to first base with her."

Lionel seemed pleased with her report. "Whatever it takes."

When the family sat down to supper, the boys were still talking about Helena's car. Lionel asked the boys a lot of details about Helena and her stunning vehicle. Mary piped in, "She wants us to come out to her farm."

Addy's heart sank. She was sure this was not what Lionel wanted to hear. Much to her surprise, Lionel said, "That would be great." Then he turned to Addy and said, "Let her fall in love with the kids." His comment went right over the children's heads, as they excused themselves to go upstairs to do their homework.

Lionel said he had to go back to the office to finish some paperwork. What a relief. Now Addy could take her time reviewing the events of her day without Lionel accusing her of being lost in space.

Lionel left, and Addy once again was alone in the kitchen. She remembered how the silence of the house the night before had inspired her to think about Greg. Tonight, however, she made a conscious effort to put Greg out of her mind. After all, what good did it do to dream about the impossible? As she cleaned up the kitchen, she reflected upon her magical day with Helena. To think she was going to the farm again next Wednesday!

Addy counted the days until Tuesday finally arrived. She had asked Lionel if it would be OK if Helena picked her up and, surprisingly, he agreed. Addy called Helena Tuesday afternoon to tell her Lionel was going to let Helena come get her.

"Great," Helena said. "I'll pick you up around ten o'clock."

Lionel had called in the afternoon to say he would not be home for dinner. Once the kids were in bed, Addy prepared a pumpkin pecan loaf to take to Helena's in the morning. By the time Addy finished baking Lionel was still not home. Addy went upstairs to bathe and get ready for bed. She soon fell into a deep, peaceful sleep, feeling that somehow her life was going to take a turn for the better.

Around ten o'clock the next morning, Helena pulled up in her shiny silver dream car. Addy grabbed her jacket and the pumpkin bread and rushed outside to greet her friend.

"What have you got there, Addy?"

"Pumpkin bread to go with our coffee."

"Fantastic. I can see what I'll be eating for dinner tonight." Addy just could not believe that Helena did not cook at all for herself. Maybe if she didn't have children, she would eat crazy like that, too.

When they arrived at the farm, Woodrow, barking loudly, wagging his tail excitedly, once again raced to meet them. On such a crisp, spotless autumn morning, the farm was like a Grandma Moses painting. Helena made the coffee while Addy went to the cupboard to get the dishes. It was amazing how quickly she had come to feel right at home at Helena's. Never in her life had she gone into someone else's cabinets or refrigerator without permission. The aunts had taught her that such actions were extremely rude.

Addy felt as if she belonged in this kitchen. Although Helena herself was far from a homemaker, her mother Mary's warm, domestic spirit still lingered in the farmhouse. Domesticity does provide a girder of strength and safety to a home.

Long ago, Addy had resigned herself to the fact that she was an unlucky person, so symbols of luck fascinated her. While in college, she had read Charles Dickens' novella, "A Cricket on the Hearth," with its themes of luck, true love, and a happy household. One of Addy's great interests had been to research the meaning of symbols across disciplines and cultures. She imagined that even in prehistoric times, the little cricket might have provided companionship to the wayfarer carefully picking his way through hostile environments. She learnt that the cricket had been a sign of household luck for thousands of years, appearing in English folktales as a symbol of good fortune, love, and a happy home. Some American Indian tribes revered the cricket and believed it was disrespectful to imitate its sound. In Asia, the cricket served as a watchdog of sorts; whenever danger was approaching, the cheerful chirping always stopped.

That is true, Addy thought. She remembered summer evenings in childhood when she would linger in the backyard until moonrise. If she approached the hedges where the crickets were happily chirping, the music would stop abruptly. In addition, Addy once visited the Museum of Fine Arts in Boston, where the collection of ancient jewelry from around the world fascinated her for hours. Early artisans from the Middle East and Europe carved images of the cricket on charms and amulets to ward off the "evil eye."

As hard as Addy tried to make her own house feel comfortable and welcoming, a sense of gloom always hung in the air. Maybe the ugly furniture and dated decor contributed to the sterile atmosphere in the house. On the other hand, perhaps the specter of fear and sadness would remain in Addy's home as long as Lionel resided there.

While Addy was lost in thought, Helena observed her actions. Addy had gone over to the cupboard and removed the plates, cups, and saucers. She then went to the silverware drawer and got out the spoons and forks. Addy's eyes appeared glazed over, her movements methodical and slow, as if she were walking in her sleep.

"A penny for your thoughts," Helena said with a smile.

Addy laughed. She was so used to Lionel flying off the handle when she drifted off into thoughts that she was stunned when Helena actually spoke casually about Addy's habit of daydreaming.

"I'm thinking about crickets." Addy then went on to share her musings about Charles Dickens, crickets, luck, folklore, and ancient jewelry.

Addy's story fascinated Helena. "That is so interesting. I remember how intelligent you always were in school." Addy blushed, and Helena laughed. "Come on, Addy. What do I have to do to convince you just how smart and creative you are?"

The two friends sipped coffee and ate cake while Duke Ellington and his Orchestra played, "I Let a Song Go Out of my Heart," on the big brown radio. They whiled away the afternoon with laughter, coffee, cake, and music. Addy swooned to Mel Torme's "Alone Together," while Helena teased her for being so romantic. When Xavier Cugat's "Cocktails for Two" came on, Helena got up and did the "cha-cha." She danced over to Addy and pulled her out of her chair.

"Please don't, I can't dance, please," Addy protested. Helena said, "Never say the word CAN'T." She grabbed Addy's hips and began shaking them to the beat. "Follow my feet."

Feeling clumsy and awkward, Addy struggled to keep time. One-two-cha-cha-cha, she counted in her head.

Helena threw her head back, laughing, "I thought you said you couldn't dance."

Addy began laughing too, put her hands on Helena's hips, and followed her steps from behind. By the time the recording was ending, they were both laughing so hard, Addy had to race to the bathroom.

When she got back to the kitchen, Helena joked, "Did you make it this time?"

"Just barely. I wonder if they make diapers for grownups?"

Helena made another pot of coffee, and they finished off the pumpkin bread. She said, "Addy, I haven't laughed so much since I was married to James." Helena stopped to explain, "He is my third husband and the love of my life. It took me three times to get it right, but as far as I'm concerned, he's my only husband."

When Helena spoke in the present tense, Addy's face brightened. Helena could see that Addy didn't understand. "He died," Helena said sadly.

Addy felt angry, not with Helena, but at life. Helena finally found true love, but it was snatched from her too soon. Why were things so unfair?

Helena continued to talk about James for the rest of the afternoon. As Helena spoke, Addy drifted off into dreamland, picturing the tall, handsome couple, deeply in love, traveling, boating, and dancing under the stars. James wore a white tuxedo, and Helena was in a long, jade green evening gown. They were on the upper deck of an ocean liner, waltzing to the strains of the orchestra playing below. The moon, full and white-bright, glistened on Helena's silver-blonde hair and sparkled on the sequins of her gown. As the vocalist was singing, "A Hundred Years from Now," Addy could imagine James pulling Helena even closer and whispering, "That's us, darling. We'll be together a hundred years from now." Helena was lost in the reverie of her memories, while Addy spun fantasies of Helena's wonderful marriage.

"And I thought I was a romantic," Addy joked.

This time, Helena actually blushed. "Stop it, Addy. James is one in a million. I got lucky."

That word---"Lucky." What did it really mean? Addy had chased after luck all her life but was never able to catch even the cuff of its sleeve. She had been unlucky since she was born.

"Helena, do you think a person's luck can change?" Addy asked in a childlike way.

"Of course," Helena replied. "We make our own luck—well, there are lots of things beyond our control, but we have to keep pushing for those things we can control."

At that moment, there was a knock on the kitchen door. Addy looked guiltily at Helena as if they had been having too much fun, and Lionel had thus arrived to put a stop to it.

"Come in," Helena called casually.

"Hi, Cosmo. I just remembered I haven't paid you since my mother died. I am so sorry," Helena said. "Addy, this is Cosmo Scortelli; Cosmo, this is Addy Blake—I mean Roberge—she's an old school friend of mine."

Wiping his hands on his overall, Cosmo, a short, stocky man with sanguine complexion, gave Addy a firm, friendly handshake. "Isa pleshur to meeta you," Cosmo said with a broad smile.

Helena got her wallet, handed Cosmo a large wad of bills and said, "Is that enough, Cosmo?"

Cosmo looked surprised. "No, Missa Helena, isa too much. Your Mama giva me thirty dolla month."

"My mother didn't have a lot, Cosmo, but I'm rich." Helena laughed. "Treat your wife to dinner."

Cosmo thanked Helena repeatedly then turned and exited the kitchen door.

Helena remarked, "Cosmo is such a dear. He can fix anything and has always been there to help my mother. The animals love him. If I didn't have Cosmo around, I would definitely have gotten rid of the animals by now."

"I'm glad you didn't get rid of them—at least not before my kids got to see them."

"Well," Helena said, "why not plan to bring them soon on one of their days off from school? I can't wait to see them again."

"Oh my God," Helena exclaimed in disbelief. "We had better get you home, Addy, or that husband of yours will be sending out the National Guard so you can be there in time to cook his dinner."

Addy realized they had not talked once about how they were going to lead Lionel on. "Helena, what should I tell him you and I discussed today?"

"Tell him that Helena got talking about her three marriages, and you just sat and listened. After all, you have to pretend to approve of my promiscuity so that I will come to trust you."

"Perfect!" Addy laughed. "We'd better get going."

As they drove, Addy felt prettier and smarter than she had in a long time. Helena acknowledged her as an intelligent, worthwhile person. Of course, her own children adored her, but that didn't really count. Most kids love their mothers, no matter what. There had never really been any adults, except for her parents and Greg, who valued Addy's uniqueness, but she had known them so briefly.

When Helena dropped Addy off at home, she made a date to pick up Addy next Wednesday morning at ten o'clock, give or take.

"We'll make plans to get your kids out to the farm. Then, we'll plot how to kill your husband."

Addy laughed, but Helena didn't sound as if she was kidding. At dinner that evening, Lionel pumped Addy for information about her visit with Helena.

"She wants the kids to come out and spend a day at the farm," Addy said nonchalantly. The kids' faces lit up.

"And...?" Lionel said impatiently. "Anything else?"

Addy raised her eyebrows and said with an air of mystery, "Yes, but we'll talk about it when the children go upstairs."

Lionel fell for her ruse. He was probably licking his chops waiting for some salacious details about Helena's wanton life, and Addy was getting crafty enough to give them to him.

"I'll take care of the dishes tonight, kids. You get an early start on your homework," Addy said.

"May we be excused?" her three sweethearts chimed in unison.

"Yes, you may," replied Lionel, preoccupied with what Addy might soon reveal to him.

Lionel sat drinking his after dinner coffee, while Addy cleaned the table and scraped the plates. She filled the dishpan with steaming hot, sudsy water and began the long chore of washing and drying the dinner dishes.

As Addy stood at the kitchen sink, she began to spin her tale. "Well, Helena has been married THREE times, and the last husband was a millionaire."

"See. You got mad at me when I said she was a slut. I told you so. She's damaged goods," Lionel said with an air of wisdom.

Addy laughed inside as she lied. "You were right. Well, she has so much money that it looks as if she doesn't care one bit about the farm. She has to pay a man to take care of it for her. I am sure she'll want to get rid of it soon enough."

"Have you mentioned the church yet?" Lionel said gullibly.

"Lionel, think about it. Helena doesn't have much use for the Catholic Church, but she is getting to really like me and wants to spend time with the kids. I think that eventually she might listen to my advice as a trusted friend. Even though she seems tough, she is grieving at the loss of her mother. Right now she's vulnerable so I have to tread gently."

"Addy, that's about the smartest thing I've ever heard you say. Just keep working on her. She's bound to come around."

Lionel went upstairs to shower so Addy dragged out the dishwashing and drying for two hours. If she stalled long enough, he might not be awake when she decided to call it a night. He eventually called down to her, "Are you coming up to bed?"

"I have to iron the kids' school clothes now. I didn't get to the ironing because I was at Helena's."

Lionel didn't answer. Addy was not lying. There was a lot of ironing to do, and she was determined to finish it tonight so Lionel would be asleep when she went to bed. Although Addy had no hope of ever leaving Lionel, she was thinking about some of the things her friend had said. Helena had not shared any details about the beatings she had received from her first husband, but look at Helena now. She was alive and well, free and rich. The rebirth of her friendship with Helena sparked a flicker of promise in Addy's heart.

There had been a great deal of rain in the summer so the foliage was exceptionally beautiful this year. No matter what happened at her house, Addy lived for Wednesday visits with Helena. Sometimes the two friends went out to lunch at nearby inns or shopped at exclusive gift and clothing stores. Helena was extravagant and insisted upon buying Addy a few beautiful items for Addy's tired wardrobe. When Lionel questioned the new periwinkle Pendleton suit she donned for church, Addy explained Helena had bought it for her. Lionel loved hearing that Helena was growing so fond of Addy.

Very often during their time together, Helena would talk about the best way to bump off Lionel. Steeped in J.M. Harrison's flawless tales of murder, Helena spoke often of elaborate plans to do away with Lionel once and for all. Of course, Addy thought she was joking.

"Criminals always make mistakes," Addy laughed. "They eventually get caught."

"I beg to differ with you, my friend," Helena said. "Take the case of The Black Dahlia. The police still do not know who killed her. There are theories and suspects, but no one has ever been prosecuted. She was cut up in pieces, and the murderer got away with it."

"Yuck. Please don't talk about that. It is so scary. Besides, I could never kill anyone, no matter what they did to me."

Helena quickly responded, "I could. That's your Catholic conscience talking now. Some people do not deserve to live. They're not worth the space they take up or the air they breathe."

Addy was beginning to think that Helena was serious so she quickly changed the subject. "Speaking of scary things, I have an idea for Halloween. Tell me what you think."

Chapter XII

Halloween

"Shoot," Helena said, smiling at her own clever word choice.

"Well, Lionel doesn't allow the kids to go trick-or-treating, so their Halloweens are pretty boring. Sometimes they go to the costume parade at school, but the boys are too old for that. What if we planned a Halloween party here at the farm? Is it brazen of me to suggest that?"

"Are you kidding? I **LOVE** Halloween; it's my favorite holiday," Helena answered.

"Halloween is on a Friday this year so we could plan to have the party after the other kids go trick-or-treating because it won't be a school night. I'm sure the mothers in town would give their eyeteeth for their kids to come to the farm. After all, you hold such intrigue for them."

"Let's start planning today," Helena said, changing immediately to her work mode. Helena got out a pen and paper from the writing desk in the parlor and made an outline of topics they needed to discuss: time; guest list; invitations; decorations; menu; activities; games; and prizes. Addy was amazed at how quickly Helena could switch gears.

"What if I hire someone to take the kids on a hayride around the farm?" Helena asked.

"Wow. That would be fantastic!" Addy exclaimed excitedly. She couldn't wait to tell the kids, especially Mary, about the party.

At dinner that evening, Addy said, "I have a surprise for you, kids." The three children quickly looked up from their plates. The only other time they had a real surprise was when they went to Maine.

"Oh, Mommy, tell us please, please," Mary shouted. Lionel

first looked at Mary sharply for her loud tone, and then glared at Addy for not consulting him about any surprise.

"Helena Kurowski is going to have a Halloween party out at her farm, and you can invite all the friends you like. It's going to be great, with games, prizes, and even a hayride."

"She doesn't seem to be in mourning," Lionel grumbled. Everyone ignored him. The kids had come to understand that anything Helena did was somehow fine with their father. They were not sure why he was approving of this fun, but who cared? Their mom hadn't looked this happy since they were on their vacation at Wells Beach.

Peter, James, and Mary had spent two Saturdays at the Kurowski farm and could not wait to go back. Helena paid Cosmo extra to work on the weekend so he could show the kids around. They gathered eggs from the henhouse; romped through the fields with the goats and sheep; and took turns riding on old "Lightning." What a misnomer. Lightning was so old she hardly galloped. After trotting around the barnyard for nearly an hour, she was ready for a long nap. Having the children ride on her pleased the old mare immensely; she felt useful again.

Addy watched wistfully through Helena's kitchen window at her three lovely children running and laughing with abandon. They looked like models for a Norman Rockwell painting. Cosmo loved kids; he had six of his own. He was very easygoing, and in spite of his thick Italian accent, he joked with the children constantly. Addy could see Jimmy falling on the ground, rolling around and laughing.

For lunch, Addy scrambled the eggs the children had gathered, serving them up with bacon and homemade corn muffins. Since the kids had had only cereal early in the morning, they loved having breakfast for lunch. That was such a sweet, simple pleasure but Lionel never approved of such things. In Lionel's world, breakfast fare was for breakfast … period.

As they all sat around the kitchen table, Helena admired Addy's handsome children. Their faces were flushed from all the running and fresh air. In spite of their having a tyrant for a father, Addy had sheltered them from the ugly side of life. They were sweet, kind, and innocent kids.

"Isn't your mom the best baker in the world?" Helena asked the kids.

Mary was the first to pipe up. "Yes, she always makes cakes for the PTA bake sale on voting day, and all of her cakes get sold."

"Yeah," Jimmy added, "we bring cupcakes to school for our birthdays, and my classmates like my mom's the best."

Blushing, Addy said, "Thanks, you guys. You sure know how to make a gal feel special."

After lunch, the kids shared their ideas for the Halloween party. The boys thought up a "Hall of Horrors," where kids go through a pitch-black hallway and stick their hands in various bowls of creepy things. Peeled grapes would be "eyeballs," and cold spaghetti, "worms." Rather than being frightened by this scheme, Mary offered some creative suggestions. As long as she was in on the planning, she was not afraid.

They would decorate the living room with orange and black crepe paper streamers, pumpkins, cats, ghosts, and skeletons. They planned to attach a heavy line of string to one wall of the living room, and stretch it tightly across to the other wall. On the day of the party, they would hang doughnuts by pieces of string attached to the line. With their hands behind their backs, the partygoers would have to catch the swinging doughnuts with their teeth. There would be dunking for apples, musical chairs, and prizes for the best costumes in categories like: scariest, funniest, and most original, but at the end of the evening, every child would go home with a prize.

Addy was in charge of the menu but made sure Helena and the kids liked her suggestions—pigs in a blanket; deviled eggs; celery sticks with cream cheese and paprika; canned cling peaches; cider; a fruited punchbowl; popcorn balls; potato chips; and several kinds of Halloween cookies, cupcakes, and candy. Helena had insisted upon paying for all the groceries, and Addy was relieved. No matter how much Lionel wanted to wheedle his way into Helena's life, he would never foot the bill for an extravaganza like this.

News of the upcoming party at the Kurowski farm spread through Chester like wildfire in the California hills. The mothers gossiped on the telephone, debating who would be the ones to drive for the carpool. In the end, the nosey women got their way. The more subdued mothers knew that they would eventually hear every detail about Helena, like it or not.

Addy's kids were amazed at the growing number of children who sent their RSVPs accepting the invitation to the Halloween party. Mary could hardly sleep from all the excitement. Fortunately, Lionel seemed very distracted of late and left Addy alone, thank goodness. She had too much to do to worry about his foolhardiness.

The day of the party was rapidly approaching, and Addy had to make all of their costumes. She had not taken out Aunt Sophia's sewing machine in years and hoped it still worked. Her aunts were accomplished seamstresses and had taught Addy to sew. Because she had spent so much time alone as a child, Addy amused herself with reading, drawing, baking, and crafts.

Helena and Addy went shopping for the costume patterns, material, and accessories. Once again, Helena funded everything. How would Addy ever repay Helena for all that she did for the children and her? Helena insisted she was the one benefiting from her time with Addy and the kids. After all, money is just money, Helena told Addy. It cannot buy health, friendship, or true happiness. Still, Addy felt guilty about letting Helena pay for everything. How she wished she had some money of her own so she could buy Helena a lovely gift, but Lionel kept track of every penny she spent.

On the Sunday before the party, Helena took the kids to a local farm to pick countless pumpkins to carve into jack-o'-lanterns. She had the clever idea to use the jack-o'-lanterns to illuminate the path leading to the farmhouse door. Helena, Addy, and the kids started the carving on Sunday, and by 10:00 p.m. on Wednesday, they finished all the jack-o'-lanterns.

Addy noticed the time and panicked. Lionel was sure to make a fuss about the children staying up so late.

"Oh my God, Helena. We have to go. It's after ten. Lionel will have a fit."

Helen rolled her eyes in exasperation. "Addy can you take even one breath without worrying about that man?"

Luckily, the kids were out of earshot. Addy's eyes immediately filled with tears of shame at her complacency and fear of Lionel. Helena walked over and put her arm around Addy's shoulders. "I'm sorry, kid. I just get so frustrated seeing you walk on egg shells because of that brute."

The kids ran into the kitchen but stopped cold when they saw their mom crying. They, too, were scared of their father's reaction and feared he'd make a scene in front of Helena. They all piled into the Rolls and rode home in silence. As they pulled up to the house, which was in total darkness, they breathed a sigh of relief, knowing Lionel was not there. Helena bid a quick, "good night" to Addy and the children.

The kids raced to get into their PJs and then hopped into bed, pretending to have been asleep for hours. Lionel must have come stumbling in during the middle of the night, but he never disturbed Addy. Upon awakening from a rare, restful sleep, Addy thought about how her luck was increasingly changing for the better. Ever since Helena had arrived on the scene, Lionel had backed off considerably. Addy laughed to herself imagining Lionel busily drawing up plans in his mind for the Monsignor Jean-Paul Roberge Center.

Helena, Addy, and the children were swept up in the excitement of preparing for the Halloween party. Little Mary had begun emulating Helena. Notebook and pencil in hand, she checked off each task as it was completed. The boys cut out ghosts from sheets of white crepe paper, black cats and orange pumpkins from construction paper, and then hung them all from black and orange crepe paper streamers. They would add orange and black balloons and the doughnuts on strings just before the party was about to begin.

In anticipation of dunking for apples, the boys had dragged large aluminum washtubs from the barn, scrubbed, and hosed them off. As the tubs dried in the sun, Addy imagined Helena's grandmother washing the family's laundry using a washboard in one of those tubs. How did women in that era find time to do everything?

Helena's grandparents, Henryk and Teresa Kurowski, were immigrant farmers from Poland. Her grandfather, Henryk, a stern and humorless tightwad, bought twenty acres of land from his widowed sister, Alina. Both Henryk and Teresa died while Helena was still young so she remembered almost nothing about them. Even if her grandparents had lived, Helena would not have been able to communicate with them because they spoke almost no English. Helena never learned Polish; Mary and her contemporaries wanted their children to speak only English and immerse themselves in the great American cultural melting pot. As much as the Kurowski children tried to remain inconspicuous and fit it, immigrant children of other nationalities taunted them, shouting, "Stupid Polanders, Stupid Polanders." The immigrant groups that had been in the United States longer ridiculed those who had arrived more recently.

Addy and Helena suspected that Henryk must have been as cruel as Lionel. Since Alina was in jeopardy of losing the farm, her heartless brother Henryk gave her almost nothing for it and then turned her away. Henryk was not only a successful farmer but also a shrewd businessman. He eventually acquired tenements and commercial buildings in town, collecting steep rents from the occupants. Henryk did not believe in banks so he hid his money in the barn. While Henryk watched his fortune accumulate, his family lived in dire poverty.

Mary Kurowski's simpleminded sister, Genevieve, got pregnant out of wedlock and gave birth to a son, Stanley. Helena never knew any details about the man who had impregnated Genevieve. In those days, having a child outside of marriage was as appalling as committing a felony. Viewed by others as damaged goods, Genevieve, of course, never married. Raised on the farm as somewhat a neglected child, Stanley was more comfortable in the chicken coops than amongst humans.

Stanley was no dummy, though; he knew exactly where his grandfather Henryk had hidden all the money. When Henryk died, Stanley raided the barn and became a rich ladies' man overnight. Although he bragged to his paramours about "inheriting" his grandfather's fortune, Stanley never shared one cent with his mother, Genevieve. Tragically, Genevieve eventually died in the Northampton Lunatic Asylum with Stanley, of course, nowhere around.

Henryk and Teresa Kurowski had five children, counting Genevieve, but Mary was the only one who turned out normal. Although Mary's marriage to Helena's father, Anthony, was ultimately a disaster, Anthony's Italian family may have helped Mary learn to enjoy life. When they were first married, Anthony's family gave Mary the cold shoulder because in those days, you did not marry outside your nationality. As was the custom, all of Anthony's brothers and sisters married Italians. When Anthony's siblings realized Mary's strength and good character, however, they embraced her as one of their own.

Anthony's family was warm, loving, and generous. Although Henryk probably had more money in his barn than Mary's Italian in-laws ever dreamed of having, one would never know it. When it came to food, family, gifts, and fun, money was no object for the Italians. Mary had treasured the memories of countless weddings, christenings, and picnics shared with Anthony's family.

In contrast, Mary had grown up under the stern hand of her father, Henryk, for whom "fun" was a dirty word. Mary's childhood was a grim, gray, existence. One day when Mary and her sisters were wearing their mother's clothes and hats, and jumping on the bed, Henryk came home unexpectedly and beat them soundly. At Christmastime, there were no presents. When her schoolmates talked about the toys Santa Claus had delivered, Mary wondered why Santa never visited her house. One Christmas, she magically received a hunk of chocolate wrapped in silver paper from a distant relative. Mary secretly planned to sneak it to school to show her classmates proudly that Santa, indeed, had stopped at the farm this year. In her eagerness to display her treasure, Mary quickly ran all the way to school, inadvertently dropping the hunk of chocolate in the mounds of snow.

Helena hated hearing these stories of Mary's unhappy childhood and vowed that when she grew up, she would do exactly as she pleased. Although a good man, Helena's father, Anthony, drank too much and constantly reminisced about the "old country." Mary never touched a drop of liquor, while Anthony repeatedly embarrassed her by getting plastered at every family gathering. Anthony's siblings drank a lot at parties, too, but they seemed to be able to handle their booze better than he did. While the men in his family mowed the grass, trimmed the hedges, and worked in their gardens on the weekends, Anthony sat on the sofa in a drunken stupor, blinking his eyes and staring at the wall. Mary often wondered if the proponents of Prohibition had firsthand experience with alcohol's part in destroying families. Anthony's drinking problem had spiraled so far out of control that he would search the medicine cabinet for Paregoric or other products that contained alcohol.

The more Anthony drank, the more Mary threw herself into hobbies and household projects. Employed outside the home, she also attended night school to learn woodworking, rug braiding, chair caning, upholstering, and hat making. Mary had learned to cook Italian food from her husband's mother and prepared meals that rivaled those of her sisters-in-law. She canned tomatoes that she and her mother-in-law picked from their garden, made pasta dough from scratch, and stood for hours wrapping the delicate little tortellini around her fingers. She was also an extremely talented baker. Her brother-in-law, Jimmy, always said her creampuffs were so light, he had to eat them all before they floated off the plate. Perhaps Mary's countless pastimes kept her from losing her mind.

Helena had one hazy memory of her father. It was afternoon, but the saloon was very dark. Her father lifted her out of her stroller and she toddled around the place. The floor was oily and sticky, the air heavy with the stench of stale cigarette smoke and beer. After a long while, her father wheeled her home.

This event was probably the beginning of the end. Mary

must have smelled the alcohol on Anthony's breath, and she was wild that he had taken little Helena to a bar. The couple must have had a terrible row, concluding with Anthony walking out.

He eventually hooked up with a woman who had come from the same town in Italy as he, and together they ran away in drunken oblivion back to the old country. Anthony's family was furious with him for abandoning Mary and Helena, but blood is thicker than water in the end. Neither Mary nor Helena ever heard from Anthony again so Mary eventually changed Helena's and her own last name back to "Kurowski." Helena was never sure why her mother did that. Maybe it was her way of finally severing ties with Anthony.

Specters from the past still haunted parts of the Kurowski farm, but this Halloween, they would be brushed away for good. Cosmo, Helena, Addy, and the children all pitched in to scour the house and barn. If only Helena's mother could see the place now. The farm had not looked this spiffy since Mary bought out her siblings' share of the place. Determined to raise her daughter Helena in a lovely country setting, Mary had toiled away on weekends and vacations, cleaning, painting, wallpapering, and planting, gradually transforming the ramshackle, foreboding farm into a bright, welcoming homestead.

The weather in New England on Halloween was always unpredictable. It could be as warm as summer one year, then snow the next. Listening intently to the weatherman on the radio, the children squealed with delight when they heard the forecast for this Halloween night: clear skies, temperatures in the high 60s, and a full moon.

Thus far, everything seemed to be falling into place. Life for Addy's children had improved considerably since Helena Kurowski came on the scene. Little Mary was convinced that "Auntie Helena" was like Glinda, the Good Witch of the North who appeared in *The Wizard of Oz* movie. After much coaxing by Mary, Helena agreed to dress up as Glinda, with the one condition that her gown be blue rather than pink. Addy sewed a stunning gown with layers and layers of Tiffany blue chiffon scattered with silver stars, trimmed with silver-sequined rickrack, and lined in blue satin.

The long-awaited Halloween day finally arrived, and the farm was buzzing with activity on the afternoon of the party. Decorations, food, costumes—so much to do. Feverish with excitement, the children dashed about placing the finishing touches on their royal banquet. Everything had to be perfect. After all, more than fifty guests were expected. The town was sopping with gossip, rumoring that a reporter from the *Chester Gazette* would be on hand to cover the event.

Helena was livid when she got word of the possibility of a reporter trespassing on her property. Had they not already violated her privacy by publishing the article about her return to Chester? However, there was one good thing that might come out of this lunacy. Hungry for status, Lionel would devour the attention showered upon the farm and his family's connection to Helena. This would be just one more nail to hammer into the coffin of deception so craftily constructed by Addy and Helena.

As the clock on the mantel chimed eight, cars began pulling up in front of the farmhouse. Addy, Helena, and the children were upstairs adjusting their costumes. Mary looked out the bedroom window and called breathlessly, "Hurry, hurry. They're here."

Helena, never one to rush, straightened her tall crown, picked up her magic wand, and seemingly floated down the staircase, an otherworldly vision of beauty in blue. The first to arrive was Carol Howie with her two children, Sadie and Daniel. Sadie was one of Mary's favorite classmates. As soon as Helena opened the door for them, Mrs. Howie said, "Hello, Helena. Do you remember me from St. Mary's? My maiden name was Nedder, Carol Nedder. These are my children, Sadie and Dan."

Helena vaguely recalled Carol but did not have any special memories of her. "You look so beautiful," Carol gushed. Helena brushed off the compliment with, "It's the gown. My friend Addison Roberge—Blake—made it. Do you remember Addison?"

"I'm afraid I don't," Carol said uncertainly.

"Well, it's Addy and her children we have to thank for this

bash," Helena said with pride. "She's an amazing person. There isn't anything she can't do."

Peeking out from behind Helena's billowing skirts, Mary said, "Sadie, I'm so happy you could come!"

Her face immediately lighting up, Sadie said, "Hi, Mary. I like your costume."

"I like yours, too," Mary said shyly. "My mom made my costume."

Carol quickly made the association between Addy and Mary. So this was the room mother whose cupcakes the students liked best. "I haven't met Addy," Carol stammered. "Shall I pick the kids up around 10:00?" Both Mary and Sadie's eyes opened wide with delight at the prospect of staying up that late.

Eager to get the fun started, Sadie grabbed Mary's hand and said, "Let's go. Bye Mom." The two girls pranced away. Sadie's brother Dan stood impatiently on the front porch, shuffling his feet. He did not know Pete and Jimmy, but his mother made him come to the party to keep an eye on Sadie. Carol pushed Dan forward, and Helena said graciously, "Welcome, Dan. There are going to be a lot of boys here ... maybe even more boys than girls."

Dan looked relieved when Pete and Jimmy came to the door to greet him. "Hey, I know you," Dan said to Jimmy excitedly. "I see you on the playground. You are in Miss Shibley's class, aren't you? She's an old grouch."

Giving Dan a sharp look, Carol said, "You are not to talk about a teacher like that. She's just strict, that's all. Someday you children will thank her for that." Dan, a rambunctious sort, rolled his eyes, and pretended to vomit, while Jimmy quietly chuckled. The ice between the boys was already broken. Without so much as a "good-bye," Dan ran inside to join the merriment. Carol walked slowly back to her car, deliberating upon Helena's description of Addy. Who could have ever imagined that a nobody like Addison Blake could turn out to be so talented and have a wealthy, prestigious friend like Helena?

A steady stream of cars wound down the road leading to the farm. Because several children brought uninvited siblings, the sum of party guests was burgeoning, well surpassing the original fifty. Addy was grateful that her dear neighbor, Joan Avery, had volunteered to help. In spite of all their planning and preparation, Helena and Addy never thought about how they would manage a throng like this.

Even with three adults, it was a challenge keeping things under control. The party guests scuttled around the food table, many filling their paper plates to overflowing. The last thing Addy wanted was for any of the kids to go home with a bellyache. Helena searched through one of the kitchen drawers to find an old whistle. When she blew it, the children quieted down immediately, as they were used to doing in school. In an authoritative voice, Helena announced, "Let's stop this commotion. If you want food, please line up, and Mrs. Roberge, Mrs. Avery, and I will serve you."

The children who still wanted to eat fell into formation like dutiful soldiers while the women filled their plates. Next were the games, but the children did not have to participate if they didn't want to. Addy crossed her fingers that some of the guests would choose not to play; with the increase in the number of kids, there were no longer enough doughnuts on strings or apples for bobbing.

Some of the older kids wanted no part of the games so Peter took them into the parlor to listen to records and bop. Mrs. Avery chaperoned the dancers, while Addy and Helena supervised the games. The old farmhouse was bursting at the seams with hilarity, and the minutes were ticking away too rapidly. Would they still have time for the hayride and costume contest? Helena whispered to Addy that they had better step up the pace of the activities. Helena blew the whistle, and said, "We still have some surprises for you. If we are going to finish by ten o'clock, we have to stop the dancing and games."

Some kids objected, claiming their mothers would let them stay until 11:00, but Helena and Addy did not want any guff from the parents. In fact, some mothers had already come to fetch the smallest guests. Several kids cried because they did not want to leave, but their mothers were adamant. Smiling affectionately, Addy brought the prize basket out and let each little cherub choose a treasure. Addy's face reddened as each mother thanked her profusely. If the mothers were sincere in their gratitude, they may well view Addy in a different light. Addy looked up at the huge orange moon and beamed. Helena was indeed a godsend.

Helena did not want to participate in the hayride so stayed behind to clean up some of the mess. It was a good thing that, at the last minute, they had decided to hire two hay wagons; sixty kids remained. Joan Avery went in one wagon and Addy in the other. By this time, the kids were getting tired and were more subdued. Countless stars flickered on the black velvet backdrop of the autumn sky. The enormous ginger pumpkin moon smiled down upon the happy group. Chilly breezes gusted, and the riders huddled under the large plaid woolen blankets provided by the hay wagon drivers.

The carefree chatter ceased as the fresh air lulled some of the children to sleep. As the hay wagons bumped along the unpaved farm roads, the mood was reverent and serene. Addy's mind expanded, as it used to do when she was in college. Helena had helped her to tap once again into her intelligent nature. Addy floated out of herself, but this time not to escape Lionel's abuse. Her spirit drifted above the hay wagons, looking down on a scene that could have taken place at any time in history. Gazing at the lovely children, cautious wagon drivers, and gentle horses, Addy saw how life should be: infinitely beautiful; safe; and good. The divine spell was broken as the wagons pulled up in front of the farmhouse. The children groaned, knowing that the lovely ride had ended.

As the wagons stopped and the kids jumped out, Jarvis Egan, a reporter from the *Chester Gazette* arrived to take pictures. Addy didn't want to be in the snapshots, but Helena called Jimmy, Peter, and Mary to pose with her. Lionel would eat that up for sure. Other kids scrambled to get into the pictures. After taking his photographs, Jarvis interviewed Helena briefly. Unlike the cub reporter who had written the first story about Helena, Jarvis was a seasoned, respectful journalist. Exiting with a wave and a smile, Jarvis reminded them to watch for their pictures in the Sunday rotogravure.

Of course, there was no time for the costume contest, but Helena and Addy had the children select a prize from either the boys' or girls' tables Helena had set up while everyone was on the hayride. The kids were genuinely pleased with the selection of prizes. The last stragglers were dozing off to sleep as their parents arrived after 11:00 p.m. Most mothers apologized copiously, claiming their dinner parties or country club soirées had run overtime.

Helena, Addy, and the children were exhausted. The Halloween party had been a huge success, elevating Jimmy, Mary, and Pete to a level of popularity they had never known. Lionel had given his permission for Addy and the children to sleep at the farm that night. Barely able to get out of their costumes, the revelers dropped into bed, drifting peacefully off to slumberland.

When Addy arrived home late Saturday afternoon, Lionel immediately began questioning her about the party. Knowing just what he wanted to hear, Addy spoke animatedly about the success of the event. She saved the best for last: A reporter came to the farm, and Peter, James, and Mary posed with Helena for the Sunday newspaper.

Lionel was well pleased. He had begun to see Addy in a different light. Maybe she wasn't such a mouse after all. He made plans to stick his penis in her vagina, then her anus, alternating between the two wildly nonstop that night. After all, he had not had sex with her in a long time, and it was a wife's duty to pleasure her husband. Lionel became aroused, but not by the notion of having his way with Addy.

His sexual urges were associated solely with Mistress Irena. In a few weeks, he would be with her again. All the secret sexual practices revealed to him by his Mistress made Lionel feel immensely clever. He fantasized about being bound and lying on the floor with his head fixed under the "queen's chair," which Mistress Irena had once described to him. In olden times, a royal woman would sit on a low chair or stool fashioned with an opening in the center of the seat. While the lady's billowy skirts covered the stool, a page lying on his back with his head under the seat would service madam with cunnilingus to her heart's content. Lionel was dreaming of doing this for Mistress, if ever allowed. First, of course, she would torture him to the brink of unconsciousness.

Addy did her best to stall going to bed that night, but when she went upstairs around 1:00 a.m., she sensed Lionel was still awake. She took a long shower and dressed in the nightgown she had left on the hook before leaving for Helena's. Addy was surprised Lionel had not thrown the nightgown into the hamper because, of course, he never liked anything out of place. When she tiptoed into the bedroom, Addy was shocked to see all the lights on and Lionel lying there naked. He ordered Addy to remove her nightgown.

"Lionel, I'm so tired from the party. Couldn't I please just go to sleep?"

"God damn you, Addy. Haven't you learned yet that a wife must be submissive to her husband? Remember your marriage vows, when you promised to love, honor, and OBEY? Drop that nightgown NOW and get into bed."

Frightened, Addy did as he said. She tried to climb under the covers, but Lionel was sprawled on top of them. "Get on your knees," he commanded. Addy knelt on the bed, and Lionel pushed her down. "Now stick your ass up in the air."

"Lionel, please ... No," Addy whimpered. To force her to keep her behind raised, Lionel grabbed two pillows and shoved them under her stomach. By this time, he was erect and went to work on Addy as he had planned. The rest was a blur. Lionel seemed to take forever to climax so Addy, as always, left her body. When he was finally done, he collapsed into a deep sleep. Addy went to the bathroom to first pee, as the urologist had advised; then she took another shower and swallowed her antibiotic.

Chapter XIII

Thanksgiving

Fall was Addy's favorite season. The colors were ineffably beautiful, but as the weather grew colder, the leaves trembled and fell to the ground. It was always sad to see the leaves die. Once the trees were bare, winter was at hand, and winters in Connecticut were awfully long and gray. Addy wished her aunts had allowed her to take skiing lessons. Skiing in New England made the season delightful. Addy fantasized about swooshing down the slopes, and then drinking hot chocolate by the fireplace in the ski lodge. Her aunts never let her do anything, and, as a result, she had come to believe she was clumsy and inept.

Helena and Addy continued their planning and trickery throughout the weeks between Halloween and Thanksgiving. Helena suggested Addy bring Lionel out to the farm for Thanksgiving dinner. That gesture would make him believe he had finally arrived, and the turning over of the farm to the church was imminent. Helena did not want Addy to cook. When Addy protested, Helena insisted she was ordering the completely extravagant dinner from Brunell's Turkey Farm, family-owned for over 75 years. You could select the live turkey of your choice for the Brunells to slaughter and either take it home to cook it yourself or have the Brunells prepare it for you. In addition to the turkey, the Brunells offered all the tasty trimmings typical of a New England Thanksgiving dinner. Of course, a meal to feed a dozen people (Helena had also invited Cosmo and his family.) would be very costly, but Helena never skimped. Living life robustly instead of frittering it away pinching pennies was Helena's philosophy.

At 10:00 a.m. on Thanksgiving morning, Cosmo drove

Helena to the Brunell farm to pick up the feast. Even with the help of the Brunell's burly sons, it took several trips to load all the food into Cosmo's truck. The gigantic turkey, warm, golden brown and wrapped in several layers of foil was ready to serve. All the tightly wrapped side dishes were prepared to place in a low-temperature oven until the guests arrived. Heating the gravy on top of the stove was about the only "cooking" Helena was planning to do. The pies were just fine the way they were.

After dropping Helena and the food off at the Kurowski farm, Cosmo drove home to pick up his wife and their brood of six who would help Helena get everything ready. When Cosmo returned to the farm an hour later, Helena hardly recognized him in his spiffy suit and tie. She was used to seeing him in grubby overalls, with dirt under his nails. Today he was spotlessly clean and quite handsome.

Cosmo's wife, Regina, elegantly dressed in black from head to toe, was still in mourning after losing her mother almost a year ago. Although Helena had told Cosmo not to bring anything, it is a rare Italian who can show up empty-handed. Betty, Cosmo's strikingly beautiful eldest daughter, proudly carried a tray of cookies she had helped Regina make. The children stood perfectly still until Cosmo told them in Italian what he wanted each of them to do. Then Cosmo translated his instructions. Helena nodded in agreement, and then showed the kids where the good china and silverware were. As Helena laid her mom's elegant lace tablecloth on the dining room table, she felt a pang of melancholy. She sometimes used to grumble at Mary for using fancy items even when it was just the two of them sitting down to Sunday dinner. Now Helena understood that, no matter how humble your circumstances, surrounding yourself with lovely things makes life just that much sweeter.

Addy's family soon arrived. They, too, were all dressed up in their Sunday best, and Lionel was carrying a large arrangement of fall flowers. The last person from whom Helena would ever want flowers would be Lionel, but she had to play along. Peter stood holding a cake carrier.

As Lionel extended the beautiful bouquet to Helena, she said coyly, "I told Addy not to bring anything, but I am glad you brought these. How did I overlook ordering flowers? Let me get a vase." Helena brought out a large Waterford vase filled with water and placed the flower arrangement in the middle of the table. "What a lovely Thanksgiving centerpiece. Thank you so much, Lionel."

Pete was still holding the cake carrier, when Helena noticed and said, "Sorry Pete. I didn't see you standing there ... now what on earth is this?" Helena said, taking the carrier from Pete.

Addy answered quickly, "It's a chocolate cake for those who may not like pie."

"Between the pies, Regina's cookies, and your cake, I can eat like a queen for a week," Helena laughed.

The crowd was too large to fit around the dining room table so the younger kids ate in the kitchen. In his usual pompous manner, Lionel said grace, thanking God for every imaginable blessing. Helena eyed him as he sat with his head bowed piously. Hypocrite, she thought to herself in disgust.

Throughout the meal, Lionel eyed the antiques, calculating the profit the church could make in an auction of the contents of the farmhouse. The dinner was scrumptious as well as bounteous, and they all overate. When Addy asked who was ready for dessert and coffee, a collective groan rose from the overfed guests. Thinking quickly, Lionel suggested they take a walk around the farm to make some room for dessert. This would give him a chance to check out the lay of the land and report back to Monsignor Roberge.

The weather was pleasant so everyone except Regina, Addy, and Helena went outside. Cosmo and Regina's children were delightful and had great fun with Addy's kids. Regina insisted she help with the dishes, but Helena would not hear of it. "With all those bambinos, you need a day off. Now go outside and get some fresh air."

Regina shrugged her shoulders and went outside to join the others. The children went to see the animals while Lionel and the Scortellis strolled along the path leading down to the brook. As Addy and Helena cleared the tables, Helena remarked, "I wonder what the hell he's talking about to them? They barely speak English."

"That's fine. Lionel won't care. He prefers to hear himself talk," Addy quipped. This struck Helena so funny; the two friends began laughing uncontrollably. As Addy raced for the bathroom, she shouted, "Darn you, Helena. Look what you've done!"

"What did I do? You were the one who started it!" Helena wheezed through peals of laughter.

Addy quickly regained her composure, knowing Lionel might walk through the door any moment now.

"They won't be back for a long time," Helena said, reading Addy's mind. "I saw them heading down to the brook, and it's a farther walk than they realize."

As Addy scraped and washed the dishes, Helena dried them. Distractedly wiping the same plate over and over, Helena said, "We haven't talked about killing Lionel for a long time."

Smiling, Addy said, "I've always thought you were joking. We can't get away with a crime. Even if you were serious, how would the children feel knowing their father was murdered? It would be devastating for them, especially if I wound up in jail."

"But no one would ever know you did it. Who would suspect YOU? Come on, Addy. You are not the kind of person who bumps anyone off. Besides, I'd be in this with you every step of the way. I've read enough true crime stories to know that some people really do get away with murder. Lots of deaths classified as accidents, illnesses, or 'unknown causes,' are actually perfect murders."

After enduring one of Lionel's beatings or rapes, Addy always wished that he would die. She sometimes thought about Helena's suggestions for his demise but quickly dismissed those thoughts from her mind. She was an unlucky person, and no matter what, she would be caught. She just knew she would. Addy could never be icy and unapproachable like Helena, who could probably talk her way out of anything and walk away unscathed. In contrast, Addy would end up cracking under the pressure of her secret and blurt out the truth.

"How's his health?" Helena quizzed.

"What?" Addy said with surprise.

"Does he have any allergies? Is his heart strong? Does he have asthma?"

"I'm not sure," Addy responded. "He gets a yearly physical. His father died of a heart attack when Lionel was a teenager."

"Now there's a possibility. If we fed him a substance that triggers a heart attack but is also untraceable in the blood, we would get away with it. After all, he has a history of heart problems in his family. You just said it. Many things can cause either a gradual or a quick death. I'd like something that would make him suffer slowly and agonizingly," Helena said in all seriousness. "I've read about putting small amounts of antifreeze in someone's beverages to initiate a long painful illness and eventually death. The hospitals can't figure out why a person keeps getting sicker. I would just have to check to see if they have a test that can detect antifreeze in the body. Of course, there is always arsenic or rat ..."

Just then, the children tumbled through the kitchen door shouting, "Is it time for dessert yet?"

Lionel and the Scortellis, in an equally good mood, followed the children.

"We've worked up an appetite," Lionel said. "I'm ready for dessert."

Helena put the coffee on, and everyone gathered in the dining room. Addy had placed stacks of glass plates, forks, and napkins on one end of the sideboard and lined the desserts up next to them so the guests could serve themselves. To see them heap the sweets on their plates, one would never know they had just eaten a huge Thanksgiving dinner.

Regina said, "Who made-da shoc-o-lat torta?"

"Me," Addy answered modestly.

"Isa bes'a shoc-o-lat torta I efer eat," Regina remarked with great sincerity.

"That's my Addy-girl," Lionel bragged. As quickly as that spurious statement rolled off Lionel's tongue, Helena's temper flared. To restrain herself from gouging out Lionel's eyes,

Helena jumped up to make another pot of coffee.

It was well past dark by the time everyone went home. Dog-tired, Helena dropped into her easy chair. As she mulled over the events of the day, she concluded that the Thanksgiving dinner was, on so many levels, a complete success. Now Lionel believed he was her friend, and that was just the way she wanted it. Helena could have won an academy award for doing such a great job pretending Lionel was an interesting, engaging person.

In spite of having to endure Lionel's presence in her home, Helena had had a great day. Her friendship with Addy and the children was enriching her life more than she could ever have envisioned; they had become like family to her. Plotting the deception and demise of the brute, Lionel, occupied Helena's imagination. Addy did not realize that Helena was dead serious.

Chapter XIV

Christmas

Soon after Thanksgiving, the weather grew cold and the foliage dry and dull. Addy looked out of her kitchen window at the gray late November skyline speckled with black India ink silhouettes of trees. Fall had been brilliant, but now the season of darkness was approaching. A mood of depression suddenly overtook Addy. What if Helena decided to go back to New York? She must surely be tired of Addy's problems and humdrum life in Chester. What would Addy do without Helena?

At that moment, the telephone rang and Addy ran to get it. Helena was the only one who called regularly.

"Hi kid. How're you doing today?" Helena asked.

Addy's voice cracked, "I'm fine."

Helena could tell Addy was not fine. "What's wrong? Is it the beast again?"

"No. I'm just feeling a little down today, that's all," Addy replied.

"Well, this should cheer you up. How about coming out to the farm for Christmas? We had such a great time on Thanksgiving, why not more of the same?"

Addy's spirits lifted. "The farm must be beautiful at Christmas, like a Currier and Ives painting. Truthfully, I was just worrying that you might be getting sick of living here, and you might decide to go back to New York."

Helena laughed. "Don't you worry your pretty little head off about that. I'm not leaving any time soon. Want to go Christmas shopping today?"

"Sure," Addy replied. "Lionel doesn't care what I do now, as long as I'm hanging around with you. What time?"

"See you at one o'clock," Helena said. "We'll have a fabulous time."

Rushing, Addy finished cleaning up the kitchen and straightened the rest of the house. It's amazing how fast you can get ready when you know you're going somewhere fun, Addy thought cheerfully. Her depression had already lifted.

As soon as Helena pulled up in front of the house, Addy was ready to go. She hopped into the car, and Helena said, "I'm famished. Want to have lunch by the ocean? I adore the Essex Inn."

Over bowls of steaming, thick New England clam chowder and plates of crispy crab cakes, the two friends discussed plans for the upcoming holiday. Helena quizzed Addy about what the children wanted for Christmas. Because Lionel established a strict budget to buy Christmas presents, Addy could rarely purchase the things the kids wrote on their Christmas lists.

Trying not to appear greedy, Addy insisted that she had enough money to purchase all the gifts; by now, Helena knew when Addy was not being completely honest with her.

"Come on, Addy, I know how cheap Lionel is. I am sure it would be impossible to shop on the skimpy stipend you will get from Scrooge."

Addy laughed. Helena always chose such humorous but true words to describe Lionel. Helena had gotten into the habit of ordering cocktails for both of them with lunch. Addy could not hold much alcohol and inevitably got tipsy. Helena saw this as a perfect opportunity to ask Addy, "If, say, you had unlimited funds, what would you buy the kids for Christmas?"

Addy wasn't usually fooled this easily, but she had had more alcohol than usual and fell into Helena's trap. "Well, Mary wants a walking doll, new ice skates because hers are too small, a velvet coat with a fur collar. Let's see, Pete wants an erector set, a pair of ice skates, and a chemistry set ... Jimmy ... an electric train set, ice skates, and a toboggan. I will be able to afford one gift for each of them."

"What about Santa Claus? Will the toys be from him, or will they be wrapped gifts under the tree from Lionel and you?" Helena persisted.

"Only Mary still believes in Santa Claus so the doll will be fine for her. The kids are used to getting one present each from Santa."

Helena paid the bill for lunch, and the two friends embarked upon their shopping adventure. The weather had grown windy and chilly, so they ducked into a children's clothing shop. "Look at these beautiful clothes," Addy whispered. "They must cost a fortune."

Hanging alone on its own rack was a girl's hunter green velvet coat trimmed with a rabbit collar dyed to look like leopard skin. At the end of the ties on the matching hat were pompoms made of the same fur. A green velvet muff completed the ensemble.

"This is just the coat for Mary," Helena exclaimed.

"Are you loony?" Addy mouthed. "Look at the price tag."

By this time, a tall, stately woman came over to ask if she could be of help. Helena asked Addy what size Mary wore. Addy did not want to look like a fool in this classy store so she said softly, "Eight."

"Do you have this in a size 8?" Helena inquired coolly.

"Yes, as a matter of fact, we do. These coats just came in so we still have one in each size."

"We'll take it in size 8," Helena said quickly. "Will you wrap it, please?"

When the saleslady went into the back room, Addy protested, "Helena you can't buy that. It is way too expensive. I could outfit all three of my kids for that price. I beg you, please don't get it."

Ignoring her, Helena said, "What sizes do the boys wear?"

Addy refused to answer so Helena walked up to the counter to find the saleslady. "After you finish wrapping the coat, will you show me the latest styles for boys?"

"Most certainly, ma'am," the saleslady replied graciously.

By the time they left the clothing store, Helena had purchased handsome outfits for both Pete and Jimmy.

"Now to Gepetto's Toy Shop," Helena directed. Off they went, with Addy protesting all the way.

Addy had never seen such a charming toy store. Christmas music was playing, and in the center stood a tall tree decorated with multi-colored lights, silver garland and tinsel, and countless miniature toy ornaments. A lighted angel perched on top, and a shiny electric train circled round the bottom. Two six-foot wooden nutcrackers flanked the doors of a life-sized gingerbread cottage, home to the teddy bear and doll departments. Helena wasted no time searching out the clerk and asking to see the walking dolls. The saleslady led them to a display of this year's rage—walking dolls with matching dresses for the little girls lucky enough to find this treasure under the Christmas tree.

Addy looked at the price tag and gasped. The doll cost more than what Addy's whole wardrobe was probably worth.

Unfazed, Helena continued, "We will take that doll in the white dotted Swiss outfit, and the matching girl's dress in size 8; and, one more thing, we want the electric train set that's under the tree in the other room."

The saleswoman went into the back to get a boxed train set. She carefully wrapped the gifts in children's Christmas paper, trimming each package with a large bow and ornament. By this time, Addy felt like a charity case.

"I can't let you buy all these things, Helena," Addy moaned weakly. "We never shop at expensive stores like this. Lionel will have a fit."

Helena countered, "I beg your pardon, my dear. Lionel will be in hog's heaven. I'll even buy HIM a gift or two—how about a muzzle and a noose?"

Addy laughed and resigned herself to the fact that what Helena wanted, Helena got. There would be no talking her out of these outlandishly priced toys.

Weighted down with many bundles, Helena suggested dropping the packages at the car and finishing off the afternoon with coffee and dessert at a café near the Essex Inn. "The only other place that has raisin tarts as delicious as these is in London, but we don't have enough time to fly there today," Helena joked. "We still have to find a sports shop to get the skates and toboggan. Let's plan on doing that next week," Helena said.

After dropping Addy off at home, Helena went straight to the farm to hide the children's presents in the attic. It was wonderful knowing she was using her money to make some incredible children happy this Christmas. This feeling was worth more than her collection of jewelry.

True to her word, Helena took Addy on a shopping excursion the following week. They purchased the skates and toboggan in a sports store in Middletown and found the chemistry and erector sets at a local hobby shop. On Thanksgiving, Lionel had mentioned he was going to Colorado on business after Christmas and hoped to get in some skiing. Wouldn't he be amazed that Helena actually listened to what he was saying and bought him a very expensive ski jacket? That would seal the deal: Helena would have him eating right out of her hand.

In spite of Helena's protestations, Addy knew she had to get something special for her friend for Christmas. What do you buy a woman who has everything? In one of her ladies' magazines, Addy had seen a beautifully etched crystal bedside carafe, and she was determined to order it for Helena. The cost of the carafe was almost equal to what Lionel had allotted Addy for Christmas shopping. Now that Helena had bought so many presents for the children, however, Addy did not have to pinch her pennies to provide the children with a memorable holiday. She still had enough money to buy the delicate carafe for Helena.

While Addy and Helena enthusiastically prepared for the perfect Norman Rockwell New England Christmas, Lionel counted the days until he could finally take off for Colorado. He had begun to wonder if Helena would ever hand over the farm to the Church, and lately he didn't much care. In fact, he was sick to death of his job, his wife, the kids, and even his brother the monsignor. The only thing that really mattered to him was his Mistress. Sometimes Lionel found it unbelievable that he, Lionel Roberge, had a secret life so very different from his boring existence in Chester, Connecticut.

Lionel loved his salacious secret, particularly because he was convinced that Mistress Irena was doling out his penance. He was well aware that he was a sinner, so he was grateful for each session with Mistress. She had promised him that their next meeting would be one he would never forget. After God, Mistress Irena was the one Lionel cared most about pleasing.

*　*　*　*　*

It had been almost three years since Lionel first laid eyes upon the most tantalizing woman he had ever met. The only person who came close to the beauty of this woman was someone Lionel had once seen in a photograph. When he was a boy, one of Lionel's friends had gotten his hands on some cheesecake photos of the alluring Bettie Page. Still emblazoned in his mind was the image of Bettie dressed in all black underwear: skimpy bra, revealing panties, sexy garter belt, and silk stockings. Sitting with her legs spread wide apart, she wore high-heeled black leather boots that zipped up the front. Shiny, raven black hair cut in thick bangs fell to her shoulders. The photo was not in color, but Lionel saw that her eyes were light, maybe blue. With a menacing, diabolic look on her face, Bettie was holding a whip in her hand. This scene was confusing to the young fellows; they knew lion tamers used whips but never appeared at the circus sporting only underwear. Although the boys had no idea what this picture was about, the photo aroused Lionel enormously. So often throughout his life, he closed his eyes and summoned every detail of this dark angel. Sometimes when he was ravishing Addy, he would visualize Bettie.

When attending a business conference in Colorado, Lionel was sitting at the hotel bar after a long day of meetings. In the dim, smoky light, he did not notice the woman sitting near him because he was engrossed in belting down his highballs. While he was waiting for the bartender to bring his next drink, Lionel glanced over at this woman, the only other patron in the place. Déjà-vu, apprehension, and an immediate sense of arousal grabbed Lionel like the talons of an eagle; sitting near him was the specter of his boyhood fantasies ... Bettie Page. He was loaded by now, so maybe he was seeing things. Straightening himself up, Lionel realized it could not be Bettie Page because she would be older by now, and this woman looked quite young. Still, the resemblance was unnerving. She had the same long, glistening black hair cut in bangs. A short, tight-fitting, black straight skirt, black seamed silk stockings, and black stiletto heels accentuated her perfect ass and legs. Her ample breasts peeked out from a low-cut, skin-tight, black cashmere sweater. Whoever she was, she exuded wealth, and Lionel could not take his eyes off this beauty.

Feeling Lionel ogling at her, the woman fired him a look of disgust, threw a wad of cash on the bar and then got up and walked away. Lionel sat motionless, dumbfounded by what had just happened. When the bartender came over to fill his glass, Lionel, gaining his composure, remarked, "Who is that skirt? She sure is a looker."

The bartender snickered, "Forget about her. That's Irene Bauer. Daughter of a big-shot senator, and married at that. A real cold fish. She pays me well to keep my mouth shut whenever she checks in. Beautiful, rich, and a bitch." The bartender smiled at his own rhyme.

Guzzling his last drink, Lionel rummaged for his wallet and tossed a few dollars on the bar. The bartender looked at the measly bills, barely enough to cover Lionel's tab. "Jerk," he mumbled under his breath.

It was nearly 3:00 a.m. as Lionel staggered up to his hotel room. Damn it. He had to get up by 7:00 a.m. He set the alarm, collapsed fully dressed onto the bed, and immediately fell into a deep sleep. The loud ringing of the alarm clock disturbed him way too soon.

His head pounding with a hangover, Lionel lumbered robotically to the bathroom to shower and shave. It was going to be another long, boring day. Every time there was a break in the meetings, Lionel looked around for the woman he had seen the previous night at the bar. The conference would be over in two days, and he just had to meet her.

While Lionel searched for Irene, she was still upstairs in bed, nursing her own hangover. Irene liked this hotel because the exquisite penthouse suite was very private. She phoned room service for coffee, and then propped pillows behind her back. Almost instantly, the waiter was at the door. Irene buzzed him in.

"Are you sure you don't want anything else besides coffee, Miss Bauer?" the butler asked attentively.

"No thanks, Ken; I'm not hungry this morning."

Ken laughed, "You mean this AFTERNOON. It's about one o'clock."

Irene smiled teasingly, then said, "I have to get my beauty sleep, you know."

She told Kenneth to take some money from her purse on the table. He showed her that he took a dollar, but she told him to take five. She liked Kenneth and always asked for him when she stayed at this hotel. He was quiet and discreet – a "live and let live" kind of guy.

Ken had wheeled the cart next to the bed, and Irene poured herself a steaming cup of coffee. Another thing Irene loved about this hotel was that their coffee was always fresh and hot.

As Irene sat back sipping her breakfast, she asked herself what the hell she was doing in this place. Hers was an aimless life. Yes, she was the daughter of Senator Neal Richter and wife of Attorney Samuel Bauer. Irene was the only child of Neal and Sally Richter. The couple met in college and was still nauseatingly in love. In fact, Irene often wondered why they had even bothered to have a child. Flossie, the same nanny who had fostered her mother, raised her. As far as Irene was concerned, Flossie was the only parent she ever had.

Irene's mother Sally had grown up in the South, where prominent families still maintained a staff to run the household. When Sally moved to Colorado after she married Neal, Flossie moved with her. Flossie had never married; her identity intertwined first with Sally's and now Irene's. She raised the two of them as if they were her own, guiding them with her love, wisdom, and kindness. A devout Christian, Flossie often quoted the Bible when she taught the girls life lessons. Irene's family, on the other hand, feigned Lutheranism, but it was all for show. They made an appearance in church every Sunday and contributed large amounts to the coffers, but that was about it.

Irene was shipped off to boarding school when she was eight years old. She and Flossie had a hard time parting, but Irene's parents assured her she would get to see Flossie during school holidays. It was traumatic sending a child so young to boarding school; perhaps that was why Irene had very few memories of the early years of her education. By the time she reached junior level, the once quiet and timid Irene had turned into a rebellious girl filled with resentment for her parents, and lashed out at them by getting herself into predicaments. On a few occasions, her father had to plead with the administration to keep Irene at the school. Senator Richter's large donations always helped convince the headmaster to give his daughter another chance. Her father's money motivated even the most upstanding of institutions to look the other way. In addition, the last thing Miss Astor's Preparatory School for Girls wanted was negative press.

Miss Astor's was not all that bad. Albeit there were a lot of silly rituals and codes, but fortunately, Irene fit in rather well. When Irene's insurrections won the admiration and respect of some of the other girls, she flourished from the attention, and her aberrant behavior escalated. Once, Irene ran away from school and convinced her schoolmate, Lisbeth Washington, to go with her. Although Lisbeth knew they were committing a grievous crime against the school, she was too much in awe of Irene to refuse her proposal. After all, Irene was smart, pretty, brave, and popular, too. The girls had not worked out a plan, and once they scaled the tall, black iron fence, terrified Lisbeth began to cry.

"Why did we do this, Irene?" she bawled. "My parents will kill me, and we'll get thrown out of school."

Calmly, Irene replied, "Trust me. My father will make sure they don't expel us. Now let's head for the train station." At least Irene had brought along a large sum of money, expecting they could hop a train to nowhere. By the time the escapees reached the train station, however, the police were already there to take them back to school.

The girls rode silently in the back of the police car while Lisbeth cried softly. All Irene could think about was they had gotten as far as the train station and were now riding home in a cruiser. At least Irene had succeeded in stirring up the administration.

It was just before dawn when Irene and Lisbeth arrived at the school, and most of the girls were in their bathrobes, peeking out their bedroom doors. The headmaster and other staff members were waiting nervously outside the front entrance. After a quiet conversation with the police officers, imploring them to keep this out of the newspapers, Headmaster Walker told Irene and Lisbeth to go up to bed. From the look of anger on his face, the girls knew this incident was far from over.

When Lisbeth and Irene went upstairs, their classmates, in hushed tones, begged the girls to tell them what had happened. The pair of delinquents was so tired, however, they promised to give their friends a blow-by-blow account of their escapade in the morning. Irene planned to embellish the tale and hoped Lisbeth would go along with it.

The maid came up earlier than usual to wake Irene and Lisbeth. Apparently, both the girls' parents were waiting in the headmaster's study. Lisbeth looked horrified knowing her family was drawn into this mess. Irene, so used to reprimand, was not the least bit concerned that her father was there again. While Lisbeth scrambled nervously to get dressed, Irene yawned and purposely dressed slowly.

When the girls got downstairs, Irene's father and both Lisbeth's parents were seated outside the headmaster's lavish study. Irene didn't expect to see her own mother there. Sally Richter maintained unpleasant encounters were too much on her delicate nerves. She was, after all, a Southern belle. The headmaster called the girls into his study individually, Lisbeth going first.

When she came out crying, Irene figured Lisbeth spilled the

beans, telling the headmaster it was all Irene's idea. Next, Irene went in for her interrogation. She took blame for the whole incident but was stunned when the headmaster said Lisbeth assumed responsibility for everything. Well, the fainthearted Lisbeth had not ratted out Irene after all. From that day on, Lisbeth became one of Irene's most trusted pals.

Lisbeth's parents and Irene's father were summoned individually followed by each girl called in with her own parents. Finally, the headmaster invited the whole flock into his kingly chambers. Irene had been a guest in there many times and always admired the shiny wood floor-to-ceiling bookcases filled with works of classical literature. Plush velvet brocade chairs, an ornately carved mahogany desk, and oriental rugs carried Irene's imagination to a scene in the life of poet Robert Browning and his forbidden courtship of poet Elizabeth Barrett.

When Irene's consciousness drifted back into the present, she caught the headmaster droning on about how, in most cases, the girls' actions would lead to expulsion. Because Lisbeth had never been in trouble, it would be unfair to dismiss her, and the headmaster did not mention Irene's former transgressions in front of Lisbeth's parents. He knew full well Irene's father would once again pay the school for keeping silent, and Miss Astor's could really use the money for dormitory renovations.

The headmaster issued a warning, and revoked all privileges until further notice. Everyone had to agree verbally that this was fair punishment, and all present signed off on the reprimand documents. The meeting ended near lunchtime so the headmaster dismissed the girls to the refectory. The parents stayed behind and exchanged pleasantries, but under his feigned cheerfulness, Lisbeth's dad, Mr. Worthington, was seething. He knew Senator Richter's daughter was untouchable and knew Irene was a bad influence on Lisbeth. He would see to it that Lisbeth stayed away from that wild child of Richter's.

For punishment, Irene and Lisbeth had to help the cook staff peel vegetables for lunch and dinner; clear the tables and sweep the refectory floor after each meal; go straight up to their rooms after dinner with no dessert; and not listen to their phonograph records. Some of the girls snickered at them, but most of their classmates felt sorry.   When their month of punishment concluded, Lisbeth and Irene had to write a five-page essay describing how they would amend their behavior to comply with the code of ethics at Miss Astor's School. In addition, they had to write letters of apology to their parents and the headmaster. The incident sealed the bond of friendship between the two renegades, and Lisbeth and Irene asked to be roommates the next school year.   Of course, Mr. Worthington adamantly opposed, but Mrs. Worthington and Lisbeth convinced him that Irene was fully reformed ... she had not gotten into any trouble and was receiving honor grades. Lisbeth was a good influence on Irene, and the two had become like sisters. The girls went on to room together through the end of junior level into their senior level.

By now, Irene and her classmates had reached the appropriate age to attend the four dances sponsored each year by Miss Astor's: Halloween Masquerade, Yuletide Formal, Spring Ball, and finally, Prom. Only one boys' academy was invited to the dances so as not to overwhelm the girls. Most often there were enough boys to go around, and the dances were heavily chaperoned by staff from Miss Astor's and the boys' academy.

With her shiny black locks, porcelain skin, and sapphire blue eyes, Irene had blossomed into a classic beauty. Some of the girls nicknamed her "Snow White," but Irene retorted, "Then where the heck is my prince charming?"

Although her dance card was always the first to be filled, Irene never found a boy who really interested her. By their last year at Miss Astor's, many girls were writing to young men who had attended one of the dances. After all, what was the purpose of finishing school if not to find the proper husband?

It was near the end of the Yuletide Formal, and although Irene had a boy's name on her dance card, she asked him if he would not mind too much if she sat that one out. Her feet hurt. Lisbeth had insisted she buy these gorgeous see-through pumps decorated with crystals, just like Cinderella's glass slippers. Well, Cinderella had gotten to take her shoes off at midnight, and Irene was just about to do the same. Lisbeth had also convinced Irene to buy a white chiffon floor-length ball gown with a strapless sweetheart neckline. The red satin sash around Irene's tiny waist matched perfectly with the red roses in her chignon. She wore simple, but terribly expensive, matching diamond earrings and necklace.

As Irene sat there trying to remove her shoes inconspicuously, she felt someone standing in front of her. Looking up with a start, she saw a young man she did not recall having seen before. He was tall, slender, and strikingly handsome, dressed to perfection in a winter-white dinner jacket, a red cummerbund, black trousers, and a red bow tie. Most of the young men wore black, but this fellow stood out from the rest.

"May I have this dance?" he said confidently. "I know I'm not on your dance card, but I just noticed you now. You are stunning."

Irene struggled to put her feet back into her shoes without using her hands, but it was impossible. She stammered, "My feet hurt so I took off my shoes." "Well, let me help you get them back on, Cinderella." The words had no sooner descended from his lips than he was down on one knee, searching discreetly under her gown.

Chapter XV

Disastrous Alliances

As this mysterious prince gently slid her feet back into her pumps, Irene noticed the young man who was originally supposed to have the last few dances with her.

Although Irene could always hold her own, this gorgeous prince rattled her, and stammering, she said, "Thanks, but that boy had signed my dance card, and I asked him if he wouldn't mind if I sat the last numbers out because my feet hurt so much ..."

"Then he should have offered to help you put your shoes back on," said the confident prince. He took both of Irene's hands, pulling her caringly to her feet. "Do you think you will be able to dance now?" he asked as he guided her cautiously to the dance floor. Irene snuck a peek at his face. As Lisbeth would say, "He is to die for!" With chiseled features like a marble statue of a Greek god, and wavy jet-black hair and intense blue eyes like hers, this young man could be her Gemini twin. Irene had heard that for some primeval reason, women find a large Adam's apple very erotic, and he had a good-sized one. As soon as he held her close, Irene felt comfortable and safe. As he pulled her closer, she could hear his breathing quicken. "You smell nice," he whispered.

"You do, too," Irene said breathlessly. She had never felt this way before. At that moment, the orchestra and vocalist broke into "The Christmas Waltz" from Frank Sinatra's dreamy album, *A Jolly Christmas*. She and Lisbeth loved Frank Sinatra and always listened to "The Christmas Waltz" to get into the holiday spirit. Neither girl ever imagined she would be floating to this song with an ideal partner.

As her prince pulled her even closer, Irene could feel a large bulge in the front of his pants. She had been aware of a bulge when other boys danced with her, but she had always quickly pulled away. This time, she wanted to get closer and closer. Her face reddened as she placed her cheek upon his hot skin. The exquisite couple, throbbing with beauty and youth, whirled passionately into oblivion.

The orchestra stopped playing "The Christmas Waltz" and moved seamlessly into "Irene Goodnight." As Irene sleepily came to, she laughed and startled her prince.

"What's so funny?" he questioned somewhat apprehensively.

"That's my name. I'm Irene."

"Well, hello Irene. I'm Glenn. Nice to meet you."

When the chaperones switched on the bright lights, a shared groan rose from the dance floor as the enchanted couples realized the magical ball had come to an end. This year's Yuletide was especially lovely. The decorating committee had worked tirelessly, transforming the ballroom into the winter scene from *The Nutcracker Ballet,* to the smallest detail of white confetti floating down gently on the dancers at the end of the night. Some of the couples scrambled to exchange addresses before the cars arrived to transport the boys back to their school.

Glenn politely asked Irene if he might write to her. Having come to her senses and not wanting to appear too eager, Irene leafed slowly through her dance card booklet to find a suitable page ... one that would show Glenn just how many boys signed her card. She scribbled the school's address and phone number on the top of the page, ripped it from the booklet, and handed it to Glenn. Without saying a word, he leaned over, gave her a kiss on the forehead, and then walked to the coatroom.

By the time all the boys had left, it was after midnight. The girls got their wraps and strolled dreamily to their dorms. Once Lisbeth and Irene were in the privacy of their rooms, Lisbeth whispered loudly, "Who was that dreamboat you were dancing with at the end of the night?"

Irene realized she never did get Glenn's last name. Trying to sound indifferent she replied, "Oh, just another boy." Then smiling joyfully, she ran over to Lisbeth and hugged her. Both girls jumped with glee. "Oh, Lisbeth, I think this is love at first sight. Do you think he'll write to me?"

Always her enthusiast, Lisbeth responded, "Of course he will. He'd have to be crazy not to. You were the most beautiful girl at the Yuletide."

Exhausted, the girls unfastened each other's gowns, throwing their dresses in a heap on the floor. Then stripping down to their undergarments, they flopped on their beds, pulled up the covers, and fell fast asleep.

Knowing the students had been up until nearly dawn, the cooks prepared a late Sunday brunch. When Lisbeth and Irene strolled into the refectory, some of the girls glared resentfully at the jovial pair. Glenn was one of the most attractive boys at the ball last night, and lucky Irene ended up with him. Irene whispered to Lisbeth, "They think I'm wild. Maybe they think I threw myself at Glenn."

"Just ignore them, Irene," Lisbeth assured her. "They are green with envy."

Two days after the dance, Irene found a letter from Glenn in her post box. She tucked the letter into her Latin book, hoping she could be disciplined enough to save it to read at bedtime.

That evening after homework and a bath, Irene propped herself up in bed to pore over her precious epistle. It was just one page and not too wordy. Glenn wrote that he was traveling to Canada with his school's hockey team right after Christmas, but he expected to return soon after New Year's. He gave Irene his home address and asked for hers so that they could make plans to meet during the winter vacation. He wished her a very "Merry Christmas," then ended the letter in French:

"Je compte les jours jusqu'à ce que je vois ta belle visage un fois de plus. S'il vous plaît attendez-moi de vous embrasser passionnément."

Lisbeth, pretending to be asleep, popped up and exclaimed, "What did he say?"

Irene, looking as if Cupid's arrow pierced her heart, said in a faraway voice, "He wants to see me during winter break ... and ... he wrote in FRENCH!"

"Do you read French?" Lisbeth asked naively.

"Of course I do. Every cultured woman should know French," said Irene with an air of sophistication.

"Well, translate it for me. I guess I'm not cultured, 'cuz I don't know French, but I'm going to take it in college."

Irene didn't really know that much French, but she bluffed her way through. "He says ... I count the days ... until we meet again ... and I want to ... KISS YOU PASSIONATELY!"

Lisbeth let out a spontaneous "WHOOPEE!"

Irene suddenly looked worried. "How will I convince my parents to let me see him?"

"Don't worry," Lisbeth assured her. "We'll think of something. Maybe you can pretend you are visiting me. Or maybe you can meet him at my house. Now go to sleep. It's late."

"Lisbeth, you are a genius and the best friend a girl could ever have. Let's always be friends, OK?"

Lisbeth did not answer. She had already drifted off to dreamland.

* * * * *

The two-day train trip from New York to Colorado gave Irene plenty of time to think. She knew her parents would not be at the station to meet her but would send the driver. Mother was always so busy at this time of year with charity work, holiday parties, and non-stop shopping. Daddy, the perpetual campaigner, would be occupied with political hobnobbing, fundraising, and speaking engagements. Her mother was an empty-headed, over-dressed, helpless Southern belle, her dad a phony self-centered blabbermouth. Irene knew these were mean thoughts to have about one's parents, but she just couldn't help herself. In the eyes of the world, Irene was the pretty, smart, privileged child of rich, important parents. Yet, Irene would gladly change places with a girl who might have less but was certain her parents wanted and loved her.

As a toddler, when Irene was sick with fever, it was Flossie who sat by her bedside, sponging her forehead with cool water. If nightmares awakened Irene, Flossie came to her room and soothed her back to sleep with lullabies.

Irene had booked a lovely private room on the Pullman sleeping car but spent the last few hours of her trip in the lounge. Although Irene was not of drinking age, the porters would never ask a wealthy young woman for identification when she needed a glass or two of wine to calm her nerves.

It was dark by the time the train finally arrived at her station, and Irene had dropped off to sleep. "Miss. We're almost here, Miss," the porter repeated gently as if he hated to disturb the young lady who had been so kind and gracious to him.

Irene, still drowsy from the wine, suddenly came to and smiled at the porter. She furtively handed him a twenty dollar bill. Surprised once again by her generosity, he thanked her profusely. After all, it was Christmastime, and she was sure he had a family.

"No ... thank YOU," Irene said sincerely, "and Merry Christmas!" Irene hated that there was one set of rules for white men and another for everyone else. Most wealthy white people expected poorer people to wait upon them. Many freed slaves made their way north and vied for the "coveted" job of Pullman porter. In fact, Flossie was proud that her own brother was a member of **The Brotherhood of Sleeping Car Porters** and made a whole $82 a month. Irene did not want to hurt Flossie's feelings, but if you divide that into at least 13 hours work a day, it's peanuts.

Hiss .... Screech, the train pulling into the station interrupted Irene's thoughts. She tried to rub the steam from the window with a napkin, but she could see nothing. Yawning and stretching, Irene reached for her train case and pocketbook and then headed toward the exit. When the door opened, a blast of freezing air blew Irene's hair across her face so she could hardly make her way down the stairs. It was snowing heavily, and as she pushed her hair away from her face, she squinted to figure out which one of the shadowy figures on the platform was the family's driver. For a moment, Irene worried that maybe no one had come to meet her. It would not be the first time her parents had forgotten when she would be arriving. Then she heard someone faintly calling, "Irene, Irene."

Irene immediately recognized the voice of her own darling Flossie. What a wonderful surprise. Flossie had never come to the station before. Maybe this was a sign that her winter vacation was going to be a good one. Irene ran to Flossie and hugged her tightly.

Overcome with joy, Flossie exclaimed, "Oh, Miss Irene, it's so good to have you home."

Irene was equally delighted and teased, "Oh, Miss Flossie, it's so good to be home."

The driver loaded Irene's fine Hartmann luggage into the car, and they drove off slowly into the snowy night. When they finally arrived at the Richter mansion, the outdoor lights, still gleaming, cast prisms and gems of color on the peaceful, fresh snow ... a scene on an expensive Christmas card. The butler greeted them warmly at the front door and told Irene the driver and he would bring her bags up to her room. As she expected, her parents were not around.

Flossie had made one of Irene's favorite wintertime dishes—chicken potpie. As she sat at the kitchen table wolfing down the scrumptious meal, Irene said between mouthfuls, "Flossie, I met a boy—a nice boy—he wants to see me during my vacation." Looking deeply concerned, Flossie said, "Now Miss Irene, you know how your parents feel about boys."

"I don't care," Irene said obstinately. "Flossie, you are always on my side. Will you help me to see him? I know you will like him."

Flossie smiled and promised she would do everything she could. By this time, Irene could hardly keep her eyes open. "Why don't you go on up to bed, precious? There are plenty of fresh nightgowns in your lingerie chest, and we can unpack your bags in the morning."

"OK, Miss Flossie," Irene yawned. "That was such a delicious meal. Thanks." Irene hugged Flossie and kissed her "good night."

* * * * *

Although Irene's parents showered her with lavish Christmas presents as usual and sponsored a glorious open house for New Year's Eve, Irene couldn't have cared less. The days dragged on as she waited impatiently to hear from Glenn. On January 4, the phone finally rang, and Irene's life changed forever. Glenn.

Irene could barely speak. At first, they made small talk about how the holidays went, and then Glenn said in a husky voice, "I can't wait to see you again." Irene could not believe that Glenn's hometown was Broomfield, Colorado, about twenty miles from her town, Golden. This must be fate. Glenn went on to say that his father was traveling to Golden for business, and Glenn wanted to accompany him to meet Irene. At that moment, Irene did not care what her parents said. She made up her mind she was going to see Glenn.

"Of course I can see you. I'm looking forward to it," Irene replied, trying to sound confident but shaking inside. Glenn sounded thrilled and told her he would call her when he arrived at the hotel where his dad and he would be staying. Irene couldn't wait to tell Flossie because she knew Flossie would tell her how to handle the situation.

When Flossie went upstairs that night to wish Irene "pleasant dreams," Irene shared her delicious secret with her confidant. At first, Flossie looked perplexed, but as she had promised, she came up with a plan. "You just have to have that boy over for lunch. That way, your parents can see him, and if he's as nice as you say he is, everything will be fine." Irene was disappointed in the plan, but she knew Flossie was right.

When Glenn finally arrived in Golden and called Irene from the hotel, she invited him over for lunch the next day. With no hesitation, he responded, "I'd love that if it's not too much trouble."

Flossie had groomed Irene's parents for Glenn's visit, telling them that Irene was of the age when girls start noticing boys. Flossie said that if parents try to keep boys and girls apart, the kids would draw even closer to one another. She hesitantly admitted that when she was young, she used to have clandestine meetings with a boy. "You, Flossie?" Irene's mother said. "Why I just don't believe it." Flossie smiled as she recalled her first love, wondering what ever did happen to him.

The next day, Irene dressed for lunch in the lovely pink angora sweater Flossie had given her for Christmas and the string of pearls her parents had presented. With her grey wool straight skirt and high-heel pumps, she looked chic and sophisticated. Fortunately, her parents had a prior commitment that day so Irene was ecstatic. She had been sure her parents would have embarrassed her, and now Flossie would be able to provide a glowing review of Glenn. The wait staff served lunch to the young couple in the formal dining room, and Flossie looked in on them from time to time.

Glenn tried not to stare at the crystal chandelier and the collection of original artwork. He knew his art and was certain he saw a breathtaking landscape by Robert Scott Duncanson. He doubted if Irene's parents, who still seemed to maintain "slaves," knew this artist was not white.

Glenn was rather reserved during lunch, and Irene asked him if everything was OK. Did he like the food?

To the contrary, he loved the food but blurted out, "I can see from your home that your parents are wealthy. I have to tell you that my family doesn't have money. My father owns a hardware store in Broomfield, and I am in prep school on a hockey scholarship."

Irene laughed. "Is that all? Don't be too impressed. My father inherited his money from his parents who were savvy enough to have invested in gold and uranium mines here in Colorado. My mother likes to pretend she is a descendant of Southern plantation owners, but I think her lineage is linked more closely to carpetbaggers. At least your father works for a living."

183

Glenn laughed and stopped thinking about Irene's wealth. After all, we cannot choose our parents. She looked so beautiful today, and he wanted to ravage her.

Instead, they retired chastely to the parlor where the maid served them coffee and dessert. Flossie had stopped popping in to check on them so Glenn had the nerve to hold Irene's hand. With one eye on the door, he put his arm around her shoulder and kissed her. This was Irene's first real kiss, and it was lovelier than she could have ever imagined.

By the time Glenn was ready to leave, the sun was setting. He asked Irene if he could see her again tomorrow, and she immediately consented. This time he would treat her to lunch at the hotel where his father and he were staying.

Glenn sought out Flossie and the wait staff to thank them for the wonderful lunch and for making his visit so enjoyable. As soon as Glenn left, Irene went immediately to work plotting how she could escape tomorrow to meet him at the hotel. Although she would feel dreadful about it, she may even have to lie to Flossie.

That night Irene called Lisbeth to ask her advice, and the two chums devised a plan. Irene would say that Lisbeth was also coming to town and would accompany Irene and Glenn to lunch. If by chance anyone saw Irene and Glenn at lunch at the hotel, she could say Lisbeth had to cancel at the last minute.

Flossie gave Irene's parents a flattering review of Glenn, describing him as a very well mannered, intelligent, and handsome young man. Her parents trusted Flossie's judgment so their misgivings about Glenn faded. Surprisingly, they agreed that Irene could go into town to meet Lisbeth and Glenn for lunch.

The next day, Irene had the driver drop her off at the train depot where she was supposedly meeting Lisbeth. Once the driver was out of view, Irene walked briskly to the hotel. Glenn was waiting for her in the lavish restaurant, and they had such fun over lunch. Irene mentioned that she would have to call the driver to pick her up, and Glenn suggested she call from his room. He whispered in her ear, "I have to have you all to myself before I go."

Irene's heart raced. How could she be alone with a boy in a hotel room? She had been warned repeatedly at school that things like this could lead to a girl "getting in trouble." Her voice quivering, Irene asked, "What about your father? What if he comes back and finds us in the room?" She continued nervously, "You have to be married to go into a hotel room together. What if the front desk clerk sees us going up in the elevator together? He might report us."

Glenn laughed. "First of all, my father isn't due back until after dinner, and second, we can take the stairs instead of the elevator. Besides, you are just coming up to use the phone."

Irene knew this was not a good idea, but she didn't want to risk losing Glenn. Hesitantly, she agreed to go upstairs.

Right after Glenn closed the hotel room door behind him, he gently led Irene over to the bed. He immediately kissed her passionately, and she responded willingly with equal desire. He slowly unbuttoned her blouse, unfastened her bra, caressing her breasts and kissing her erect nipples. Moving his hand up her leg to her garter belt and stockings, he pushed the crotch of her panties aside and tenderly inserted his finger into her vagina then slowly moved his finger in and out, in and out. Moaning with pleasure, he moved his finger more rapidly, in and out, in and out. Suddenly he stopped. "You had better call the driver," he said. Irene was devastated. What had gone wrong? Glenn offered an immediate explanation. "You haven't been with a boy before, have you?" Irene did not know if she should lie and say, "Of course I have." Then he might think she was a nymphomaniac. She had better tell the truth.

Glenn said he had never "gone all the way" with a girl because he didn't want to get her pregnant. Boys could not go into drugstores and buy rubbers as grown married men could. At first, Irene was disappointed that Glenn had stopped but then realized the wisdom of his words. The last thing she needed was to get pregnant out of wedlock. They were too young to get married so it was good that Glenn had self-control.

Irene disappeared into the bathroom to freshen up, and then came out to call the driver. She told him to pick her up at the train depot. Glowing with womanliness, Irene gave Glenn a passionate kiss. They were both aroused, but Glenn once again applied the brakes. Although neither of them verbalized it, the afternoon created a bond between them that nothing could break. They belonged to each other.

For the rest of their time at prep school, Glenn and Irene wrote every night and managed to see each other as often as possible. Glenn got a scholarship to Brown, and Irene was going to Skidmore. They had tried to arrange it so they could attend college closer to one another, but Glenn had to accept the scholarship.

Throughout college, neither of them dated anyone else. Irene's parents liked Glenn well enough, however, frequently made reference to the fact that Glenn's family did not have money. Glenn's family adored Irene, but they, too, had misgivings. Irene's parents were so rich.

Glenn presented Irene with an engagement ring at the end of their senior year in college, and they each vowed not to tell their parents. Neither of them obtained degrees that prepared them to work, but they did not care. Glenn had saved up money from summer jobs, and he was going to buy a motorcycle. Irene had her own money. They would travel around the United States, working odd jobs if necessary, enjoying the freedom and adventure of life on the road.

Although Irene trusted Flossie implicitly, she could not share her secret with even Flossie. Flossie would never betray Irene, yet once a secret is spoken, it takes on a life of its own. Ironically, Irene inadvertently betrayed herself.

Right after graduation, Irene moved back home. She still had not figured out how she would sneak away with Glenn so she called Lisbeth for advice. Although Lisbeth had gone to Swarthmore, she and Irene remained as close as ever. Irene was excitingly telling Lisbeth about Glenn's and her plan to take off. Unaware that her bedroom door was open, and her father was listening, Irene talked freely to Lisbeth about her upcoming adventure.

Irene's father never let on that he knew about Glenn and his daughter's clandestine plans. One evening when Irene was up in her room reading, the doorbell rang. Her father answered, and Irene was sure she heard Glenn's father speaking. She tiptoed to the staircase, hunching down behind the rails.

Her father was saying, "I'm sure you can understand our position. Irene and Glenn are so young, and as much as they think they are in love, it's just puppy love." Irene could not make out everything Glenn's father was saying, but he left soon after he arrived. She did catch what was probably the most important part of the conversation: "Thank you so much, Mr. Richter. Glenn's brother will start college next year, and there is no scholarship for him. This will really help."

Irene was confused. Had her eyes deceived her, or had her father passed money to Glenn's dad? If so, then why? Overcome by curiosity, Irene marched downstairs to find out why Glenn's father had come to their house. At first, her father was tongue-tied. Pulling on the knot of his necktie as if it were a noose, Irene's father stated coldly, "I paid him so Glenn will not run off with you."

Irene was dumbfounded. How in the hell did he find this out? Her father continued, "I heard you talking to Lisbeth the other evening, and I had to put a stop to this. You aren't thinking straight, Irene. You can't marry that boy. How will he ever support you?"

Her father's words stabbed her heart. Screaming, she raced up to her room to call Glenn.

His mother answered the phone, and Irene could tell she was upset, too. "Mrs. Devereux, may I please speak to Glenn?"

"Sure, dear, I'll go get him." The phone was silent as Mrs. Devereux went upstairs to Glenn's room. When he came downstairs to get the phone, Irene immediately uttered, "Glenn, do you know about my father's dirty dealings? He is paying your father so you won't marry me."

Glenn was mute at first. His voice cracked as he responded, "Yes, I do."

Irene shouted, "You are not going to go along with it, are you?"

Glenn said, "I have no choice. Your father will disown you if you marry me."

"I don't care, Glenn. You and I can earn our own money," Irene begged.

"Your father said he'll make sure I never get a job anywhere. My parents are sending me to France to live with my uncle."

Irene began to wail loudly and hung up the phone. Sobbing uncontrollably, she threw herself on to the bed. Flossie came to her aid, but she didn't even feel like talking to Flossie.

Glenn called every day, but she would not speak to him. Finally, he showed up at her house. She was alone. Irene just had to see him before he left for France, so she let him in. He held her close, and they both cried. Then Irene had an idea. Before he left, they should go all the way. They hadn't done that before, but what did they have to lose now? Glenn agreed. He even said that if she became pregnant, their parents would have to let them get married. Irene and Glenn went up to her room, crawled into her bed, and made love for the first time. It was more wonderful than Irene could have ever imagined.

Glenn was to leave in a week, so he came to pick up Irene whenever he could. They drove to a remote wooded area, took a blanket out of the car trunk, and made sweet love repeatedly, each time they met. Irene knew she belonged to Glenn, and he belonged to her. They would eventually be together. When Irene was old enough to have access to her trust fund from her grandmother, she would take the money and go to France.

On the day that Glenn left, Irene stayed in her room crying. After three days, Irene received a letter from Glenn telling her how much he missed and longed for her. They wrote to each other every night. Glenn was an accomplished writer. His descriptions of France made Irene feel as if she were right there with him.

After Glenn had been in France for three months, his letters became more sporadic. Irene panicked, writing him daily, asking him why he didn't write as often. He told her he had found a job teaching English, and he was also busy helping his uncle in the bakery.

Irene had been feeling awfully sick lately. In fact, she had thrown up several mornings. Flossie kept a careful eye on Irene and feared the worst. What if she were pregnant? Flossie came into her room one evening and pulled a chair up next to Irene's bed.

"Honey," Flossie began, "I've been noticing that you are sick in the mornings. Tell me, how long has it been since you had your last menstruation?" At first, Irene was taken aback by Flossie's intimate question. "Why do you ask, Flossie?" Irene queried.

"Miss Irene, I think you may be pregnant. Did you have sexual intercourse with that boy?"

Irene hesitated, put her head down, and then said softly, "Yes. I did."

Flossie put her hands to her face and said, "Oh God. Your parents are sure to blame me. I was the one who helped you to date Glenn."

"Sometimes my menstrual period isn't regular, Flossie," Irene said, now starting to panic.

"Irene, I am going to take you to my doctor; he will tell you for sure. Meanwhile, let's just pray it's not true."

Irene laughed and said, "Don't worry, Flossie. Glenn and I hoped I would get pregnant so he would have to marry me. We want to be married."

With a worried look on her face, Flossie said, "Good night now, child. I have to figure out how to get you to my doctor without your mother knowing."

Irene did go to Flossie's doctor and found out that she was, indeed, pregnant. She immediately started imagining how her child would look, and what she would name him or her. At the same time, Flossie felt overwhelmingly distressed by the news.

She knew that Irene's parents would never let her keep Glenn's child.

Irene wanted to wait a short time before she wrote to Glenn about the good news of her pregnancy. She hadn't heard from him in several days, and in the back of her mind, she feared he might not be pleased with her news. What if he no longer wanted to marry her?

Glenn's letter arrived before Irene could write to him. It said, "Irene, darling, I don't know how to tell you this. You were my one and only love, but it is not realistic for us to think we can ever marry. Now that I am so far away from home, I have had a chance to really think things over. I love it here in France, and I have met a French girl. She does not have your qualities, but she has things about her that are marvelous. She is from a working class family, and to her, I seem rich. I am sorry to hurt you, Irene, but I know in time you will heal and find a man who is better suited to your station in life." Irene read the letter again. She could not believe what it said and started to whimper like a wounded animal.

"Flossie, Flossie, please come here."

"What's wrong baby?" Terrorized, Flossie came running to her room.

"Flossie, he has another girl. He doesn't want to marry me. What am I going to do?"

"But did you tell him about the baby?" Flossie said, hopefully.

"No, and I'm not going to tell him. He knew there was a chance of this happening, but he still went and found himself a French whore," Irene cried.

"Irene, we have to tell your mother. That baby's in you to stay, and we have to see what your mother wants you to do with it. You'll be showing soon."

"MY MOTHER?"

"Irene, she will help you, I know she will. She has a good heart. I will tell her if you want me to."

Irene was numb. What would she do with a baby? Would her parents send her away and make her put the baby up for adoption? Why should she suffer through a pregnancy so another woman could have her baby? Should she keep the baby? That would ruin her chances of ever finding a husband. No, she wanted to get rid of it, if she could. She didn't want Glenn's demon growing inside her.

Flossie broke the news to Mrs. Richter, and Irene's mom cried brokenheartedly. "Flossie, you are going to take Irene to London. She can get an abortion there. That is what we have to do."

Flossie's heart broke to think poor Miss Irene would have to go through that. She grieved, too, for the baby that would never be, but it wasn't her place to tell Irene what to do. After all, she was the one who condoned Irene's romance with Glenn. Flossie never dreamed Glenn would be the kind of boy to take advantage of a girl.

Mrs. Richter told her husband that because Irene had been so devastated by the news of Glenn's having found another girl, Irene needed to get away. Mrs. Richter loved London, but had too many commitments to make the trip with Flossie and Irene. Mr. Richter thought it was a splendid idea. He was sick of seeing Irene moping around the house like a lovesick puppy.

Mrs. Richter procured a lavish suite in the beautiful Browns Hotel in London. Although abortion was against the law in the United States as well as in England, the British didn't seem to be as hysterical about it. One of Mrs. Richter's married socialite friends got pregnant by her lover and had gone to a doctor in London. She found this doctor to have a spotless clinic with great follow-up care. The procedure was without incident. All the time, this woman's husband thought she was on a shopping trip in England.

Luckily, Mrs. Richter remembered the name of the doctor because it was much like her own last name. It was Rich—Alcott Rich—thank God she could recall it. The last thing she wanted to do was to consult that blabbermouth socialite about Irene's abortion. It would be all over town that Sally Richter was inquiring about an abortion.

* * * * *

When Flossie and Irene arrived in London, they took a sightseeing bus around the city. Irene's heart wasn't in it, but she knew that this was a once-in-a-lifetime trip for Flossie. Mrs. Richter had given them plenty of money to shop and eat, so they did a lot of that, too.

The appointment with Dr. Rich was scheduled for the third day of their trip. Irene was very nervous, but Flossie assured her that Mrs. Richter's wealthy friend would never go to a doctor who was not the cream of the crop. Flossie and Irene rode to the clinic in a taxi. Irene told Flossie that she didn't have to stay with her, but she knew Flossie would never let her go through this by herself. Irene had never had an internal examination, and she dreaded the thought of it.

Dr. Rich gave a mild anesthesia. He didn't want her to be too groggy because this was not a hospital setting. The nurse had Irene get undressed and change into a hospital gown. Irene had to climb up onto the examining table and put her feet up in the stirrups, which forced her to spread her legs. She shook with fear and embarrassment. Then, the nurse draped a sheet across her abdomen, so Irene could not see what the doctor would be doing.

When the doctor came into the room, he immediately stuck a freezing cold tool inside Irene's vagina and turned something on the side of the tool to allow the vagina to open wide. This was so humiliating and painful. The pain was just beginning. He then inserted something like a dental drill into Irene to go up into her uterus and scrape out the baby. Irene let out a low scream, and the doctor said, "It won't be much longer. Hang on."

It was much longer, and Irene could feel blood gushing out all over her thighs and the table. After what seemed like an eternity of pain, the doctor said, "That's it. How do you feel?"

"Sore," Irene said truthfully.

Dr. Rich said quietly, "That is to be expected. You will have a heavy menstrual period for a few days and will need extra thick sanitary napkins. The nurse will give you a box to take with you. Just rest here on the table for as long as you want."

"You mean I am not going to stay overnight in a hospital?" Irene asked, frightened.

"No, this isn't a serious operation, and my clinic isn't open all night. Do you have a place to stay?"

Irene did not want to tell him Flossie and she were staying at the Browns Hotel, probably one of the most high-class places in town.

"Don't take a shower for two days. You may sponge yourself off if the blood gets thick. The nurse will give you Darvon for the pain. I want to see you back in four days."

Irene lay back on the table and closed her eyes. What had she just done? Even though she was lucky not to have had to resort to some back-alley butcher and clothes hangers like women without money did, she still felt filthy and defiled.

After about a half hour, Flossie came in to see her. The nurse had given Flossie a cup of orange juice and some biscuits to bring to Irene. Flossie was so glad to see that Irene was okay and know that this horrible ordeal was over.

"Do you think you are strong enough to go back to the hotel yet?" Flossie asked with great concern.

"I think so. I want to get back to the room and just sleep."

The nurse came in and gave Irene a sanitary napkin to place in her panties for the taxi ride home. "Don't be alarmed, dear, if you bleed a lot. That is normal."

Flossie thanked the doctor and nurse, and then helped Irene to the taxi that the nurse had so kindly called for them. Irene was sure the taxi driver knew why she was there. He had probably driven many women to and from this clinic before.

When they got back to the room, Irene just dropped into bed. She had nightmares about Glenn and his new woman. She envisioned Glenn as the doctor, insanely hacking their baby from her womb, shouting, "Whore. Slut. You are all used up now. No man will ever marry you."

For the next four days, Irene had her meals brought up to her. She begged Flossie to go out and enjoy the sights in

London, but Flossie never left her side. They were scheduled to fly back to America the day after Irene had her follow-up examination with the doctor.

"What if he didn't get it all out, Flossie, and there is still a baby in there?" Irene worried.

"Don't fret, child. These doctors know what they are doing. You will feel better before you know it."

The plane ride back to the U.S. was grueling. The turbulence made Irene throw up more than once. Poor Flossie. This surely hadn't been a pleasant trip for her.

After they finally arrived in Colorado, Irene went straight up to bed. She tried to feign cheerfulness in front of her father, but said the flight home was so bumpy, she had gotten sick. Flossie took the cue and exclaimed about how much sightseeing and shopping they did. She once again thanked Mr. and Mrs. Richter profusely for paying for her trip to London.

Irene's mother came up to see her after dinner. She quietly asked, "How was it?"

"Painful," Irene answered. "Now, I'm going to sleep."

"One day this will all be behind you. You'll be happy you did this so you can have a normal married life."

After the abortion, severe depression seized Irene's soul. She second-guessed her actions, wondering if she should have told Glenn about the pregnancy. Maybe he would have left his girlfriend and come back to her. Maybe they could have gotten married after all. He was probably lonely in France, and perhaps the girl was just filling the void left by Irene's absence.

Obsessing about her actions day and night, Irene couldn't sleep or eat. She shut herself up in her room, and didn't even feel like bathing. She was taking the painkiller, Darvon, which Dr. Rich had given her in London. Maybe that was making her crazy, but she liked the way it numbed her feelings. She spent most days sleeping or sitting in a chair, gazing out the window.

Her father could not figure out why, after a vacation in London, Irene was so down. Although Irene didn't think so, he did love his daughter deeply. Maybe he had been foolish to have insisted Glenn be sent away. After all, Glenn was a nice enough guy, and smart too. Senator Richter had plenty of connections who could give Glenn a job. Maybe he would send the boy to law school himself. No matter what, Senator Richter could not bear to see Irene suffering so much and had to figure out what he could do to help her. The next day Senator Richter drove to Broomfield to Glenn's dad's hardware store. Mr. Devereux didn't have many customers, so Senator Richter asked if he would have time to talk.

"Sure. I'll just put up the 'be back in an hour' sign, and we can go have lunch."

Homey coffee shops and restaurants lined the Main Street of Broomfield. Mr. Devereux led the way to a quiet café. The two men, feeling somewhat awkward, sat in a booth.

Mr. Richter didn't waste any time getting to the point. "Look, Charles, I am having second thoughts about having had you send Glenn to France. It doesn't seem like my Irene can forget him, and she is making herself sick. Maybe I was wrong. I could have helped Glenn get a good job. Frankly, I am ashamed of the way I reacted to their plans to get married. Now I think they must have really loved each other. Is there any chance Glenn might come back?"

Mr. Devereux sat silently, his spoon clinking the sides of his coffee cup as he stirred distractedly. "Neal, I have something to tell you." He was silent again and finally said, "Glenn is already married, and his wife is expecting a child. I am deeply disappointed in my son. My brother, his uncle, tells me that when Glenn used to go to France during summer vacations, he used to chum around with this girl. They ran into each other again, and the next thing you know, he got her pregnant. Now her parents are forcing them to get married. Glenn is happy, though, because he realized he has always been in love with this girl. He was unfair to your Irene, and I am so sorry, Neal."

Senator Richter could not believe what he was hearing. So, Glenn had a true love all along, and now he had married her? How would Irene react to this news? She had been so devoted to this God-damned Glenn. The two men finished their sandwiches and bid each other farewell. They knew they would never meet again.

When Senator Richter got home, he told Sally about his meeting with Glenn's father. Sally said, "That dirty rat. He had probably always planned to go to France after he graduated. How could he do this to Irene?"

As usual, Irene was lying in bed when her father rapped on her door. She did not answer, but he entered anyway.

"Irene, I have something to tell you. It may hurt now, but in the long run, you will see that it is for the best."

He then went on to tell her how he had had a change of heart about Irene and Glenn, so he went to see Glenn's father in Broomfield to ask if Glenn could come back to the United States. That's when Glenn's father told him that Glenn is married, and his wife is expecting a child. He spared no details; even sharing the crushing news that Glenn had loved this girl all along.

Irene wanted to cover her ears and scream but maintained her composure. Just to get rid of her father she said, "Daddy, you were smart to have his parents send him to France. It turns out he's no good. He's a liar and a cheat, and I would never want to marry a man like that."

That was just what her father wanted to hear. He kissed her on the cheek and was relieved that she had absolved him of his guilty feelings for having paid Mr. Devereux to send Glenn away.

The next night, Irene's parents were out at a gala, Flossie was attending choir practice, and the maid and butler had the evening off. It was a rare occasion for Irene to be all alone in that huge house. As she listened to the deep silence, Irene began to wonder why she was even living. What purpose did she have in this world? Although she had healed physically from the abortion, the wound that this dirty secret left upon her heart and soul would never heal. Irene, sickened by her wretched life, swallowed one Darvon after the other to numb her thoughts. Then she remembered where her father kept the key to the liquor cabinet. When she was little, she was proud to open the ornate bar when her parents had guests.

Irene went downstairs to the cabinet and removed one of her father's rare bottles of scotch. She took the scotch and glass up to her room and swigged shots in between pills. She was feeling more and more groggy, and that was good. She hungered for obliteration. Soon, she passed out on the bed.

Flossie came home from choir practice about nine o'clock and called to Irene. When Irene didn't answer, Flossie figured she must be asleep already. Tiptoeing upstairs so as not to disturb her dear charge, Flossie peeped into Irene's room. At first, she thought Irene had dozed off sprawled across the bed, not even pulling back the night covers. When Flossie came closer, however, she saw the empty bottle of scotch and the pills on the nightstand.

Panicking, she felt Irene's pulse ... it was almost nonexistent. She put her ear near Irene's mouth and nose, but the girl's breathing was inaudible. Flossie ran downstairs to call the ambulance. She prayed that Irene would make it.

The ambulance came and rushed Irene to Wesson Hospital. Flossie sat in the lobby of the emergency department, crying softly. Why did this have to happen to Irene? She did nothing wrong but love a boy who did not love her back.

Flossie had left a note for Irene's parents about the emergency, so as soon as they arrived home, they sped to the hospital. Of course, Senator Richter immediately started demanding to know about Irene's condition. The doctor calmly assured Senator and Mrs. Richter that Irene had a close call, but they pumped her stomach, and she was out of danger. He advised them all to go home and come back in the morning. Senator Richter was worried that this incident might leak out to the press, but the doctor assured him that he would never violate his patient's privacy. As far as they knew, Irene's attempted suicide would remain a lifelong secret.

From that moment on, Irene's parents never let her out of their sight. Although her effort to end her life was unsuccessful, Irene had died inside. Her resolve was gone, and she just went along with whatever her parents wanted. They regarded her transformation as an indication that she had finally come to her senses. Irene, on the other hand, considered herself a zombie.

* * * * *

Mrs. Richter was a good friend of Attorney Samuel Bauer's wife, Nancy Bauer. The two women put their heads together to see how they could get Irene to meet Mrs. Bauer's son, Samuel III. Neither Irene nor Sam dated anyone, and their parents were concerned. After all, most kids were married by the time they were twenty-three.

The Bauers and their son accepted an invitation to the Richter's holiday open house. In spite of her troubled life, Irene had become increasingly beautiful. That night, she was wearing a black silk sheath and diamond jewelry. Irene had never been aware just how attractive she really was; unpretentious, she exuded an air of sophistication and charm.

Samuel Bauer III was a shy young man, but well-built and ruggedly handsome. He had played football for Dartmouth and was now attending Yale University School of Law, as his father and grandfather had done before him. He was an athlete, not an academic by nature; still his parents wanted more than anything for Sam to become a lawyer.

The rest of the evening unfolded like a dime-store novel. The Bauers introduced their son to the Richter's daughter, and the two young people hit it off. Sam was smitten, but Irene, whose heart had already turned to stone, pretended to be interested. After all, what did she have to lose? Sam had blonde hair and green eyes and a perfect physique. He was definitely not an intellectual, but was unassuming and straightforward. By the end of the evening, he worked up the courage to ask Irene to go skiing, and much to her parents' surprise, Irene accepted.

While Sam was home on holiday, Irene and he went skiing almost every day. The chilly air and exercise gave Irene a new lease on life. She felt healthy and hopeful once again. Sam was not Glenn, but he was OK. He and Irene dated while he was in law school, and eventually Sam asked her to marry him.

At first, Irene refused. She told him that he really didn't know her, and she was bound to hurt him in the end. Sam vowed to make her happy and take care of her forever. When Sam presented Irene with an engagement ring, and Irene accepted his proposal, Flossie and Irene's parents were ecstatic. They believed that Irene had found happiness at last.

Irene should have known better than to have gotten married. She and Sam never had sexual intercourse before they were married. For all Sam knew, she was a virgin bride. On the first night of their honeymoon in Hawaii, Sam made the disastrous discovery that Irene was frigid. Because Sam and she had not had relations before their marriage, Irene did not know she had developed a psychological aversion to sex. Sam attributed her response to him as the honeymoon jitters and was confident that, in time, Irene would become a loving wife. Sam and Irene had an enjoyable holiday in Hawaii, but the consummation of their marriage did not occur.

Sam had given up trying to make love to his wife, and Irene was relieved that she no longer had to deal with his attempts. The two slept in separate rooms. Very soon after coming to live with them, Flossie knew something was wrong with Irene's marriage. It was heartbreaking for Flossie to realize that Irene's troubles were not over, and there would probably be no children from this union.

Chapter XVI

Mistress Irena

In a rare volume of the works of Aubrey Beardsley she had purchased, Irene stumbled upon an illicit yet extremely erotic illustration with which she became strangely obsessed. In the drawing, a slender lady robed in a long, Victorian-era dress, with the gown's sleeves falling off her shoulders, grasped the dress between her breast with her delicate right hand and wielded a whip in her left hand. A slender young man with just a white sheet draped around his thighs kneeled down in deference to the older woman. The whip was poised, ready to strike a blow on the tender backside of the submissive young male. Irene was not sure if the original illustration showed the young fellow's face, but his features were indistinguishable in this print. His thin body and full head of coal black hair reminded Irene so much of Glenn.

Maybe Beardsley purposely omitted the boy's face so the observer could feel the power the woman wields over the young man. To Irene, this image represented her dark and tainted view of herself. Yes, here is Irene beating the lying, cheating Glenn to a bloody pulp. While the general society believed that the Victorian era was pervasively prudish, pockets of deviant behavior flourished in the streets of England. Perhaps the repression during the Victorian age had the same effect that Prohibition had on America; the more alcohol was banned, the harder people tried to get it.

The most shocking yet titillating of Irene's readings described flogging establishments that existed in London in the 1800s. The men who visited these elite bordellos did not turn up to have sex with the women; instead, they came to be spanked and whipped. Most of the gentlemen were wealthy aristocrats. Sometimes, girls apprenticed to become accomplished flagellants, learning how to employ the birch rod with the utmost skill and grace. Theresa Berkely, who ran a high-class flagellation house, was very imaginative in her approach to her role as "governess," or "dominatrix," and used a variety of tools to inflict painful pleasure upon her patrons. Berkely was purported to have invented a "flogging machine," a clumsy apparatus to which the receiver of the whipping could be strapped. This device was named the "Berkely Horse." These readings were about the only thing that inspired Irene to smile and laugh. What strange stuff, she thought. Yet, she could not get her fill of this erotic material.

On one level, Irene felt these things were perverse, aberrant, and downright sick. Nonetheless, she repeatedly asked herself why she was attracted to such abnormal behavior. English noblemen, and even some noblewomen, frequented these flogging establishments, finding great pleasure in their experiences. Is there pleasure in pain? Maybe for some. Maybe for her. Maybe inflicting pain upon a man would give pleasure to Irene. She knew she could get no pleasure from regular sexual relationships, nor did she want to try. She was not sure why she was frigid, but expected it was from the trauma of Glenn and the abortion. Alternatively, maybe it was the underlying boredom, despair, and emptiness that often plague the rich. It was nice to be able to buy whatever your heart desires, but the final question always remained: To what end?

Irene did not hate men. She was just not attracted to them in a romantic way anymore. If some men derived pleasure from being whipped, then by fulfilling that desire, a woman is still providing sexual satisfaction to her partner, just not in the normal way. This thinking justified Irene's descent into this bizarre world.

* * * * *

The discovery of the Aubrey Beardsley print was Irene's first baby step into the secret life she had now lived for many years.

It was comical to her when the men offered to pay her. She always refused the money and told the submissive men to go out and buy something nice for their wives or girlfriends. The last thing Irene needed was money, particularly not for something from which she also derived great pleasure.

Understandably, Sam had had several affairs, but Irene knew that it was Sam's secretary, Lola, who was the love of his life. Lola got flustered and sounded guilty when Irene called Sam's office. Poor little fool. Of course, Irene knew about Sam's relationship with Lola, and Irene, in fact, condoned it. Sam was a good man, and he deserved to have his needs met. Irene and Sam stayed married for appearances' sake only. A divorce would detract from their prominent families' impeccable reputations.

* * * * *

When Irene looked out the window of her hotel suite, she was astounded to see that it was already dark. She must have been musing about her past for several hours. Famished, she called down to room service to bring her a meal.

It had been quite some time since she had met a man suitable for flogging. The main reason she liked this hotel was that men from all over the country came here for conferences and were, for the most part, married fellows who needed a little spice in their lives. Irene also liked the fact that most of the guys lived far away and did not want to start a relationship with her. That was exactly the way she wanted it; anonymity was important to both Irene and the men she dominated.

After she ate, she showered, got dressed, and went down to the bar, the place where she usually met her partners. This evening, she noticed a man gawking at her, the same chump she caught staring at her the previous night. She remembered having dismissed him with a glance of scorn. On second thought, he was not bad looking, but he certainly was not polished. Irene did not care for men who stared. They gave her the creeps. She glanced away from Lionel, but the next thing she knew, he was asking the bartender to send over her favorite drink. The bartender knew Irene well and poured a glass of Scotch whisky for her, telling her that the man sitting at the other end of the bar had bought her that round. She scrutinized Lionel and mouthed a stern, "No thank you."

Lionel continued to drink his bourbon while Irene paid for her own Scotch. Both were getting reasonably inebriated. As she gave Lionel the once-over, she thought she might just be able to ignore his indelicacy. She knew from the way that he had been eyeballing her that he may sense what she was all about.

Finally, Lionel moved closer to Irene and introduced himself. Irene, calm and unruffled, said nothing while Lionel nattered on nervously. Both of them were sloshed by now, and Irene self-assuredly leaned over near Lionel's ear, whispering, "Have you ever had a woman whip you?"

Lionel, caught off guard, questioned whether he had heard her correctly. "What did you say?" he asked apprehensively.

Irene refused to repeat it. She said with irritation, "You heard me."

Stumbling over his words, Lionel, attempting to be suave, replied, "Never. But I would love to try."

Irene slowly looked Lionel up and down. He'll do, she thought. She asked him when he was going home, and he muttered, "In two days."

"How would you like a beating before then?"

On one level, Lionel was afraid of this woman. He did not know her, and maybe she was a killer. Yet he wasted no time to respond that he would like that very much.

"Good," Irene said. I am in the penthouse suite and expect to see you there tomorrow night at 9:00 p.m. If you don't show up at that time precisely, don't bother coming at all."

Was this really happening to him? "I will be there. By the way, what is your name?"

"To you, I am Mistress Irena. That's all you need to know."

Lionel could not concentrate on the meetings the next day. He was fantasizing about the beautiful woman he had met the previous night, a spitting image of Bettie Page. That evening there was going to be a farewell banquet for the conference participants, as most people would be leaving by the afternoon of the next day.

With booze flowing and inhibitions lowering, many attendees coupled up after dinner. Leanne Abney, one of the secretaries who traveled to the conventions with her boss, had a fondness for Lionel and always sought him out after the closing banquet. When she went up to him this time, though, he said he was going to bed early because he was taking off in the morning. Disappointed, Leanne spied Marty Jackson standing alone and went over immediately to cozy up to him. Most of the men knew that Leanne was a slut. Marty and Leanne disappeared down the corridor, heading for Leanne's room.

Lionel knew he could not be late to see Mistress Irena, so he rushed back up to his room to shower and change. He was nervous but eager. Never in his life had he had such an opportunity, and he didn't want to miss this chance.

The penthouse had its own private elevator, and Lionel was the only person on it. When he arrived at Irene's door, she called from another room, "It's open. Come in. I'll only be a minute. Pour yourself a drink."

The penthouse suite was beyond description. His dinky room on the eighth floor looked like a dump compared to this one. He went over to the fully equipped bar and poured himself two quick shots of bourbon.

Soon, Mistress Irena called him into another huge parlor. He was dumbfounded when he saw her. Wearing a form-fitting black corset-like garment, black fishnet stockings, high black leather boots with stiletto heels, long black satin gloves, and a black masquerade sequined mask, she looked like a heroine from fantasy comics. Around her neck was a black velvet ribbon choker, dripping with rubies in the shape of droplets of blood. Her persona was completely different: uncompromising, severe, and formidable.

She hissed at Lionel in harsh tones. "I am going to speak, and I do not want you to say a word. As of now, you are under my control. If you cry out in pain, the lashes will get harder.

204

Before I begin, you have a chance to back out. Do you want to proceed?"

Lionel did not answer because she had told him he was not to speak.

"Answer me, you mute. Say 'yes' if you want to go forward, or 'no' if you want to stop now."

Lionel replied, "Yes."

Mistress Irena told Lionel to strip naked and kneel on the floor facing away from her. She continued, "Listen carefully. Although I am tough, I am not a cruel sadist. If the lashes become unbearable, you can let me know by using the word "Red." When I hear you say "Red," I will stop immediately. This is your first time, so do not try to be a hero. I will not think less of you if the pain becomes intolerable. Are you sure you understand?"

Lionel was beginning to feel humiliated kneeling there completely nude. "Now tell me what your safety word is, clown," Mistress Irena demanded.

"Red," Lionel replied.

"Fine, we are ready to begin. Kneel upright," Mistress Irena barked at Lionel.

Lionel straightened up quickly, gritting his teeth as he waited for the first blow. In an instant, Mistress Irena raised her whip and dealt a stinging strike. Lionel cringed with pain but managed to remain straight, as Mistress instructed. The whip whizzed through the air with no pauses between the "cracks." Burning red welts swelled on Lionel's back.

Time stood still as Lionel moved from consciousness of pain to the stark white realm beyond agony. He could not see, hear, or feel. When Lionel finally opened his eyes, he recognized he was lying on the floor in a hotel room, alone. Weak and disoriented, Lionel, the wounded antelope, struggled to his feet. His whole body throbbed unremittingly. He staggered over to the sofa, and then collapsed.

When he awakened, it was already morning, and Mistress Irena was gone. Lionel pieced together the events of the night before and still wondered if it was all a dream. He limped to the bathroom, gradually becoming aware of the burning wounds on his back. Showering made the pain even more excruciating. What had he done, and why had he let himself partake in this experience. Was he crazy? Was he a pervert? He had not even had sex with this woman. In spite of the present agony, he remembered the whipping arousing him more than any sexual relations he had ever had in his life. It may be sick, but he wanted more. Why had Mistress Irena left him there alone? Would he ever see her again?

As Lionel was heading toward the door to go back down to his own room, he caught sight of a handwritten note on the elegant mirrored *mezza luna* foyer table. Maybe Mistress Irena did have something to say to him after all.

"Dear Lionel, You were a brave soul, and I hope you achieved satisfaction from our session. However, I must warn you not to fall for me. If you are planning to be in this area again, you can write a note to my post office box, and I will try to meet you. No strings attached."

Lionel couldn't believe that Mistress Irena wanted to see him again. She was so beautiful, so strong, so demanding, yet he must have pleased her. Even if he didn't have business meetings to attend, he would pretend he did just so he could see her. She would be his passage to Heaven; his atonement for his transgressions. Saying a few "Our Fathers" and "Hail Marys" was such an insubstantial penance. It was no wonder Catholics return to the same sins over and over again.

Lionel wanted to be more like the monks who offered their flagellation to God as repentance for their wickedness. Although he was suffering from the whipping he had received at the hands of Mistress Irena, Lionel felt as if he was walking on air. He had a new purpose in life, something that would satisfy him, and he was going to pursue it to the fullest.

* * * * *

Three years had passed since this first session with Irene, but in spite of Mistress Irena's warning about becoming attached,

Lionel had fallen in love with her. She, on the other hand, was not capable of loving any man, a fact that Lionel did not realize. He believed that as she continued to meet with him, she would one day love him in return. Lionel had convinced himself that Addy was mentally ill on the day she married him, so he could easily obtain an annulment for his marriage to her. Having a brother who is a monsignor would help his cause; Lionel would then be free to marry Irene.

He was particularly excited about the upcoming visit with Irene because she had invited him to her private ski lodge hidden in the mountains near Fairplay, Colorado. Their other meetings had been at hotels, so Mistress Irena had to practice some restraint. Lionel suspected that, after three years, Mistress considered him ready to experience full submission in what might turn out to be a real dungeon setting.

Addy had noticed that every time Lionel traveled to Colorado for business, he was distracted and on edge. One of the many good things about these trips was that he paid no attention to Addy while he was preoccupied with upcoming trips. When Lionel was in this state of mind, he didn't scrutinize the children's actions nor did he pinch Addy for sex.

Lionel was scheduled to leave for Colorado the day after Christmas and return some time after the New Year. Addy thought it rather odd that business meetings would take place during the holidays; but, of course, she didn't care. She, Helena and the kids would have a ball at the farm.

Chapter XVII

There is a God

Helena and Addy had been gradually redecorating the farmhouse. There were five bedrooms, one for each of them. Helena spoiled Addy's children so; but the kids were none the worse for it. Compared to Lionel's unpleasant attitude toward them, the kids viewed Addy and Helena as fairy godmothers.

For her room, Mary picked out pink rose-patterned wallpaper with a pearlite finish. Helena had bought a white canopy bed with a bedspread and canopy that matched the wallpaper. The room was so light and airy, with white organdy curtains on the windows. Mary even had her own dressing table with a skirt made from the same fabric as the bedspread and canopy, and, of course, a writing desk and stuffed chair. This redecorating project cost a fortune, but to Helena, when she loved someone, money was no object. She loved little Mary deeply; a sweet child named after Helena's mom.

Jimmy had chosen tan cowboy-themed wallpaper, and Helena bought new maple furniture for his room. Pete liked aviation, so he selected light blue wallpaper printed with airplanes from various eras in history. He, too, had all new bedroom furniture. The second floor of the farmhouse was decorated like the lovely rooms Addy had seen in her women's magazines. Never in her life could she have imagined her children and she would share in such fantasies.

Addy's wallpaper was her favorite color, yellow. Located on the side of the house that received the most sun in the morning, Addy always awakened in a good mood. She had chosen a bedspread dotted with daisies, but she would not allow Helena to buy her new furniture. Mary had kept her mahogany bedroom set in pristine condition, and Addy convinced Helena that it would be an honor to use Mary's furniture.

Helena had redecorated her bedroom with new ivory-colored French provincial furniture. The walls were pale blue, and the padded headboard matched the ivory and light blue printed drapes and bedspread.   Above each window was an ivory-colored cornice outlined with wide, light blue grosgrain ribbon. Helena designed this room to resemble one of her favorite rooms in the elegant, yet inviting, Paris hotel James and she had frequented.   Always cognizant of the possibility that Lionel might one day try to put a stop to her friendship with Addy and the children, Helena left the first floor exactly the way it was. She locked the upstairs bedrooms so that Lionel would never be able to see the havens she had created for her best friend and the children.

Halloween and Thanksgiving at the farm had been wonderful, but neither could surpass the sheer magic of Noel. Lionel let Addy and the kids sleep at Helena's on Christmas Eve. Addy made eggnog and turned on the radio to listen to carols. At around ten o'clock, after they had all had their fill of eggnog and cookies, Addy coaxed the children up to bed. Mary knew Santa would not come while she was still awake.

"What if Santa doesn't know I'm here, and he goes to our house instead?" Mary asked, suddenly frightened.

Helena thought quickly, and said, "Mary, Santa knows where you are no matter what. Remember the song, 'He knows when you are sleeping; he knows when you're awake ...'"

Relieved, Mary laughed, kissed Addy and Helena "good night" and skipped upstairs to her beautiful new room. Mary could not remember ever having been this happy on Christmas Eve.   She never imagined lovely bedrooms and pretty, calm houses existed outside the pictures in storybooks.

The boys asked if they could play a board game until they got tired. Addy agreed, just as long as they did not keep Mary awake. When the kids were all upstairs, Helena and Addy both flopped on the sofa, sitting silently in the gentle glow of the Christmas tree, immersed in the ineffable tranquility and beauty of the moment. Helena had never experienced the holidays with children, and Addy had not experienced peace at Christmas for so long. Could the two women have ever imagined just how much the rekindling of their friendship would change their lives? It had only been a matter of a few months since the death of Helena's mother, but in such a short time, a small window of hope had opened in Addy's heart. She was afraid that at any instant, the panes might shatter, and she would be, once again, unprotected and afraid. Addy pushed those fears out of her mind. Tonight was Christmas Eve, Lionel was nowhere around, and she was with Helena, her sister of the heart.

Addy turned to look at Helena, who was admiring the beauty of the tree. "You sure know how to decorate a Christmas tree," Helena remarked.

Addy replied with, "At least I'm good at something ..."

"You stop that, Addy. You excel at a lot of things. Look at the job you've done with your kids, and you are a remarkable cook. Most of all, you're a phenomenal person. It's that beast of a husband of yours who has knocked the life out of you. When ARE we going to kill him?"

Addy laughed, "You forgot to say that I'm also a great seamstress. Remember the Halloween costumes?"

Helena tossed a throw pillow at Addy. "Don't go getting a swelled head. Well I guess we will let that brute Lionel live through Christmas. Now let me go spike the eggnog. We have a lot of work ahead of us, so we may as well get plastered."

Helena rifled through the kitchen cupboards to find the bottle of Jamaican rum her mother had used solely for baking, and then poured the rum into the punchbowl of eggnog. She filled two cups and brought them into the living room. "Cheers, Addy, here's to many more glorious holidays together."

Addy raised her cup high, and said, "Cheers, Helena, I'll drink to that."

The two friends drank and laughed late into the night. They managed to put the train together and set out everything that Santa was supposed to have delivered. Then they arranged the presents around the tree.

By this time, Addy could barely stand up. She wobbled over to Helena to give her a hug. "Helena, I don't know how I can ever repay you for all that you have done for us." Then, Addy began to cry.

Helena held her close, gently stroking her hair. "Shhh ... you'll wake up the kids. It will be all right, you'll see. You are going to be fine. I promise you. Now, don't be a weepy drunk."

Addy laughed between sobs. Her nose was running like a little kid's. The thought of how she must look with snots dribbling down her face struck her funny. She laughed so hard she had to make a beeline for the bathroom. Thank God, she made it. Having a snotty nose and pissy pants at the same time would be the last straw.

"I'm going to turn in," Helena yawned. After a last long look at the tree, she reminded Addy to unplug the Christmas lights. "Good night, Addy. Sweet dreams. I'll set my alarm for six, so we can try to be up before the kids."

Addy lingered downstairs; she had always loved to be alone with the tree. It was sad that such beautiful trees had to give up their lives at Christmas, but Addy used to console herself with the thought that these trees were selected for this moment of crowning glory. There had been a few times when Addy was a child that she saw the tree as a symbol of the life of Jesus. He was born an innocent babe in a wooden stable, and the reason for his coming was to give up his life for the sins of humankind. He hung on a tree, but overcame death on Easter Sunday. In the end, it was a triumphant story, for Jesus ascended into Heaven.

As Addy grew older, she had difficulty understanding that if God is all-knowing, then had he known beforehand that Adam and Eve would sin. Was he naïve? He could not be ingenuous because that is a human quality, and God is not supposed to be human. Several times during her Catholic schooling, Addy had tried to raise such questions, but her queries were quickly dismissed with, "You cannot question your religion."

Tonight, she did not want to fall down the rabbit hole of over thinking. All she knew was Christmas cast a magic spell upon her, and she did not care to analyze why. Addy went to the window to see the fresh snow falling. If the flakes were large, you could catch them on your sleeve and inspect each crystal. She went outside to the edge of the porch and stuck out her arm. Sure enough, the flakes gathered on the sleeve of her nightgown and remained there for a few seconds so Addy could admire their individual beauty. The sky was clear black, dotted with sparkling stars. As Addy looked upward, she whispered a little prayer, "I don't know who I'm praying to. Is it God? Is it my parents? Is it the universe? All I know is that right now I am filled with humble gratitude for my life. Oh, please let me carry this thankfulness in my heart, no matter what happens."

Addy surprised herself. She had given up praying long ago. Once she identified herself as an unlucky person, she had relinquished all hope of her life ever improving. The wind picked up and Addy was shivering. She went inside to take one last cup of eggnog to help her sleep then climbed the stairs to her room, where no Lionel was waiting to pinch her bottom.

Mary awakened around five thirty and tiptoed into the boy's rooms. She whispered excitedly, "It's Christmas!" The three had always crept downstairs early to see if Santa had come. Although the boys had stayed up really late and would rather have pulled the covers over their heads, they could never disappoint Mary. Dragging themselves out of bed, the groggy brothers tiptoed downstairs with Mary.

The children were speechless when they saw the mounds of gifts piled around the tree. Peter and Jimmy looked at each other in amazement; maybe there really is a Santa Claus. Mary squealed with delight when she saw the walking doll and the new skates. Helena didn't feel that just two gifts from Santa were enough for Mary, so she had also bought a small model kitchen with tiny accessories. Jimmy's electric train was set up around the tree. He immediately flipped the switch, and the little train chugged off, blowing its whistle proudly. He was so enthralled with his train set that he hadn't noticed there were skates and a toboggan for him, too. Pete marveled at the erector and chemistry sets, and new skates. He just could not believe that he had received so many gifts.

By this time, Helena's alarm clock had buzzed, and she rolled over to turn it off. Then she remembered it was Christmas morning, so she forced herself to get out of bed and drag her tired body to the bathroom. Addy was knocked out from the rum, and Helena had to shake her vigorously to wake her up. Addy was disoriented. Where was she? Why was she in this pretty room? Where was Lionel? As Addy slowly came to, she was relieved to know she was at Helena's.

"Merry Christmas, sleepyhead," Helena said cheerfully.

"Merry Christmas to you, Helena. Are the kids up yet?"

"They sure are. Can't you hear them? It sounds like they're thrilled with the toys."

As Addy tried to lift her head from the pillow, a pounding headache overwhelmed her. "Wow, do I ever have a headache."

Helena laughed, "I'll give you a couple of aspirin. What you have is better known as a hangover."

Addy smiled, rolled out of bed, and gave Helena a hug. "Helena, I love you."

"I love you too, Addy. Now get your carcass out of bed. It's Christmas."

The two women slunk sleepily down the stairs, just as Addy's aunts had done so many years ago. When Addy saw her children laughing with complete abandon, she once again sent up a prayer of gratitude. Lionel would not be arriving until dinnertime, so they had the whole morning to relax and enjoy themselves. Thank God, Addy had convinced him not to come over and fetch them for Mass. Lately, he actually listened to her sometimes.

Helena played Christmas records on her phonograph, and making believe she was a conductor, directed everyone to sing along. The morning flew by, and it was time to start getting everything ready for Christmas dinner. Lionel was bringing his brother the Monsignor, so Helena reminded herself to be on her best behavior, lay it on thick, and pretend she was poised to hand over the farm any day now.

Lionel and the Monsignor arrived promptly at 2:00 p.m., wine and presents in tow. Helena greeted them warmly, and the children shouted, "Merry Christmas, Daddy. Merry Christmas, Monsignor."

Much to Helena's surprise, Monsignor Roberge hurried over to the children and gave them each a warm hug. "Merry Christmas, and God bless you." He seemed much nicer than Lionel did, but then again, he might be putting on the dog to impress her. She was no fool.

After Monsignor said a long grace, they dined on a fabulous ham dinner. Of course, when his brother raved about Addy's cooking, Lionel smiled toward Addy and said those familiar but revolting words: "That's my Addy girl."

Addy almost choked on her food, wishing Lionel had kept his big, fat mouth shut. Every time he said that, Addy shuddered, thinking, "If they only knew."

After dinner, everyone retired to the living room to open presents. Of course, Helena had made sure that each person received about the same number of gifts. The boxes were wrapped in beautiful Christmas paper with coordinated package decorations that could be used as tree ornaments next year. Helena studied the Monsignor carefully. She saw his eyes open wide at the opulence around him, but he did not appear covetous or sneaky like his brother. He was thrilled with the sweater, pipe, tobacco, and black leather belt. Even Lionel seemed genuinely appreciative of his ski jacket and other gifts.

By the time they finished opening the presents, it was already getting dark. They returned to the dining room for dessert and coffee, and the Monsignor had to leave because he said daily Mass at 7:30 a.m. and had to get to bed early. He thanked Addy and Helena profusely, saying he could not remember when he had had such a lovely Christmas.

Addy was relieved that Lionel did not say when she and the kids would have to return to their home. She asked him if he needed help packing for his trip but was delighted when he declined. He gave Addy a peck on the cheek, shook the boys' hands, and bent down to hug Mary. He said he would be leaving tomorrow and would be back after the New Year. He thanked Helena again and then turned to the door.

As Helena watched Lionel and Monsignor Roberge walking down the path to the car, she noticed the difference in their gaits and auras. Lionel took quick, sharp steps like a Russian soldier. His whole body appeared tense and prepared to pounce at any moment. In contrast, the Monsignor made long, smooth strides, and he seemed encircled with peace. How could two brothers be so different?

Helena spoke that thought aloud, and Addy responded, "I wonder that myself sometimes. The Monsignor really isn't a bad guy. He does try. Maybe Lionel turned out the way he did because his family always bragged about Jean-Paul's going into the priesthood."

"OK, Sigmund Freud. Don't go psychoanalyzing Lionel. People have suffered worse injuries but still turn out normal. Look at us, for instance ...."

Addy laughed. "*Us*? Normal? Hold on there. I never claimed to be normal."

"Well, for your information, you are normal and so am I. Normal people don't intimidate or hurt others. Normal people have empathy and compassion. Come on, Addy. We were Girl Scouts, for God's sake."

Addy laughed even harder. "Oh I FORGOT about that. Of course, I'm normal. Thanks for reminding me. Want another cup of coffee?"

"Sure. Let's just rinse the dishes and leave them in the sink until morning. I can't face them tonight, can you?"

"Wasn't it a nice day, Helena? The kids were so happy, and Lionel didn't ruin things. It's good that his brother came for dinner because Lionel behaves when the Monsignor is around."

The children were exhausted, and try as they may to wring the last drops out of Christmas day, they were dozing on the sofa. Addy gently shook each child, then shooed the three off to bed. She followed them to be sure they didn't fall asleep in their clothes. This had been an extraordinary day for everyone. Addy wanted to stop the clock at this very moment for eternity. She hated to release loveliness from her hands because she always feared loveliness would never return. The future scared her because her self-fulfilling prophecy of doom often came true. If only she could just relax and trust life to be good to her. When misfortune inevitably arrived, she wished she had the fortitude to fight back. Addy wished she was not so weak. She desired strength and confidence like Helena. At least Helena was around for Addy to admire.

When Addy returned downstairs, Helena was sitting at the kitchen table drinking coffee. She had removed the crystal carafe from its box and was admiring it.

"You know, Addy, I have always wanted one of these but never got around to getting one for myself. The only place I remember having a bedside carafe was either in Europe or in the hospital. Thank you so much for this. It's Waterford crystal, and I know how expensive it must have been. You shouldn't have spent all that money."

"Shut your mouth," Addy joked. "After all you have spent on my family, even LIONEL and his brother, for God's sake; I could never repay you if I tried for the rest of my life. My gift is measly compared to what you bought all of us."

"No, YOU be quiet," countered Helena. "How many times do I have to tell you that the kids and you have breathed the life back into me? I'm sick of saying it. Now, let's go to bed. I'm EXHAUSTED."

It was a very silent night as Addy stared up at the ceiling in her cozy, inn-like bedroom. She surprised herself when a prayer came to mind. "Oh, God," she found herself whispering, "if you are listening, I want to thank you for this blessed day. May angels watch over Helena and my children forever. Please let us be happy, even if it is for just a little while longer."

Addy fell into a deep, peaceful sleep. Her dream that night was particularly realistic. She was walking through a strange and snowy land, and wicked people were chasing her. They mistakenly thought Addy had done something wrong. Addy kept protesting her innocence and shouting to her pursuers, "I just want to find my way home."

Suddenly the skies opened up, and Herculean men riding in golden chariots and wielding silver shields appeared. Addy knew they had come to rescue her, but she said to these guardians, "Don't hurt those people who are trying to hurt me. Just please guide me home."

When Addy awoke in the morning, she recalled the dream and puzzled over its meanings. All she knew was that it had left her with a sense of relief. Then it dawned on her ... she felt truly at home at Helena's farm and once before ... in Greg's arms.

Chapter XVIII

Fair Play, Colorado

While Addy and the kids passed halcyon days at the farm, Lionel busily prepared for his trip to Denver. He was scheduled to arrive at Stapleton Airfield on December 28 at 6:00 p.m., but hadn't a clue if Mistress Irena would be there to pick him up. She was always aloof and mysterious, qualities that drove Lionel wild.

Lionel smiled smugly as he packed the expensive ski jacket Helena gave him for Christmas. He interpreted her generous gesture as a sign of affection and was certain the farm would soon be in his brother's hands. In the days leading up to his departure, Lionel could not concentrate on his work. He told his new protégé, Michael Russell, he would be out of town for a few days checking on some accounts in Colorado. Crafty Lionel did not want the higher-ups knowing too much about his travels, or they might examine the books more carefully. The company was thriving, and most of the executives were out of town for the holidays. They trusted Lionel and rarely questioned anything that he did. He would be back before they even noticed he was gone.

Lionel asked Mike to keep the information about the Colorado trip close to the vest, just in case the accounts did not result in sales. As an incentive, Lionel offered Mike the use of his office while he was away. Wet behind the ears and eager to please, Michael assured Lionel that he would not breathe a word about the trip, but he asked Lionel what he should say in case anyone asked. Thinking for a moment, Lionel responded, "Just tell them I had to go out of town suddenly for a family matter. Then if I score big on these accounts, they'll have a hell of a surprise, right Mike?"

"Right, right, you betcha, Mr. Roberge," Mike agreed enthusiastically.

"Don't be so formal, son. Call me Lionel," he said, stretching his hand out to Michael ingratiatingly.

On the morning of December 28, a snowstorm hit Connecticut, and Lionel worried about his flight. Fortunately, the storm subsided by early afternoon, the runways were cleared, and planes departed as scheduled. Lionel had arranged for a taxi to pick him up in plenty of time for his reservation.

As soon as he arrived at Bradley International Airport, Lionel headed straight for the bar. He was not afraid to fly, but when the plane hit turbulence, he got nervous. Knowing he would soon experience a session with Mistress Irena always made him a little jumpy. What would she do this time? Would he make a fool of himself? Maybe she would get disgusted and refuse to see him ever again. His uneasiness mixed with a sense of dread.

Lionel often questioned why he kept going back for more of these meetings. He had figured out that the pain of bondage and discipline served as atonement for his fallen nature. In addition, his time with Mistress Irena was incredibly arousing and a replacement for the satisfaction his wife should be providing. His wife. Addy. What a huge mistake that was. Sure, he had gotten his Catholic virgin but had to accept her peculiarities along with it. She had no interest in pleasing him. If she had, maybe he would not lose his temper and have to beat and rape her. Maybe if she put on a sexy negligee and sucked his dick regularly, he would treat her better. There was no hope for Addy. She was getting worse. To hell with Addy. Lionel was on his way to see a real woman.

When his plane finally touched down in Denver, Lionel searched the faces of the people waiting at the arrival gate, but he did not see Mistress Irena among the crowd. Disappointed, he took a taxi to his hotel, checked in, and went up to his room to wait for her call. She did not call. What if this time, she never shows up?

Lionel stirred fitfully in his bed, waiting for the phone to ring. No call came through—not during the night; nor the morning; not even by afternoon. He was getting hungry and headed for the hotel restaurant. Afraid he may have missed his call, Lionel checked at the front desk to see if he had any messages.

The front desk manager assured him that guests were promptly notified of calls. Lionel ordered a sandwich and a few shots of bourbon then headed back upstairs. While turning his key in his room door, Lionel heard the phone ring. He tripped over his feet, and his heart raced as he ran to answer it.

"Lionel?" Mistress Irena said in a flat tone. "I couldn't pick you up at the airport because I had some problems out at the cabin. They're fixed so I'm leaving soon to come get you. Be ready. Good-bye."

Lionel was speechless. He had not had a chance to say anything. That is how she was, though: all business most of the time. Elated that she had called, Lionel became aroused in anticipation of what was to come. He watched the clock until the front desk finally telephoned him to say he had a visitor. Lionel rushed down to check out, and the desk clerk informed him his visitor said she would wait for him outside in her car.

Mistress Irena was driving a shiny black Lincoln Capri hardtop. Boy, could Lionel get used to a vehicle like that; nice-looking and fast, too. He placed his suitcases on the back seat and then slid across the supple, beige leather front seat.

Starting the ignition, Mistress Irena looked straight ahead and asked distractedly, "Did you have a good flight?"

Knowing that details bored Irena, Lionel replied quickly, "It was fine."

Mistress Irena sped through small villages until they were far from any civilization. The sky suddenly seemed blacker and the stars brighter than Lionel had ever seen in his life. He wondered how far they had left to drive but did not dare to ask. He was hungry and tired. The snow was falling more heavily now, the roads becoming more slippery.

In spite of the slick roads, Mistress Irena continued speeding, losing control of the vehicle a few times. She seemed to enjoy recovering from the spins, but Lionel feared she would kill them both for sure. After what seemed like days on the dark and treacherous mountain passages, they finally reached the lodge.

Lionel had imagined that Mistress Irena's ski chalet would resemble a scary dungeon. To the contrary, it was a large, pleasant-looking log home with warm lights glowing invitingly through the icicled windows. Irena pulled into the long driveway. Lionel removed his luggage from the back seat and dutifully followed behind his Mistress up the front path.

When she unlocked the heavy door and Lionel got his first glimpse of the place, he was dumbfounded. The only time he had seen anything like this was in a travel magazine: post and beams; cathedral ceilings; one whole wall of windows that looked out onto the wilderness in back; a huge fieldstone fireplace ... it was magnificent.

Before Lionel had a chance to look around, Mistress Irena said, "There is supper on the stove. Your suite is the first one on the right at the top of the stairs. I'm tired and am going to bed now. See you in the morning."

Lionel barely had time to set his bags down, and Mistress Irena was already gone. She was an enigma. Lionel went into the kitchen and found a pot of beef stew simmering on the stove. There were biscuits in a basket, some bottles of beer, and an apple pie. Good food. Very good food.

The wind howled all night, and Lionel slept late. He dressed quickly, hoping Mistress Irena would not think him a slug. When he got downstairs, she was sitting at the dining room table, drinking coffee. She seemed to be in better spirits this morning, and smiling, she asked, "Did you sleep well?"

"Great, great," Lionel stammered. "I hope I didn't sleep too late."

"No worries. This is your vacation. You can sleep as long as you like. How was the supper?"

"Delicious. Thank you. You're a great cook."

Irene laughed. "I don't cook. We have a regular cook, but when I come up here, Flossie always packs special meals. She's a living doll. She has been with me since I was a child and was with my mother before that."

Flossie had also prepared a breakfast strata, which was warming in the oven. "I DO make coffee. Would you like some?"

"Oh, don't wait on me. I can get it myself," Lionel said.

Mistress Irena laughed once again. "Don't worry. You'll be doing as I say soon enough."

It was a gorgeous day. The snow had stopped, and sun streamed into the wall of windows. Mistress Irena made a fire, and the two unlikely companions sat on the sofa eating strata and sipping coffee. After breakfast, Mistress told Lionel she was going out for a walk, and he could amuse himself as he liked. Obviously, she did not want Lionel to accompany her. Anything that smacked of romance or relationship was never on her agenda.

Lionel cleaned up the breakfast dishes and then looked around the chalet. He expected to find a room filled with equipment that Mistress Irena would use to dominate her slave, but he found nothing. Maybe there was a secret locked dungeon. He dozed in front of the fire until he was hungry again and found some sandwiches in the icebox.

The sun had nearly set when Lionel heard someone walking up the front path. He hoped to hell that it was Irena because he did not know how he would explain his presence there to anyone else. Irena burst through the front door, carrying an armload of wood. Her cheeks were pink from her long walk in the woods and wisps of her raven hair framed her beautiful face. Lionel stood gaping at her until she became irritated and barked, "Don't just stand there. Help me unload the wood."

Lionel quickly obeyed, taking the logs from her arms and piling them into the woodbin. One night and nearly a whole day had passed, but Mistress Irena had made no moves toward him. Maybe she had changed her mind and decided Lionel was not suitable.

Mistress Irena said she was going upstairs to take a nap and told Lionel to put supper in the oven to heat. Flossie had made chicken croquettes with cream sauce and peas and even included a note explaining the warming instructions. Lionel did as she said. In the vegetable drawer, he found lettuce, tomatoes, and cucumbers so he put together a salad. He grabbed a bottle of beer and waited for Mistress Irena to come downstairs for dinner.

She must have set her alarm because as soon as the oven timer dinged, she was in the kitchen. Lionel carried the food into the dining room, where he had set a festive table with a red and green tartan plaid cloth and red candles. If Mistress Irena was impressed, she did not show it.

Before they sat down to eat, Irena asked Lionel to go into the wine cellar and bring up a bottle of Austrian white wine, "The Chateau Mouton Rothschild, '49."

Lionel panicked. He did not want to appear the fool, but he had never been in a wine cellar. What if the bottles were classified by a system he did not understand, and he was unable to find the wine his Mistress requested?

When he went down into the wine cellar, Lionel was relieved to discover that the wines were sorted by regions, with producers and vintages grouped together. It took him no time at all to spot the bottle Irena wanted.

They quickly finished off that bottle, and Mistress Irena required another and another, each wine from a different country and vintage. Although these rare wines were not strong, Lionel and Irena drank so many bottles that Lionel was getting drunk. Mistress handled her alcohol well and never lost decorum.

After Lionel lost count of how many times he brought another bottle up from the basement, Mistress Irena finally said, "I think it is time. Go upstairs and take a shower."

Lionel tried not to stumble as he made his way upstairs to his bathroom. He was tempted to collapse on his bed, but he knew it was now or never. He had been waiting so long for this opportunity, and nothing was going to get in his way.

While Lionel showered, Mistress Irena changed into one of her many dominatrix outfits. She most always wore black leather, but tonight she chose gold. "Why not get into the spirit of the season?" she said to herself wryly. She stripped naked and then slipped into her gold leather cat suit, pulled a tight-fitting gold hood over her head, donned her gold stilettos, and found her gold whip. This instrument was one of her favorites. She got out her bag of fetish bondage devices, took one last look in the mirror and was pleased with what she saw. Now she was truly MISTRESS IRENA. She could escape into the world in which she was in charge; where she meted out the pain that was stored inside of her. Only now did she feel alive.

Lionel was not sure how he should dress so he nervously pulled his bathrobe over his naked body. When he got downstairs, Mistress Irena was not there. His heart pounded with anticipation. After what seemed like hours, his Mistress Irena, breathtakingly beautiful, slowly descended the staircase. In her outfit of gold, she seemed an avenging angel, ready to punish him with her golden whip that sported many studded leather straps.

The post and beam construction of the chalet had large, smooth tree trunks that held up the second floor balcony, and the balcony wrapped around the living room. There were arms of wood jutting out from the main beams, forming right triangles to support the second floor. Lionel had not noticed before, but he suddenly realized these structures resembled crosses.

Mistress Irena demanded that he remove his robe. She first got a ball gag for his mouth and covered the gag with a locking leather cover. She got the step stool and told Lionel to stand up on it, facing the tree trunk beam. Lionel followed her instructions while she went up a few stairs. She then had him stretch out his arms and raise them above his head while she bound his wrists to the cross beams. Irena came back downstairs, tied Lionel's ankles together, and then pulled the stool out from under him.

Lionel was hanging from the posts by his wrists. Mistress Irena knew that this position could not be maintained safely for a long time so she had plenty of other tortures planned for the rest of the evening. She began flogging Lionel first lightly, then progressively harder. He did not cry out because the ball gag silenced any screams. Although Mistress Irena was always in control of herself, she had had more wine than usual. She beat and whipped relentlessly, losing track of time.

When she awakened from her frenzied zone of domination, Mistress Irena suddenly realized Lionel was hanging there longer than what was advisable. She quickly put the step stool under his feet so that he could climb down, and she untied the ropes from around his ankles. She would give him a chance to rest until they moved on to their next session.

"Step down," she commanded. Lionel did not move. "Step down," she repeated harshly.

For an instant, Mistress Irena felt foolish. His wrists were still tied. Lionel hung there completely limp. I must be losing it ... I forgot to untie him, Irena thought seriously, as she rushed upstairs to loosen his bloodied wrists from the crossbeams. As soon as she undid the knots, Lionel's flaccid body crashed to the floor. Irene ran downstairs to remove Lionel's ball gag. He was not participating. He seemed comatose. His eyes were closed and saliva was dripping from his mouth. Shaking him, she shouted, "Wake up! WAKE UP! It's over!"

But Lionel did not wake up. She put her ear to his chest to listen for his breathing. She felt his pulse, frantically searching for a heartbeat. Nothing. She tried compressing his chest repeatedly. She tried mouth-to-mouth resuscitation. Nothing. Nothing.

Irene panicked. Had she killed a man? She had played like this countless times before, and no one ever got hurt. What should she do? Whenever Irene was in trouble, the first person who always came to mind was Flossie. She ran to the telephone and dialed her home number, praying that Flossie would answer.

Providentially, Flossie picked up the phone. "Good evening, the Bauer residence."

"Oh, thank God, it's you, Flossie,"

"Why, Miss Irene. Are you having a nice retreat at your cabin? Did you like the food I fixed?"

Irene felt as if she would vomit at any second. "Flossie," she pleaded. "I'm in trouble. I need your help. Can you get Otis to drive you out here as soon as possible? I can take you home tomorrow. Oh, please, Flossie. I need you."

Flossie didn't like the tone of Irene's voice. She and Irene had been through many trials together, but Flossie never remembered Irene sounding this desperate.

"OK, child. I'll get my things together and come just as soon as I can."

"Hurry Flossy, hurry—and don't let Otis come in."

Irene paced the floor, wondering what she should do. Should she call the police? How would she explain this dead man in her house? What should she say happened? She ran upstairs to get a bed sheet and threw it over Lionel's body. Then she sat of the sofa, immobilized with fear, waiting for Flossie to come.

The ride out to Irene's chalet was a long and hazardous one, and Flossie kept praying Otis would keep the car on the road. His eyesight was not what it used to be, and he did not fancy driving at night. Flossie prayed, too, that whatever Irene had done this time could be fixed.

When they finally found the chalet, Otis asked Flossie if he could walk her up to the door, but Flossie quickly joked, "I'm old, but I'm not THAT old yet. I can make it just fine, thank you, Mr. Otis."

Otis laughed and told Flossie to call if she and Miss Irene needed anything at all. Flossie waited for Otis to pull out of the driveway, and then she rapped on the front door. Irene went running to answer the knock, forgetting she was still dressed in her gold dominatrix cat suit.

"Well, I'll be, Miss Irene. Were you having a costume party?" Flossie queried innocently.

By this time Irene began to cry uncontrollably, and Flossie spied what looked like a body covered with a bed sheet. Frightened, she slowly walked over to the sheet and gently pulled it aside. When she saw a naked dead man lying there, she let out a howl, "Oh, Glory Be to God!"

Wailing, she knelt down, pulled the sheet back up over the man, and automatically began reciting Psalm 20:

"The Lord hear thee in thy day of trouble; the names of the God of Jacob defend thee; Send thee help from the sanctuary, a ..."

Irene shouted wildly, "Flossie, you can't take time to pray. You have to help me. You have to help me get his body out of here."

"Miss Irene. I cannot help you with that. I would be covering up a murder. That would be too great a sin for me to bear. We have to call the police."

"Flossie, I didn't murder him, I swear. He died. He just died. I think he had a heart attack. I can't let the police come here. You know what it would do to my family. Oh, Flossie, I know I have asked you to do so many things that went against your conscience, but I promise I will never ask you again. Please, please, help me."

Flossie wept silently. She knew she could never refuse Irene anything. Irene was in so many ways her own daughter. If Irene had gone wrong, then Flossie must be at fault. After all, she raised her.

Irene tucked the sheet around Lionel and went upstairs to get a blanket. She had Flossie lift Lionel under his shoulders while she lifted his legs, and they moved him onto the blanket. Then they dragged his body out to Irene's car. Lionel was heavy, and his body left drag marks in the snow.

"What are we going to do with him, Miss Irene?" Flossie asked in disbelief.

"We can throw his body off Peregrine Cliff. The snow down in the valley is so deep no one will find him."

"Lord, forgive us," Flossie prayed.

They stuffed his body into the back seat, but had trouble getting the back door to close all the way. Flossie climbed into the front passenger seat, and Irene sped off.

"Slow down, slow down, honey," Flossie cautioned. "No use getting us killed, too."

Irene kept speeding, frantic to unload Lionel as quickly as

she could. What had gone wrong? Why had he died? Maybe he had choked to death or had a heart attack. Lost in thought, Irene pushed the pedal to the floor. She did not see the huge bull elk bounding toward the road. Even if she had seen him in time, there would be no way of avoiding him. He was colossal, maybe 500 pounds or more, with giant antlers. Disoriented by the headlights, the elk ran straight in front of the car. The impact was so strong that the car lifted off the ground—there was bloody screaming, shattering glass, crushing metal, cracking bones, shredding flesh—an unidentifiable mass of ugly chaos. The elk lay lifeless, entrails steaming, guts spilling onto the pristine white snow.

The rear door of the car, not tightly closed, flew open, and Lionel, tossed like a bag of trash, landed in the bloodied mess. If Helena could see Lionel's naked body lying next to the elk, she would likely think, "What a fitting ending for a bully like Lionel. Now he can't push Addy around anymore. Good riddance to bad rubbish."

* * * * *

The Richters and Bauers went regularly to see Flossie in the Jefferson County Hospital. She was the only one who had miraculously survived the car crash, but she remained in a coma. Both Irene and Sam's parents knew that in order to protect their reputations, they had to keep the details of the accident out of the papers. The members of the first aid squad were paid to keep their mouths shut. As far as they were concerned, the only two people discovered at the scene of the accident were Irene and Flossie.

Flossie may have known what really happened, but the doctors were uncertain when or even if she would awaken from her coma. Weeks passed, and Flossie remained asleep. Visits from the Richters and Bauers became less frequent, but there was one person who came almost daily to sit by Flossie's hospital bed: Reverend Edward Thomas, the pastor of Flossie's church. He read Bible passages aloud to her, confident that she could hear him. Other church members came regularly to pray with Pastor Thomas. They trusted that in His time, God would awaken Flossie from her deep sleep.

That glorious day finally came. Flossie opened her eyes, and much to her great surprise, found herself in a hospital bed with Reverend Thomas seated next to her. She could hear but could not speak. Reverend Thomas gently explained that she had been in a car accident and had been asleep for quite some time.

Flossie had no recollection of the accident. The last thing she remembered was Otis driving her out to Irene's ski house. Eventually, Flossie was able to form words. Once she started speaking coherently, the Bauers and Richters immediately came to visit. Although they loved Flossie dearly, they had secretly hoped she might not wake up from the coma so that there would be no chance of her revealing the details of the crash. The first question Flossie asked was, "Is Otis OK?"

Mrs. Richter explained that Otis was fine but that Irene was killed. Flossie was in shock and cried and cried. Try as she may, she could not recollect anything about that night. Somehow, she had escaped alive, but poor, dear little Irene was gone. Even when the police came to question Flossie, she was of no help. When she tried to think, her head would hurt something fierce.

Flossie could remember so many particulars of Irene's life from when she was first born until she was grown. She just couldn't remember how Irene died. With all the privilege and money in the world, Irene still had an unhappy life in the end. Flossie prayed that her angel was safely at peace in the arms of Jesus. That poor child never had a chance in this life. That young man Glenn had ruined her. Maybe she was better off.

The Reverend continued to visit Flossie until she was feeling stronger and almost ready to go home. But Flossie didn't want to go home now that Irene was gone. She had never really had a place of her own, and maybe it was time. Flossie asked the Reverend to check if anyone in the congregation had a room to rent. He promised he would do as she asked, and then shyly turning the brim of his hat round and round in his hands added, "Sister Butler, when you get settled in your new place, may I come to call on you?"

Flossie looked at Reverend Thomas as if he had just stepped out of a flying saucer. Come to call, she thought. Why would Reverend Thomas want to call on ME? Then she remembered he was a widower. Flossie had admired him for all the years she was in the choir. He was a gentleman, and not bad to look at, either. Oh how Irene would tease her if she could see her now.

"That would be fine, Reverend Thomas. Maybe you could help me in my Bible study. I appreciate your Biblical wisdom so."

"First, I would like to invite you out to dinner," Reverend Thomas said nervously. Then he got up quickly with a hasty, "Good day, Miss Butler. See you soon."

Flossie was astounded. She had never married, and at her age, she never considered doing so. Now you stop that, Flossie, she chided herself. The Reverend must just feel sorry for you because of the accident and the loss of your dear Irene. That must be what it's about.

Flossie shut her eyes and turned on her side. Who would have ever imagined she might be leaving the Richters and Bauers to live on her own? She knew they would object, but now that Irene was gone, her work for them was done. As she drifted off, Flossie imagined herself in her finest blue silk suit and hat, serving punch and pastries in the fellowship hall after the Sunday service. Emma Brown would come up to Flossie and whisper, "Reverend Thomas gave such a fine sermon this morning. He was always good, but since he married you, he's even better." With that sweet fantasy in her heart, Flossie fell into a deep, peaceful slumber.

The police had also been paid off generously to keep quiet about the naked man found in the snow near Irene's car. The stiff obviously had no identification on him, and the rope burns on his wrists and welts up and down his back puzzled the medical examiner. One thing was certain: he had been dead before the accident. The coroner listed the cause of death as "cardiac arrest resulting from asphyxiation."

* * * * *

While Addy and the children were at the farm, Lionel had never called. Addy was getting anxious, but not because she wanted Lionel to return. She liked to be let down slowly, not taken off guard when he was suddenly back in town. Addy mentioned to Helena that it was odd that Lionel had not called once since he left for Colorado.

"What's wrong? Do you miss the beast?" Helena joked.

"Of course not. I wish he would stay away forever, but I have to come down off my cloud and gradually face reality."

"Don't give it a second thought. It's New Year's Eve, and we are going to celebrate. Just think. For all our lives, we have had to listen to Guy Lombardo and his Royal Canadians on the radio and count as the ball we couldn't see dropped in Times Square. How boring. This year we can watch it on my snazzy new TELEVISION!" Helena had bought a beautiful 17-inch Zenith console TV as a Christmas present to herself, and for the kids, of course.

"Now, you're going to let the kids stay up and watch Guy Lombardo, aren't you, Addy? We can get drunk after they go to bed."

Helena had another surprise for Addy and the kids. She had purchased TV trays and Swanson frozen TV dinners, something that had recently come on the market. Addy always insisted upon making everything from scratch, but Helena planned to start the New Year off right by getting Addy out of the kitchen. Helena bought several frozen turkey dinners. These TV dinners were nifty little things, really; her kind of cooking. The aluminum pans were sectioned off with compartments for meat, potatoes, and vegetables. All you had to do was pop them in the oven, heat, and enjoy.

As soon as Addy started bustling around the kitchen to prepare a fancy New Year's Eve dinner, Helena, with a flourish, opened the freezer door. "Ta Dah. No cooking for you tonight, my dear. We are now part of the new American frontier. Television and dinners to eat in front of the television."

Addy was aghast at the suggestion. The kids had talked about their friends having these new frozen dinners, but Lionel would never have allowed them in his home. In fact, they didn't even have a TV yet. Not wanting to seem unappreciative of Helena's surprise, Addy remained quiet. She had a flashback of the Italian ladies laboring over the steaming pots of pasta at Sound View Beach and imagined them shaking their heads in disgust at this new invention. "You calla-data FOOD?" Maybe it was best that most of them had passed on. This world was moving much too quickly for folks from "the old country."

"Don't you like my surprise, Addy? It will save you hours of cooking. Besides, it's about time we got MODERN!"

The weather was exceptionally mild for December, and the kids had been playing outside all day. They would have to return to school on January 3, but until then they pretended that Christmas vacation on the farm would last forever.

Unlike Addy, the kids loved the idea of watching the ball drop in Times Square and eating their dinner in front of the TV. Guy Lombardo's New Year's Eve party at the Waldorf Astoria started around ten o'clock, with formally dressed revelers dancing to the sweet sounds of the orchestra. Mary marveled at the women's beautiful gowns and wondered how people got invited to that party. The ballroom was packed, and the dancers seemed to push their way in front of the TV camera. Mary thought that maybe someday, if she were important enough, she could wear a gorgeous gown and dance on TV, too.

The kids could barely keep their eyes open until midnight but were determined to stay awake and watch, for the first time, the ball dropping from a tall building in New York. When the counting began, everyone came to life again, jumped up, and counted along. New Year's Eve was always magical to Addy. In spite of her dreary existence in the past, she held out the hope that something good just might happen in the New Year. At 11:59, just as the ball was touching down, they all jumped and shouted, "HAPPY NEW YEAR!" hugging and kissing one another. Then the Guy Lombardo Orchestra broke into its famous, "Auld Lang Syne." The people in the streets at Times

Square were going wild; waving banners, blowing party horns, releasing balloons. How wonderful it was to see the festivities for the first time. The kids felt as if they were right there.

Addy walked the kids up to bed while Helena started shaking the whiskey sours. The kids fell asleep as soon as their heads hit their pillows.

Helena and Addy sat at the kitchen table gazing out the window. The air had turned cold and large snowflakes were flying. The silent peace of the first day of the New Year was impalpable. Addy hated to break the spell of this beautiful scene, but she was worrying about something. Because the kids would have to return to school on the third, she would have to leave tomorrow to start getting their clothes ready.

When Addy mentioned what was on her mind, Helena said dreamily, "Don't talk about it tonight, OK? We still have plenty of time to make plans."

Addy breathed a sigh of relief and put her hand over Helena's, saying, "You always make me feel better."

After several whiskey sours, the two friends helped one another up the stairs and collapsed in their beds.

Everyone slept late the next morning. Jimmy asked Helena if there were TV breakfasts, but Helena said she didn't think they were invented yet. They all lazed around on New Year's Day, and before they knew it, January 2 snuck up on them. Helena asked Addy if she would like to go home and get the children's clothes and things ready to go back to school. The thought of going back to her house left Addy with a sinking feeling in her stomach, but she knew she had to return sometime. Cosmo was working around the farm, so Addy felt comfortable leaving the kids there with him for a while.

Helena drove Addy home and offered to come inside to help her. Addy did not refuse. She hated to face her house alone. It was cold and gloomy in there so Helena went around opening the drapes and blinds. Addy made some coffee and then went upstairs to collect the kids' school outfits from their closets and hampers. Addy came downstairs with a basket full of laundry and headed toward the basement.

The phone rang, and Addy's heart sunk ... it must be Lionel. Addy put the laundry basket down on the couch and ran to answer the call. She did not recognize the voice on the other end. "Hello, may I please speak to Mrs. Roberge?"

"Yes. I'm Mrs. Roberge. May I ask who is calling?"

"This is Michael Russell, your husband's assistant at work."

Since when does Lionel have an assistant? Addy thought to herself.

"Mrs. Roberge, has Mr. Roberge returned from Colorado yet?" Michael asked nervously.

"Why, no," Addy quickly replied.

"He was supposed to be back by January 2 at the latest, but no one at the office has heard from him. The boss is expecting him for a meeting, and we're all wondering if there might be something wrong."

"Sometimes he misses his flight from Colorado because of all the snow they have there," Addy fibbed. "I'm sure he will be back soon."

Addy was ashamed to admit to this fellow that she had not heard from Lionel at all.

"Will you please have him call the office just as soon as he gets in?" Michael asked.

"Of course. Of course. He must be on his way right now. It's not like him to ever miss a meeting at work," said Addy, trying to sound convincing.

Placing the receiver down slowly, Addy turned to Helena and said, "I think something has happened to Lionel. No one at his work has heard from him—he may not call me at times—but he always checks in at the job."

"If you're lucky, he might have run off with some tramp," Helena joked.

Addy look worried. "No, Helena, I really think something has happened to him. He knows the phone number at the farm, but he never called once ... not there; not at work."

Helen became serious. "We can call the hospitals and police stations in Colorado. Do you know where he went, exactly?"

Addy suddenly realized that Lionel never told her precisely

where he would be staying. She knew that he went to conventions in the Denver area so Addy said quickly, "It's usually Denver."

"That's Jefferson County," Helena said. "Let's get busy calling."

Helena phoned all the police stations and hospitals in Jefferson County, but still came up empty. Then she remembered that when she gave Lionel the new ski jacket for Christmas, he had mentioned he might get some skiing in on his next trip to Colorado. Maybe they should try surrounding counties like Park and Arapahoe.

When they finally reached the police station near Fair Play, they began to get some answers. At first, the captain was hesitant about giving them any information. Then Addy got on the phone and explained that her husband had gone to Colorado, but no one had heard from him since, and she was worried that he had met with some harm.

The police captain knew that they found the body of an unidentified man at the scene of a grizzly car accident, but the details of his death had been sealed. Although Lionel's identification was at the ski chalet, Irene's parents had gone there before the police arrived and destroyed Lionel's belongings.

It seemed plausible to the captain that Lionel's body was the one waiting to be identified at the morgue, but he did not want to alarm Mrs. Roberge.

He proceeded cautiously, "There was a car accident here in the mountains recently. A driver hit an elk. A man was involved, but we still don't know who he is."

"Is he dead?" Addy whispered in disbelief.

"I'm sorry, ma'am. I am not at liberty to share any information with you at this time. You would have to come out here and prove that you know this man."

Helena took the phone from Addy. "What's going on?" Helena inquired impatiently.

"Who are you?" the captain snapped back in an equally sharp tone.

"I am Mrs. Roberge's sister. We need more information."

"I apologize, ma'am, but I am not the one to give you that information. My suggestion to you is that you fly out here just as soon as you can."

"Should we expect a man in a coma, or a corpse, or what?" Helena persisted.

The captain would not budge. "When you get into Denver, call me at the station, same number you just called. Ask for Captain Brewster. I'll drive out to the airport and meet you."

Helena hung up and immediately got the wheels in motion. She called Addy's best neighbor, Joan Avery, to see if she could watch the kids for a few days. Helena explained that Addy and she had to fly out to Colorado because Lionel had never returned from his business trip there, and it was likely he had been in a serious accident.

Addy wandered around the house, feeling as if she was out of her body. She did not know what to do first. She had to pack her clothes to go to Colorado. Should she pack a suitcase for Lionel? She still had to get the children's clothes ready for school.

Helena could see that Addy was a mess. She reminded Addy that the children had gotten some new outfits for Christmas, and those clothes would get them through the short week until Addy returned. She did not have to bother doing laundry.

"You're right, Helena. We have to get ourselves ready to go. Do you think I should bring clothes for Lionel?"

Helena strongly suspected Lionel would not be needing any clothes, but she said, "Sure. Bring him a change of clothes. If he was in an accident, I'm sure all he has now is a hospital johnnie."

Addy went upstairs and packed a small bag for Lionel and one for herself.

Then Helena and Addy drove back out to the farm to get Helena's travel clothes. What would they tell the children? Mary sensed something bad had happened. "What's wrong, Mommy?"

Addy said that Lionel had been in an accident in Colorado, and Helena and she had to go there to help him. She assured

Mary she would not be gone long and said, "You kids are going to stay at Joan Avery's house. You love going there, and this time you can sleep over. It will be so much fun."

The boys, overhearing Addy, questioned, "Why can't we go with you?"

"You have to go back to school, and besides, it costs a lot of money for all those plane tickets. I won't be gone long, I promise."

Mary was frightened. Pete and Jimmy didn't know what to think.

Helena made all the arrangements for the trip. She and Addy would be leaving the next morning before dawn, weather permitting.

Addy watched amazed at the brilliant sunrise, as she flew for the first time. Remarkably, she was not afraid but felt she no longer knew who she was. She and Lionel had a brutal, loveless marriage, but she had never lived on her own. If Lionel were dead, then what? Or, if Lionel were crippled, would she have to take care of him for the rest of her life?

The sky was tinged with pinks and oranges, and the flight was so smooth. How Addy wished she and Helena were taking off on some happy adventure instead of traveling to Colorado to find...who knows what? More heartache? Addy knew the life she and the children shared with Helena was too good to last. She thumbed mindlessly through the pages of her women's magazines until the stewardess came to take their orders for breakfast.

By the time they arrived in Colorado, it was evening. They decided to check into their hotel and wait until morning to phone Captain Brewster. They ordered dinner through room service and then got ready for bed. Addy tossed and turned all night, dreading the morning.

Helena called the police station after breakfast. She got Captain Brewster on the line, and he agreed to meet them at the hotel. They waited for him in the lobby. Captain Brewster looked nervous as he searched out the two women. Helena noticed him first, and she walked over and introduced Addy and herself to him.

"Did you rent a vehicle?" he asked Helena who, as always, looked like the more competent one.

"We didn't have a chance because we got in late last night."

"That's fine," Captain Brewster said. "I'll give you a ride. The roads here can be tricky."

As they drove along in the squad car, no one wanted to be the first to speak. Captain Brewster chose his words carefully. "The unidentified man who was in the accident is at the morgue. We have no way of knowing if he is your husband, Mrs. Roberge."

Addy knew that when a woman in a movie learned of her husband's possible death, she would get hysterical; maybe even faint. Someone would carry the grieving widow over to a sofa and bring smelling salts.

Addy, however, was numb. To draw attention from Addy's failure to react, Helena quickly said, "We don't know anything for sure yet. My sister is in complete shock."

Captain Brewster was more at ease now. "It seems that this fellow was in the mountains at night, probably coming back from a ski trip. His car hit a huge elk. These things are enormous. It's like hitting a brick wall. Poor guy ... didn't stand a chance."

They drove the rest of the way to the morgue in silence.

Addy was terrified. She had never been to a morgue before. What a horribly gruesome thing to have to do. Helena took Addy's arm as they got out of the car. When they were inside, Captain Brewster said something in a hushed tone to the man at the desk. The man disappeared down the corridor and returned about five minutes later.

"We're ready," he announced somberly.

Addy's instinct was to turn and run. She did not want to see a dead person. Helena had linked arms with her and was literally pushing her down the hallway. They entered a small, depressing private room. On the gurney in the middle of the room was a body covered with a white cloth. There was no point of reference for Addy. Who has experience entering the hall of death? In funeral homes, the bodies are spruced up and ready for viewing. This is no different, thought Addy, until she saw a tag tied to the big toe of the corpse.

As the attendant pulled the sheet away from the dead man's face, Helena and Captain Brewster braced Addy from both sides. Addy gasped and immediately looked away. She tried to form the words, "That's my husband," but nothing came out of her mouth. Helena looked over at Captain Brewster and shook her head in acknowledgement.

Of course, Addy was in shock. As much as she often wished Lionel would die, she didn't really mean it. Not die. Maybe just go away and never come back. No normal person could be happy about someone else's death. That would be warped. How would she tell the children? What would she do?

Addy heard Captain Brewster and Helena discussing plans to have Lionel's body flown back to Connecticut. Her mind flashed with recollections of her existence with Lionel. There had been some good times; there really had. She remembered how he looked at her when he first saw her in her wedding dress. He had provided for the children and her. He did try to be the best father he could. Maybe she was at fault. Maybe if she had been different, Lionel would not have struck her. Lionel knew she went to Confession begrudgingly. Did that anger him? She wasn't sexy enough. She didn't know how to please a man. He may have had a good reason to hit her. Oh, why, why hadn't she tried harder? What a failure she was as a wife. At least he liked her cooking ... why did she ever get married? She didn't know how to be feminine ... what a worthless excuse for a human being she was.

Watching Addy from the corner of her eye, Helena could almost read her thoughts. She was certain Addy was somehow blaming herself for Lionel's death. She knew Addy so well by now. If things went terribly wrong, Addy would irrationally take responsibility.

Captain Brewster drove them back to the hotel, and as he opened the car door for them, he spoke earnestly to the women. "This is the part of my job I hate. I can't tell you how sorry I am for your loss. Let me know if there is anything else I can do."

Helena thanked the captain while Addy walked like a zombie up to the hotel entrance. Helena needed a drink and told Addy she was going to the bar. "Why don't you go up to the room and get some rest. Do you want me to call room service to bring up some food or a cocktail? Are you OK to be alone for a little while?"

Addy just shook her head "Yes" or "No" in response to Helena's questions. In the elevator, a young couple was laughing hysterically, in complete oblivion to their mortality. How could anything be funny? Addy had just looked death squarely in the face. The decay swallowed her, and she wondered if the young couple could smell her decomposing.

The rest of the time in Colorado was a blur. Helena respected Addy's silence and spoke only when necessary. She could see that it might be a tough road ahead for Addy. Although in the end, Addy was better off without Lionel, the wounds were still too fresh. If Addy could conquer her guilt, she would move on to a happier life. Helena was convinced of that.

Chapter XIX

Possibilities

Monsignor Roberge, badly shaken by the news of the sudden death of his brother Lionel, maintained his composure and was more than helpful consoling the children and assisting with the final arrangements.

As Addy and the children sat in the front row of Blanchard's Funeral Home, waiting for the mourners to file past Lionel's casket, Addy's mind drifted off to the day she had first seen Helena again. It was in this same room, at the wake of dear Mary Kurowski, Helena's mom. That time seemed far away; their lives had changed so much since then. Addy stood up quickly as the first few people in the line of sympathizers came over to greet the children and her. The funeral home was crowded: neighbors, church members, Lionel's co-workers, the children's teachers and schoolmates—an endless stream of faces awk-wardly muttering condolences.

After the funeral Mass and rite of burial at the cemetery, Monsignor Roberge extended an invitation to everyone present to join the Roberge family for lunch at "Lido's," the new Italian restaurant in town. The crowd thinned out considerably, and Helena was relieved that there would not be an overabundance of supporters at the restaurant. She recalled the day of her mom's funeral and how dreadfully hot it had been. Thank God it was still winter. All she wanted to do was get back to the farm, kick off her high heels, and get drunk. Never in her wildest fantasies about killing Lionel off, did she ever imagine that an elk would be the demise of the poor slob.

Helena insisted that after the funeral Addy and the kids stay on at the farm indefinitely. Addy did not protest. She dreaded going back to her house, which was plagued by Lionel's dark spirit. Addy was superstitious about people who met with violent deaths. She believed that they could never rest in peace and returned to disturb the lives of those they had left behind.

In a week, the children returned to school. Addy still wandered about aimlessly in Helena's house. She could not even cook, but people had brought them enough meals to last a month. Helena did not push Addy but knew some plans had to be made eventually. Did Lionel have a will? Did he own life insurance? What about the mortgage on the house?

There were some storms in January, so the kids got several snow days. Addy was glad to have them around, even though she didn't know what to say about their father. The three children tried to act as if nothing had ever happened. Addy doubted she was handling the situation responsibly, but she just didn't know what to do. These were the times she wished she was more religious. Perhaps then, she could reassure the children that their dad was in "a better place."

Come February, Addy had still not talked about what she was going to do next. Helena felt it was time to discuss how they would sort out Lionel's financial affairs. One bright, chilly morning, while the two friends finished their coffee and marveled at how sunny it was for February, Helena broached the topic.

"Addy, did Lionel have a lawyer?" she asked gently.

Addy thought for a moment and then remembered that he did. "Yes. He's Turner Boyd, the same lawyers my aunts had."

"We are going to have to see him soon. Do you know if Lionel had a will?"

Addy was embarrassed to say she did not know. It would seem a husband would share such information with his wife, but Lionel always said Addy was dense when it came to financial matters.

Helena asked Addy if it would be OK for her to call and make an appointment to see Attorney Boyd, and said, "I'll go with you."

"Sure," Addy agreed, relieved that she did not have to see the lawyer alone. Sometimes she wondered if she was becoming a burden to her friend.

Attorney Boyd had an opening for that Friday. Addy dreaded going. She hated to appear so stupid about her husband's finances. When Addy saw Attorney Boyd, however, she felt very much at ease. He was a gentle soul, but extremely competent.

After Counselor Boyd expressed his condolences, he opened a folder containing a thick stack of papers.

"Lionel has provided well for you," Attorney Boyd began. "He purchased mortgage insurance so your house will be paid off due to his death. We just have to deliver his death certificate to the bank. In addition, he had a life insurance policy with a cash value of ... $500,000 for accidental death."

Addy looked at Helena with disbelief. Lionel with THAT much life insurance?

Attorney Boyd continued, "Lionel was relatively young and in good health so he was able to purchase a large amount of life insurance with considerably low premiums. Insurance companies bank on people living longer than, unfortunately, Lionel did."

"Is there a will?" Helena asked. She was afraid that Lionel might have left all his assets to the church.

"There's a simple will," Attorney Boyd replied. "$450,000 goes to Mrs. Roberge, with the stipulation that she establishes a trust fund for the children's education, and $50,000 goes to Lionel's brother, The Monsignor Roberge."

Tears welled in Addy's eyes. She couldn't believe that Lionel had arranged for them to be taken care of so generously. As usual, Helena could almost read Addy's mind. She had to bite her tongue to keep from blurting, "You have the bruises to show for it."

After their visit to the lawyer's office, Helena took Addy out to lunch to "celebrate," although she was careful not to use that word. Addy was square, had always been square, and would always remain square. Reveling about a windfall that had come at the expense of Lionel's very life was something Addy could never imagine doing. "No matter what, one must never be happy about something horrible happening to another person,"

Addy always told the children.

As Helena looked at Addy sitting across the table, she noticed that, in spite of recent events, Addy looked lovelier and more serene. She had lost a lot of weight during this ordeal, and her narrower face highlighted her delicate features. "So now that you've seen the lawyer, what are your plans?'

"About what?" Addy looked startled.

"About what you will do with all that money?"

Addy said, in all seriousness, "Why, I haven't even thought about it, have you?"

"Of course," Helena answered animatedly. "Do you want to hear my plans? First, you must sell your house. The farm is your home now."

"But we can't move in with you permanently. I know what a private person you are. It would be an infringement," Addy protested.

"Wait. Here's what I was thinking. If you would feel better, you can buy the house from me for a dollar. I still have a lot of business to attend to in New York. I keep an apartment there, you know, and besides, I'm not quite ready to put myself out to pasture in CHESTER. Still have miles to go before I sleep."

A look of anxiety clouded Addy's face. How would she ever live without Helena in Chester? She had come to depend upon her so much. How had she been so stupid to think Helena would ever settle down on the farm? What an idiot she was at times. Just because she and the kids were happy there, it didn't mean Helena was. After all, Helena was a woman of the world, used to an exciting life.

Helena said, "Hey, don't look so worried. I'm not planning to leave any time soon, and I'll be back and forth. Before I go ANYWHERE, I'm going to teach you how to DRIVE."

Addy was terrified to drive, but now that Lionel was gone and Helena might be moving back to New York, she really had no choice. Before Addy got behind the wheel with Helena, she would take a few driving lessons. Helena was, of course, a great driver, albeit, a little heavy on the pedal, but Addy was just too ashamed to have Helena witness her ineptitude. Helena thought

Addy was being foolish to waste her money on driving school, but Addy insisted.

"Hmm ..." Helena mused. "You are growing a backbone, Mon Cheri. I can count on one hand those who dare defy my decrees." Then, they both laughed. What a warm and easy friendship they shared. To have someone you trust implicitly, and who is always in your corner, is a priceless gift. Addy and Helena shared this blessing and would remain ever-grateful for it the rest of their lives.

Learning to drive was grueling for Addy. Her biggest fear was that she would have an accident and kill someone. She took several lessons but could tell her driving instructor did not have any confidence in her ability. Helena took her to empty parking lots when all the stores were closed on Sundays. They practiced ceaselessly. Helena assured Addy that winter was the best time to learn to drive because if you can drive in icy conditions, you can drive anywhere. Addy wasn't so sure about that. When she felt the car spinning out of control, she panicked. Eventually they decided to put the remainder of the lessons on hold until spring.

"I'm not letting you off the hook, you know," Helena warned. "We're just taking a little respite, but we'll pick up in April."

Helena decided that the only time Addy and she would return to Addy's house was to make cosmetic improvements to put it up for sale.

"Look at it objectively," Helena told Addy. "Look at it as projects ... like you never lived there."

They did hire painters to freshen up all the rooms, had new carpet installed, and cheery slipcovers made for the living room furniture. They scrubbed the bathroom, changed the shower curtain, had all the windows in the house washed, and hired a landscaper to beautify the front and back yards. Cosmo and the kids cleaned out the basement and gathered items to donate to the Salvation Army. Spring was a particularly good time to sell a home because families fleeing from larger cities often wanted to get their children situated in a suburban school system come fall.

The house seemed to take on a new life, and Addy, in her characteristic mindset of regret, mused, "Why couldn't the house have looked like this when I lived here?"

Addy knew the answer. Although she did not want to malign the deceased, she recognized that Lionel had never let her fix up their home. She had several times offered to do the wallpapering and painting herself, but Lionel wouldn't agree to even the cost of one gallon of paint. Their home remained as it was when they were first married, and although Addy was ashamed of its dingy appearance, she had long ago given up on its beautification. How ironic that Lionel had been such a tightwad all his life, and now his money was funding what he would most assuredly have considered an extravagant, unnecessary makeover.

Attorney Boyd's wife was one of the few female real estate agents, and she worked diligently to help Addy sell the house. Because Addy had the insurance money, she priced the house to sell, and it did. Just two weeks after the house went on the market, several buyers expressed an interest. Judy Boyd particularly liked one young family and asked Addy and Helena to meet them at the property.

In spite of her eagerness to rid herself of the memories the house held for her, Addy had a difficult time with change. On the day that Helena and she were scheduled to meet the couple, Addy was noticeably uneasy. Helena, who knew Addy almost as well as she knew herself asked, "What's wrong, kid?"

Addy said, "I'm a nervous wreck and don't know why. Now that the time has come to sell the place, I'm scared."

That was all Helena needed to hear. "Oh, I forgot. You have those tender memories of your love nest with dearest Lionel; how he worshipped and coddled you; how your wish was his command. I don't blame you for not wanting to sell the place— shall we take it off the market? How about making it into a shrine for lovers?"

Helena's ribbing snapped Addy back into reality. They both began to laugh, sending Addy running to the bathroom. It was a beautiful spring day, but Addy was far from trusting that things would turn out all right.

Both Addy and Helena loved the people who were interested in buying Addy's house. The couple had two small boys, and the wife was pregnant with another child. Ever since they were first married, they had been living in New Haven on the second floor of the three-story house that belonged to the young man's parents. The tenement was getting too small for their growing family, and the fellow's parents, who lived on the first floor, frequently complained about the noise the boys made. It had been nice of the parents to charge them only half rent, but this financial break came at a cost. The young man's parents were Italian immigrants, and the father ruled with an iron hand. He bossed his son and daughter-in-law, expecting them to raise their boys as he said as well as doing all the maintenance around the property. Of course, the old man's attitude made for a good deal of marital strife for the couple. All they wanted was to move into a home of their own.

Addy was sold on this young family. She knew they must have been sinking every cent into buying the house so in private negotiations with Judy Boyd, Addy dropped the selling price down by $2,000 and said the couple could have any or all of the contents of the house.

The young couple could not believe how they had stumbled upon such a generous seller. Their luck was certainly changing. After they moved into their new home, Addy brought over one of her coffee cakes, and she exchanged phone numbers with them. Helena and she just had to know whether the new baby would be a girl or boy. Maybe their family would even like to come out to the farm someday.

Helena knew Addy had a long way to go before she began to believe in herself. Learning to drive was the first step, but there were still many obstacles remaining. One evening after dinner while Helena and Addy were sitting alone in the farmhouse kitchen drinking coffee and eating tomato soup cake, Helena revealed her latest idea to Addy.

"My next plan for you is—are you ready for this—to open a BAKERY!"

Addy looked at her friend as if she had finally snapped. "Are you crazy? I don't even want to discuss it. I have no idea how to run a business, and even if I did, it would be sure to fail."

Helena was weary of handling Addy with kid gloves and said tetchily, "Look, you are a widow with three children to support. You have plenty of money so if the bakery fails, you can just write it off. Nobody needs to know Lionel left insurance money. People will just think you are using the money you got for your house. Besides, who cares what people think? They'll feel sorry for the poor widow and buy your cakes. I hate to say this, Addy, but it's time for you to stand on your own two feet."

All Addy heard was, "time to stand on your own two feet," and immediately spiraled into shame and self-hatred. Her eyes welled with tears, suspecting Helena had most definitely grown tired of her and thought she was a worthless, helpless, baby.

"Addy, I didn't mean to upset you. All I want is for the kids and you to enjoy some of the happiness you've missed out on in life. The bakery can be a family affair, and the kids can work there, too. Can't you just see Mary bustling around, waiting on customers?"

Helena was right. Addy knew she had been a disgraceful mouse all her life, and she did not want to be a weakling anymore. She had to show her kids that she was someone upon whom they could always depend. Helena was the only strong person in their lives; what would they do if Helena went away?

The next day, Addy told the kids she had something to talk about with them. The kids seemed delighted because ever since Lionel died and the house had been sold, no one seemed to say much to them about anything. Addy explained how Helena had the idea of opening a bakery. At first, it seemed like an outlandish notion, but after she contemplated, it didn't seem like such a crazy idea after all. She told the kids that as a child, she always dreamed of having a bakery of her own. Even after the kids went off to college, Addy said, they could work in the bakery in the summers. Before she got too excited about the prospect of a business, however, Addy wanted to see what the kids thought.

Of course, the children loved the idea. They could see the sparkle in their mom's eye while she was talking about it; a gleam they had rarely seen before. Straightaway, they started thinking of names for their pastry shop. When Helena heard the enthusiastic chatter, she rushed into the room. Suspecting the kids had given their stamp of approval on the bakery idea, she piped in with, "How about 'Addy's Dream?' Isn't that a DREAMY name for a bakery?"

The boys rolled their eyes at Helena's pun.

"Hold it a minute, everyone!" Peter shouted excitedly. "First we have to figure out where we can find a building for the bakery, and all that other stuff." As the eldest, Peter felt he was now the man of the family and was enjoying his new status.

"You're right, Pete," Addy said. "I'll have to do some investigating first. We have a lot to learn about the 'dough' business before we start making any 'dough.'"

The boys groaned at her corny joke, but Helena said, "Good one, Addy."

Helena was always self-assured, but now she felt like "Wonder Woman," the Justice League Heroine. Boy am I good, she thought smugly. She had been instrumental in changing Addy from a shrinking violet into an Amazon—well, maybe not an Amazon yet, but a Jane Eyre, at least.

Addy could not sleep that night. Opening a bakery was a far-fetched idea, and, of course, she was scared to death. Yet, she wanted to show Helena and the children that she was self-reliant and brave. Addy didn't know how to be courageous, but maybe by doing things that built self-confidence, she would learn. What if the bakery was a huge flop? Well, others greater than she had failed but tried again. Addy had always liked to read about famous people who overcame great obstacles and never gave up.

She recalled that Henry Ford failed and went broke five times before succeeding. F.W. Woolworth wasn't allowed to wait on customers when he worked in a dry goods store because his boss said he didn't have any sense. Why even Albert Einstein did not speak until he was four or read until he was seven. His parents and teachers thought he was mentally slow. Now, Addy, don't even think about comparing yourself to Einstein, she thought and smiled, falling into a pleasant sleep.

The next morning, Addy awakened to the smell of fresh coffee that Helena had just made. It was Saturday, and the kids were already down in the barn helping Cosmo. Addy was embarrassed that she had slept in while Helena fixed breakfast for the children. She grabbed her robe and rushed downstairs.

"I'm so sorry you had to make breakfast. I don't know why I slept so late," Addy apologized.

"Hey, I may be no cook, but at least I scramble a mean egg and make good coffee. Besides, if we're ever going to get this bakery opened, I have to start learning so I can help you out. What do you think ... should we serve breakfast there?"

"That might be trying to take on too much at once. Maybe just coffee and pastries to start? Do you remember the bakery near our school when we were kids? We used to buy a bag of crumbs for a nickel. My aunts always said the crumbs were swept up from the floor, but we didn't care. How odd when I think of it now—selling crumbs—maybe they were supposed to be for the birds?"

Helena laughed. "You have such a good memory, Addy. I had forgotten all about that. Those crumbs were good, though. I would lick my finger and put it in the bag so the crumbs would stick to it."

"Such simple times, right?" Addy mused.

"Now, don't change the subject. We are going to see our realtor next week and have her locate a building for us. She did a great job selling your house, don't you think?"

Addy nodded in agreement. "You know what? I'm going to go through my recipes and find the ones that can be doubled or tripled without losing their flavor. The Protestant churches always have church suppers so they must have recipes that can feed a crowd. Maybe there are cookbooks at the library or maybe I can ask at one of the churches ..."

Pleased that Addy's train of thought was back on track, Helena said, "The first thing we have to do is develop a business plan, and I can help with that. Then, of course, we have to decide if we want to buy a bakery that's already established or purchase a building and then buy the equipment. It would be more feasible to buy one that has all the ovens and machines, but chances of our finding one like that might be slim."

In the next few weeks, Judy Boyd took Addy and Helena to several potential buildings, but the negatives of each outweighed the positives. Either the location was bad or the building would be too difficult to convert to a bakery. Finally, Helena decided to become proactive and approach bakery owners about selling their businesses.

Most pastry shops had sprung up in ethnic neighborhoods and had been passed down through the generations, like *Faranelli's*, famous for its rum cakes and Italian cookies. Helena visited every bakery in the vicinity, but none seemed positioned to sell.

One possibility might be *Mother Emmanuelson's Scandinavian Bakery* on the same street as St. Michael's Church. This shop had been in town for years and enjoyed a steady flow of customers after Mass. When Helena stopped in, the bakery was very busy, and the elderly couple who owned it didn't come up for air. They had to be in their seventies and looked totally overwhelmed. Helena heard that their son was part owner of the business, but he was not around that day. Helena went back a couple of times just to evaluate the situation. She bought a cup of coffee and a fabulous Danish and then brought a box of pastries home for Addy and the kids.

When Helena returned to *Emmanuelson's* a third time, she got lucky. The son, Jensen, was working, and the parents were not there. He had to be in his fifties, so maybe the parents were older than she thought. He also looked worn out. The shop was not busy, and Helena wasted no time turning on her charm and flirting a bit. He was wearing a name badge so Helena pounced on that immediately.

"Good morning, Jensen," Helena quipped. "Smells great in here."

The weary shopkeeper looked up, smiled, and said, "Good

morning. May I help you?"

Helena ordered a cherry-cheese Danish and coffee. She sat down at one of the four marble tables, and Jensen quickly brought her order. As he turned to go back to work, Helena said demurely, "Jensen, could you sit down and talk for just a minute?"

Her request caught Jensen off guard, and before he had time to think, he answered, "Sure. Let me get myself a cup of coffee." He seemed relieved to take a break from his work. After he joined Helena, they made small talk, and when Jensen seemed more relaxed, Helena broached the topic of selling the bakery. She was prepared for any response from outrage to acceptance.

Surprisingly, Jensen was somewhat receptive. "You know, we haven't ever considered selling the business, but you have got me to thinking. My parents are almost ninety, and they don't have half the energy they once had. I've been part of the business since I was a kid. Frankly, I am sick of it. We don't need the money anymore, but this bakery is my parents' life. They have too much pride to admit they are getting too old for this. I don't want to end up like them."

Jensen looked worried. He knew it would be a hard sell. Impossible even, but he could give it a try. Helena finished her coffee and left her phone number. "Thanks for hearing me out. After you talk to your parents, and they have time to consider our outlandish proposal, give me a call."

Helena then flashed her killer smile at Jensen, just as if he were the only man on the planet.

"I will call you," Jensen said. "Can't promise you anything, but it's worth a shot. My parents are stubborn."

Helena decided to let it be until she heard from Jensen. The last thing she wanted was to badger him or his parents. If she behaved badly, she might ruin her plans for Addy's big chance.

Three weeks passed before Helena heard from Jensen. He apologized for keeping her waiting so long, but his mother had been hospitalized, and his dad and he had been running the bakery alone. Jensen had always wanted to hire help, but his parents would never hear of it. Maybe now that Mama was ill, his parents would realize they just could not do it by themselves anymore. He told Helena that he was going to first try talking with his mother.

Of course, Jensen did not have the power to make decisions about the business, but while his mom was resting in the hospital and his dad was out of earshot, Jensen brought up the topic of the bakery. His mother, Anesa, was far more reasonable than his father was, and she was strong enough now so this discussion would not contribute to her infirmity. She was surprisingly interested in the idea. Mama told Jensen she had approached Papa many times about retiring, but he had always said he would never close the bakery.

"What if instead of closing the bakery, he sold it to someone? Maybe the people would let him stay on as long as he wanted so he could show them how to run things. He would like that, don't you think, Mama?"

"Jensen you know how your Papa is. He's *stædig som en okse* (stubborn like an ox)."

"I know, I know, Mama. Why do you think I never argue with him? He won't stop until he wins ... I don't even bother," Jensen agreed in a frustrated tone.

Jensen's mother looked sad. "Papa has not been fair to you. If he didn't make you stay in the bakery all your life, maybe you would have gone to college or maybe you would have found a wife."

"Don't blame Papa because I didn't find a wife. I guess I was just too busy to find one, but I am getting sick and tired of the bakery. My dream is to travel ... maybe see the old country ... maybe you and Papa could come with me."

Anesa's cloudy blue eyes suddenly sparkled. "I have longed to see my country again before I die, but we have always been too busy with the bakery. That would be wonderful, and I could show you all the places I knew as a girl ..."

"That's it, Mama. We are going. Papa likes to pretend he is as strong as he was when he was younger, but he is getting old. I notice how he walks slower and takes longer to fill the orders. His hearing is failing, too."

Anesa said she wanted to rest now so Jensen kissed her "good-bye," and said he would be back the next day. When he returned home, he called Helena to update her on the progress.

"I talked to my mother today, and she seems like she would be for the idea. I'm not sure how you feel about this, but I suggested that the new owner might let my father stay on to help run the bakery. I'm sure he would be proud to show off all his knowledge, but I don't know how you feel about that," Jensen said somewhat nervously.

Helena thought for a moment. They certainly didn't have any deadlines, and they did not know the first thing about running a bakery. Maybe having the old man stay on wouldn't be such a bad idea.

"We would consider that, sure," Helena said agreeably. "Just try getting your father to see the benefits of selling the business. Then we can work out all the details."

"That's good. When my mother comes home from the hospital, I will bring up the subject with my father. Right now, he's fretting over Mama's health, and I know he's not in the mood to talk about anything ..."

After speaking with Jensen, Helena felt confident that she could make this deal a reality for Addy and the kids. It would take patience, diplomacy, and probably a lot of fawning over the old man. After all, the couple had no grandchildren so they might take a liking to Addy's brood. Plus, Addy and the children were not only sweet creatures, but Addy was a widow and the children now fatherless. Maybe the old fellow's heart would soften after he has gotten to know the Roberge family. Time would tell.

Helena and Addy put the prospect of a bakery on the back burner while they had the first floor of the farmhouse renovated. This time Addy insisted on paying for the work. Part of her felt guilty for using the money she had received from the sale of her house and Lionel's insurance money to fund the renovations. They wanted to keep the integrity of the old home intact so made only a few necessary and decorative changes like having new windows installed; refinishing the hardwood floors; and wallpapering and painting all the rooms. Would people look at her as the greedy widow spending blood money? As much as she tried to feel sorrow about Lionel's death, she felt only emptiness. Addy continually reminded herself that Lionel was, after all, the father of her beautiful children. He had supported them while he was alive and had provided handsomely for them upon his death.

The children had mixed feelings, too. They knew that when a dad dies, kids should be crying inconsolably. Mary was the only emotional one of the three, and even she had cried for just a little while. How could life be progressing so smoothly—in fact, even better than before? Guilt, such an integral part of their Catholic upbringing, was having somewhat of an effect upon them all but was, fortunately, not eating them up inside.

Now that Lionel had died, Addy was free to think about Greg without feeling adulterous. She wondered how Allison and he were doing up in Maine. Did he have a woman by now? Most likely ... he was so desirable. How he had found her attractive, Addy would never know. He was lonely and desperate. That must be it. One of the things that had kept Addy back in life was the fear of making a fool of herself. Had she done that with Greg? What if she had been laughable and repulsive in bed, but Greg was so lonely that he put up with her? At times, she thought about contacting him but was afraid to do so. Sure, things had been going her way since Helena came to town. Addy had always thought of herself as a very unlucky person, and although her luck seemed to be changing, she dare not let down her guard. Helena brought her luck, but every person's run of good luck has to end eventually. She made up her mind never to contact Greg. If he rejected her, all the good that had entered her life would evaporate, and she would spiral into obsessive thinking about her inadequacies. Why invite trouble?

Chapter XX

Unspeakable Joy

Wells, Maine

Greg had made the decision to move permanently to Wells, Maine. He winterized the cottage and transformed it into a comfortable year-round home. Allison was enrolled in a small, friendly school where the teachers were sensitive to her medical issues and aware that she did not have a mother.

Greg's sister Caroline and her family came to visit frequently, even celebrating holidays with them at the cottage. As always, Caroline was trying to set Greg up with someone. When she attended the Christmas pageant at Allison's school, she observed that one of the teachers had an eye for him, but Greg had no interest. He was too busy juggling work and taking care of Allison. Caroline sometimes brought up Addy, but Greg did not want to discuss her.

In reality, Addy had inadvertently ruined it for him to find any other woman. He knew she was off limits, but he still savored the special memories of Addy and her children. He had had his share of romances, yet he had never met anyone as sincere and tender as Addy. His blood boiled when he thought about her suffering abuse at the hands of her husband, and numerous times, he almost got in his car to drive down to Connecticut. Of course, he always stopped himself. That tyrant by no means intimidated Greg, but a lunatic bully like Lionel can do great harm to his wife and children when threatened. If he killed Lionel, Greg would go to jail, and who would look after Allison?

When he was first married, Greg's wife Diane seemed loving

and caring, but when she got pregnant with Allison, she changed. She had never been the motherly type, but she chose to have a child for Greg's sake. The pregnancy was a difficult one. Diane experienced drastic mood swings, and the morning sickness lasted almost nine months. Allison was premature, and a callous doctor told them, "Don't get too attached to this baby because the chances of her surviving are not good." Greg wanted to punch that doctor in the face. Now that he looked back, his wife had probably wished that grim prediction had come true.

Allison spent her first three months in the hospital barely clinging to life. Greg went every day after work to sit by Allison's incubator and talk softly to her. Diane rarely accompanied him. She always found some excuse to stay home. Had the fact that she had been unable to bond with Allison made Diane exhibit so little interest in being a mother? Against all odds, Allison did make it, and when that glorious day to pick her up from the hospital arrived, Greg went alone.

His sister Caroline was waiting at his house to greet tiny Allison, but his wife barely glanced at the baby. Greg told himself that the difficult pregnancy had worn Diane out, and she would surely come around. Over the next few months, Allison experienced recurring infections with fever, restlessness, and inconsolable crying. The pediatrician assured Greg that because Allison was premature, she had a hard time fighting off germs. He counseled Greg to bundle up the baby and take her outside in her carriage. He also advised keeping Allison away from young children and crowds.

Greg followed the doctor's instructions but noticed Allison had difficulty breathing at times. Again, the pediatrician attributed these symptoms to Allison's underdeveloped lungs. She did not seem to have an appetite and was losing weight. During one of her examinations, Greg mentioned he had read about babies diagnosed with "failure to thrive."

The doctor dismissed Greg's concerns with the statement that not all babies grow at the same rate, and some babies lose weight in the first few months.

"You're a nervous first-time father. Stop worrying so much, and enjoy your baby," the pediatrician laughed.

Soon, however, Allison began to develop bruises on her body from activities as simple as having her diaper changed. As Greg watched his listless, pale, and thin little girl deteriorating further, he felt helpless and broken-hearted. He had that parental instinct that something was seriously wrong with Allison, and it was time to seek another opinion. His wife Diane told him he was being a worrywart and should listen to the pediatrician. That was easy for her to say because she rarely interacted with Allison. Greg had become the primary caregiver.

Greg decided to make an appointment for Allison at Boston Children's Hospital and asked his sister Caroline to go with him so that she could hold the baby in the car. By this time, it was obvious that Allison's mother wanted nothing to do with motherhood. One evening in the midst of an intense argument, Diane shouted at Greg, "I wasn't cut out to be a wife and mother. I had no idea what this would be like. I'm suffocating!"

From that moment, Greg knew he was in this alone. It took quite a while to get an appointment with Dr. Samuel Hirschfield, a pediatrician who specialized in childhood diseases. Greg counted the days until he could finally take Allison to Boston. Dr. Hirschfield was recognized for his dedication to research of illnesses for which cures had not yet been found. If anyone could find out what was wrong with Allison, this doctor could.

As Dr. Hirschfield took notes about Allison's short medical history and then examined her, he looked gravely concerned. He informed Greg that before he could make an accurate diagnosis, he had to order blood tests. Greg had done a lot of his own research and feared his suspicions might be correct.

"I know I have to wait for the test results, but do you have ANY idea by examining Allison what might be wrong with her?" Greg entreated.

"Many different illnesses can exhibit these same symptoms. I don't want to alarm you unnecessarily. Try not to think the worst and relax until I call you with the results."

And that was that. The doctor shook Greg's hand and exited

the examining room.

Several days had passed, and Greg still had not heard from Boston Children's Hospital. He was overcome with worry, but his wife seemed unfazed. Sometimes Greg tried to give Diane the benefit of the doubt, telling himself that she was in denial, and this was the only way she could cope with Allison's poor health. Diane rarely prepared dinner and had plans most evenings to go out with "the girls." Greg was by no means a mouse, but he was also not a controlling husband and never asked where she was going or what time she expected to be home. After all, they had a live-in helper to take care of Allison while Greg was at work.

When the phone rang early one morning, Greg knew instinctively that it must be the Boston Children's Hospital. Dr. Hirschfield proceeded in very measured words, "Greg, we have Allison's test results back. I am sorry to have to tell you this, but Allison has acute leukemia." Greg had reached that conclusion long ago, but he had hoped it would turn out not to be true.

He knew the statistics. Babies with leukemia had only a few months life expectancy. The treatments in use were arsenic and chemotherapy. How could a baby ever survive these radical therapies?

Dr. Hirschfield continued, "Our hospital has one of the best treatment centers in the world. Will you call my office and make an appointment to bring Allison in again?"

Greg thanked the doctor and hung up the phone. Life had been pretty good to him so far, but today everything came crashing down. How could his sweet baby have this awful disease? When Allison was born, the doctors warned him not to become too attached, but that was the most ridiculous statement anyone had ever made—let alone a doctor. How could you not love your baby?

Greg did not have to wait long to find an answer to that question. When he broke the news about Allison's diagnosis to Diane, she acted as if he had just informed her of some calamity he read about in the newspaper.

"That's a shame. I just can't believe I didn't have a normal baby." It was all about her. No thought of the suffering and inevitable short life their child was facing. In that moment, Greg realized he had married the wrong person.

Greg was a New Englander whose ancestors had come to America in the 1700s. Some had fought in the American Revolution. He was raised in a close-knit Catholic family who put God and children above all else. Surrounded by dedicated wives and mothers while he was growing up, Greg assumed all women were like that once they got married.

Greg had first met Diane at college when she was a tall, blonde beauty queen from California. All the guys in his fraternity wanted to date her, but she chose Greg. She knew how to have a good time and made his college years exciting. As their relationship grew more serious, Greg brought Diane home to meet his family. He could tell immediately that his mother did not approve of her. First, she was not Catholic and had no affiliation with any religion. His family's displeasure with Diane served only to push Greg even closer to her. After all, what did they know about love? They all seemed to base their marriages upon commonplace things like religion or nationality. This was the twentieth century and time for people to marry because they were in love not because they shared similar backgrounds.

Because Diane was not a Catholic, she and Greg could not get married in the Church. This was one of his mother's greatest heartaches. They eventually eloped and found a justice of the peace to perform the ceremony. The first few years of their marriage were romantic, and Greg believed he had made the right decision.

Greg eventually realized that his mother's misgivings about Diane were accurate, and he only wished that his mom were still around so that he could tell her. Diane was a very beautiful but superficial woman whose world revolved around herself and her enjoyment. Would she ever mature? Diane reminded Greg of "Fanny Trellis," the character Betty Davis played in the film, *Mr. Skeffington*. Fanny was an attractive socialite who could not face getting old. She even rejected her own daughter because she did not want any competition. Greg loathed the character of

Fanny Trellis, and he now despised Diane.

Greg did not have to be the one to tell Diane to get lost. One day while he was at work, Diane left him. She did not tell the live-in nanny where she was going, but she had taken her vast wardrobe with her. In a note she left on Greg's pillow, Diane simply stated:

"We had some good times, but I am finished with this marriage. All you care about is Allison, and I need someone who puts me first. Good-bye and good luck."

What a cold, cruel woman she was in the end. Greg was relieved she had left him. He could not bear watching her ignore Allison; her blasé manner just added to his anxiety. She had plenty of her own money, so Greg doubted she would try to get alimony from him.

Diane moved to California and never looked back. She resumed her carefree existence as a socialite, watchful not to reveal she had a daughter. As Greg suspected, Diane did not sue him for alimony so they never had to interact again. The whole situation was sad; maybe some women just do not have any maternal instinct. During his childhood, Greg had a female cat who gave birth to four kittens. The mother cat nurtured three of her babies but ignored the fourth one and refused to nurse it. Greg tried feeding the poor little runt with an eyedropper, but that did not work. The neglected kitten died soon after birth, and Greg was furious with this mother cat. His parents told him that occasionally, if an animal senses there is something wrong with one of its babies, the animal ignores that baby. Maybe Diane was like that mother cat. In her case, she could not face the fact that she had given birth to a less than perfect child. Greg eventually reached the conclusion that it was a waste of time to try to figure out some people. He tried to put Diane out of his mind forever.

Being both mother and father to his daughter was not easy, but Greg certainly tried. Allison defied the statistics. She survived the grueling treatments, and her leukemia was in remission. Although there was no known cure for her disease, as long as she remained in remission, she would live. The physicians at Boston Children's Hospital were amazed at Allison's progress, and they frequently praised Greg for his devotion to his daughter. Still, Greg was humiliated that Allison's mother had taken off on them. Mothers are not supposed to do those things.

One evening when Allison was in bed, Greg was reading the *Boston Sunday Globe* and listening to classical music on the radio. He looked forward to this quiet time just before his workweek began. His eye caught the headline on an article: **"Scandal uncovered upon death of Colorado Senator Neal Richter"**

Greg enjoyed following national politics and knew that Senator Richter, a conservative Republican with an impeccable record, had been in office for years. The press was so often cruel. Why would they dig up a scandal after a man dies?

The article stated that Senator Richter had not been well ever since his only child, Irene Bauer, was killed in an automobile accident. The details of the crash had been sealed but were leaked to the newspapers when Senator Richter passed away. Apparently, Irene's car hit an elk, and she died instantly. Her maid survived the accident but was in a coma for some time and recalled nothing. The shocking secret was that the body of a naked man with ligature marks around his wrists and ankles was also discovered at the scene. The man was identified as Lionel Roberge, of Chester, Connecticut. No further information about the deceased man or his connection to Irene Bauer was available.

Greg thought, that's pretty weird. Then it struck him—LIONEL ROBERGE. If he remembered correctly, that was the name of Addy's husband. It couldn't be the same Lionel Roberge. What would he be doing naked in the Colorado mountains in the middle of the winter? Yet, Chester, Connecticut, was the name of the town where Addy lived. There could be a chance that there was more than one man in Chester named "Lionel Roberge."

Although Greg tried to forget about what he had read, this bizarre story was bedeviling. If this was, indeed, Addy's husband, does it mean she is now a free woman? How was she supporting herself and her children? Addy was fragile, and maybe this news had humiliated her beyond healing. She was the somewhat vulnerable, innocent woman a man instinctively wants to protect.

Greg shared the story with his sister Caroline, and she encouraged him to take a ride down to Connecticut to investigate the matter. Ever the optimist, Caroline reminded Greg that he and Addy had a lot in common, and maybe they were meant for each other. This time Greg took Caroline's words to heart. What did he have to lose? If the outcome were to see Addy and the kids again, however briefly, it would be worth the trip.

Before Greg set out on his journey, he made plans to have Allison stay with Caroline. Although he might have been able to get Addy's number from the Connecticut telephone operator, he decided against calling her. It would be better to somehow assess the situation first. The ride from Wells to Chester would take him about five or six hours. The pleasant route would give Greg time to relax and figure out how to approach Addy. He did not want the people in her small town to get the impression that his intentions were less than honorable. Maybe he would pretend to be a distant cousin.

Because it took him longer than expected to get Allison settled at his sister's, Greg hit the road later than planned. He was less than halfway to Chester, and it was already growing dark. Greg was getting sleepy but wondered where in this uninhabited stretch of woodlands he might find a motel. As a last resort, he could pull over to the side of the road and take a snooze, but he did not want to be nabbed by a police officer.

The Connecticut shoreline was a popular vacation spot, so there had to be some places to stay on this god-forsaken road. Greg had almost given up the prospect of finding a place to sleep when he spotted a dim neon sign flashing, "Dew Drop Inn." Hallelujah! If he was not hallucinating, he had not only stumbled upon a motel, but it had the name his sister and he used to think was hilarious when they were kids. Granted, it took their young brains a while to figure out the double meaning of those words, but once they did, "Dew Drop Inn" never ceased to amuse them.

Greg was relieved that when he reached the motel, the office was still open. The couple who ran the place was one for the books. The husband had a bum leg, and his wife was the spitting image of the bulldog yapping in the background. The motel was clean and cozy. After Greg finished checking in, the man asked him if he wanted to join them in a nightcap. Greg had not eaten, and all he wanted to do was flop in his bed, but he did not want to be rude.

The wife brought out a large bowl of peanuts, and the husband poured some shots of scotch. The couple seemed hungry for conversation so Greg just listened and took it all in. Apparently, the woman was a nurse and met her husband in the hospital when he was recovering from a motorcycle accident, in which, unfortunately, his left leg was severed. The couple bought the motel early in their marriage when she was still working as a nurse and he, a pattern maker in Holyoke, Massachusetts. Someone else managed the motel for them, but the owners came down on weekends to keep an eye on things. They had two of the motel rooms converted into a lovely apartment for themselves, and when they retired, they moved permanently to "The Dew Drop Inn." Because the scotch was getting to Greg, he had to try hard to suppress his laughter when the man prattled on about their motel being a "respectable" establishment, and not a "hot pillow joint." The man admitted that it was difficult for him to get up from his recliner so he held a hand mirror over his shoulder to check out the cars that pulled up in front of the office. If the prospective guests looked suspicious, he would warn his wife to say there were no vacancies. In addition, they always asked for identification to be sure a man and woman who were checking in together were married.

The man said after a staid-looking couple checked out one weekend, the maid reported that the couple had removed the mirror from over the dresser and placed it down against the wall on the carpeted floor. Greg almost choked on his drink, but when he saw the looks of horror and disgust on the faces of the owners, he had to maintain his composure. This couple was a riot and didn't even know it. Now, Greg could belt them back as well as any Irishman, but with just a few peanuts in his stomach, he was getting woozy. When there was finally a break in the conversation, Greg politely excused himself, saying he had to get an early start in the morning. The couple apologized for having kept him so long, but he assured them he had enjoyed every minute of it. What is a white lie when you are sparing someone's feelings? They told him to drop into the office in the morning for coffee.

When Greg got to his room, he could no longer contain his laughter. He pictured the old man spying over his shoulder with the hand mirror, the "hot pillow joint," the mirror on the floor ... it was a wonder they had any business. All this wackiness put Greg in a great mood, and he was confident he would accomplish what he set out to do. It was lucky the couple did all the talking. If the liquor had loosened his lips, and he blabbed about his affair with Addy, the self-righteous owners of "The Dew Drop Inn" may have given him the boot.

The soft ring of his travel alarm clock awakened Greg the next morning. Boy, his head was pounding. He dropped his room key into the mailbox on the motel office door, hoping the couple would not ask him in for coffee. Fortunately, they must still have been asleep.

He drove for a couple hours and then stopped at a bustling diner for breakfast. Greg asked the waitress how far it was to Chester because the map he had did not show many small towns. The girl looked at Greg as if she did not know what he was talking about, and then she went into the back and got one of the busboys to come out. This kid knew exactly where Chester was located and was proud to explain the route to Greg.

Greg followed the lad's instructions precisely, but he did not end up in Chester. How prejudiced of him to even think this, but Greg had been told that people in Connecticut sometimes tended to be "backwards." Hopefully, a gas station attendant might be able to help him.

When he finally arrived in the tiny downtown area of Chester, Greg stopped at the first telephone booth he saw so that he could look up Addy's address in the directory. There was only one "Lionel Roberge" listed for Chester, so it must have been Addy's husband who had been killed in that accident. Greg copied down this address: 17 Colonial Road, Chester, Connecticut.

Greg stopped at the drugstore on the corner to ask directions to "Colonial Road" and then started out on the very last leg of his journey. Wow, was he happy. He had such a good feeling about all this. It was a crystal blue day, and Greg's heart was light. Addy, my dearest, here I come. Not until Greg pulled up in front of 17 Colonial Road did his heart start beating out of control. What the hell was he up to, anyways? Greg walked up the front sidewalk to a very pleasant home. He was practicing what he would say if Addy were to answer the door.

To his dismay, Addy did not come to the door. Instead, a young woman with a baby girl in her arms and twin boys at her skirts answered. "May I help you?" she asked.

Greg was dumbfounded. "I'm looking for the Roberge family. I thought this was their address."

The young woman smiled and said, "Yes. This used to be their house. We bought it from Mrs. Roberge after her husband died."

"Husband died ..." That was music to Greg's ears. Struggling to look somber, Greg said, "I'm sorry. I wasn't aware Lionel had passed away ... how tragic."

The trusting mother continued, "Addy and the kids are still in Chester, but they went to live on the Kurowski farm. It doesn't really have an address, but I can tell you how to get there, if you want to see them."

"Thanks so much. What beautiful children you have," Greg said after he jotted down the directions to the farm.

"Zippity-Do-Dah!" Greg hummed to himself, as corny as anyone could be. He was following the yellow brick road to find his angel. When he arrived, Greg marveled at the storybook setting. What a beautiful, happy place. He wasted no time sprinting up the stairs to the farmhouse, turning the knob on the old-fashioned bell, and waiting breathlessly for Addy to answer. Instead, Peter, Jimmy, and Mary came to the door.

"Greg!" all three children shouted. He instinctively knelt down and tried to scoop all three of them up in his arms.

"Where's Allison?" Mary asked cautiously.

"She's with my sister, but WHERE IS YOUR MOM?" Greg teased. Talking all at once, the children told Greg excitedly that their mom was opening a bakery, and she was there working on it with her friend.

Greg hoped "her friend" was not a man. His first instinct was to have the kids pile in his car and show him how to get to the bakery. If the friend turned out to be a man, however, this would be a dumb move. Instead, he asked directions to the bakery. Pete outlined the route, and Greg promised he would drop back to visit with them longer. The kids just could not believe that this wonderful man from Maine who they thought they would never see again had just appeared on their doorstep.

As Greg drove to the bakery, he thought about how much Addy must have blossomed now that Lionel was out of her life. Her own BAKERY? The Addy he had met would never have had the confidence to start a business. Hopefully, it was not a man who had boosted her ego, but even if that were so, good for Addy. Greg realized that although the time they spent together was brief and under ideal circumstances, he believed he loved Addy. When you truly love someone, you want the best for that person, whether or not it includes you.

Greg drove to the location Pete had explained, and pulled up in front of a neat old brick building that appeared to be abuzz with activity. There was no sign that the place was "Open for Business," but the door was unlocked so Greg went inside. The wood floors of the bakery were highly polished, you could almost see your reflection. Greg was looking down at the sheen of the wood, when a woman's voice said in a gentle tone, "I'm sorry sir. We are not open yet, but we should be open ..."

Addy glanced at the tall, handsome man who was admiring her floors. Oh God, she suddenly thought to herself. I cannot be experiencing this in real life. If this is really Greg, then I may as well stop living and become a character in a book.

Addy lowered her eyes, and tears began streaming down her face. Rushing over, Greg pulled Addy close to him, gently stroking her hair, and, whispering, "Shh. Shh, it's me, Addy," Greg consoled her. "Everything's going to be all right. I won't ever let you go."

Helena, looking most unglamorous with hair tied back in a red bandana and overalls speckled with paint, looked over at the two lovebirds and quipped, "Enough histrionics for the day, kiddies, WE HAVE A BAKERY TO OPEN."

Author's Note

ABUSE IS NEVER OKAY

If you or someone you know
is in an abusive situation please go to:

http://helpguide.org

for resources on abuse toward women,
children, men, the elderly, bullying, and cyber-bullying

You can also contact
The National Domestic Violence Hotline at:

http://www.thehotline.org
1-800-799-SAFE (7233)
or for TTY 1-800-787-3224

Nearly every city and town in the United States has an organization to help individuals who are in an abusive situation. Seek out someone in whom you can confide and ask that person to find where you may go for help. Remember, never assume that a restraining order will guarantee your family's safety.